THE CORPSE WHISPERER

CORPSE WHISPERER
THE SERIES

H.R. BOLDWOOD

OLIVERHEBERBOOKS

Cover art by Dar Albert at Wicked Smart Designs

Published by Oliver-Heber Books

This title was previously published.

0 9 8 7 6 5 4 3 2 1

PRAISE FOR H.R. BOLDWOOD

"If Anita Blake and Stephanie Plum had a lovechild, it would be Allie Nighthawk. One of the funniest and freshest takes on the zombie genre I've read, with genuine heart at the core of the humor and gore."

— DANA FREDSTI, AUTHOR OF THE *ASHLEY PARKER* SERIES AND THE *SPAWN OF LILITH* SERIES

"Anita Blake and October Daye, scoot over to make room for Allie Nighthawk, the fiercest and funniest heroine to hit the streets since Buffy first quipped while laying the undead to rest. *The Corpse Whisperer* is smart, witty, and so much fun you may just start it again as soon as you finish it."

— LISA MORTON, SIX-TIME BRAM STOKER AWARD-WINNING AUTHOR AND CO-EDITOR OF HAUNTED NIGHTS

"The Corpse Whisperer redefines the zombie genre. Allie Nighthawk is the hero we all need more of."

— TOM DEADY, BRAM STOKER AWARD-WINNING AUTHOR

"H.R. Boldwood is the Janet Evanovich of zombie hunters. She's fierce and funny and smart, just like her heroine. She's rejuvenated the zombie genre with a kick-ass, take-no-prisoners, balls-to-the-wall, laugh-out-loud series you're going to want to read, time and again."

— CHRISTIANA MILLER, AUTHOR OF
SOMEBODY TELL AUNT TILLIE SHE'S DEAD

CONTENTS

1. The World Is Batshit Crazy 1
2. Raising Cephus 7
3. You Can't Fight City Hall 18
4. Slicing the Pie 28
5. Dealing with the Devil 40
6. Life in the Tar Pits 53
7. Life Without Rules is Zushi 66
8. The Damned ACLU 78
9. Everyone Always Wants Something 87
10. Who's Killing Who? 99
11. Genghis Khan: Corpse Whisperer 107
12. When is a Black Lexus Just a Black Lexus? ... 117
13. For the Love of Lasagna 127
14. Shit Got Real 137
15. Tick-Tock, Tick-Tock 146
16. Damn It, I'm Busy 154
17. End of Watch 162
18. Bitches and Snitches 169
19. We Don't Need No Stinking Plan 180
20. Oh, No She Di'nt 190
21. Ain't Nothing But A Thing 198
22. Can't We All Just Get Along? 207
23. No Wonder Health Care Is A Mess 215
24. Nighthawk Down 226
25. The Best Laid Plans 230
26. Trouble in Paradise 238
27. Did Someone Say Dark and Gritty? 247
28. Eeny, Meeny, Miny, Moe 256
29. By the Light of the Silvery Moon 262
30. Gotcha! 270
31. Why? 279
32. Some Days Suck Worse than Others 286
33. The Weight of the World 292

34. The Last Dance   299
    Excerpt: Corpse Whisperer Sworn   309

Acknowledgments   311
About the Author   313
Also By H.R. Boldwood   315

This book is affectionately dedicated to Lisa Morton, friend and mentor, without whose unfailing support The Corpse Whisperer would not exist. Thank you for believing in me— even when my own confidence wavered.

It is also dedicated to my awesome brother, H. Richard Burdick, Jr., Retired Lieutenant/Blue Ash Police Department. Your encyclopedic knowledge of law enforcement and weaponry kept me from making many a rookie mistake. You answered my every question, sometimes more than once. Where would Allie and I be without you?

Last, but not least, this book is dedicated to Barbara Kuroff, one of Allie Nighthawk's biggest fans. I so wish you were here to see her debut. But I know you're up there smiling.

1

THE WORLD IS BATSHIT CRAZY

There aren't many good reasons for raising the dead, but there are plenty of bad ones—greed, revenge, and absolute lunacy top the list. I'm Allie Nighthawk and raising the dead happens to be my only talent. People are willing to pay for it. Go figure.

I'm also one of the few corpse whisperers who puts the 'toys' away when clients are finished playing with them. *Away,* as in hermetically sealed back in their coffins, with their disease-ravaged brains neutralized. That's shop talk for scattered, smothered, covered and chunked. The last thing we need is zombies clawing up through the dirt like demented whack-a-moles, and gnawing on the residents of Cincinnati.

I was born a corpse whisperer, twenty-six years and too many zombies ago to count. It's a genetic thing, like blonde hair or blue eyes, except that it's...raising the dead. Yeah. Okay. It's not exactly the same. It involves different genetic markers.

Buy a vowel, people. The concept's the same.

The supernatural abilities that come with this *gift* have increased with each generation. That makes me very good at what I do. And a little dangerous. If you raise deadheads, you'd better be able to put 'em down. Whisperers like me take care of business.

I can remember a time when you never saw biters shambling in the streets. But things have changed. Vampires aren't just for breakfast anymore, and the dead have become disposable pawns for necromancers. Someone had to ante up. Looks like I won the lotto. Imagine my delight.

You should thank me, really, because the world is batshit crazy.

No matter how much the rotters reek like sun-baked sushi, no matter how many of their orphaned body parts skitter after me like flesh-bots in search of a host, at the end of the day, reruns of *Dancing with the Stars*, a bag of Doritos and a Jack Daniel's slushie have always been enough to take off the edge.

At least they were, until a couple of months ago, when my nemesis—a very spiteful necromancer—took his vengeance on me by doing something so heinous, I swore I'd never raise the dead again. *Ever.* I'd still hunt down your occasional, garden-variety deadhead. I mean, *somebody* has to put the freaking flesh-eaters down. But raisings were off the table.

I haven't told the Cincinnati Police Department about my updated business model—yet. They pay me as a sub-contractor to raise schmucks for evidentiary reasons, and they weren't going to appreciate my change of heart. I'd been ducking their calls for a while, until a CPD cop banged on my door and forced the issue.

"Allie Nighthawk?"

"Get lost." I said, slamming the door, but he blocked it with his foot.

"Jesus, lady. Don't you ever answer your phone?"

"Don't you take a hint?"

"I'm Rico De Palma. The department's new liaison for the Paranormal Crimes Unit. Your ah...*partner.*"

The guy sounded like he'd swallowed a pinecone.

I gave him two sarcastic thumbs up and used my Mister Rogers voice. "Well, aren't you special."

He peered at me over the top of his Oakleys. "Six of us drew straws, lady. And I lost. I need you to raise Cephas McCoy for questioning in the disappearance of Twila Harris, a six-year-old from Price Hill."

I'd read about that case in the paper. Cute kid snatched right out of her own home. Rico had piqued my interest.

"McCoy...that's the scumbag you guys fingered for the Highpoint child abduction murders."

"Yeah. We were bringing him in for questioning, when some kid's father got wind of it and took him out with a .32 to the chest." Rico stepped aside and held the door open. "Grab your coat. Let's go."

Seriously. He wanted me to raise a *child killer*.

"I'm not going," I said.

"Excuse me?"

"I don't do raisings anymore. And even if I did, I wouldn't raise a child killer. Sorry. My game, my rules."

"Screw your rules. This kid needs you."

I reached for the door again, but his gunboat was still parked on the threshold.

"Move it or lose it," I said.

"Corpse whisperer, my ass. You're nothing but hype. No wonder your last partner didn't last very long."

He was referring to Harry Delk. A damn fine cop. Why De Palma thought he could fill Harry's shoes was a mystery.

He curled his lip and turned to walk away. "Thanks for nothing. Why don't you stick your rules up that hard-case ass of yours and rotate?"

The smug bastard. Who did he think he was?

I plowed forward, knocking us both onto the porch floor, and clocked him so hard, his sunglasses flew into the bushes.

Then, for some inexplicable reason, even though I didn't have to explain myself to anyone, I told him the truth.

"Bite me, blue boy. Those *rules* are all I've got."

People with my talents aren't standing on every street corner, you know. And the lawmakers left whisperers like me hanging in the breeze. As if the courts didn't have enough trouble defining *life,* once *un-death* came into the mix, they all but threw up their hands. Legislation governing zombie wrangling was intentionally vague because courts wanted wiggle room in sentencing.

Me? I don't like gray. So, I made my own set of rules. I wouldn't raise children or murderers. Children, because the angel you buried isn't what you'd get back, and murderers because re-animation brings out the worst in a corpse. If you were a killer in life, the odds *against* you coming back like Mother Theresa are higher than the odds of a positive DNA hit on your own spit.

Besides, it's a boundaries thing. A re-animator with no boundaries is a soulless whore. I had limits. I had a line.

But Rico wasn't giving up. He rubbed his chin and got to his feet. "You crazy-ass bit... If I didn't need your help, I'd haul you in. Twila went missing three days ago. They just buried McCoy yesterday. She could still be alive out there somewhere, cold, scared or hurt. Jesus, Nighthawk, she's just a baby. You can't walk away from this."

"Don't tell me what I can or can't do. You don't know anything about me."

"I know you're a coward."

A coward?

Well. That was ballsy. I moved in to smash... I moved in to respond in a more personal manner, when he simply stepped back, dropped his hands to his sides, and shook his head.

"Just tell me why," he said. "Why won't you raise this one insignificant piece of shit, if it'll save her life?"

I counted to ten and then schooled him on the facts of life —well, the facts of *un-death* anyway.

"Everyone, good or bad, has the right to rest in peace. Just because I can raise corpses, doesn't mean I should. Every corpse I raise becomes a zombie, and every zombie has to be put down."

"And your point?"

"You think it's easy deciding who gets raised and why? Well, let me enlighten you. Sometimes people raise corpses for the wrong reasons, and then people like me have to clean up after them. But not me. Not anymore. I'm done."

Rico's voice went flat. "I don't know why you stopped raising. Hell, I don't even care. But can you really let this kid die?"

He pulled her picture out of his pocket and stuck it in my face. Pretty little thing, freckles, pig-tails, the whole nine yards.

Then he went for gold. "It's your call, sweetheart. But you need to make it quick. It's the end of March. Colder than shit out there. If Twila isn't dead, she's running out of time. And if you let her die—it's on you."

Well, *crap*. The freckles got me. It's so much easier when you don't let freckles, and feelings, and people in. Then it doesn't hurt so bad when you lose them.

I wanted to find her too, damn it. Just what I needed, a reason to start raising the dead again.

I tried to ignore Little Allie, the voice in the back of my brain that screams like a banshee when she thinks I'm screwing up. She was having an apoplectic fit, telling me Rico was right. She was telling me to go all in, balls to the wall, to save that girl.

So what if she was right? She could have used her indoor voice. The crazy bitch must think I'm deaf.

I took a deep breath and stuck my finger in Rico's face. "Let's get one thing straight, De Palma. I'm not your sweetheart. The next time I hear anything close to that come out of your mouth, I'm gonna feed your lips to—"

"Roger that, Nighthawk. Get your gear."

Game time, baby.

I tucked my hair under my *Ungrateful Dead* ball cap. Long hair is an easy handhold for a deadhead and besides, in the moonlight, my black hair shines like a hundred-watt bull's-eye.

I put on a pair of black khakis, stuck my Swiss army knife into the back pocket, pulled on my boots, and yanked my good luck *Zom-B-Gone* T-shirt over my head. The right sleeve was in tatters. Like I said, it was my lucky shirt. It could have been my arm.

Next came my shoulder holster, where my main man, Hawk, hangs out. He's a custom 9mm semi-auto Nighthawk. What else would I carry?

Last, but not least, I grabbed a bag of Lays barbecue chips and a roll of duct tape, and shoved them into my go bag with an extra set of clothes. What can I say? Mine is a messy job.

Then I slipped into my black leather duster and became *Allie Nighthawk, the best of the bad-ass zombie hunters.*

"Out of my way, De Palma."

As I pulled the door shut behind us, my bulldog, Headbutt, barely glanced at me from his throne on top of the air-conditioning vent. He would still be there when I got back, not having moved an inch. He's what you'd call *kinetically-challenged*, but he can smell a rotter a mile away.

His partner in crime, an African Grey parrot named Kulu, hung upside down on her perch. She turned her yellow eye toward me and took a parting shot. "Box-o-rocks."

Yeah? Well. Bite me, bird.

I climbed onto my Harley Low Rider and went looking for trouble.

2

RAISING CEPHUS

The cemetery would be a freaking obstacle course, but Rico insisted we wait until sundown to raise our rotter. As we climbed over the retaining wall, he explained that mommies don't want their children watching me chase decomped deadheads down Central Parkway, with a flamethrower.

I get that. I got no problem being discreet. It's not like I want to do this work in the daylight anyway. You spike one zombie's head, the ACLU and the paparazzi are all over you like stink on a flesh-eater. Besides, biters tend to hole up during the day, since they can't see in sunlight. Wrangling them is easier in the dark, when they're on the prowl.

Fallen tombstones, mole holes, and titanium flower vases, all vying to take out my knees, are the problem. That's why the art of negotiation comes in handy.

"Hire me," I said as we sprinted though the headstones. "I'm tired of this independent contractor shit. I want double-time for field work, full medical coverage, and disability benefits. Call it hazardous duty pay."

Rico stopped and swung his flashlight in my direction.

"Captain Dorsey said you've already discussed that with him. You're not in the budget."

"Really, De Palma? It's not smart to screw with the one person who can keep your ass from getting corpsified."

"That's Cap's call, not mine," Rico said, taking off with long, powerful strides toward the gravesite.

———

The backhoe had done the hard work. I stared at McCoy's low-rent casket shining in the moonlight and gave Rico one last chance to bail.

"You know, this isn't as easy as I make it look. Raising a rotter is a lot like doing a rain dance. You might get a drizzle or you might need a freaking ark. McCoy's a freshy. He hasn't even been dead a week. Raising him will screw with the cognitive function of his brain—the part that processes information. He won't be capable of lying, that requires deliberation and intent. But whatever else happens is anybody's guess. You sure you want to do this?"

"She's six years old, Nighthawk. We don't have a choice."

"Open the lid." I closed my eyes and let the power surge through me, like God's own hand.

Make no mistake, the ability to raise the dead is a God-given gift that comes with a moral obligation to protect the living *and* the dead. The gift itself isn't evil, but misuse of that gift is as ugly as it gets.

The mortician had done an impressive job, given the circumstances. McCoy looked like he was napping, like his eyes could open at any moment, and he'd be confused by his surroundings. Sometimes appearances aren't deceiving.

"Cephas Allen McCoy, in the name of God, I command you to rise!"

Cephas moaned, low and steady.

I spread my hands over him and whispered a single word. "Awaken."

Tiny rivers of light streamed from my hands into his body, causing him to pitch and thrash. Teeth clenched, limbs flailing, he sprang upright and opened his eyes—crazed, animal-like eyes that showed fear but nothing else.

He grabbed the edge of the casket and leapt to the ground above. *Shit.* That's what I'd been afraid of. His muscles still had memory. The .32 he took to the heart hadn't caused peripheral tissue damage. Climbing out of that grave, for him, was no more difficult than climbing out of bed to take a leak.

We stood, face to face—almost. He looked about six-two, giving him a good eight inches on me.

"Cephas, stop!"

He froze and stared at me, like he was trying to figure out who I was, trying to use the cognitive part of his brain that no longer worked.

Then he twitched.

God. I hate when they twitch.

"Cephas, where's Twila Harris?"

He growled and drooled on my feet.

"Answer me, damn it!" I pulled the bag of barbecue chips out of my pocket, opened it, and waved it under his nose. "Tell me where she is and they're yours."

Rico's eyes went wide. "*Potato chips?* You've got to be—"

"Hey. You mind? I'm working here."

Cephas grabbed at the chips and slurred, "Duck blind on Lake Chetac. Shush...it's a secret."

Now for the tough question. "Is Twila still alive?"

"Yes. Yes. Pretty. Go play with her. Need to play. Need her." His mouth quivered, and a long string of saliva that dangled from his lip bounced like a bungee cord.

Then he snarled, snatched the chips out of my hand, and bolted across the cemetery.

"Ah, shit!" I took off after him, the freaking twitcher.

Cephas hadn't gotten a big head start, but he was running on freshy legs, making me work to close the distance between us.

When Rico started to run with me, I yelled, "No, go get the girl! I can handle McCoy."

I was so busy keeping Cephas in my sights, I didn't notice the plastic tarp in my path. It gave way beneath me into six feet of nothingness.

The air *whooshed* out of my lungs, as I did a face plant into the open grave. My hands absorbed some of the impact and probably saved me from a broken nose, but my left wrist jammed when I landed.

Son of a bitch.

Did I happen to mention I'm left-handed?

Something warm and sticky ran down my face—blood bubbling out of the top of my head. Alone, hurt and six-feet under, with no easy way out...*perfect.*

Kulu's words came back to haunt me: *box-o-rocks.* She's an insightful little bitch.

A large, titanium flower vase stared down at me from the gravesite, as if mocking my stupidity. An idea began to form.

I stood beneath the vase, faced sideways, then pushed my back against one dirt wall and my feet against the other. I inched up the walls, feet and shoulders in tandem, doing a horizontal mambo toward the top. When I got to the surface, I reached over and grabbed the vase, which was anchored into the ground, with my right hand.

What I did next looked pretty much like my *5-Minute No Flab Ab* routine, trying to rock myself up and over to the ground. Sound easy? Not so much. By the time my body made it out onto the grass and I rolled to my feet, pain washed through me in waves.

Cephas couldn't have gone far. The stucco walls around Rose Hill Cemetery were a good twelve feet high, built for privacy and protection. And the gate was locked. That's why we'd scaled the wall.

I caught sight of my deadhead across the grounds, in an older section of plots—only there were three of him, moving in perfect synchronization. So, I focused on the Cephas in the middle, as he backed himself into a corner, between the wall and Louis Kapiniski's mausoleum (which I have to say was impressive, as mausoleums go).

I eased down, onto a concrete garden bench across from Louis's crypt, and checked my aching wrist. That sucker had swollen to twice its normal size. No way I could pull Hawk, let alone fire him. Hawk was going to have to keep his pants on. So much for Plan A.

I didn't have a Plan B.

I looked around for inspiration, but the pickings were slim —tombstones, grass, backhoe. *Backhoe.* Parked on the service road, across from Cephas's grave, it was big and powerful, simply waiting for the next hole that needed to be dug.

Cephas paced back and forth like a brain-dead pinball, bouncing from the perimeter wall to the mausoleum, and back again.

I whistled to get his attention. "Yo! You and me, pal? We're not done. Be right back."

Closing my left eye to streamline the double vision, I trekked across the grounds toward the backhoe. Pulling myself up to the driver's cage with my right hand was a piece of cake. Removing the control panel screws was a challenge. My right hand didn't recognize the feel of my knife. Turning the screws felt awkward, but after finally exposing the wires, I bypassed the ignition and twisted them together. The backhoe roared to life.

What happened next was collateral damage. At least, that's my story and I'm sticking to it.

Sometimes, you have to break a few eggs to make an omelette. If the damage scale begins with a single egg, think of mine in terms of a big-ass, family-sized frittata. Just because I could hot wire a backhoe did not mean I knew how to operate it. And trying to do things right-handed didn't make it any easier.

There were a few additional incidents, as I drove across the grounds on my way back to Cephas.

Barely worth mentioning, really.

He hadn't strayed far. I wrangled him with the bucket of the backhoe, moving him toward the Kapinski mausoleum. He snarled and snapped, gnashing his teeth, scrambling to get at me. I tried to run him over, but those freshies are so damn agile.

He grabbed hold of the bucket and hoisted himself inside it. Next thing I knew, he'd launched himself from the bucket onto the driver's cage, and was gnawing on the bars.

Shaking Cephas loose was like trying to shake gum off the bottom of my shoe. I made a sharp right turn, then jerked the wheel to the left, throwing him off the backhoe.

When he fell to the ground, I raised the bucket as high as it would go and stared into his eyes. He wanted nothing more than to chew off my face. And I wanted nothing more than for the night to end.

Once I yanked the control lever down, the bucket smashed into his head with surprising speed, spewing brains, bone, and embalming fluid outward in an angry arc. The bucket continued downward, pile-driving him into the earth. When it came to rest, an odd arrangement of arms and legs protruded from beneath it.

Juicy, but effective. I just put 'em down. I don't get paid for clean-up. The maintenance workers were going to have a meltdown.

I said the only thing that can, or should, be said at a moment like that. "Rest in pieces, Cephas."

I needed to get to Lake Chetac fast and all I had was my Harley. Once I got it into gear, my right hand could take over. But using the clutch was going to be a bitch. So, I pulled out the duct tape and wrapped my wrist.

That bike and I must have hit a thousand bumps as we tore up the road to Lake Chetac. Rico had called in the cavalry to search every duck blind, cabin and outhouse on the grounds. They found Twila Harris right where Cephas had said she'd be. He hadn't had time to play out whatever sick fantasy he'd had in store for her.

Rico walked toward me with Twila cradled in his arms. I'm not sure who was holding on tighter.

She was alive and in one piece. Sometimes miracles do happen. And maybe, sometimes, bending the rules, even my rules, was the only way to make them happen.

Rico's eyes twinkled. "I was right about you. I knew you'd come through."

"You just impress the hell out of yourself, don't you?" I asked, doubling over, feeling like I might hurl.

"Go ahead. Say it."

"Say what?"

"Say, Rico was right."

"Rico's an asshole."

Our debate ended when the Deerfield Township EMS arrived for Twila. When the paramedics saw my bleeding head and swollen wrist, they nodded curtly, tossed me a band-aid and an ace wrap, and then moved on.

Rico tried to call them back, but I cut him off.

"We've run into each other before," I explained. "They value their lives too much to screw with me."

A television news van pulled up and a low growl hummed in my throat. "If it isn't my good friends from Channel Ten."

"Oh, hell no," Rico said. "Cap warned me about this. Nighthawk. Retract your claws."

I cracked my neck from side to side to loosen up, producing an audible pop from my spine. The fun was just getting started.

Jade Chen and her pet cameraman, Rip Sacca, burst out of the van.

Rip grinned and raised his camera to his shoulder. "Hi, Allie. You can run but you can't hide."

Hide? How hard was it to find us?

The press monitored the scanners, and CPD had the place lit with so many search lights, it looked like a used car lot. Still, I was a little surprised to see them. Jade had the journalistic instincts of lint.

She flashed her pearly white caps at the camera. "Good evening, Cincinnati. I'm Jade Chen, reporting to you live from Lake Chetac. We're here tonight to follow two breaking stories. The recovery of young Twila Harris, kidnapped just days ago. And the escape of a freshly risen corpse, Cephas Allen McCoy." Jade turned to Rico. "Detective Rico De Palma, of the Cincinnati Police Department, what can you tell us?"

"Only that Twila has been recovered alive and well. Due to the ongoing nature of the investigation, I'm not at liberty to discuss specifics at this time."

Jade tucked a strand of long, black hair behind her ear, and squeezed his bicep, clinging to him like a barnacle.

"Thank you, Detective De Palma. Greater Cincinnati is fortunate to be protected by such a brave and dedicated officer."

Her nostrils flared as she turned to me. "Ms. Nighthawk,

Cincinnati's resident cadaver diver. It appears things got a little out of control tonight. Someone took out the north wall of Rose Hill Cemetery with a backhoe. What can you tell us about that?"

"No comment."

"Can you explain why the Kapinski Mausoleum, the resting place of the city's founding father, is now a pile of rubble?"

"No comment."

"Did you obtain a warrant to raise McCoy's corpse? The ACLU has issued a statement condemning your actions tonight as desecration of a corpse. Would you care to comment?"

"Yeah, sure. You should use a smaller trowel to pack on that eye shadow, honey. You look a little like a corpsicle—"

"Nighthawk!" Rico whispered from off-camera.

Jade smirked and addressed the faithful viewers at home. "This is Jade Chen for ABC news affiliate, Channel Ten, dedicated to giving you yesterday's news, today."

Rip lowered the camera and gave her a look that wiped the smug off her face.

"*Crap*," she mumbled. "Cut. Take two."

Rip gave her a thumbs up and started rolling.

"This is Jade Chen for ABC news affiliate, Channel Ten, dedicated to giving you tomorrow's news, today."

What a freaking moron. Rip moved in tight for Jade's signature closing.

"May I never appear on your doorstep, microphone in hand, searching for the truth. Goodnight, Cincinnati."

Rip lowered his camera. "Cut. And that's a wrap."

Jade quickly regrouped and batted her onyx eyes at Rico.

"Looks like your partner's going to be on the disabled list for a while," she said, side-eying me. "If you get bored, text me."

She slipped her hand into his jacket and pulled out his cell phone. He froze as she punched in her number, and then slowly slid the phone into the bottom of his pants pocket.

"I'm on speed dial, sugar." She winked and walked back to the news van, working her ass like a curve ball.

Jade and Rip left with no more details than they had when they arrived, yet their story was destined to headline the eleven o'clock news. They'd pull a forty-three percent market share, thanks to the draw of deadheads and Jade's Double-D's.

Pulitzer Prize, my ass.

Rico magically rediscovered his ability to speak when the van drove out of sight. "Jesus, she's hot!"

"If you go for the annoying type," I said, feeling a little green.

It was time to change the subject.

"She was right about one thing. I am going to be out of commission for a while. That's why I asked for full benefits. What the hell am I supposed to do for money, while I'm laid-up? You'd better tell Cap to stick a crow bar in that budget, De Palma, and pull something out other than his thumb. I want salary plus three weeks paid vacation, full medical, disability, and expenses. Small arms ammo and flamethrowers don't come cheap, you know."

I tried to punctuate my point with a finger to his chest, but missed his body completely.

"Why are there three of you? Stop moving around!"

Rico laughed. "You might be able to bulldoze the EMTs, but not me, Nighthawk. You're going to the emergency room, even if I have to carry you."

"Feeling froggy? Go ahead and leap, Mister 'I Drew the Smallest Straw'. I can take your scrawny ass."

I swung so hard, I spun full circle and nailed the air with a deadly left cross. My follow through would have ended in my second face-plant of the day, except that Rico ducked beneath my outstretched arm and rolled me over his shoulder.

"Jesus, you're exasperating. I'll get back to Cap about the

budget. I've got some other connections, too. We'll find you some kind of paying gig while you're off work."

Though I couldn't see it from my vantage point, hanging upside down over Rico's shoulder, I heard the smile in his voice.

Despite the pain in my head that throbbed with his every step, I flashed a little grin of my own. Three of the finest asses this side of the Ohio River were bouncing in my face. Even concussed, I was fairly certain they were his, not mine.

That bimbo reporter, Jade Chen, might have been hot, but I was Allie Nighthawk, the best of the bad-ass zombie hunters. And I was exasperating.

The last things I remember before everything went black, were Rico cursing when I puked into the back of his shoe, and wondering what the hell kind of light-duty options would be available for a zombie hunter.

3

YOU CAN'T FIGHT CITY HALL

About a week after the Rose Hill Cemetery ~~debacle~~...
~~incident~~...case, Captain Dorsey arranged for me to cover
Zombie Combat with the cops of the 51st Precinct. He scheduled
the lecture in an auditorium at City Hall. It sounded like the
perfect restricted duty gig, given my sprained wrist. I'd never
held a training session before. But how hard could it be?

With all the chairs set up, the room felt a little tight. It had
to be ninety degrees in there. My hands turned sweaty and then
my stomach went south. I started fidgeting with my notes and
dropped them on the floor.

Relax, I told myself. Everything will be fine.

Since Cap offered to pay me, I went all-out and brought a
visual aid—a deadhead chained to a two-wheel dolly, with a
catcher's mask strapped to its face. Eighty cops rose to their
feet, locked and loaded.

I stepped to the left. Far, far to the left.

So, sue me if I got a little creative. I had their attention, at
least for the moment.

"At ease, officers," I said, moving to the lectern. "I brought my friend...Hannibal...along for show and tell. Say hello, Hannibal."

Hannibal growled. Strings of slobber clung to the bottom of his catcher's mask and swayed back and forth. The left side of his forehead was gone, but his brain was functioning. You could see it peeking out from between the metal bars of his face-plate.

"Notice he's parked on an eight-by-ten sheet of white plastic," I said. "By the end of our session, it won't be white anymore. I hope that won't offend your delicate sensibilities."

Great line, I thought, looking out into the audience. And then...my mind went blank.

One-hundred and sixty eyes—one-hundred and sixty-two if you count Hannibal's—stared at me, waiting for me to speak. And I didn't have squat.

Sweat dripped from my forehead. My mouth went dry, and my freaking knees shook like a pair of maracas.

Rico joined me onstage and covered the mic with his hand. "What's wrong? You don't look so good."

"Apparently, I hate public speaking. Who knew?" I said from behind gritted teeth. "Thanks, anyway. Bye-bye now."

I turned to leave, but he grabbed my arm and leaned in toward the mic. "How about a warm welcome for our guest lecturer, Ms. Allie Nighthawk, better known as the Corpse Whisperer."

Random claps drifted through the room like tumbleweeds through the desert.

Rico smiled at the sea of cops. "I know it's a mandatory lecture, but let's give Ms. Nighthawk our undivided attention."

Mandatory lecture. Yay. They hated me already, and I hadn't even started.

Rico took a parting shot as he walked to his seat. "Suck it up, buttercup. You're on."

Douche-waffle.

If I could raise the dead and take down zombies, I could do this, damn it. Mind over matter.

I cleared my throat and started again. "As I was saying, this is Hannibal. I found him wandering around Liberty Street, near the abandoned subway entrance. You'll find deadheads there, and most anywhere else you find society's throwaways. If you look close enough, you might even recognize a few of them from the streets. Indigents are a small segment of the population and may not be your top priority, but they're perfect MREs for biters."

I raised my bandaged wrist. "I collared Hannibal here with one good hand. Zombie wrangling isn't magic. It's technique. That's what I'm going to teach you today. Now, some of you might think it's cold, making an example out of Hannibal. He was human once. He had a name. It probably wasn't Hannibal, but he had a name. But the minute you start thinking of these biters as human, the minute you hesitate to pull the trigger because they used to be somebody, you're dead meat. Never, ever forget that."

I paused, searching the crowd for signs of life. It was too late. The bastards had flat-lined. I was dying up there. The thought of diving out an open window crossed my mind, but that's not my style. A train wreck, with my name on it, awaited me, so I pulled up my big girl panties, embraced the suck, and carried on.

"People ask me why, since I can raise the dead, I can't just wave my hand and lay them back to rest. The answer's simple. This gift doesn't come with a reverse gear, folks. If it did, I wouldn't have to train my butt off to fight like *Xena: Warrior Princess*. The only thing that will take a biter down is physical destruction of its brain or brain stem.

"The next thing we're going to discuss today is zombie physiology. The medical term for the disease is *Carovescitis*. There are only two ways to become a zombie—being raised from the dead by someone like me—or being bitten by a raised zombie, if you have a specific genetic marker that predisposes you to the disease.

"Raised corpses show immediate symptomology, whereas bite victims can begin to manifest symptoms in as little as fifteen minutes, with a massive delivery of toxin, to months later, if they're treated with a newly developed medication, *Nacarotoxin*. Currently, there's no vaccine for Carovescitis."

A long, loud snore broke my train of thought, followed by another, a few seconds later. *Found him.* Row three, aisle seat, on the left. I clipped on the lavalier mic and moved out into the audience, smacking Rip Van Winkle up the side of his head with my elbow.

He jumped and almost fell off his chair. Snickers rolled through the room.

"Shall we continue?" I asked. "There are actually four stages of infection. First, you have latents, bite victims who've contracted the disease, but use medication to delay their symptoms. That's the honeymoon phase. It doesn't last. Sooner or later, even with the meds, they turn into deadheads.

"Second, you have freshies, victims who were either raised within seven days of death, or who are genetically predisposed, were bitten less than seven days earlier, and are not taking meds to delay their symptoms. Once turned, they need to eat within twelve hours. It doesn't matter whether it's road kill, roof shingles or license plates, they need to eat."

I glanced at Rico, remembering Cephas and his potato chips at the cemetery. "They do show a marked preference for greasy junk food."

Rico nodded and I turned back to the crowd.

"Scientists think the fat used in processed foods stimulates the development of the zombie's appetite for flesh, which kicks in after the seventh day. Freshies are able to speak and answer questions, but do not retain the ability to problem-solve or lie.

But, if they start twitching, lock and load, folks. Things are about to get real ugly.

"Next, you've got flesh-eaters, raised, or genetically predisposed and bitten between eight and sixty days earlier. They've got seventy-five percent of their reflexes and eat exclusively human or animal flesh and brains. They are still somewhat agile, highly unpredictable, and your worst nightmare.

"Last, but not least, you have corpsicles, raised or genetically predisposed and bitten more than sixty days earlier. You'll smell them long before you see them. They're slow, but if one gets the drop on you and takes a bite, you'd better hope you don't have that marker.

"For those lucky ducks who don't have the genetic marker, bite damage can run anywhere from a grossly infected wound, to an agonizing death, watching yourself being eaten alive. Any questions so far?"

Thwack, bang, crash, bwauk!

What the hell... I knew those sounds. I played that game every day. *Angry Birds* was squawking from a nearby phone. My, my, my. Someone had a death wish. But *who*?

I followed the commotion straight to its source, before he could silence his phone. The guy saw me approach and slunk into his seat, shoving the phone in his pocket and looking the other way.

Busted, dumbass.

My hands were already reaching out to shove that phone up his left nostril, when who showed up but that head-squatting bitch fairy, Little Allie, her panties in an uproar, lecturing me about restraint.

Restraint? Does she even know me?

She's pretty ballsy for a voice in a head. Sometimes I wonder if her real name is Sybil. That might actually explain a few things.

So what if she's never wrong? She sucks the joy out of life.

I wanted to hear birds squawking out of that guy's nose. But in the end, I opted for a better plan. Maybe the bitch fairy's counsel did have something to do with that, but hindsight being twenty-twenty, I doubt she wants the credit.

I flashed a full set of teeth at the guy.

He glanced around the room like he was searching for the nearest exit.

My fingers dug into his bicep, as I hauled him to his feet. "Hi, I'm Allie. What's your name?"

"D-D-Donald," he said, trying to sit back down.

No dice, Donald. I pulled him out into the aisle, and escorted him up the steps to the stage, toward Hannibal.

"This is some boring shit, isn't it, D-D-Donald? Everyone knows you shoot zombies in the head. But what if you're in a packed room...like this one? Or on a crowded street?" I glanced at his utility belt. "What if...you don't have your gun?"

I held out my hand, waiting for him to give me his Glock. He balked. Of course, he did. A cop doesn't just hand over his gun.

"It's okay, Officer. I promise you. This is a training exercise. Please."

Captain Dorsey glared at me, but then he turned and gave Donald the nod. Donald hesitated, like he was trying to find a way out of the jam he'd gotten himself into.

When he finally turned over his piece, little beads of sweat glistened on his upper lip.

I unlocked Hannibal's chains, letting them fall. They clanged against the two-wheeler. Then, I stepped behind him, out of his line of sight, and took off his catcher's mask.

The cops shifted in their seats, eyes snapped front and center. D-D-Donald swore under his breath. Hannibal stepped toward him.

"Obviously, you know how to handle this situation, Donald, or you would have been paying attention instead of playing games on your phone. Why don't you show the group how to take down a biter without a gun?"

He darted his eyes around the room. "Wh...what am I supposed to use?"

"Your imagination. Think on your feet—and whatever you do, go for the head."

Hannibal lurched forward across the plastic. His shriveling brain slid forward in his skull and pushed out through the hole in his forehead. He waddled with his arms outstretched, grasping at Donald, snapping his jaws up and down, grinding them bone-on-bone.

Donald's feet got tangled and he stumbled backward onto his butt.

"Ewww. Rough start," I mumbled into my mic.

Donald did a backwards crab walk across the stage, with Hannibal in pursuit. They worked their way across and off the plastic in no time.

That's when I remembered that Hannibal was a corpsicle. Even one-handed, I'd planned on doing the demo myself. Since he was strapped into the dolly, I could slice into his brainstem, *quick in, quick out,* and take Hannibal down, right there on the plastic.

But then Donald decided to become an asshat.

Unfortunately, D-D-Donald shuffled backwards too far, and rolled down the steps to the floor, with Hannibal staggering after him.

"What the hell!" Donald screamed. "Call this thing off!"

"He's all yours," I said. "Don't let him get close enough to bite you."

"No shit, Nighthawk!"

Jesus, give me strength. "Use your damn baton, Donald!"

He followed my directions and beat the crap out of Hannibal, but in his panic, he threw all body blows.

Being a corpsicle, Hannibal was in an advanced state of

decay. Thick chunks of flesh, bone and zombie goo sailed through the air.

It reminded me a little of the chum scene from *Jaws*.

The guys in the first few rows took direct hits. They turned their chairs upside down and used them as shields.

"The head!" I yelled. "Go for the head!"

Freaking moron.

Donald took his head out of his ass, backed up about ten feet, and then charged Hannibal, holding the baton high. But he skidded on the slick floor and went ass-over-elbows, dropping his baton and flying across the floor, like it was a slime-covered slip-n-slide. He ended up at Hannibal's feet—with no weapon.

Talk about FUBAR.

I launched myself off the stage, onto Hannibal's back, Ka-Bar knife in hand. Since my left wrist was still iffy, I used both hands to bury the knife straight into his brain stem, just as he was about to take a chunk out of D-D-Donald's face.

You'd think the fact that I saved Donald's life would have put a positive spin on the whole episode. And it might have, if Captain Dorsey hadn't dived across the floor, on his stomach, to pull Donald out of Hannibal's reach. My Ka-Bar attack sent brain matter and zombie sushi (better known as *zushi*) spraying every which way, but mostly into Cap's face.

You could have heard a pin drop in that room. The only sound was Donald's hyperventilating.

Rico moved out from behind his chair shield, rushed over to Cap and knelt on the floor beside him, wiping biter bits off his face with his sleeve. When he finished, Rico stood up and glanced around the room to check out the carnage.

"Would you look at that," he said. "There isn't one speck of biter on that drop cloth you brought. You sure nailed Cap, though."

Way to have my six, partner.

I gotta say, I wasn't liking this light-duty thing too much. I was supposed to get paid for this gig, but when Cap calmed down enough to speak, he told me I'd have to pay for the clean-up. I tried to explain that since this was my first training session, I was just trying to make a big splash. But it was still a little too fresh, so to speak. I'll fight that battle another day.

Good thing I've got my own crime scene cleaners on speed-dial—a company named Splatz. I'm in tight with the owner, and I get their Diamond Club preferred customer discount.

If you ask me, the day wasn't a complete disaster. The cops got their training and after a few...slight complications...D-D-Donald and the other officers learned how to take down a biter without using their guns. Mission accomplished.

Everything else was just zushi.

My homeowners association has never liked me much. To be fair, peculiar things have happened at my house that have had the neighbors peering out their windows, with binoculars, for years.

The night of the City Hall episode, I pulled my Harley into the driveway around dinner time and Nonnie Nussbaum, the widow-lady next door, flew outside to give me an earful.

"That monstrosity, it hurts my ears! *Vroom, vroom.* Always so loud when you come home. And that *schmendrick* bird of yours —I tend my garden on such a beautiful spring day as this, and what do I hear but that *fakakta* bird screaming at me through your windows. It stares at me from behind the glass. I think it wants to eat me."

Nonnie's a 5'2", cranky, 200 lb., 70-year-old, gum-grinding busybody with short, bottle-blue helmet hair. Her eyes are glued on my house 24/7.

I waved at her as I walked inside. "Don't worry, Mrs. Nuss-baum. Kulu doesn't keep kosher. You're safe."

Oy, vey.

In lieu of dinner, I'd grabbed a bag of Doritos and a Jack Daniel's slushie when Jade Chen's face loomed back at me from my fifty-two-inch Sony.

"A police training session at city hall today, led by noted zombie wrangler Allie Nighthawk, results in chaos and a biohazard clean-up. Details at six."

Perfect.

The phone rang, right on cue.

It was Rico, calling to yank my chain. "Think you'll ever be allowed back in city hall?"

"Let them bar me out. See if I care. They might change their minds if a corpsicle shows up for a council meeting, someday."

Rico snickered. "You can stop pouting. The doctor sent your full-duty release for Monday."

"Thank you, God," I sighed. "I'll be in at nine."

"No. You'll be at the range by eight. The doctor might have released you, but I want to see you shoot with that hand before I sign off on your return."

"You're killing me, De Palma," I sighed. "Fine. But I'm bringing my custom targets."

I'd designed them myself: Jade Chen's head photoshopped onto a corpsicle's body. What better way to celebrate my first day back to work, than doing what I do best—hunting zombies.

4

SLICING THE PIE

There's a certain zen at Brasshole's Firing Range in the early morning hours. Later in the day, there are too many yahoos breathing my air. But when the sun comes up, the range's dingy, pockmarked walls and chaw-stained floors tell the story of an old boys' club.

Somehow, that works for me.

Once I start shooting, the smell of burnt gun powder and the *plink* of shell casings zinging off the ceiling, puts me in the zone. It's quiet at that hour for a firing range, just me and a couple other guys settling in, getting lost in the rhythm, honing the skills that make shooting more about instinct and less about aim.

Poor Hawk hadn't tasted brass in two weeks. He was starved, so I filled the mag pouch on my shoulder holster and slid Baby, my backup Glock model 26, into my ankle holster. She's a semi-auto, but smaller than Hawk, and she gets a little jealous when I don't show her some love once in a while.

One by one, each mag would disappear before the day was through, because practice makes perfect. Right? Rico would be arriving at Brasshole's any minute to sign off on my release. I knew I'd pass. It wasn't about that. For some reason, I wanted to impress him.

By the time he arrived, I'd burned through two mags. He got a load of my custom Jade Chen zombie targets and laughed so hard, he snorted. That was the first time I saw him laugh. It was genuine and straight from the belly. Even his brooding brown eyes joined in.

The laugh suited him, and though I tried not to notice, he's as hot as they come. Not that it mattered. A guy like him would never be interested in me.

He clipped his target to the T-rail, sent it out fifteen yards, slammed a mag into his Glock 34 Safe Action Long Slide, and grinned. "Show me what you got, cadaver diver."

Damn. That was just plain mean.

After we emptied our mags, Rico had seventeen center-mass hits. Impressive. All of mine hit slightly above and to the sides of center-mass, carving Jade's Double-D's down to mosquito bites, with room to spare for band-aids over her nipples.

Booyah, baby. Bullseye.

Rico smirked. "I'm guessing you hit what you were aiming at, but there's one more test. Cap's orders. I'm supposed to take you for a walk down Main Street."

I laid down my gun and gave him my sharpest Allie eye.

He didn't even blink. "I know you're not a cop, but you're going to be out on the streets with us, carrying. Cap wants to know you can protect yourself, and that you're not going to accidentally take out some civilian."

"It's not the same. Zombies don't shoot back," I said.

"Neither do the pop-ups."

Behind Brasshole's is a tiny shell of a village, named Perptown. It's a private SWAT training facility, owned by the city, with pop-up targets consisting of civilians, officers and bad guys. I'd heard of it, but I never had the chance to walk the gauntlet. It sounded like fun. On the other hand, for the first time ever, I was being asked to qualify.

What was I going to do? Shoot the *wrong* corpse running loose in a cemetery?

I know. I know. It's not that simple. But the little brain bitch didn't even give me a minute to process this new development before blowing a gasket, preaching at me about not getting my ass in a pucker.

Let's face it, people. This is *my* ass we're talking about. And it was born puckered.

We walked behind Brasshole's to Perptown and stopped at the entrance, the intersection of Main Street and Watch-Your-Six.

Rico grinned. "We don't have any zombie targets. Just pretend the pop-up perps are biters. Use the cover that's out there. Condition one, Allie."

Allie? Wow. That was a first.

"Cocked and locked," I said. "That's how I carry."

"Slice the pie. Center mass."

"De Palma, please. I don't do center mass. Zombies...head shots, remember? Thanks for the tip, but I know what I'm doing."

He climbed the steps to the control tower that overlooked Perptown, and then turned back to me. "Signal when ready. I'll be watching you on the monitor."

I'd been scoping out the place since we got there. Thanks to a wet March and no drainage, Main Street, about an eighth-of-a-mile long, was nothing more than a continuous mud slick connected by a series of chuck holes.

On my right, was a supermarket, a bank, and an alley alongside a hardware store with a second-floor walk-up. On my left, an Italian restaurant, an open lot, and the police station. Telephone poles, a mailbox, and a few vehicles lined the concrete curbs, including a UPS truck on my left, about twenty feet down range.

I took a deep breath, exhaling long and slow, then drew Hawk and signaled Rico.

A beep came over the loudspeaker. The clock started.

I sprinted toward the UPS truck, taking cover behind the front bumper. Both the supermarket and the restaurant were still ahead of me, the restaurant a little closer. I kept low, extended my left leg toward the end of the bumper, and leaned as far to the side as I could, without passing the corner of the truck. Clear.

Then stretching to my right, I did the same. Clear again, so I rolled out from behind the bumper and did a duck-and-run for the side of the restaurant. Adrenaline soared through my veins as I slammed up against the side of the building.

Breathe. Just breathe.

I moved toward the corner of the restaurant, tucked in my elbows, both hands on Hawk's grip, and slowly sliced the pie, edging forward until I had a clear view of Main Street. An armed bogey popped up in the doorway of the supermarket across the road. I squared and squeezed. *Tango down. Good to go.*

I jumped back behind the corner to take cover. It was close to fifty feet through the parking lot to the police station. After clearing the field at the corner, I tore through the lot like my ass was on fire. About halfway there, a target flew up, not five yards ahead, to my right.

I aimed and started to squeeze the trigger. *Shit, shit, shit!* A mommy and her baby out for a stroll. *No joy. Repeat, no joy.* Holy crap, I almost shot her.

Multiple targets popped, behind me, and to the right. I dove behind the mailbox and turned. Two more bogies, two head shots, problem solved.

The targets flew fast and furious.

I made it to the police station and pressed up against the wall, halfway hoping some officers might wander out and lend a hand. Like that was going to happen. I took a knee and sucked air like a Hoover, all the while keeping my eye on the far side of the street.

A computerized voice blared over the loudspeaker, "Shooter proceed to the alleyway and ascend the stairs. Clean and clear the walk-up."

Are you shitting me? What the actual fu... Get a grip. Focus. I closed my eyes and pulled myself together. *Steady now, breathe. In. Out. In. Out. Woosah. Woosah.* My mind cleared and I was ready to rock.

One last scramble across the street to the alley. Thankfully, no targets popped along the way, but that made me anxious as hell about what was inside the walk-up.

I plastered myself against the stair rail, pivoting to see as much as possible at the top, and then took the steps one at a time, scanning right-to-left, left-to-right, listening to the *thrum* of my heartbeat and the *squeak* of the boards beneath my feet.

It was quiet.

Too quiet.

I cleared the top of the stairway and hugged the building, reached across the door, and turned the knob. It was locked, so I kicked the door in and stepped back alongside the wall.

Clearing the right side of the room, I caught a reflection in the mirror. Bad guy number four. Nailed him with a shot through the door.

Two more rooms to go. I moved down the hall toward the

first door and a target dropped from the ceiling behind me. I dove to the floor, rolled and turned, then squeezed the trigger and blew off its head.

Last room. I sprang back to my feet and kicked in the door. A bogey at twelve o'clock had me in his sights. I dropped to my ass and took him out with one sweet shot.

It's over, I thought. Thank God.

Until another scumbag dropped from the roof on a rope just outside the window. One final squeeze of the trigger put him down with a dose of ballistic therapy.

Six up, six down. *Who's your momma?*

The loudspeaker crackled. "Exercise complete. Shooter return to the top of the course."

I was halfway back to the entrance of the walk-up when a damn biter busted through the closet door and jumped me.

The bastard jostled my hand and sent poor Hawk flying across the room.

That deadhead was on me faster than flies on a flesh-eater. And wouldn't you know it? He *was* a stinking flesh-eater, the meanest, most unpredictable deadhead of all.

I body-slammed it to the floor and scrambled for my gun, but the biter grabbed my right foot and bit down hard.

Damn, that hurt! I flipped onto my back and rocked a scissors kick straight into its face, knocking it on its ass, and pulverizing everything from its eyes to its chin. Then I reached into my left boot, pulled Baby from my ankle holster, and tapped that mother right between the eyes.

Allie: One. Biter: Zero.

Seconds later, Rico raced through the door. "You okay?"

"Just peachy." I glanced down at the tooth-shaped hole in

the side of my boot, fighting the urge to yank out my foot and look for blood.

That damn biter shook me up, but Rico didn't need to know that.

He picked his way across the brain splatter on the floor, stared at the remains of my rotter, and pulled on some nitrile gloves. "I don't understand. This is a private range. There're security cameras everywhere. How'd that thing get in here?"

That was the $64,000 question. How indeed?

Rico turned a little green as he stuck his hand in the biter's pants looking for some ID.

"Nothing," he said, sounding annoyed that his first ever pat-down of a deadhead had come up empty.

"The mystery doesn't end there." I shook my left foot a few times and splattered what was left of the biter's face across the wall. "Zombies don't come out in the daytime. They're blind in the sunlight. But this one grabbed my foot when he fell. He s*aw* me."

Rico and I stared at each other in silence, letting that factoid sink in.

Rico's phone rang and I was glad for the intrusion. Biters that can see in the daylight. That was a game-changing event. Had the virus mutated? Or had someone altered it?

After a brief conversation, Rico hung up and said, "Cap wants to see us. We've got a new case." He took one last look at the fresh coat of bio-goo on the walls and floor. "Looks like a job for Splatz."

"Hey, I get a fifty-dollar credit for referrals. Tell Jack, Allie sent you."

"So, what does this mean—the Z's changing?"

"Hard to say." I ducked into the hallway before he had a chance to ask anything else.

If my hunch was correct, we'd be up to our butts in biters before you could say *Jack Splatz.*

The 51st Precinct, a brownstone at the corner of Erie and Melbourne, smelled like stale smoke and marinara from Ricardo's Pizzeria next door. Its walls were a dingy yellow, which might have passed for white fifty years ago. A double-row of solid-oak desks faced each other and divided the bullpen.

What was probably the original flooring, a black and white checkerboard linoleum, was scuffed and worn with the occasional cigarette burn and unrecognizable stain. Add the empty pizza boxes and sticky coffee cups, and it was pretty indistinguishable from any other station I'd seen.

I ducked into the john as soon as we got there, to clean up and check my foot. An angry purple bruise had bloomed, but the skin wasn't broken.

That turned out to be the only good news of the day.

Cap's admin, an aging fussbudget named Miriam Miller, buzzed him to let him know we were there. His office was the first door on the right, past the bullpen. We hung in his doorway, waiting for him to wave us in.

Cap, aka Philip Dorsey, was in his 50s, almost as round as he was tall, and bald as a cue-ball. Old-school and hard-boiled, he preferred his skells living. He's had a hard time wrapping his mind around me and my *freaky Voodoo shit*. That's made me the proverbial fly in his ointment.

He looked lost in thought, gazing at a photo of a woman on the corner of his desk. When he realized we were there, he turned the picture around and waved us toward some chairs.

"How'd the qualification go?" he asked.

I started to answer but Rico jumped in. "She did great, Cap, but somehow a biter got into the walk-up and attacked her—in broad daylight."

"Piece of cake. No problem." I said, catching Rico's eye. "Just some random biter stuck in a closet."

Really? Stuck in a closet?

"Nothing I couldn't handle."

I didn't want to start fielding questions that I didn't have the answers to, so I changed the subject. "Cap, I wanted to talk to you about hiring me full-time."

Rico groaned and melted into his chair.

"You did? What a coincidence! I wanted to talk to you, too, Nighthawk." Cap's face blazed.

He picked up a piece of paper, wadded it into a ball, and threw it at my head.

"$13,456.17 for...*mausoleum repairs*?" Then he picked up another piece of paper. "$5,621.42, biohazard cleanup at city hall?"

"I can get you a better deal than that, Cap. I use Splatz. The owner—"

"*Ah, ah, ahhh.* I'm not finished yet." He held up yet another document, my employment application. "Hire you? *Hire you!* Nighthawk, I can't afford you. And while I'm at it, why are these bills coming here? You do have liability coverage, don't you?"

He peered over a pile of paperwork, like a vulture waiting to swoop.

"Of course, I do!"

Truthfully, I was only sixty-percent sure I did. I didn't keep track of all that minutiae. I'm a freaking *corpse whisperer*, damn it. I've got more important things to worry about—like saving the world from meatbags.

Little Allie was banging on my brain to let her speak, but I blew the little bitch fairy off. Screw her. She could save her own ass. It was every man for himself.

"For now," Cap continued, "You'll stay an independent contractor. I'll pay you a hundred bucks an hour. When you find a way to conduct your business using something other than the scorched earth method, we can revisit this conversation."

He leaned back in his chair. "Now, if you don't mind, I'd like to circle back to the corpsicle in the closet. How the hell did it get in there? That's our facility. No one else has access."

"We're already looking into that," Rico said.

"I'll call in Internal Affairs, if I have to. *I want answers*. It's not going to be *my* ass in a sling."

Rico winced "Roger that, Cap."

"Um... It was a flesh-eater, not a corpsicle," I mumbled. "There's a difference, you know."

Cap rolled up his sleeves and loosened his collar. "I may not like all this paranormal hoodoo, but I do keep up on it. That's my job. As I understand it, deadheads can't see during the day. So, how is it that this one broke form?"

I couldn't skirt the issue anymore. "To be honest, I don't know. But I've got some connections. I'll be reaching out as soon as we're finished here."

Like any moment now... Just get me the hell out of here.

Rico heard the word 'finished' and jumped up like he'd been shot out of a cannon.

But Cap wasn't finished yet. "How can these things, all of a sudden, start seeing in the light? Are they evolving? Has the disease mutated? If this gets out, the press will have a field day."

Oh, sweet Lord, the press. Chen would be like a rotter gnawing on a rib bone.

Cap pointed at me. "I want answers, Nighthawk. *Before* the mayor calls me and asks what the hell's going on."

"Yes, sir."

"Who're these connections of yours?"

"I have several, Cap. I'm not the only corpse whisperer in the world, or even in this country. I thought I'd contact Sandoval Latka, a European protégé of mine. He's a scientist with the *European Centre for Disease Prevention and Control* in Stockholm—Europe's version of our CDC. He's on the cutting edge of Carovescology, the study of the zombie virus. If there's any precedent for this, he'll know."

Cap leaned forward. "All right, then. Keep me posted. Now, on to new business. I've got another case for you. The FBI has requested your assistance with a mob informant, by the name of Leo Abruzzi. He's the financial wizard who cooked the books for the Giordano Family, and shuffled their money from one invisible holding company to another. Abruzzi contracted the virus several weeks back, when a biter sunk its teeth into him. He couldn't stomach the thought of turning, and lacked the intestinal fortitude to swallow his own gun, so he offered to turn state's evidence in return for a supply of Narco... Naco... Necro..."

He'd never get it, so I helped him out. "Nacarotoxin. The drug that slows the progression of symptoms."

"Whatever," Cap said, waving me off. "Abruzzi's a few weeks into treatment. He knows the drug will stop working someday. The FBI deposed him, so they have his testimony on file, but they're still gathering physical evidence for the indictment. They want to keep him safe until he testifies before the grand jury."

Crap, crap, crappity, crap. Talk about the icing on the turd cake.

Rico went slack-jawed. "You want us to babysit the numbers guy?"

"Call it what you will," said Cap. "Between the two of you, keep him out of harm's way."

"What am I supposed to do?" I asked. "I can't make the drug work any better, or longer, than it was designed to."

Cap shrugged. "True, but if anyone can pick up on signs that he's deteriorating, or outright turning, it's you. If he doesn't make it to the stand, the FBI wants to be sure to get a final deposition from him while he's still mentally competent, just in case he's been holding back. He's flying in tonight, on the redeye, with an agent escort. So, here's what's going to happen. De Palma, tomorrow morning, you're going to play Uber driver for Abruzzi, pick him up from the Kenwood FBI office at nine, and bring him back here for a little chat about his security detail."

Cap turned to me. "You're going to call that Latka guy in Stockholm and find out if there are any more of these mutant meatbags showing up."

Rico got up to leave, but Cap had something else on his mind.

"Wait a minute, Nighthawk." He shot a quick glance toward the photo on his desk and hesitated like he was collecting his thoughts. "Tell me something. These creatures...these...dead-heads. How long have they been around?"

"Forever." I let out a sigh. "When people like me get it right, they're almost invisible. They're like the derelicts living under railroad trestles or the addicts wandering the alleys. They're just another monster no one wants to see."

That was so sad and true, that it hurt.

I flashed a half-hearted smile, tired and paper-thin. "Not to worry. We whisperers always manage to keep them in check."

Cap lowered his voice. "Don't get me wrong, but if the game is changing—if the disease is changing—can you still do that? Keep them in check?"

"Damn straight, I can. I'm the best of the bad-ass zombie hunters. Remember?" I threw him a wink, spun on my heel and walked out the door.

No sense in letting the man lose sleep over something he couldn't control.

Me? I wasn't sure I'd ever sleep again.

5

DEALING WITH THE DEVIL

Stockholm is six hours ahead of Cincinnati, so I sipped my morning coffee and considered giving Sandoval a call. Then I heard Nussbaum and Headbutt going at it in the back-yard. I didn't need to look out the window to see what was going on. It was a daily ritual that never got old: Headbutt whizzing on Nussbaum's rosebushes through the chain-link fence and Nussbaum vaulting off her porch, brandishing a broom, support hose billowing around her cankles, flying after him like the Wicked Witch of the West.

I had to give the old bat some props. She was spry for a fossil. She swung that broom like a battle-axe—straight into the top of the metal fence rail, making her batwings jiggle like jello in a wave tank.

"Mrs. Nighthawk," she yelled. "Keep that four-legged golem away from my bushes. Always, every day is same. He has no manners. Your father—God rest his soul—would never allow such monkeyshines. The dog is like spoilt child. *Feh!*"

I inherited the house when my father passed away three years ago. My mother died when I was eleven. I've never been married a day in my life, and yet for some reason, this nut-job blue-hair always referred to me as Mrs. Nighthawk.

I knew Headbutt shouldn't pee on her bushes, and Headbutt knew he shouldn't pee on her bushes. But it was one of his few pleasures in life. What can I say? Rules aren't his thing. Mine either.

I waved at her from the backdoor. "Sorry, Mrs. Nussbaum. Headbutt, come in here!"

He waddled inside as fast as his short legs could carry him, wearing a proud, accomplished smile. It earned him a dog biscuit.

"Could you at least *try* to not pee on her bushes? It drives her crazy."

He snorted and walked away, a dog that bowed to no man. He and I were more alike than either of us would have cared to admit.

I refilled my coffee cup and called Sandoval, aka Sandy, to ask if he'd heard tales of sighted Z's popping up. Sandy, an old friend, a man who'd dedicated his work at the European CPDC to the study of Carovescology, was a leading authority on the virus. His research had saved me more than once. I'd have walked through fire for the man, and he the same for me.

"Good to hear from you, my dear," Sandy said. "You must have read my mind. I was about to call and ask you the same. Since yesterday, we've received several reports, three in Germany, two in Argentina, and one here in Sweden. I expect more in the coming days. The sightings are too wide-spread to be coincidence."

"What's happening?" I asked. "Is the virus mutating?"

"Always in such a hurry, my Allie. You know I don't have that answer yet. But I'm taking some tissue samples from the zombie that turned up in Gothenburg, about four hours from here. I'll contact you when I know more. You must call sometime when you simply want to chat, my friend. I love you and I miss you."

"Me too, Sandy. Gotta run. Take care, now." I hung up and turned my thoughts to the rest of the day. Looking back later, I wished that I'd told him I loved him, too. Those were words he deserved to hear.

Between Kulu and Headbutt my doorbell had become obsolete. Visitors, strangers within fifty yards of my house and tiny, blowing leaves were thoroughly announced, long before they ever reached my porch.

I opened the front door to find Rico, and a short guy I presumed to be Leo, chatting with Mrs. Nussbaum in my driveway.

Damn. She was fast for a fossil.

"I didn't know you were receiving today, Mrs. Nighthawk," she said. "Such lovely gentlemen, too."

She followed them to my door. "It was pleasure to meet you, Mr. De Palma, and Mr...? I'm sure we see each other again—"

"Bye-bye, Nonnie," Rico said, as they stepped inside.

Nonnie was still talking as he eased the door closed in her face. The short guy eyed me from head-to-toe, like he was picking a hooker for the evening.

"So, this is the ballbuster?" he asked. "*The* Allie Nighthawk? You yanking my chain, De Palma? Lay youse fifty-to-one the girls on the shore could take her in five."

Even the brain bitch wanted him dead.

Rico flushed. "Nighthawk meet Leo Abruzzi."

Leo elbowed Rico. "A little make-up, the right clothes, she could be a looker. Am I right?" Then the douche-canoe winked at me. "Hey, baby. I'm Leo—the lion."

I needed a shower. In less than a minute, I already knew

more about Leo Abruzzi than any woman should ever want to know—all 5'6" of him, with his oily black hair and his tailored red silk shirt. He wore a thick gold chain and charcoal-colored slacks that were a size too small. His tiny brown eyes scanned from side-to-side, like he was casing the joint.

The douche-nozzle. I considered shoving his nose through his brain, but shot him the Allie eye, instead.

Then it occurred to me the nimrod might think I was flirting, so I turned to Rico and said, "Why don't you and Mr. Brylcreem wait for me in the car? I'll be right out."

Headbutt and Kulu needed to be fed and I had to lock up. When I finally closed the door, Kulu gave me a long, loud raspberry.

You can't buy that kind of love.

From the time we left my driveway, Leo's mouth ran like a duck's ass. He leaned forward in the backseat, his mouth next to the steel-mesh cage.

"What kind of nightlife you got in this podunk town, anyway? One thing about Leo, he go, go, goes. You stay moving, you make a harder target. Am I right? Every town's got a strip joint. It's almost noon, they gotta be open. Seven-sevens, on me. C'mon. What do you say?"

I turned around and smacked the cage with the palm of my hand. He didn't take the hint.

"What's a matter, baby? You don't want to share Leo with other women? Leo's a lot to handle, if you get my drift. Magnum-sized, but hey, I'm willing—"

"That's it. Pull over," I said.

Rico groaned. "Jesus, Nighthawk. Chill out."

Leo never stopped for a breath. "A spitfire! Leo likes a spitfire. Listen, sweetheart—"

I spun around, pushed my face against the wire mesh, and let my bitch flag fly.

"*Shut the hell up.* Either lose the third-person bullshit or lose your head. Your choice. And if you ever call me *baby* or *sweetheart* again, I'm going to pull a magnum-sized condom over your cheesy face and turn you into a balloon animal."

Leo paused, then glanced at Rico and said, "That was cold, man. You told me she liked that shit."

Rico's eyes sparkled.

That's okay, mi amigo. Payback's a bitch, I thought.

The sparkle in his eyes faded.

"What's up?" I asked.

"Maybe nothing." He looked at me and mouthed, "Black Lexus. Four cars back."

I shrugged and whispered, "Only one way to find out."

Rico took a series of lefts and rights. The Lexus stayed with us, lurking a few cars back, never catching us, but never losing pace. Then, Rico jerked the steering wheel to the left, onto the entrance ramp of I-71S, and hit the gas.

Leo grabbed the mesh cage to keep from sliding across the back seat. "What the hell, De Palma?"

"You got any friends that drive a black Lexus, Leo?" Rico asked.

"Half the damn country drives a black Lexus. How the hell should I know?"

Then the lightbulb went on and his eyes flew wide open.

"Ah, shit. Shit. Somebody tailing us?" Leo whipped his head around to look out the back window. "I don't see no black Lexus. Fucking mob. I knew this grand jury shit would come back to bite me."

We were doing eighty-five. Leo was right, the Lexus was nowhere to be seen. Apparently, it hadn't made the bat-turn onto the expressway. Whoever the tail had been, we'd lost them. At least, for the time being.

Cap's admin, Miriam, snarled as she watched us approach through the bullpen. Her hair, knotted tightly in a bun, pulled her eyes toward the sides of her head, making them look like two tiny almonds stuck in pastry dough.

There wasn't a smidgeon of dust on her desk. Her stapler and other supplies were turned at ninety-degree angles, flanking her like tiny desktop warriors. Someone was seriously OCD.

She rounded her desk and planted herself between us and Cap's office. "I'll see if he's in," she snipped.

"No need," I said, flicking over her stapler. "I can see him from here. Hey, Cap!"

Miriam's face blanched as she leaned into Cap's office. "Officer De Palma and that Nighthawk woman have arrived with Mr. Abruzzi."

"I can see that, Miriam. Thank you. Have a seat," he said, motioning us forward.

Miriam stood at the door, watching us file in. Leo hesitated as he walked by her, then leaned in and nibbled her ear. She recoiled faster than a semi-automatic.

I gave the door a push, and saw her eyes blaze as it swung closed in her face. Then, I slapped the back of Leo's head as she scurried back to her desk.

"Watch the hair. Watch the hair," he said, slicking it back into place.

The three of us sat lined up across from Cap's desk, like rowdy kids reporting to the school principal.

Cap started with Rico. "I take it Mr. Abruzzi's financial books were logged into evidence at the FBI office?"

"Yes, sir. They're digitized on a thumb drive that's tagged into evidence. But, before we go any further, you should know that we think we were tailed on our way here. Black Lexus, no plate number. Whoever it was, we lost them."

"Is that right? Welcome to the world of a protected witness, Mr. Abruzzi. Keep your eyes open, listen to what I'm about to say, and you just might make it to the grand jury," Cap said. "Officer De Palma and Ms. Nighthawk will be your primary security detail. They'll be relieved by Officers Powell and Ortega. You'll be staying at a safe house in Oakley, about ten miles north of town. There are rules that apply to an individual with protected witness status. You are to tell no one of your whereabouts, Mr. Abruzzi. Not only for your safety, but for that of my officers and Ms. Nighthawk. You will follow their directions, at all times. And you will, without fail, use the alias, *David McGee*. Am I understood?"

Leo winked at Cap. "Gotcha. *No problemo*. Leo's not great with rules, but—"

I reached over and dug my fingernails into his thigh, to stop the third-person bullshit.

Leo winced. "I mean, yeah. Sure thing, Cap. I'd never endanger your guys. You got my back, right?" He laughed, then suddenly sucked in a breath and froze.

His forehead glistened with sweat, and his face grew pale. He clutched the arms of his chair in a death-grip, gouging his fingernails into the wood until they bled. His teeth chattered like one of those wind-up skulls, then they clenched so hard, I thought they'd crack. In a violent spasm, he flew out of the chair and flopped onto the floor, convulsing.

Cap jumped to his feet. "What the hell's happening?"

I looked at Rico. "When's the last time he had his meds?"

"Hell, I don't know." Rico grabbed his wallet and shoved it between Leo's teeth. Then, he turned Leo's pockets inside-out, and found his pre-dosed, capped syringes. "How do we know that's what's wrong with him? Do we give him the medicine or call 911?"

Cap and Rico stared at me, waiting for an answer. I was a freaking *corpse whisperer*, damn it, not a doctor, not a pharmacist, and not a chemist. On a good day, I was lucky if I had on two shoes that matched. And yet, there I was, once again, making a life-and-death decision, based only on a hunch. For all I knew, the seizure could have been caused by an allergy we knew nothing about. The shot might save him, or it might kill him. But, one way or the other, he'd either go full-on zombie or be flat-out dead, by the time an ambulance arrived. What choice did we have?

I grabbed one of the syringes and jabbed it into Leo's thigh.

He stopped twitching, and in a matter of seconds, lay still on the floor, his eyes open, his breathing almost normal.

Rico took his wallet out of Leo's mouth and laid his sport coat over the top of him.

Leo gave it a couple of minutes and then struggled to sit up. "Am I turning? Is this it?"

"What time were you supposed to take your medication, Leo?" I asked.

His voice shimmied. "Same time I take it every day. Noon. Why?"

I looked at my watch. It was almost one-thirty. He'd missed it by an hour and a half.

"Leo, didn't the doctor explain to you how important it is that you take your medicine on time? Every day? If you miss a dose, you run the risk of turning."

"Holy shit." Leo shook his head and mopped his face with his hand. "Yeah. Yeah, they told me. What with flying out here and all this talk about depositions, I didn't think about it."

"*Didn't think about it?*" I screamed. "You little fuck-stick! You turned state's evidence to get that shit. How about taking some responsibility? Keeping yourself alive to honor your end of the bargain? Monitor your own damn meds. Jesus. Do we need to breathe for you, too?"

"That's enough, Nighthawk." Cap helped Leo up off the floor. "You think you're okay, now? Or do you want to go to the hospital?"

"I'm fine," Leo said, his face crimson, like I'd spanked him in front of his classmates. "It won't happen again."

Cap nodded. "Good. I'm glad we're all on the same page. Now, back to the safe house. De Palma, coordinate with Powell and Ortega—twelve-hour shifts. Electronic clocking. By the book. Tight as a drum. I want the shift changes documented."

Twelve-hour shifts?

My head snapped up. "Cap, I've got pets at home. I need to make arrangements for someone to care for them while I'm on detail."

I had no idea how I was going to do that. It's not like I could afford doggy daycare. For crapsake, all three of us were eating dog biscuits. The chicken-flavored ones weren't so bad, once you got past the smell. But Kulu usually snapped those up.

"Fine. Whatever you have to do. Just do it. If neither of you have anything else, I think we're through here." Cap stood, signaling us to leave. "Oh, Nighthawk, hold on a minute."

Leo sighed. "If it's okay with youse, I gotta use the can."

Rico led him out of the room, shutting the door behind them.

"Did you get hold of Latka?" Cap asked. "What's the story on the daytime deadheads?"

"Yes, sir. There've been a few scattered reports of sightings, worldwide. One of the biters wasn't too far from Stockholm. Latka's doing some tissue testing. He'll get back to me when he knows more."

"Keep me updated," Cap said, turning to a file on his desk.

I opened the door, and almost fell over a twitchy little janitor named Ottis. I'd seen him around, and had taken to calling him *The Squirrel* because he had small, pinched features and he scurried when he moved. He'd been bent over, sweeping nuts or something into a dust pan, and bolted upright when the door opened.

A smile jittered across his face, as he stepped aside to let me pass. The guy made my skin crawl—and I dealt with deadheads.

I caught up with the guys back at Rico's car. Rico opened the rear passenger-side door to let Leo in, and casually tossed out the only plausible solution to my pet-sitting problem. Even if it did make me want to shove a needle into my eye.

"Why don't you ask that nosy neighbor of yours to watch Headbutt and Kulu?"

Leo snorted. "Headbutt and Kulu? What the hell kind of names are those? What's wrong with Spot and Max?"

He stooped to clear the roof as he climbed into the car, and I gave him a shove. "Shut up, *David*."

Damn it. Rico was right. Mrs. Nussbaum was my only choice.

When we pulled into my driveway, Mrs. Nussbaum burst through her front door, and swooped in on us, like a turkey vulture. I'd rather have done anything than ask her for help. At least she wasn't carrying her broom.

"Mrs. Nighthawk, you and your friends are back! How nice. Come. Come have some rugelach. Not the dry kind tastes like sand. My kind, with the chocolate and cream cheese and apricot jam. Come. I bake all day. Just for you."

I've known this woman my entire life. She'd never baked anything for me or my father. Not even the things that tasted like sand. She must have the hots for Rico. God knows, it couldn't be Leo. Nonnie and her hormones were going to have to chill.

Wow. *Nonnie* and *hormones* in the same sentence. Disturbing.

I needed to get Leo inside, out of sight, somewhere that I could protect him. For the moment, that was my house.

"Thank you, Mrs. Nussbaum, but we'll have to pass. *David's* tired after his long day of travel."

She looked like I'd just peed on her rosebushes. And I still needed to ask for her help. *Shit.*

"If anyone cares," mumbled Leo, "I vote for the chocolate cream cheese things. Just sayin'."

"It was so nice of you to think of us, Mrs. Nussbaum," I said. "Maybe you could bring the rugu...the stuff you fixed...here, to my house. We can eat them inside while David rests. Would that work?"

"Yes. Yes, of course. I bring milk, too. Very good with milk."

I kept Rico and Leo behind me when we walked inside the house, making sure no one got bit or pooped on. Headbutt glanced up from his throne on the floor vent. Seeing me calm and unconcerned, he promptly closed his eyes. Kulu, however, kept her distance, mumbling curse words and shaking her wings, clearly more concerned about stranger danger.

My house, an old Cape Cod, was small but cozy. I didn't have an eye for decorating. The worn, early-American furniture might have been a good clue. The place was quiet, but if it ever caught on fire, the neighborhood would be toast. The basement and spare bedroom were packed with napalm and small arms ammo.

Mrs. Nussbaum appeared at the backdoor, rugelach in hand.

Headbutt scrambled to his feet and farted, then began barking non-stop.

Kulu spread her wings and paced back-and-forth on her perch, screaming "Crazy bitch! Crazy bitch!"

I threw my shoe at Kulu, intentionally missing her by a mile.

"Allie's mad. Allie's mad," she muttered, sulking on her perch.

It took a while for me to get Headbutt settled. He kept a bloodshot eye on Mrs. Nussbaum and woofed periodically, reminding everyone that he was ready for action.

At last, the menagerie quieted and the party commenced. We ate. We drank. We laughed. I gagged when I realized Nonnie was interested in Leo, and nearly puked when I caught him winking back at her. *The hound.*

I couldn't put it off any longer. "Mrs. Nussbaum. We've had such a lovely evening. Maybe we can be friends, not just neighbors. Wouldn't that be nice?"

Her smile froze.

"I have to ask you something—a favor. I need your help."

"What you want?" she asked, giving me the hairy eyeball.

"I need you to watch Headbutt and Kulu for me."

She grabbed her chest, and looked at me like I'd asked her for a kidney.

"Just for a little while," I pleaded. "My work schedule changed. I have to leave now for my shift. Can you watch them for me, for the next twelve hours? And maybe...every day, until my schedule changes back?"

"When that?"

"As soon as humanly possible."

Nonnie whined. "The dog, it farts and pees on my roses. And the bird is very scary."

"Headbutt needs manners, right? Maybe you could teach him manners. You could feed Kulu some treats and teach her some *nice* words."

"This, I could do." She smiled shyly at Leo. "I stay here with your friend, David, while you working and watch them."

"David has to go to work with me, but you're welcome to watch them here or at your house. Your choice."

"Here," she sighed. "No peeing and pooping my house."

Headbutt and Kulu stared in silence as I grabbed the keys to my Harley.

"You be good," I said, pointing at them. "C'mon, Rico, David. Time for work."

As we headed out the door, I took one last look at the unholy trinity—Nussbaum, Headbutt and Kulu—and couldn't shake the feeling that I'd just made a deal with the devil.

6

LIFE IN THE TAR PITS

As we turned onto Jora Lane, folks were trimming bushes, edging their lawns, and taking leisurely strolls in the late afternoon sun. Cozy, red-bricked Cape Cods stood side-by-side on the quiet, tree-lined street of Oakley. Locals kept their houses neat and clean, and their yards manicured and green. Crime was nearly unheard of. The residents, many of them members of the Neighborhood Watch Association, made it their business to keep it that way.

It was Every Street, U.S.A., anonymous and ordinary, the perfect place for a safe house, despite Leo's reservations.

"You're killing me!" He gawked out the car window at his new neighbors. "Look at those dinosaurs. Not one of 'em's under ninety. It's the La Brea tar pits—only without the tar."

I figured at least he wouldn't be sneaking out for booty calls. But then I remembered him going moon-eyed over Nonnie, and realized that keeping track of Leo could be like herding cats.

Rico did a quick sweep of the house before Leo and I climbed out of the car. When we got the *all clear*, we walked inside and found ourselves smack-dab in the middle of the 1960s.

A metallic sunburst clock stretched across the living room wall like an enormous golden spider. The hardwood floors were covered by a puke-green shag rug, anchored by an ugly plaid sofa and two faded, flowered chairs, all of which wore plastic slipcovers.

Accessories included a laminate coffee table with chipped edges, a set of matching end tables, and some cheesy Lucite lamps. But the crowning glory, a huge console television, squatted in the corner like an ancient wooden behemoth. No satellite dish on the roof, no cable box in sight, and no strip-club at the corner. Poor Leo.

In a brief but blessed moment of silence, Leo stood speechless. The kitchen, with its white steel cabinets, canary yellow countertops, and ugly-ass linoleum floor seemed to break the spell. He opened the cabinet beside the refrigerator, put his medicine on the shelf, and then rummaged around beneath the sink, pulling out spray cleaner and a roll of paper towels.

For some reason, when he walked back into the living room, he tore off a wad of towels and threw them at me.

"You take the chair on the right. I got the couch." He drenched them both in spray cleaner.

I tossed the towels back. "Sorry, guy. I don't do windows."

A vein on the side of his head began to pulse. "Do you know how old this piece of shit furniture is? It was here when Kennedy was president. Who the hell has furniture this old? The FBI, that's who. Cheap bastards. Hello? This is the twenty-first century calling. Can we please have furniture that isn't dry-rotted and shrink-wrapped?"

Leo scrubbed the cooties off the fifty-year-old slipcovers, I supervised, and Rico scavenged for food.

"Coffee filters," Rico said. "But no coffee. Nothing in the

freezer. Ketchup, mustard, and something green and shriveled stuck to the bottom of the vegetable bin in the refrigerator."

Leo threw up his hands. "No food, Leo. *No food!* Of course, there's no food. Why would there be food? Just starve me before I get to the grand jury. What's a matter with you people? I'm doing you a favor, here. Is it too much to ask for a cracker crumb?!"

In Leo's defense, it was almost dinnertime. We were all hungry.

He disappeared down the hallway with the spray cleaner, paper towels and his clothes, ranting about the place not having been cleaned since Kennedy was president. While he did that, I ordered an extra-large pie with everything except anchovies from Ricardo's Pizzeria.

Ricardo's had the best pizza in town. Their delivery guy, Toby, a tall, skinny kid about twenty-years-old, four-eyed and curly-haired, always got the pies out hot. And they were never stuck to the top of the box. All the cops at the 51st knew Toby. He was in and out of the precinct, all day long.

To be completely honest, Ricardo's was the only restaurant phone number I knew because they were the only joint in town that would still deliver to me. I mentioned that to Toby once, and he said my house was on some top-secret delivery blacklist. The reason Ricardo's would still deliver to me is because Toby said he didn't mind stopping by. But they made him sign a waiver. He was fascinated with deadheads, worshipped me like a goddess, and despite the odd goings on at my place, never once left me hanging in need of my mozzarella. Good man, Toby.

I walked down the hall to Leo's bedroom, to let him know dinner was on its way, and found him wiping out the inside of the dresser drawers. The paper towels were almost gone. I looked for more and, in the process, discovered the house had exactly one roll of toilet paper. Someone would need to go grocery shopping.

Once again, that wasn't going to be me.

Leo, the prissy little weasel, put his clothes away exactly like you'd think a numbers guy would, every pleat creased and every collar crisped.

When he finished sanitizing the bedroom, he moved to the kitchen and scrubbed the table and chairs. Then we drew up his grocery list. Every time I thought we were finished, we weren't.

"Swiffers, SOS pads, and rubber gloves. And Frosted Flakes. And a half-gallon of Johnnie Walker."

The scotch drew a side glance from Rico.

"This place gives me the willies," Leo said. "I'm going to need something to help me sleep. You don't got any Ambien, do you?"

A knock came at the door.

Rico peered out the window from behind a dusty, pinch-pleated drape and smiled. "It's Toby."

I held out my hand to Rico for money. "Don't look at me. I'm not getting paid to feed this Sicilian greaseball."

When Toby walked in with a steaming hot pie, napkins and paper plates, I handed him the thirty bucks Rico had given me and told him to keep the change.

Rico's jaw dropped.

I didn't care. I liked Toby. He deserved a good tip, especially when it wasn't coming out of my pocket.

"Hey, guys," Toby asked. "What're you doing here?"

I set the stage. "My...uncle...moved here from New Jersey and he's renting this house. His name is David. Say hello, David."

Leo grabbed hold of the pizza box and tried to walk away.

"*Uncle David*," I said, refusing to let go of the box. "Don't be rude. Say hi to Toby. He'll be delivering your pizzas, from now on."

"Yeah? What if I don't like it? Maybe I'll order from somewhere else. Gimme that," Leo said, opening the lid and jamming a slice into his mouth.

I stared a hole through his head. "Impossible. *Everyone* loves Ricardo's Pizza. And besides, *we know them and trust them,* Uncle David."

Leo shrugged and jerked the box out of my hands with a nod. "Yo, Toby."

"Nice to meet you, Uncle David. I gotta bounce. More pies to fly," Toby said, as he walked out the door.

Leo winced and spit a bite back onto his plate. "There's pineapple on this. Nobody puts pineapple on pizza. It's un-American."

I reached over and flicked another chunk of pineapple off the top of his slice.

It skittered across the table and fell to the floor.

"There. Problem solved."

"Get your fingers off my pie."

What a freaking whiner.

Rico and I drew straws to see who would get the groceries. I won, which meant I got to stay at the house. Like I would have gone, anyway.

But, Rico put up a good fight. "You should go, Nighthawk. I'm the cop. This is my job, watching Leo."

"Hey, I'm qualified. I shot my way through Perptown. Besides, if you wait for me to go, he'll starve."

So, Rico went to the store, leaving Leo and me sitting at the kitchen table, sipping some iced tea.

Motormouth had so much nervous energy that he stopped in the middle of a rant, frowned, and jumped up to open the cabinet over the stove. He glanced inside at his meds, like he was making sure they were there, then shut the door with a sigh. For the next few minutes, he yacked about nothing and paced around the kitchen like a caged animal.

He could be such a sleazebag, it was easy to forget how he'd gotten here in the first place.

I waited until he sat back down to revisit a memory he might rather forget. "If you don't mind me asking, how'd you get bit?"

At first, he didn't answer. I figured maybe he thought it was none of my business and he was blowing me off.

But then he opened up, sounding almost shy, maybe even humble, nothing like the Jersey bad-ass he'd been all along.

"I can tell you what happened, but why? Who the hell knows? I was in town, seeing a...a...a...client in the Carew Tower."

The tower was a high-rise not far from the riverfront. That's a busy part of town, especially during the day. Security every-where, cameras and alarms.

"How any freaking biter could get into that parking garage, I'll never know," Leo said. "The thing staggered out of the shad-ows, from between the parked cars, and headed my way. At first, I thought it had to be a prank, right? Or maybe I'd walked into the middle of a movie set."

His voice caught in his throat. "I mean, seriously—a freaking zombie in the middle of town? No fucking way. And it seemed like the damn thing came right at me. It shuffled past cars and other people *to get to me.*"

His story set off all kinds of alarm bells. Little Allie went nutso inside my head. I had to shut the brain bitch off, so I could hear the rest of what he had to say.

"Some guy whaled on the deadhead with his briefcase, connected real good, too, right at its chest. The son of a bitching biter just absorbed the blow and kept moving. Another guy tried to back over it with his Beamer. It just rolled off the trunk of the car and *kept coming at me.* People started running and diving, scrambling for cover. I can still hear them screaming."

His eyes grew moist. "And I still see it, too. Every night, when I close my eyes, that meatbag lurching at me like a fucking juggernaut, nothing stopping it. The smell, that sweet, sick stench when it was on top of me. So strong. It stuck inside my nose and liked to never go away. That motherfucker tore a chunk out of my side."

He yanked up his shirt and showed me the bite wound beneath his ribcage. "That's a whole new kind of pain, let me tell you. But I got lucky, if you can call it that. Somebody'd called the cops. They shot the bastard off the top of me when it was going in for seconds."

He pointed toward his med stash in the cabinet. "The EMTs gave me a needle full of that stuff. Do you know how much that shit costs? One month's worth is more than I make in a year. What's that they say about 'necessity making strange bedfellows'?" Leo swiped at his face. "Excuse me."

He shuffled down the hall to the bathroom looking twenty years older than when he'd sat down.

He might have mixed his proverbs, but his message was clear. He'd never be trapped in this 1960s time warp, waiting to testify before the grand jury, if not for that bite.

When he came back into the kitchen, his eyes were red-rimmed and swollen.

I pretended not to notice and asked, "You said it seemed like the deadhead was coming after you, specifically. Did it act like it could see you?"

"Well, yeah. It had to have seen me. When I moved, it moved with me."

"How long ago was this, Leo?"

"Three weeks, yesterday. Hand to God, Nighthawk," he said. "When this medicine stops working, I ain't coming back as no filthy, stinking meatbag. I had them write it into my witness protection agreement. Somebody's going to have to scramble my brains but good."

He was right. I closed my eyes and tried not to think about who that somebody would be.

In a surprising move, he turned the tables on me. "So, what's it like to be a corpse whisperer? Must be a rush, huh? The power of life and death in your hands?"

I squirmed in my crappy vinyl chair and glanced at the clock above the sink. "Yeah, well, it's not all it's cracked up to be."

This wasn't a conversation I wanted to have with anyone, let alone Leo.

I got up and looked out the window. "Rico should be back any time now. Maybe he picked up some of that Johnnie Walker."

Leo wasn't going to let it drop. "Where does this power of yours come from?"

Damn, if he wasn't an annoying little dipshit.

"It's hereditary. On my mother's side."

"Hereditary. *Wow*. How old were you when you raised your first corpse?"

Son of a bitching, Leo. Why couldn't he just let it lie?

And just like that, I wasn't the corpse whisperer sitting in that 1960s piece of shit kitchen anymore. I was a little girl in a pink sun dress, standing with my momma in Rose Hill Cemetery, late one August night, my small hands shaking as they stretched over the body of Red Jameson.

Red had been out hunting in Adams County with his eight-year-old son, Noah. When they didn't make it back home, a search party found Red in the woods, dead of a snake bite. No sign of Noah.

"Feel the heat in your hands?" Momma said. "Don't be afraid. You can do it, Allie. Try again. Let the power flow through you."

I had been trying. Blood dripped out of my nose onto my sun dress. I let out a sob. "I don't want to, mommy! I don't want to. Let him sleep. Please. Please. Let him sleep."

She knelt beside me, put her hands on my shoulders, and said something that would stay with me all my life.

"This is God's work we're doing, Little Allie. God's work. He gave us this gift for a reason. You need to know how and when to use it. Now, you wake Mr. Jameson up and ask where Noah went. After you do that, go on home to your daddy, and I'll put Mr. Jameson back to sleep. I promise. I'll teach you that part when you're older. You never, ever raise a soul you don't put back to rest. That's a sin before God and man."

The sound of the kitchen door brought me out of my reverie. In walked Rico with Leo's Johnnie Walker, and suddenly it didn't matter to Leo how old I was the day my life changed forever—a memory that, despite my best efforts and untold quantities of Jack, I could never erase.

"I knew I liked you, De Palma. Drinks all around!" Leo said, pouring himself a double.

I could have used one about then, too, after my trip down memory lane.

But Rico cut me off. "Sorry, Leo. We're on duty. Thanks anyway."

Well, *crap*.

Since Leo had killed all the couch cooties, we took the party into the living room. I flopped on the sofa and stretched out, leaving the chairs for the guys.

Rico sipped some tea and asked Leo how he got hooked up with the Giordano Family.

Leo waved us off. "Ah, you don't want to hear that shit."

Rico kicked back in his ugly flowered chair and said, "Why the hell not? What else have we got to do?"

Leo rubbed his hand through his greasy black hair and fidgeted on the plasticized chair that groaned with his every move.

Finally, he leaned back and closed his eyes. "I grew up in Newark. I never knew my dad. My mom...she did what she needed to do, to put food on the table. Let's just say, I had an endless parade of uncles coming in and out of our apartment. Know what I'm saying? Most nights I'd sit on the stoop and wait for Mom to get done...transacting business. Even when it was cold, I'd sit out there. What kid wants to hear that shit going on with his mom? Right?

"So, this guy who lived in our burg, Paulie DeVito, a made guy, you know. Nice as hell. Used to bring me and mom food sometimes. And he never touched my mom, or made me call him uncle, or nothing. When I was maybe eight years old, he asked me if I wanted to make some money running numbers. It wasn't a question of wanting to make money. We needed money. He knew that, but he didn't want to *make* me do it. He wanted it to be my choice. See?

"And he...he was so cool, why wouldn't I want to do what he did? Of course, I ran numbers for him. And when I got older and had enough street smarts, I did some drops for him, too. Paulie always made sure I had money for clothes. He never let us go hungry. If we needed help with the rent, he was there. We needed someone to pay utilities, he was there." Leo went quiet, lost in his thoughts for a second.

I looked at him and wondered if everyone with a fucked-up childhood ended up loud and bigger than life. Maybe we had more in common than I ever would have thought.

Leo leaned forward and rested his forearms on his knees. "Paulie could see I had a head for figures, so he helped me with tuition, so I could get a degree. He didn't make me go to work for the Family, but Jesus, I owed them that and more. When I got out of school, there was a job waiting for me. No small potatoes shit, either. I was finally making some serious dough and supporting mom, so she didn't have to sell her soul to live hand-to-mouth anymore."

Rico wrinkled his nose. "But did you ever stop to think, in all those years, what the Giordano Family was into? Drugs, gaming, extortion, murder? You had a degree. You said it yourself, the Family gave you a choice. You could've gone straight."

Leo face fell. "I was a banker for chrissake! Moving money around, just like those Wall Street yahoos. Only, I made a helluva lot more dough than they did, 'cause the Family was good to me. I sat behind a fucking desk!"

He slammed his fist on the coffee table and stared Rico down. "I never did no wet work. You hear me? I never killed no one. And don't you go thinking I did."

Rico blanched. "I don't think that, Leo. You're not the type. You don't have it in you."

That awkward little Kodak moment was interrupted by the sound of Rico's phone. He pulled it out of his pocket. His eyebrows raised when he glanced at the display.

"De Palma," he answered, but not in his usual macho-cop tone. "Hi, Ms. Chen, how can I help you?"

He listened for a moment, then got up with a smile and moved past me toward the kitchen, blushing like a school-boy. I craned my neck to watch him, from my seat on the couch.

After a few nods, a couple of chuckles, and a mock groan he said, "Wow, that sounds like a *lot* more fun than I'm in for tonight, but unfortunately, I can't. I'm working."

He went quiet for a bit, like he was listening, and then said, "Sorry. I really can't say. Police business. You know."

He'd moved deeper into the kitchen, damn it. It was getting harder to hear him.

Leo sighed. "You realize that's rude, right? It's obviously a chick. Let the man work."

"Shut up, Leo. Can't you see I'm listening?"

"Oh, I get it," he said. "You got the hots for him! Ha! That's funny."

"Bite your tongue, you greasy little weasel."

Rico let loose a few more laughs and a husky, "Yes ma'am," followed by a flirty, "Looking forward to it."

Rico's feet echoed across the linoleum, his steps growing louder as he neared the living room. He stood in the archway and glanced in at us. I jerked my head around, like I was looking out the window, and almost gave myself whiplash.

He turned back to his phone and lowered his voice, but he didn't turn away. "I know," he said. "I'd tell you if I could."

Whatever she said next caused his face to flame.

"No," he snickered. "I won't tell you, even if you do that. But do it anyway." He laughed again. "Okay. See you about one. Bye."

There was way too much laughing going on for my taste. And *see you at one*? Our shift was over at midnight. She sure wasn't wasting time, the little barracuda.

"My man," Leo said, raising his hand for a high-five. "The honeys are calling *you*. You got some game."

I couldn't help myself. "What he has is you, Leo. The biggest news story to hit Cincinnati in a long time. Don't let her play you, De Palma. She wants a story. Nothing else."

"So what, if she's got an angle?" Rico asked. "She's hot...and I'm a big boy. If she wants to play, I can play. Like Leo said, I got game."

She was going to chew him up and spit him out alive, the dumbass.

Anytime that ditzy, conniving, pea-brained bitch got involved, she had a way of turning everything upside down. And I always came out on the bottom—usually in front of God and everybody, on the eleven o'clock news. Thank heaven, the night was almost over.

Powell and Ortega showed up about fifteen minutes early for the midnight shift. *Halle-freaking-lujah.* I shot out of there like a .50 caliber cannon, climbed onto my Harley and headed home. Color me done. Rico could have that bubble-headed twat-waffle.

I'd never been so glad to leave the 60s in my entire life.

7

LIFE WITHOUT RULES IS ZUSHI

Nothing good ever comes from a phone call at four in the morning. I scrambled out of bed, tripping over Headbutt in the process, and opened my phone in the dark.

It was Rico.

I did my best to keep a civil tongue. "What the fuck do you want?"

"Sorry to wake you," he said. "Cap called. There's been a murder. He wants us at the scene."

"What the hell? Why now, instead of say, three or four hours from now? Is the damn body going to get up and walk away?"

"I'm just the messenger, Nighthawk. When the boss says come, you come. I don't make the rules."

I pulled on my black khakis, the same ones I wore the day before, slipped into a clean T-shirt with *Zombies Hate Fast Food* plastered across the chest, and threw on my duster.

There was no telling how long I might be gone. Later in the morning, I'd have to call Mrs. Nussbaum and dig my pet-sitting grave a little deeper.

When I took off on my Low Rider, the cool night air slapped

me awake. A very simple question occurred to me. Why the hell was I being called to a murder scene? That was Rico's deal. Just because we were partners on paranormal crimes didn't mean I signed on for getting up at the crack of four, to ogle random stiffs. Somebody was going to answer for this.

The crime scene, the parking lot behind an apartment building on Cleves-Warsaw Road in Walnut Hills, had already been roped off with yellow crime scene tape.

Rico knelt beside the body, doing his thing, and didn't hear me walk up.

"I don't see any biters," I said. "There'd better be biters involved or you're in deep shit, De Palma."

Rico sat back on his heels, giving me a clear view of the body.

It was Cap's admin, Miriam Miller.

"She looks pastier than usual," I said.

"Wow. You really *don't* have a filter, do you?" Rico said.

He was right. That was cold, even for me. I didn't know Miriam very well. But Rico had known her for years.

"Sorry," I said, fidgeting with the zipper on my coat.

"I'll finish up here. After that, Cap wants to see us in his office."

"Who called it in?"

"That woman over there." Rico pointed to an older woman standing beside a CPD cruiser, dabbing at her eyes. "Martha Carmichael. She found Miriam lying here dead when she was leaving for work, the early shift at Busken's Bakery. She knew Miriam. She's taking it kind of hard."

"Did she see anything? Any cars? Any people hanging around?"

He fixed me in a tired stare. "No, Nighthawk, she didn't. I've already taken her statement. Is there something *specific* you'd like me to ask her?"

"Hey, you're the one who called me, remember? Don't get pissy with me, because your booty call got cut short."

I walked back to my bike and called over my shoulder, "There's no need for me to be here. I'll see you at the station."

Something told me this day was going to suck.

The 51st is a quiet place at five in the morning. I walked back to Cap's office and glanced at Miriam's work station. Something stopped me cold. Her desktop wasn't in order. In fact, it was decidedly out of order, like someone had been looking for something. Miriam would've never have left her desktop supplies scattered willy-nilly.

I peeked into Cap's office and found him staring at the photo on his desk.

"Morning, Cap. Who's the pretty lady?"

He turned to me, face ashen and eyes dull. "That's Ingrid, my wife. She died a long time ago."

"I'm sorry. I shouldn't have asked."

"Nonsense," he said, rubbing his face with his hands and then settling back in his chair. "I take it you've been to the crime scene?"

I nodded.

"Come on in. Have a seat. We'll wait for De Palma before we get started."

It didn't take long for the sound of Rico's size thirteens, clomping down the aisle, to fill the awkward silence.

"Morning, Cap. My condolences," Rico said with downcast eyes. "I know you and Miriam were friends. She was real good to you when Ingrid died. She'd been your secretary for what, twenty years?"

Cap sighed. "Twenty-five years, to be exact. And yes. She was a godsend."

Rico cleared his throat. "The uniforms secured the scene before I got there. I did my prelim and interviewed the woman who found Miriam. The crime scene techs were just getting there as I was leaving. First light, we'll check out her apartment. We're going to find whoever did this."

Cap seemed to have aged since I sat in his office, just the day before. His shoulders were hunched. The gray in his whiskers glared white under the florescent lights.

"She was one of ours," he murmured.

"I know, Cap. Believe me, nobody's gonna drop the ball on this," Rico said.

"What's your read on it?"

"She was found outside her residence, stabbed once. No other signs of assault. Not much blood. It looks like the body might've been moved. Rigor was setting in. That puts her death somewhere around 2 a.m., give or take. The M.E. will be able to tell us more," Rico said. "Her purse was stolen. If I had to guess, I'd say robbery."

I thought of the jumble on her desktop and had my doubts. But with nothing to go on, other than my intuition, it seemed smarter to talk to Rico about that in private.

"What would Miriam be doing out at that hour?" I asked.

"I wish I knew," Rico said. "Single older lady, maybe she..." He glanced at Cap and decided to let that drop. "We'll find out."

Cap turned to me and hesitated, before spitting out the reason I was there—what I'd known in my heart had been the reason, since the moment I'd laid eyes on the newly dead Miriam Miller.

"I want you to raise Miriam, Nighthawk. I want her to tell us who did this. And when I find that piece of shit, I'm going to grind him into the ground with my boot heel, until there's nothing left of him but pulp, blood and bone splinters."

Cap and I had never had occasion to discuss my "rules"

before. Trying to talk about them now, when he was so emotionally charged, wouldn't be the best time.

I could try to be gentle, hem and haw, or I could give him my answer straight. In the end, it wouldn't matter whether I yanked the Band-Aid off or teased it off, a little at a time. Either way, this conversation was going to be a whole mess of ugly.

I went with short and sweet. "No."

"What do you mean 'no'?" His eyes narrowed. "That wasn't a request. It was an order."

"I don't take orders from you—not when it comes to raising."

Cap's face blazed. "We're a family, damn it. Miriam was part of that family. People need to understand, when you attack one of us, you attack us all. There'll be no escaping justice."

"That's exactly why she shouldn't be raised. Miriam was too close to you. There are other ways to get justice, ones that don't require raising her."

He pounded his fist on his desk. "Her body should be at the morgue by now, or it will be soon. Go there, raise her in private, and get me that information." His eyes were dark as thunderheads. "Do it, or you'll never work with us again. Is that clear enough?"

That sounded like the pain talking, but even if it wasn't, he'd never keep that threat. The city needed me. He needed me. Still, there were smarter ways to change his mind than by bulldozing him.

"Cap, you don't want to do this. She was your friend. She scheduled your life. Hell, she was *part* of your life. She cared for you through some tough times. You don't want me to raise someone that close to you, only to turn around and put her back down. It's ugly and it's sad. She'll be cold, confused, even fearful. After everything she's been through, do you really want to do that to her? Why? Because you're angry? Or hurt? You and

Rico can obtain the information you need through standard investigative techniques."

I softened my voice and drove home the truth. "It's a case that can be solved without my intervention."

Cap's lips grew taut. "Raise her, Nighthawk."

"I have rules—a moral code. It's what keeps me grounded. No. I won't. I won't do it."

"You feel that strongly? You'd openly defy me?"

"Yes, sir."

"Why?"

"Because I'm right. And if you weren't so close to this, you'd see that, too."

Cap lapsed into silence.

While I waited for him to reconsider, memories of my sister, Anna, began to surface. Sitting there, in the 51st, across from Cap, my time with Anna seemed so long ago. But some nights, when I'm having trouble sleeping, it seems like only yesterday.

She died when I was eight and she was three. We were playing tag in our yard, and I chased her into the street. She got hit by a car and died in the hospital that night.

I was inconsolable. My mother was heartbroken. But my father...my father was lost.

He begged my mom to bring her back. Young as I was, I knew the power inside my mom, and I felt that same power stirring inside me. Mom sobbed, telling dad she wouldn't bring Anna back. That it was wrong. She said that with every gift from God came rules, and that in spite of my father's pain, he knew that, too. Grief over the loss of a loved one wasn't a reason to raise the dead. That was rule number one, right before rule number two, always put down those you raise.

Over the years, I'd made a few more rules, but sitting there in the 51st wasn't the time to think about them. I pulled myself out of the past and focused on Cap.

When he finally spoke, he sounded troubled. "Maybe you're

right. Maybe it's best to leave her in peace." There was a tear in his eye. "I was out of the office yesterday afternoon. Miriam left me a voicemail saying she wanted to talk to me about something important, first thing this morning. I wonder what it was."

I thought of the shamble on her desktop and wondered if the two things were related.

Cap pointed at Rico. "You find whoever did this, and find them fast. I know you're on detail with Leo. Coordinate with the other detectives. This case gets top priority until it's solved. Update me as soon as you have information to share. Anything else?" he asked.

Rico and I shook our heads.

"Then get to work."

Rico closed Cap's door behind us.

When he heard it latch, Rico said, "One of these days, you're going to have to tell me *all* your rules."

I shrugged. "It's a long list."

As we walked past Miriam's desk, I grabbed his arm and asked. "You see anything odd here?"

Rico gave her desktop the once over. "It's a little messier than usual."

"She'd never leave it this way."

"Yeah. Maybe. I'll check with the desk sergeant to see who might have been back here tonight. I'll get one of the guys to dust for prints after Cap leaves." Rico made a point of catching my eye. "We don't want him worrying whether it's an inside job until we can prove it."

"Yeah. Sure." I thought of the photo on Cap's desk and asked a random question. "How'd Cap's wife die, anyway?"

Rico glanced at Cap's closed door and pulled me further down the hallway.

"She had a flat tire on I-71S. It was late. Cap was stuck at work. She wanted him to come change it, but he couldn't get free. He had dispatch send one of the units out to help her. But, by the time they got there, she was gone. No sign of her anywhere. They called in extra cars and searched the surrounding area near the expressway. That's where they found her—dead. A biter had gotten hold of her. They think it must have been holed up beneath the overpass, and took her before the units got there."

Suddenly, it hit me. Both Ingrid and Miriam, arguably the two women closest to Cap, had come to him for help, and he hadn't been there for them. No wonder he looked haunted.

Rico and I walked to the bullpen, so he could check on the progress of the biter investigation at the shooting range.

While we had a minute alone, there was another topic I wanted to revisit. "So, I guess little Miss Double-D's wasn't too happy about you having to take off in the middle of the night."

He kept walking, acting like he didn't hear me.

"No response?" I asked

"It wasn't a question."

I grabbed his arm and stopped him midstride. "What do you see in her?"

"She's nice. She's fun." His tone sounded defensive. "And she didn't slug me in the jaw the first time we met."

That was it? That was the draw? I can do nice. I'm fun...ish. And the bruise I left on his face was next to nothing, like one, maybe two knuckle's worth. But the real question was why did I care?

He must have read my mind. "What's it matter to you anyway, Nighthawk?"

"Fine. Be a chump," I said, avoiding the question in both our minds. "But don't come crying to me when she dumps you for an even bigger schmuck. If she can find one."

Schmuck? I must have been channeling Mrs. Nussbaum,

which reminded me that I needed to make sure she hadn't changed her mind about pet sitting.

Rico went to his desk and turned on his laptop, to check the status of the firing range investigation.

I found a vacant desk and called Sweden to check in with Sandy. It was noon there. At least one of us would be awake. But I got his voicemail, so I left him a message to give me a yell.

Then, I laid my head on the desk and closed my eyes, telling myself I just needed to rest for a minute.

The next thing I knew, a voice called to me from beyond. "Wake up, slacker."

The heavenly aroma of coffee wafted up my nose. I opened my eyes to find a steaming cup of Maxwell House.

"Thanks," I said with a stretch and a yawn. "What'd you find out about Brasshole's?"

"There were dozens of fingerprints near and in the walk-up, but they all belonged to cops. That doesn't rule them in or out, but it could mean the unsub was on the job."

"Or he wore gloves."

Rico bobbed his head. "On the other hand, the only door to the walk-up, the door you entered, was locked. Security footage, from shortly before you kicked the door in, showed no sign of forced entry. And there were no scratch marks to indicate the lock had been picked. In order for someone to deposit a biter before you got there, the door would had to have been unlocked, and then relocked after they left. That suggests the dirtbag had a key. Coincidentally, the security video went black for about twenty minutes around 4:00 a.m."

He scratched his chin. "Looks like it could be an inside job. The biggest question is, who would have access to both a key and a biter?"

That *was* an interesting question.

"Oh, by the way," he added, "Sergeant Clawson said the only person he saw near Miriam's desk overnight was that oddball janitor, Ottis. Clawson didn't see him rifle through anything. He was just moseying along, cleaning, like he always does."

The squirrel. Now, he was a strange ranger. He seemed like a long shot, but you never know.

After a big swig of coffee, Rico settled into a chair and put his feet up on the desk. "In just over two days," he said, "someone planted a deadhead at the firing range, we were followed to the safe house, and Miriam Miller ended up dead in what looks like a random mugging."

"Are you assuming they're related?" I asked.

"I can't assume anything, but it's an interesting theory, isn't it?"

Rico had paperwork to finish and I had a shower calling my name. We went our separate ways and agreed to meet back at the safe house at noon.

On the ride home, my mind kept spinning. There wasn't an obvious connection between the events, but the timing was bizarre. Were they related? And if so, how?

There was a certain hinkiness to my house when I walked inside.

Kulu had replaced his typical greeting, *"Hi, dumbass,"* with *"Buongiorno, mamma."*

I froze in place, eyes scanning left to right, and back again, searching for the intruder who stole my snarky feather duster and replaced her with a sweet, gentle birdie.

Kulu, bird of prey, stood atop her perch, wings unfolded, head held high, clearly impressed with herself.

I let Headbutt out the door and listened for the daily war of the rosebushes to begin. Hearing nothing, I glanced out the window, past the tool shed, to find Headbutt hiking his leg across the yard, on the opposite fence post.

That would be where the Winstel's vining Wisteria bloomed. An amazing victory for Nonnie's roses—and yet, a new-found problem for another day.

Mrs. Nussbaum opened her screen door and called, "*Buongiorno*, Mrs. Nighthawk!"

I nodded back. "Yes, good morning. And thanks for pet-sitting. I noticed Kulu's already picking up...more appropriate words, and Headbutt's peeing on the Winstel's flowers instead. Progress. Very nice," I said with a big smile. "You're coming back today around 11:30, right?"

"Of course! And I'll have a little something for your friend David to nosh on."

"That's really not necessary, Mrs. Nussbaum."

"Call me Nonnie, dearie. Is no problem. See you soon." She ducked her head back inside.

I took my shower, swept up the birdseed and dog hair, and started an emergency load of laundry. That's what happens when you have no clean underwear left.

Within minutes, Nonnie returned, carrying a piping-hot, homemade lasagna. It smelled heavenly.

"For your friend David," she said, beaming. "He is only a friend, Mrs. Nighthawk. Is that right?"

God help me. Little red hearts were flying out of her eyes. Nonnie was on the prowl, a little long in the tooth to be a cougar, and stalking Leo, no less.

"Yes, David is only a friend. And please, call me Allie," I said, walking out the door.

She shuffled to the porch to see me off. "Wonderful, Miss Allie. Tell David I said hello."

"Will do." I strapped the lasagna onto my bike. "Thanks for

your help. You're the best, Mrs. Nuss...Nonnie. I'll be back a little after midnight."

Nonnie waved goodbye, with Headbutt at her feet, and Kulu watching me through the living room picture window.

You're the best, Nonnie? Wow. Maybe Leo had it right after all. Necessity does make for strange bedfellows.

8

THE DAMNED ACLU

Within seconds of walking through the kitchen door of the safe house and unzipping the casserole carrier filled with Nonnie's lasagna, I was surrounded by Leo and Officers Greg Powell and Danny Ortega. The lasagna, still steaming, wafted the heavenly combination of beef, cheeses, tomatoes and herbs through the air.

Despite their shift having ended, Powell and Ortega announced they weren't going anywhere without lunch. By the time Rico walked through the door, ten minutes later, half the casserole was gone. He filled a plate and joined in.

"You didn't tell me your neighbor could cook like this," Leo said. "We need her on retainer over here. No offense to Ricardo's, but even great pizza is just pizza. This," he said, shoveling in a mouthful, "Is the food of my people. *Mangia! Molte grazie la mia bella*, Nonnie."

Leo had met Mrs. Nussbaum once and was already on a first-name basis with her. I'd known her all my life, and had just gotten permission to call her Nonnie that very morning.

"For some reason, she's into you, Leo," I said, shaking my

head. "She's an old woman. I saw you hitting on her. That's pathetic, you little sleazeball. Stop it."

Leo sat back in his chair and let his Italian temper fly. "What the hell, Nighthawk? So what if she's old? She's still a woman. You think it don't make her feel good when a young stud throws a wink her way? What's the matter with you? You've got no...what do you call it...no empathy."

I laughed so hard, I almost choked on my lasagna. "Young stud? That's how you think of yourself?"

Rico and the other guys howled.

"I'm young compared to her, damn it!" He refilled his plate and carried it into the living room. "You really are a ballbuster, aren't you? I can't even enjoy my lunch without you giving me an enema. Screw you."

The rest of us finished our meals at the table, after which, Powell and Ortega took off. Rico checked his messages, while I covered the leftover lasagna and put it in the fridge. Then, I carried the dishes to the sink. That was the extent of my domestic assistance. Rico and Leo could wash and dry them.

I walked into to the living room and asked Leo if he was finished with his plate.

He ignored me and turned up the TV.

What a girl.

"Leo," I said, choosing my words as if they might explode, "I didn't mean anything by that stud crack. It was just a joke."

"Yeah? Well you're always dumping on me, calling me a sleazeball, or a weasel, or a whatever. You don't have to be such a hardcore bitch all the time."

He wasn't going to make this easy.

"Okay," I said, "Fair enough. And you don't have to hit on Nonnie."

"*Jesus*, Nighthawk. It's not like I was trying to *do* her. I was flirting. You know, winking, giving her a reason to smile. I wasn't gonna take advantage of her, for chrissake. What do you think I am? She's a nice, lonely old woman who baked me a lasagna. She ever bake you a lasagna? Huh? Didn't think so. That's because you don't know how to be nice. Now, leave me alone."

"Sorry." Damn, if that word didn't stick in my throat like a fishbone. "I guess in some...weird Leo way...you were being nice. I get it. Are we good?"

"Whatever. It wouldn't kill *you* to be nice once in a while."

"Yeah. Okay," I said, taking a deep cleansing breath. "Leo, will you *please* give me your empty pla... Hell, don't make me do this. Give me the damn plate before I have an aneurysm, moron."

"You know what?" he screamed, throwing the plate at me. "*You're a fucking onion, Nighthawk.* From one layer to the next. You're a bitter, raw, tear-inducing onion."

I ducked and watched the plate shatter as it slammed into the wall. Finally, Leo and I understood each other. That had been harder than pulling teeth.

He flipped through the three local TV stations, the only ones we could get without cable or Dish.

"Who doesn't have cable?" he whined. "No ESPN! Who the hell doesn't get ESPN?"

Rico strolled in from the kitchen with a shit-eating grin. "The FBI, right?"

He sat in one of the chairs and plunked his big-ass size thirteens on the laminate coffee table. "You must have some juicy information for the FBI to be footing the bill for your medical treatment. What do you know, anyway?"

Leo smirked and leaned back on the couch. "I know it all, baby. It's all up here," he said, pointing to his head. "I owe the Family a lot, but I ain't dying any faster than I have to. Between my brain and the Family's books, I can bury everybody on the Giordano payroll. Twenty-five years' worth of names, dates, amounts, anything you want to know, including what the payments were for. Extortion, murder, you name it. That's the part that's in my noggin."

"No wonder the DA's hiding you," I said.

Then the sad but real truth ran through my mind. *No wonder they want you to testify before your brain turns to mush.*

The doorbell rang and Leo jumped. "Who is it?" he whispered. "Is it them? Ah, God, I knew they'd find me. Shit! And all I got is you guys? Jesus. This is it."

I peeked out the window and frowned. "It's Weston. What's he doing here?"

Bill Weston was one of the shields out of the 51st.

Rico got up to answer the door. "He's running the investigation into Miriam's death, since I'm stuck here like a potted plant with Leo."

"Again, why is he *here*?" I asked.

"You heard Cap. He said to coordinate the investigation. Bill's doing the leg work and I'm calling the shots. I went through the Academy with him. He's a stand-up guy."

I rolled my eyes. "So much for a *secret* safe house."

"Consider him vouched for. I'd trust this guy with my life," Rico snapped, as he opened the door.

"You just did," I mumbled.

"Hey, dude." Bill nodded at Rico as he walked in and sat on the couch next to Leo. "Something smells awesome. I've been working all morning. Any leftovers?"

Bill was everything Leo wasn't. Tall, blue-eyed, and built like a fortress.

"No," Leo lied. "Not even a crumb."

"What you got for me, Bill?" Rico asked, returning to his chair.

"We got Miriam's cell phone records. She got a call about six-fifteen last night. We ran the number. It was from a burner phone that made three more calls, two to another burner phone in Orlando, and one to a phone number registered to Excelsior Moving and Storage."

"That's a front company for the Giordano's," Leo said.

Rico nodded at Bill. "Find out who our perp called and why."

"Sure thing, boss. Miriam's phone pinged about eight last night in OTR."

Over-the-Rhine was an area just north of town.

"We showed her picture around," Weston said. "Got a hit on it at Rhinegeist Brewery. A waitress there served Miriam last night. Some guy came in and plopped into the booth next to her. She said Miriam looked a little nervous."

Rico leaned forward with his elbows on his knees. "Any surveillance video?"

"I'm way ahead of you, boss. We pulled the tape. It was Miriam, all right. We got a still shot of the guy's face. It's in your email."

Rico pulled up the picture on his phone. "You ever see this guy before?"

Bill shook his head, and then I took a look. He wasn't familiar to me, either.

Rico started to put his phone away when Leo yelled, "Hello! Am I invisible? I have connections. I know some people. Let me see that thing."

He ripped the phone out of Rico's hand and then handed it back. "Nope. He doesn't work with the Family."

Rico glared at Leo, then turned back to Weston. "Put out a BOLO on the guy. Make sure to include his picture."

"Already done, dude. We've got the jump on him. He's as good as caught." Weston walked toward the door, but stopped short. "Oh, yeah. We did a sweep of Miriam's apartment. It was trashed big time. Who knows what they were looking for or if they found it. We dusted for prints. Didn't find any."

Rico whistled. "Trashed. Wow. Good work. You guys were all over this. I'll let Cap know. Stay in touch."

He closed the door behind Weston and looked at me. "There goes my mugging theory."

"Maybe," I said. "Or maybe, since the mugger stole her purse, he went inside her apartment, and helped himself to whatever he could find."

Rico's phone rang. He picked it up on the second ring. "Hey, Cap. Perfect timi—"

He stopped mid-sentence, furrowed his brow, and then walked into the kitchen. Clearly, he was doing the listening. He'd walked far enough around the corner that I couldn't hear much, even when he got a word in edgewise.

Leo got up to change the channel on the TV. As he darted across the room, I noticed sweat beading on his forehead.

"When's the last time you took your medicine?"

"I've been on time since that episode the other day. But about an hour before I'm due for the next dose, I start sweating like a whore in church."

"Why didn't you tell me?"

He looked away. "Maybe I don't like thinking about it."

"You need to tell me these things," I said. "I have to talk to my guy in Sweden today anyway. Maybe we need to up your dosage."

Leo lowered himself slowly to the couch. "Listen up. I'm only going to say this once. Most of my time is spent trying to forget that someday this shit is going to kill me. I spend the rest of my time scared shitless that I'm going to turn into one of those damn...abominations. Some mindless walking corpse, rotting on my feet, stinking worse than a dead deer on a high-way. It's in my agreement, when the time comes, somebody'll put me down. I'd like that to be you."

He swiped his eyes with the back of his hand. "Just make

sure they plant me within twenty-four hours and...and...say Kaddish, and all the rest of that shit."

"Say *what*?"

"I'm an Italian Jew. One of the few, the proud."

I bit my lip and shrugged.

"Jesus, Nighthawk. Just get Nonnie Nussbaum to help you plan my service. I know it's asking a lot, but I trust you. If you tell me you'll do it, I'll believe you."

Poor guy. It would have likely been me putting him down anyway. Thank God, Nonnie was Jewish. I didn't know *Kaddish* from *Kosher*.

"Sure, if that's the way you want it, Leo. I'd be honored."

We sat in silence, digesting the moment, then he snickered and shook his head. "Honored? You'll be honored to *scramble my brains*? Jesus."

"Hey. You asked me to."

The mood in the room lightened, but not for long.

Rico entered the doorway with a scowl on his face. "Cap got an envelope in the mail today, postmarked from Miriam last night. There were pictures of her niece enclosed, along with a note that said Miriam had twenty-four hours to provide Leo's location, or her niece would disappear. Miriam tried to call Cap, and when she couldn't reach him, she left him a message that they needed to talk first thing this morning. Then she got to feeling hinky, like maybe she wasn't safe, so she mailed copies of everything to Cap just in case."

"Smart lady," I said.

My ring tone blared *Don't Fear the Reaper*. It was the M.E.'s office. "Nighthawk here."

"Doc Blanchard. We've completed the prelim on Miriam Miller. Your vic may not have died from the stab wound to her chest. She had an injection site behind her right ear. We took some blood samples and sent them to toxicology. We'll know more when the results come back."

An injection site? The brain bitch started River Dancing in my head. "What are you saying, Doc?"

"Until her tox screen comes in, I can't determine the actual cause of her death. Normally, we wouldn't get those results back for weeks, but I know someone who can push them through."

"I got a bad feeling about this, Doc. You'd better destroy her brain stem now, just in case."

"What are you thinking?"

"Who knows what she was injected with? It could be anything. What if it's the Z-virus?"

Doc snorted "It can't be. It's not transmitted intravenously."

"It's never been before, but something's happening with this virus, Doc. We can't know for sure what that is, until the tissue results from Sweden come back. It's best to destroy her brain stem now—just in case."

"I don't have the authority to do that. And I won't. Not on the wild supposition that she was injected with the Z-virus, as opposed to any of the hundreds of other known toxins. Nobody's going to charge me with desecration of a corpse."

Damned ACLU.

"Fine," I said. "I'll come down and do it myself."

"Not on my watch, you won't."

Jesus.

"Then you'd better strap her down good. Truss her up tight as a Thanksgiving turkey inside a cold storage drawer. If she still hasn't turned by morning, it's probably safe to say that either she wasn't injected with the Z-virus, or if she was, she doesn't have the marker and can be released for burial. If she does turn, give me a call. I'll put her down myself."

"If that makes you feel better, Nighthawk, sure, I'll strap her down."

"Thanks, Doc." I hung up and looked at Rico, but couldn't bring myself to speak.

What the hell was going on? Sighted deadheads? It would be a serious stretch to think that could be caused by some organic mutation. And if she had been injected with the virus, there wasn't a damn thing organic about it.

There were only a handful of people in the world who could manipulate that virus, and fewer still who would intentionally make it worse. Little Allie kept chanting one name, over and over again, in my brain.

Sweet Jesus, I thought. *Please let her be wrong.*

9

EVERYONE ALWAYS WANTS
SOMETHING

I came home from the safe house to find Nonnie asleep on the couch, with Headbutt curled at her feet and Kulu perched affectionately, head beneath wing, on Nonnie's shoulder. Someone creative might have snapped a pic on their phone and made a poignant meme out of that precious moment, but it was more cuteness than I could handle after a twelve-hour plus day.

So, I thumped my holster onto the kitchen table and intentionally woke Nonnie up. She halfway opened her eyes and sleepwalked across the lawn to her house, while the trouble-makers and I settled in for a good night's sleep.

I hadn't even finished my first cup of coffee the next morning when the phone rang.

It was Doc Blanchard. "You need to get over here *now*."

I could barely hear him over all the crashing and banging in the background.

"Miriam turned overnight," he said. "She broke out of the cold storage drawer and she's tearing up my morgue."

Sweet Jesus.

"Didn't you tie her up like I told you to?"

"No. I... I just didn't think she'd turn, Nighthawk, since the Z-virus has never been transmitted by injection. I was sure she'd been slipped some kind of poison. I didn't see the need for restraints. For God's sake," he whined. "She's a corpse, damn it. Lloyd opened the drawer this morning to get her body ready for release, and she bolted like a one-legged cat in a swimming pool."

Freaking nimrod. I *told* him to put her down.

After quick calls to Rico and Nonnie, I got dressed and said goodbye to Headbutt and Kulu. They knew the routine. Headbutt returned to his post on the floor vent, while Kulu hung upside down from the bars of her cage and gave me the stink eye. I'd like to say they looked sad at my impending departure, but I think they were secretly counting the minutes until Nonnie-time.

I threw on my *Terminus BBQ* T-shirt, tucked my Ka-bar knife into its sheath, and put Hawk in my shoulder holster. The situation only involved one deadhead, and Miriam at that, but you can never have too many weapons.

When I pulled up to the curb outside of the city morgue, Rico had already arrived. The noise of Miriam's zombie-fueled fury carried all the way to the street.

Doc Blanchard saw us through the lobby doors and let us inside.

A hulk with red Brillo-pad hair stood beside Doc, dwarfing his six-foot frame. The guy's lab coat was at least two sizes too small, its sleeves ending about mid-forearm. He wore black glasses with coke-bottle lenses and had translucent, fish-belly skin.

"This is Lloyd, my morgue attendant," Doc said.

Lloyd wore a creepy lopsided grin that gave him the look of a serial killer.

"You enjoying this a little too much, Lloyd?" I asked, as I barged past him.

The morgue office had a glass window in the door with the word *Medical Examiner* painted across it. We stood in the vestibule looking through the window and watched Miriam go full-on zombie.

Freshies are crazy unpredictable, but they can still communicate. Even better, they can't lie. We needed to get Miriam under control and ask her a few questions before we put her down.

"You ready? On three," I said, looking at Rico.

I drew Hawk from my holster. "Unlock the door, Doc. Then go wait in the lobby. We've got this."

Doc almost had a coronary. "You can't just fire a nine millimeter into her brain and splatter it like a piñata. I've got other bodies in there. We'll end up with cross-contamination. It'll be my ass."

"Let me get this straight," I said, giving him my coldest Allie-eye. "We need to play twenty questions with Meatbag Miriam before we put her down, and you, who didn't take care of her when you had the chance, want me to kill her in a plastic bubble. Any other special requests?"

"Oh! Oh!" Lloyd blurted. "Can I put her down? Please?"

"*No*," the rest of us said, in unison.

Jade Chen raced up the sidewalk to the lobby doors and banged on the glass. "Channel Ten News Team. We're covering this story. Let us in."

I spun toward Rico. "Oh, my God! You told her we were here?"

"*No,*" he said, jerking like I'd slapped him into next Tuesday. "I didn't tell her. I swear."

"Then how could she possibly know we were here? We haven't even gotten inside, yet."

"I don't know, but I'm about to find out."

"Forget about her. We've got work to do." I looked at Doc. "Do you have any junk food around here?"

"I have a bag of tortilla chips in my lunch," Lloyd said. "But you'll have to eat them in the cafeteria." He glowered at Doc. "We're not allowed to eat in the lab."

Doc sighed, and shook his head. "Get your chips, Lloyd."

Lloyd hurried down the hallway toward the employees' lounge.

"Are all the other bodies in drawers?" I asked.

"Yeah," Doc said, nodding.

"Anything in the cooler?"

"No. Why?"

"Okay, I've got a plan," I said, as Doc unlocked the morgue door with his thumbprint.

Lloyd sprinted back down the hall with his tortilla chips.

"Go on outside, Doc. But leave him." I ran my eyes up to the top of Lloyd's head. "I can use Igor here inside the lab, to help keep Miriam under control."

I waved goodbye to Jade with my middle finger, and peered inside the morgue door window.

"Congratulations, dude," I said, giving Lloyd a pat on the back. "You've been promoted to zombie wrangler."

Miriam was facing the back of the room, slurping the innards off a pair of rib spreaders.

I eased open the door and crept inside, followed by Lloyd and Rico, who locked the door behind us. Then I knocked on the front of the cold storage unit to get her attention.

"Hey, Miriam," I yelled, as she gnawed on the rib spreaders. "Wassup, girl?"

She whirled around and issued a series of snarls and grunts, then began to advance.

"We've got a few questions. Can you help us out?"

She lowered her head and growled.

Rico pulled Lloyd behind a gurney and stared at me in disbelief. "This? This is your big plan? What could possibly go wrong?"

I took out my Ka-bar knife and held it by my side. Sweat trickled from my temples, as I joined Rico and Lloyd behind the gurney.

Lloyd pushed me away. "Get your own gurney, lady. This one's full."

"Careful, Lloyd, if she doesn't bite you, I might." I waved at Miriam to get her to focus on me. "Who killed you, Ms. Miller?"

She lashed out like a psychotic, flesh-eating windmill, whipping the Ka-bar out of my hand. It skittered across the floor and slid deep beneath the stainless-steel sink.

Hells bells. Things were getting out of hand.

"Abort! Abort!" I yelled.

Lloyd pulled the gurney backwards, sweeping us out of her reach, but Miriam followed. As we steered the gurney past the cold storage unit, I reached over and yanked open one of the drawers.

Miriam was running full speed, and fell into the open drawer.

"Plan B," I said, slamming the drawer closed. "Igor, give me the chips."

"*Now?*" he asked.

"No. Like in ten or fifteen minutes, you know, when you go on break. *Yes, now!* Hand them over, Igor."

"Call me Lloyd."

Rico grabbed the chips and tossed them to me.

"Here's the deal," I said. "Give me some room. I'm going to open the drawer and lead Miriam into the cooler with these chips. Rico, you're going to have to ask your questions quick. When she and I make it inside, shut the door behind us."

I looked at Rico and Lloyd, and sighed. "If this goes south, it'll go quick. Rico, pull your gun. I know what Doc said about cross-contamination. Only shoot as a last resort."

I locked eyes with Lloyd. "You grab a scalpel off that tray on the sink. Do *not* move toward her. Only use it in self-defense. You got that, Igor?"

He nodded and tried to pick up the scalpel, but fumbled it. I closed my eyes and tried to think happy thoughts.

"Miriam," I called, knocking on the drawer. "Oh, Miriam?"

She growled and banged against the inside of the cold storage unit.

"Three...two...one," I said, yanking open the drawer.

Miriam popped her head up like a meatbag meerkat.

Rico raised his gun and spooked her.

She leapt out of the drawer and onto the gurney, coming face to face with Rico and Lloyd.

"Nighthawk," Rico yelled, as he and Lloyd dove behind another gurney. "A little help?"

"Miriam! *Miriam*. Over here."

She turned toward the sound of my voice, and I held up the bag of chips. "Come and get 'em, girl. That's it."

For each step she advanced, I moved one step closer to the cooler.

Rico paced alongside her, a couple of arm lengths away. "Keep her steady, Nighthawk."

Miriam swiped at him and growled.

He held out the photo of BOLO Guy and asked, "Is this the man who killed you?"

"Yesss," she hissed, snatching at the picture.

I waved the chips in her face. "Do you know his name? Or who he worked for?"

"No." Miriam's eyes were glued to the chips.

She snarled, so I threw some on the floor in front of her, and asked, "What was your killer after?"

Half-chewed tortilla chips spewed from her mouth, like cracker crumbs. "To know where Leo is."

"Did you tell him?"

She shook her head.

"Here, Miriam," I coaxed. "Have some more chips. Mmm... Salty."

I threw a handful in front of the cooler door. When she dove for them, I was suddenly struck by how mortified the prissy Ms. Miller would have been to find herself diving for food, and spraying chip bits when she spoke.

The brain bitch suddenly woke up and screamed about how wildly inappropriate that was, even if it *was* a freaking hilarious visual, and then she shamed me into focusing on the task at hand.

"We're about to run out of food. Is there anything else you want to ask her? Maybe her sign? If she likes rain or long walks on the beach? Anything?"

Rico scowled. "Nope. Got it."

I lured her into the cooler, then nodded at Rico. He closed the door behind us.

There we stood, face to face. It wasn't the best time to remember that my Ka-bar knife was somewhere under the stainless-steel sink.

I glanced around the cooler. It was maybe eight-feet by eight-feet, tops, and completely empty. Not a weapon in sight, and my back pressed against the far wall.

Sorry, Doc.

I pulled Hawk and looked into Miriam's eyes. "You never did like me, but you didn't deserve this. Rest in peace, Miriam."

She reached out and grabbed my left arm, ripping the sleeve of my T-shirt to shreds.

My arm jerked as I pulled the trigger, and the bullet struck her neck, spraying flesh and blood across the cooler.

But Miriam wasn't finished just yet. She whirled back around, and I squeezed the trigger again, hitting her point blank in the forehead.

The back half of her head exploded like a watermelon, bathing the cooler in a random burst of bloody chum. Bits of zushi plastered themselves to the ceiling and walls.

Rico threw open the cooler door and took it all in, silent, slack-jawed and wide-eyed. He finally said something, though I had no idea what it was.

"*What?*" I yelled. "I can't hear you. That was very *loud*."

Brain bits began to fall from the ceiling, willy-nilly like tiny flesh bombs, pelting me and splattering onto the floor.

Lloyd took one look at the mess, shook his head and walked away.

I slid a couple of zushi-covered fingers inside the pocket of my khakis and fished out my cellphone. Despite slipping off the keypad a couple of times, my fingers finally dialed the number to Splatz.

"Hey, Jimmy. It's Allie. I can't hear right now, so you need to listen. I've got a rush job for you at the morgue. Do me a favor, send the bill to the attention of Doctor Blanchard at the M.E.'s Office. Give him my discount. Okay? You're the best, dude. Thanks."

Doc burst through the doors, his hands to the heavens, with Jade and her cameraman, Rip, close at his heels.

"I... You... Damn it, Nighthawk. What'd you do to my cooler?"

"Get her out of here!" I screamed, running toward Jade.

That's when I noticed that Rip was filming.

"Give me that camera, peckerhead!" I changed direction, and dove across the room at him.

Tiny bits of Miriam sprang from me, soaring like tiny

missiles through the air. And Rip captured it all, in glorious technicolor.

Rico got to Rip first, and snatched the camera out of his hands.

"Hey, give that back!" Rip yelled. "That's property of Channel Ten, damn it!"

Rico dashed past me to Jade, and took her by the arm. "I don't know how you found out what was going on here, but right now you're contaminating a crime scene. Get the hell out of here. *Now*. We'll talk later."

"We most certainly will," Jade snipped. "I'm sure Channel Ten's attorneys will have a lot to say."

She stomped out the door with Rip, looking like a kid who'd lost her lollipop.

But I wasn't finished with her yet. I tore out the door behind her and Rico chased after me. All set to unload the wrath of Allie on her, I stopped mid-stride, as I watched Jade climb into her black Lexus.

"Nice car, news hack," I shouted. Then I turned to Rico. "There's your tail from the day we took Leo to the safe house."

Rico shrugged. "There are a zillion black Lexuses. That doesn't mean anything."

Doc, who joined us at the curb, clearly wasn't ready to drop the issue of the damage to his cooler. "I told you, *no guns*. I'm going to take so much shit on this—"

"No, you aren't," I said, massaging my ringing ears. "The bodies are in the drawers and I've got Splatz on the way over to clean up the cooler. Problem solved."

"Why the hell did you have to shoot her?" he asked. "Now, I have to wait for the cleaners. I'm far enough behind as it is."

"Because my knife slid under your sink somewhere. That's why. Now I have to crawl under there and find it. I didn't have anything else to put her down with, Doc. If you'd have listened to me yesterday, and put her down when I told you to, we could have avoided all this."

Doc's face turned a glorious shade of magenta. "Nighthawk, you're a one-person wrecking crew."

"Don't bother to thank me," I said, walking back inside to retrieve my knife. "You'll be getting the bill from Splatz."

I'd have given Rico's left nut to *not* be the person who had to tell Cap that Miriam didn't go down like a graceful swan. But since Doc would no doubt be on the phone whining to Cap anytime now, I figured it was best to get out in front of this and spin the situation myself.

After a quick shower and a change of clothes from my go bag, I joined Rico.

We sat across from Cap in his office, while I explained what happened. As if that weren't bad enough, that squirrelly little janitor, Ottis, picked the middle of my one-man show to empty trash cans and tidy up the place.

It's always nice to have an audience when you're getting reamed.

Cap's face went white. "What do you mean, Miriam *turned*? How could that happen? She wasn't bitten."

"According to Doc, Miriam was injected with something. It must have been the virus. Testing has never shown the virus to be transmitted by injection before, but we know the virus is changing—take the sighted zombies, for example."

"Jesus. Poor Miriam," Cap whispered, staring at the photo of his wife on his desk.

"There's more," I said, squirming in my chair.

Rico pinched the bridge of his nose and groaned softly.

"When Doc told me Miriam had been injected yesterday, I

suggested that he...disconnect her brain stem...right then and there, but he didn't have his tox screen results. He figured since the Z-virus had never been transmitted through injection before, it was more likely she was injected with a known toxic agent. He was afraid of repercussions with the ACLU. Against my best advice, the M.E.'s office didn't use sufficient precautions when they put Miriam in the drawer. We all know what happened next..."

Cap waited for me to continue.

"She went batshi—she was very unpredictable, moving randomly, flailing her arms. She smacked my hand and my knife flew under the sink. We lured her into the cooler. There weren't any other weapons within reach. So, I had to use my gun."

Cap closed his eyes. "I see. It sounds like you didn't have a choice, really."

I felt sweat pop out on my upper lip. "That's true, Cap. But there's a tiny bit more."

He leaned forward in his chair, and folded his hands beneath his chin. "Do tell."

"We were in the cooler when I shot her, and the...ah...force of the nine millimeter made a...mess. But Splatz is already on it. We'll have Doc back in business, in no time. The mess was contained to the cooler. Mostly," I said, remembering my mad dash to annihilate Rip and his camera.

Cap leaned back and muttered, "And where is Splatz sending the bill?"

"To the M.E.'s office," I said not missing a beat.

"Good. Let it come out of their budget."

I almost asked about where to send my bill, but given his reaction, I decided to send it on to the M.E.'s office, too. I don't do this shit for free, you know.

When we left Cap's office, I felt a little better about the morning's events. Rico went to check his messages and I found an empty desk to call Sandy. But I got his voicemail again, so I transferred over to his secretary.

"Hi Ilse, it's Allie. Is Sandy around? I called him yesterday, but he never called back."

"No, I'm sorry. He hasn't been in since the night he took the tissue samples. That's not like him, really. He usually lets us know when he's working from home."

"Did he run the tests yet?"

"No. The samples are still in the freezer."

"I really need to talk to him. My bite victim here is showing increased symptoms between doses. I think his meds might need to be adjusted."

"Hold on, Allie. Let me ask Dr. Christian. He'll know. Be right back."

Ilse placed me on hold and little Allie went ballistic, screeching at me that Sandy should have called back by now. Something wasn't right.

Then Ilse picked up the line. "Hello, Allie? Dr. Christian said to up the dosage by one mil. Hopefully, that'll help. If not, let us know."

"Thanks, Ilse. Nice talking to you. Have Sandy give me a yell."

"I will."

I hung up with a case of the heebie-jeebies, and started to fill Rico in, when Weston charged up the aisle.

"Where the hell have you been, dude? I've been looking all over for you. A beat cop found your BOLO suspect in Miriam's death. You'd better sit down for this one. It ain't looking good."

10

WHO'S KILLING WHO?

"What do you mean BOLO guy's *dead*? Who killed him?" Rico slammed his palm against his desk and glared at Weston. "We needed to talk to that son of a bitch. Jesus. Cap's going to have a meltdown."

"It's not like we had a choice," Weston said. "He went biter. We had to put him down."

Biter?

My ears perked. "With a head shot, right? You put him down with a head shot?"

Visions of *Carnage in the Coroner's Office, Part Deux* made my stomach roll.

Weston snickered. "Nighthawk, after your training session in the auditorium with Donald and Hannibal, I don't think there's a cop in this city who will ever make that mistake again."

Vindicated, at last. I knew a successful training session when I gave one.

"Your guy didn't have any ID on him," Weston said, "but he had two grand in cash, in his wallet. Facial recognition software came up empty and his prints didn't hit in AFIS. We did find a scrap of paper in his pocket with *Metropole Hotel #312* scribbled on it."

Rico leaned back in his chair, eyes bloodshot, face drawn and shadowed with a day's stubble.

"What're you waiting for?" he growled. "Check it out. We've got to go babysit Leo. Call me when you've got something."

"Already in progress, boss," Weston said. "No worries. I've got your back."

It hadn't taken us long to settle into a routine at the safe house. We brought Leo lunch or ordered in from Ricardo's. Rico scrambled to juggle his case load, like a plate spinner at a circus. I scanned the Internet for outbreaks of strange Z-virus activity, making sure to check in with Nonnie from time to time. And Leo, bored to death watching the same three local TV channels, would annoy the crap out of both of us.

As I sat at the kitchen table, scouring sites for research articles on the recent Z-virus mutation, Little Allie kept clamoring about the alternative possibility—manipulation. An abundance of dark genius saturated cyber-land, but the amount related to viral manipulation could fit in a thimble.

Rico took a break and joined Leo in the living room, to watch *Days of Our Lives* and play gin rummy at the commercial breaks. I wasn't listening in on their conversations. Hell, maybe I was. But even if I hadn't been listening, I'd have heard them anyway.

Out of nowhere, Leo asked Rico why he became a cop. I scooted forward and peeked around the kitchen corner.

"None of your business," Rico said.

Rico could get testy when he was running on empty. But then, he wasn't exactly Mr. Congeniality when he had a full tank, either.

"C'mon," Leo chided. "You're like the fucking sphinx over there. All stoic and pissing vinegar. If I wanted to get bitch-slapped, I'd go in the kitchen and talk to Nighthawk."

Well. That was uncalled for.

Rico sat forward on the edge of what had become his favorite plastic-coated chair and glared at Leo. "Why do you care?"

"I like to know what makes people tick. Especially people who are supposed to keep me alive."

"Don't read too much into it," Rico said. "It's a living."

Leo wrinkled his nose. "I don't buy that. You got passion. People like you, they get up every day and believe they're going to make a difference. What's the real story?"

"You'd have made a decent detective, Leo." Rico leaned back in his chair, making the plastic fart. "I'm a third-generation cop. My grandpa, Marco, died on the job trying to stop a bank heist. He was a good man. Maybe I'm just trying to be a good man, too."

"Third generation. That must mean your dad was a cop, too."

"Your point?"

"No heroic stories about him? No, 'I wanted to be like my daddy'?"

A cone of silence descended over the living room.

Apparently, Leo sensed he'd hit a nerve and let things settle a minute before he mined for gold. "So, how'd you end up with Nighthawk for a partner?"

I scrambled to turn up the audio on my phone. I didn't want to hear this story again. But Rico's answer came too quick.

"Six of us drew straws. I lost."

The bastard.

Leo burst out laughing. "You lying bastard! You dig this paranormal shit. Hell, you even like working with Nighthawk.

What's more, you like *her*. The truth this time, hand to God, no bullshit. How'd you end up her partner?"

I ducked back behind the corner, afraid to hear his answer, but too intrigued to stop listening. What came next blew me away.

"I saw the position posted and asked Cap for it. There were a few other guys who posted too, but I scored highest. Cap offered it and I accepted. End of story."

Shut the hell up!

What a lying sack of shit. Someday, when he least expected it, I would throw out that little pearl and watch the color drain from his face. But, in that particular moment, I almost cried. *Almost* being the operative word. There's no crying in corpse whispering.

"Ha! I was right," Leo said. "Let me guess. She don't know that, does she?"

"No. And keep it that way, unless you want to die young."

I cringed and waited for the awkward moment to pass.

"Sorry," Rico said, "I wasn't thinking."

Leo cleared his throat. "No sweat. Sometimes, I almost forget about it...dying...you know? Then *pow*. Something brings it back and the air whooshes out of my lungs. It sucks to have that hanging over my head."

I was thinking he was right about that when my phone rang. It was Ilse.

"Allie, dear. I'm so worried. When I wasn't able to reach Sandy at home or on his cell, I went to his house. The back door had been kicked in and there'd been a struggle. His car was still there and his wallet too, along with his phone with all our messages on it. I've called the local police. They're at his house now. My God," she blurted between sobs. "What could have happened to him?"

Little Allie spit out more theories than I wanted to contemplate. "Jesus, Ilse. I'm so sorry. Please, please let me know the minute you hear something. If I can help in any way, let me know."

As I was about to disconnect, a thought occurred to me. "I hate to ask about the tissue samples now, with Sandy missing, but maybe the potential findings could have something to do with his disappearance. Is Dr. Christian qualified to do the tests Sandy intended to run?"

"Absolutely. He's worked with Sandy every step of the way. In fact, he thought about starting the tests, but didn't want to interfere with Sandy's protocol."

"Since we don't know when,"—*or if,* I thought,—"Sandy will be back, it might be a good idea to have Dr. Christian get started on them. Ask him to call me the minute he has the results, okay?"

Poor Ilse hung up sounding scared to death. She had every right to be scared. I was.

When I started into the living room to tell Rico about Sandy, I heard Leo's voice and realized he was still pursuing their prior conversation.

"You never did answer my question about why you wanted to work with Nighthawk, or what got you so interested in this paranormal crap in the first place."

Rico balked. Once again, it seemed Leo had hit a nerve, but after a short, stony silence, Rico's answer stunned me.

"Back when I was a kid and my dad was on the force, biters seemed more like bogeymen. Not real, nothing anyone ever had to worry about. And that was close enough to the truth, at least, close enough for a ten-year-old. Then, one night, my old man came home drunk. That wasn't unusual, he did that a lot, but he was crying. I hid in the stairwell, while he told my mom what happened during his shift that night.

"He and his partner, Conner O'Dell, took a call for a prowler at the projects over on Twelfth Street. They got there and heard noises coming from inside an abandoned building, so they went to check it out. Dad first, Conner taking his six. Next thing dad knows, Conner lets loose this high-pitched scream. Dad turns around and this biter's got his teeth sunk into Conner's face, chewing it off his skull. Conner's screaming for help, calling for my dad, over and over."

Rico stopped for a minute and rubbed his hands through his hair. When he settled himself and continued the story, his voice shook. "My dad was so scared shitless, he ran out the door and left Conner. Just left him to that son-of-a-bitch biter. By the time dad called it in and backup arrived, Conner was gone."

I stood silently at the corner of the kitchen and watched the light fade from Rico's eyes.

"My father left his fucking partner to die. You want to know *why Allie?* And *why* the paranormal crimes unit? That's why. That's also why I can't tell you stories about wanting to be like my dad. You heard enough of my life story? Or is there some other scab you'd like to pick?"

Rico's phone rang. I'd never been happier for an interruption in all my life. He strolled into the kitchen with the phone pressed to his ear, and I pretended to be absorbed in my research.

"Hey, Weston. Whatcha got?" Rico listened without speaking, nodding here and there, before finally blowing a gasket. "*What do you mean he's dead?* Stop shooting the damn dirtbags before we have a chance to talk to them, will you?"

"What's going on?" I whispered.

"Hold on a minute, Weston." Rico filled me in. "They checked the registry at the Metropole. Room 312 was registered to a Joey Fingers. He checked in three days ago, and was supposed to have checked out this morning, but didn't. They went to his room and knocked. Nobody answered, so the manager let them in. They found Fingers dead, with a single stab wound to the heart, just like Miriam. His ID matched the registry and his phone showed he made a couple calls to Jersey. They're checking out the numbers."

Leo scurried in from the living room. "Joey Fingers? I know that name. That's an alias for Joey Fingerello. He's a lieutenant with the Giordano Family. Holy crap. He ain't here, is he?"

Rico nodded. "What's he in charge of?"

"Shit. Shit. Shit." The color drained from Leo's face. "He's like three pay-grades above me, De Palma. I don't know. He's over high-level shit, not penny ante crap. I'm turning state's evidence here. Somebody want to connect the dots?"

I grabbed Rico's arm and held my head near his phone, so I could listen in.

"Did you get all that, Weston?" Rico asked. "A Jersey mob boss shows up in Cincinnati, while Leo here is under wraps. First, Miriam dies of a stab wound to the heart, then roughly twenty-four hours later, her killer ends up zombified, and the Jersey mob boss gets murdered the same way Miriam did. That's way too hinky for me."

"It's obvious why the mob wants Leo dead," Weston said. "And I get why they tried to blackmail Miriam for his location. But how did Miriam's killer end up a biter? And who killed the mob boss?"

Rico pinched the bridge of his nose and sighed. "Damn it. There's a connection here. We're just not seeing it. And now that these dirtbags are dead, we may never know what happened."

"Not necessarily," I said, joining the conversation. "Weston, have Fingerello's body taken to the M.E.'s office. Tell Doc Blanchard to look for hidden injection sites, just in case. But tell him to hold off on the autopsy for now."

"Sure thing, Nighthawk."

"Good job, Bill," Rico said. "Thanks. Keep me in the loop. Later, man."

As soon as the call ended, I told Rico about Sandy.

"Just when I think this case can't get any stranger," he said, "something happens to prove me wrong."

Suddenly, he cocked his head and smiled. The fire had returned to his eyes. "You told Weston to have Doc Blanchard hold off on the autopsy. Are you thinking what I'm thinking?"

"Yep. First thing tomorrow, you and I need to have a chat with the recently-deceased Joey Fingers."

11

GENGHIS KHAN: CORPSE WHISPERER

I magine my delight, returning home around twelve-thirty, after my shift at the safe house, to find Nonnie and the terrible twins, Headbutt and Kulu, waiting for me at the door. Nonnie handed me her shoe—at least, I think that's what it had been, before Headbutt turned it into a leather chew toy. To an uneducated eye, Headbutt, who lay prostrate on the kitchen floor, might have appeared to be wallowing in shame. But I knew this dog. He was laying low, waiting for the *Payless Shoes* storm to pass.

Kulu, roosting on Nonnie's shoulder, cast him an unsympathetic eye, ruffled her feathers, and muttered, "Bad golem. Bad. Bad. Bad."

That bird had her head stuck so far up Nonnie's ass, we were going to need a headlamp and barbecue tongs to pull it out.

And as for Headbutt, it's a good thing he had a nose for deadheads. That stubborn, fur-covered basketball was stretching my non-existent patience.

I pulled thirty bucks, the last of my money, out of my wallet. "Ah, geez, I'm sorry, Nonnie. Will this cover it?"

She pushed my hand away and shook her finger at Headbutt. "Bad Golem. Bad. Bad. Bad."

Was Kulu learning from Nonnie, or was Nonnie learning from Kulu?

"Is okay, Miss Allie. Keep your money," Nonnie said, shooting Headbutt the evil eye. "He will learn. I *make* him learn."

Headbutt moaned and rolled his sad brown eyes toward me.

"Nice try, you four-legged doorstop. Don't give me that *poor little puppy* crap. You do the crime, you do the time."

I thanked Nonnie and sent her home with a spare copy of my house key, telling her I'd be leaving early again, in the morning.

When I finally turned out the lights, deadheads filled my dreams.

Something invisible pinned me to the ground. An army of deadheads stretched as far as I could see, shuffling, crawling, dragging themselves closer and closer still, until they nearly covered me.

The rotters snapped their mossy teeth in my face and clawed at my skin. Their stink flooded my nose, and their raspy growls rumbled in my ears.

A tall hooded figure commanded the battalion of biters, urging them on. The zombies weren't randomly attacking like they usually do. They were organized and following the hooded man's direction.

Headbutt fought the horde, trying to protect me. The deadheads took him down, biting him again and again, tearing the flesh from his bones and drinking the blood from his veins.

I watched, powerless to save him.

His high-pitched cries morphed into screams, and I sprung awake to find that the screams were actually mine. Headbutt, who had been sleeping at my feet, now stood over me, head held high, nose to the air, peering into the darkness.

"Good boy," I murmured, kissing his muzzle.

He might be a shoe-chewing, fur-covered basketball, but he'd give his life for me in a heartbeat.

I lay back in bed, closed my eyes, and wondered who the hooded commander of my dreams had been. But part of me, the part I keep buried deep inside, was afraid to accept the truth.

Little Allie whispered a name. It whirred like a fly through the darkness, into my ear. And as I drifted off to sleep, there came a dark, familiar laugh. The hooded man had returned.

In that soft gray space between sleep and wakefulness, I wondered if he'd ever really been away.

I arrived at the M.E.'s office bright and early. Nothing like dreams of being devoured by an army of deadheads to get the blood pumping. The lobby door was already unlocked.

I walked down the hall, around the corner, and dipped into Doc Blanchard's conversation. He was having a hissy.

"No disrespect, Cap, but I'll strap myself to an ant hill, covered with honey, before I let Nighthawk raise that gangster in here. It's not going to happen. Did you see pictures of what she did to my morgue when she took Miriam down? I thought she was supposed to be good at this shit."

Ouch. Low blow. But I had to have some sympathy for the guy. This really hadn't been his week.

I opened Doc's office door and his jaw dropped. "She's already here, Cap. I'll let you talk to her."

I took the phone with a smile. "Good morning, Captain Sunshine. How're you today?"

Cap was short and not all that sweet. "Do what you need to do, but give Doc a break. You've pissed in his Wheaties enough this week. Is that clear?"

The call disconnected.

Rico walked in the door with Lloyd on his heels.

"I've got shit to do," Rico said. "Let's get this party started." He threw his jacket across Doc's guest chair. "How we gonna do this?"

Doc's quiet tone made me nervous. "I lost two day's work after that mess with Miriam. You can't do that to me again, Nighthawk."

"Doc, we can argue about who's fault that was later. But you're right. We need to think this through." I spun toward Rico. "Remember all those *stupid* rules of mine about who gets raised? Keep in mind that if putting down mild-mannered Miriam made a big-ass mess, raising *and* putting down Funky Fingers Fingerello—a freaking mobster—will be like spitting into a tornado and hoping you don't get F5'd all the way to Kansas. Get my drift?"

Rico nodded, but Doc squished his eyebrows together and frowned.

"Think of it this way, Doc. This guy was a bad-ass mobster. When I bring him back, he'll be a bad-ass freshy. And a bad-ass freshy is a corpse on crack."

"That's exactly why," Doc said, "you *cannot* do this in my morgue."

"What's in the basement?" Rico asked.

"Supplies—body bags, sterilized trays, surgical gowns, embalming fluid. Why?"

Rico glanced at me. "We could raise him down there."

"For God's sake," Doc said. "Embalming fluid is flammable.

Let me move it upstairs, before you light the building up like the Fourth of July."

The thought of Jade Chen reading that headline on the five o'clock news raced a shiver up my spine.

Together, we reconfigured the basement as best we could for a one-man zombie apocalypse. Doc and Lloyd brought Joey 'Fingers' Fingerello down in the elevator and wheeled him into the center of the room.

"Here, sign this," Doc said, handing me a sheet of paper.

"What's this?"

"It's a release. I took pictures of the basement as it is now. This statement says that you are raising this corpse, against my express consent, with the intention of extracting certain information and further, that you intend to put the corpse back down, once your objective has been accomplished. You will be held responsible for any and all damages that may occur in the process. On behalf of the Coroner's Office, I refuse to be held accountable or financially responsible."

"Sure, Doc."

I took his pen and laid the form on the counter behind me, to sign it. With my back to Doc, I crossed out my name and scrawled *The City of Cincinnati* in its place. Then I signed it *Genghis Khan*.

"There. Happy?" I handed it back to Doc, folded in half.

"Now go away," I said, and walked him back to the elevator. "Igor. You stay here. We might need you."

"It's Lloyd," he said, sliding his black-framed glasses up his nose.

"Whatever." I pushed the elevator button and sent Doc back upstairs to the morgue.

The basement measured around twenty by thirty—large

enough for Rico, Lloyd and me to maneuver, but throwing a freshy into that mix made it feel more like a linen closet. Overhead pipes ran across the ceiling lengthwise. There were a couple of support beams, some stationary tubs, shelving units and a floor drain. Not a lot to work with.

It was show time, but I couldn't shake the feeling I was forgetting something. I turned to find Rico holding out a family-size bag of Doritos.

"I brought them from home," he said. "It's all I had."

Junk food for the freshy. That's what we were missing. What a waste of perfectly good Doritos.

Joey Fingers, snug inside a black body bag, lay on a gurney in the center of the basement.

I put my fingers on the zipper and set the stage. "Rico, you stand across the gurney from me. Lloyd, you stand in front of the steps and block Joey if he tries to escape. Tackle him if you have to. Everybody ready?"

I eased the zipper down and got my first peak at Joey 'Fingers' Fingerello. He was a short, stout, fireplug of a guy, with curly black hair and a small jagged scar on his chin. Dollars to donuts, raising this guy was going to be a real treat.

Every corpse is different. Take Cephus, the kiddie-diddler, for example. He jumped out of his casket, ate a couple of chips, answered my questions, and then lit off like a bottle rocket across the cemetery, confused and fearful. But Fingerello, being a gangster, might wake up a lot more aggressive.

I shrugged and put my hands over Joey. "You know the drill, De Palma. This is always a crapshoot, but I'm not expecting Al Capone here to come back with flowers and a bottle of wine. You feel me?"

Rico raised his eyebrows. "Hold on, I've got an idea."

He rolled the gurney alongside a metal shelving unit anchored to the wall, and handcuffed Joey's left wrist to the support bar. "There. That's better."

I closed my eyes, placed my hands back over Joey's body, and felt the familiar, searing heat rush from my chest, through my arms, and into my palms.

Ribbons of light streamed from my fingertips, calling Joey from his eternal rest.

When the energy blazed in a solid arc, I raised my head and called upon a higher power. "Rise, Joseph Fingerello. In the name of God, I command you to rise."

His eyelids flickered.

"Joseph, hear me. *You will rise.*"

He didn't budge.

My palms were on fire, and he hadn't even opened his eyes. I pushed myself harder, generating more energy and transferring it into him, but he absorbed it like a sponge.

"Nighthawk," Rico whispered, "Your nose is bleeding."

I sucked in a deep breath and yelled, "Joseph Fingerello, you cannot resist. You will rise, *now!*"

Joey's body began to smoke. The unzipped body bag melted against his sides. His eyes snapped open and he flew straight off that gurney like a galvanized Pop-Tart.

He jerked his handcuffed arm against the shelving unit and roared, then threw a right uppercut into Rico's jaw with the opposite fist, sending him sprawling ten-feet back.

I cleared Hawk from my holster, but Joey thrashed his free arm back around, smashing into my elbow as I squeezed the trigger. The bullet went wide, striking what turned out to be the water pipe that fed the sprinkler system. Water gushed from the rusty old pipe onto the floor and the fire alarm sounded.

Miraculously, Joey was still handcuffed to the shelving unit.

"Did you have Miriam killed?" I yelled over the blaring alarm.

"*No.*" He growled and stared at me, eyes glazed.

He lunged forward, nearly pulling the shelves over. I didn't have much time. And damned if Rico hadn't fallen on top of the Doritos.

"Why were you in town?"

Joey pulled against the handcuffs, rocking the shelving unit back and forth. "Scare her. Find Leo."

Holy Shit. Did the mob know where Leo was?

"Joey," I shouted above the rushing water. "Did Miriam tell you where Leo is?"

"No," he snapped. "She dead. Dead. Already dead."

Sirens from the approaching fire trucks grew louder. I sloshed through the pooling water toward Rico. He stirred as I grabbed the picture of BOLO Guy from his pocket.

Holding it up, I asked Joey. "Do you recognize this man?"

Joey heaved forward with a shriek, straining against the handcuffs. "Killed me! He. Killed. Me!"

The shelving unit teetered on its front legs, and my brain shifted into overdrive. *BOLO Guy killed mob guy?* Who the hell *was* BOLO Guy, and who did he work for?

The brain bitch blew her top, screaming a name over and over again, a name I'd tried hard to forget, for a very long time. Joey yanked the shelving unit one last time, and brought it down with a crash. I saw it coming and backed up, but not fast enough. The corner of the unit knocked Hawk out of my hand and into the drink.

"Joey," I yelled, stumbling backward through the rising water. "Is the man who killed you with the mob?"

"No!" he bellowed. "Not mob. Kill him. Kill him. *Now!*" He dragged the shelving unit across the floor behind him, on his way toward me.

With my Ka-Bar knife in hand, I squared off to battle one seriously pissed-off freshy.

The sound of feet pounding down the steps caught my ear. It wasn't likely Lloyd. He'd disappeared once Joey went airborne off the gurney.

A blue uniform popped into view. "Stop! Police," he yelled.

Not that Joey cared.

"Just shoot!" I screamed.

One shot to the head and Joey went down. Now, there was an officer who knew how to take out a biter.

I breathed a sigh of relief. "Thanks for the assist, man. Good job."

"No problem, Nighthawk."

I knew that voice. The cop joined me at Rico's side, and I finally realized who he was.

"Holy shit! D-D-Donald—from the training session at City Hall. It's you!"

His face turned crimson. "Please. I just saved your life. Can you let that shit go?"

I threw him a wink. "No problem, Donald. Nice shooting. Let's get my partner to his feet."

I fished Hawk out of the water, and then Donald and I grabbed Rico by his shoulders and helped him up the steps, water running off us, as if we'd taken a dip in a swimming hole.

Rico, with a massive bruise on his chin and possibly a broken jaw, did his best to get his feet back beneath him.

Doc threw open the basement door as we neared the top of the stairs and came out with both barrels blazing.

"Damn it, Nighthawk! How could you possibly inflict this much damage from the freaking basement? *You're a human wrecking ball. A one-man demolition service.*"

Firemen poured through the door.

Doc stepped out of their way and sneered at me. "Well, at

least I was smart enough to have you sign that release. Thank God this clusterfuck won't be coming out of my budget."

I let that go. Low-hanging fruit's just too easy to pick.

Doc took a deep cleansing breath and calmed himself. "You should know, Miriam's killer, BOLO Guy, wasn't bitten. And I didn't find any injection site on his body, either."

The hair on the back of my neck stood up. *How the hell did he turn?*

I tried to sound nonchalant. "Since I haven't heard from Sweden yet, why don't you send a tissue sample from BOLO Guy to the CDC? Maybe they can figure out what's going on."

Doc walked away, but turned and called over his shoulder, "Oh. Remember the rush order on Miriam's test results? They're back. She had the Z-virus in her system, but she didn't have the genetic marker for turning."

"What?"

"Yeah. I don't get it, either." Doc scratched his head. "What the hell's going on? BOLO Guy wasn't bitten or injected, but he turns, and Miriam *was* injected—didn't have the genetic marker—and turned anyway. What do you make of all that?"

Little Allie moaned, and my heart thrummed in my chest. "I don't know, Doc. But I'm sure as hell going to find out."

12

WHEN IS A BLACK LEXUS JUST A BLACK LEXUS?

While police officers and firemen converged on the Coroner's Office, I took the opportunity to clean up.

The EMTs sat Rico down, so they could check his jaw. Although a dark angry bruise had already bloomed, his jaw didn't appear to be broken. When they suggested an x-ray just to be sure, Rico's only answer was the thin set of his lips and the thundercloud over his brow.

When my phone began to ring. I didn't need to look at the display to know who was calling, but the ringtone taunted me: *Don't be shy. Have a quick look-see. It's only the train wreck you've been waiting for since your bullet punched a hole in the building's sprinkler line.*

I pulled the phone from my pocket and took a deep breath. "Hi, Cap."

I held the phone several inches from my head. It was hard to know which was louder, Cap or the damned fire alarm that continued to blare in the background.

Getting a word in edgewise wasn't easy. "Yeah, but... Yeah, but... Yeah, but... Okay. You bet. It's not as ba—"

He hung up in my ear and I winced, turning toward Rico. "We've been summoned."

Bill Weston, Rico and I sat across from Cap, listening to his colorful rendition of our bone-headed fuck-ups. It was hard not to agree with him.

He started with our stalled investigation into the zombie at the gun-range, threw in Miriam's death (which, so far, had produced more questions than answers), then summarized the list of damages I'd "wreaked upon the city" *(au contraire),* before finally ending with this morning's flood in the morgue basement.

He didn't take a breath until he hit the bottom of the list and for a moment, I thought he might pass out.

But he pulled himself together and continued. "Let's recap our findings, shall we? We determined that there were no signs of forced entry, or any unusual fingerprints at the gun-range, which led us to believe there could be a badge involved, right? Any more on that front?"

Rico wriggled like a six-year-old and rubbed the back of his neck. "Not really. It comes down to a question of who might have had access to biters as well as a key to the walk-up."

"And the black Lexus that tailed you on the way to the safe house. Any leads on it?"

"No." Rico closed his eyes and sighed. "We couldn't get a plate number, and we haven't seen it since."

I threw some shit up on the wall, hoping it would stick. "Well, Jade Chen, the reporter from Channel Ten drives a Black Lexus. It could have been her. She's always sniffing around for a story."

"You don't know that," Rico said. "Stop accusing her. She said it wasn't her. Let it go."

Cap crossed his arms and leaned back, putting his feet on the desk. "But the car hasn't been back. Maybe you're both wrong. Maybe it was just a random black Lexus."

Neither Rico, nor I, said a word.

"So...maybe, we have a mole," Cap said. "Someone who knew you'd be taking a stroll through Perptown and managed to slip a biter inside the walk-up. Someone who may, or may not, have followed you on your way to the safe house. If we have a mole, who could it be?"

I glanced at Rico. "I still say Jade. She has the means, the motive, and," I rolled my eyes, "the opportunity."

Rico's stare bored a hole through my head.

Cap glanced back and forth between Rico and me, as if he were trying to figure out what *wasn't* being said. "Is there something I should know?"

I chewed on my fingernail and glowered at the floor while Rico twitched in his chair like a freaking freshy.

"Has Leo's location been compromised?" Cap asked.

Rico waved his hand. "No. Of course not."

"Then what the hell's the problem?" Cap turned to me, "Is there *anything*, anything at all you need to say Nighthawk? If so, now's the time."

"No, Cap. I got nothing."

"Then, if you two are finished dancing, let's get back to our discussion on possible moles."

Someone knocked at Cap's door and without waiting for an answer, barged in. That squirrelly janitor, Ottis. He walked straight to the wastebasket, as if no one else was in the room, and started to pick it up, but Cap stopped him.

"Not now, Ottis. We're in the middle of something here. Come back later. And when you do, wait for me to answer your knock before you enter."

Ottis tilted his head and studied us like we were a new species of insect, then nodded and left.

Weston leaned forward. "What about him? My money's on that little weasel. He never talks. He's always around, almost invisible, rummaging through garbage cans like a little ferret. He could have grabbed the keys to the walk-up."

"And he was here, in the precinct, the night Miriam was murdered," Rico said. "Clawson told me so."

"Ottis?" Cap said. "Not likely, but maybe. Anybody else?" He looked at Rico.

"I don't know, Cap. It could be anyone with access to both the precinct and the firing range. That's a big pool of suspects."

My phone rang, interrupting our little circle jerk. It was Ilse.

"Cap I need to take this," I said, walking out into the hall.

"Hey, girl, give me good news." I listened to what she had to say, at least the part I could understand between her sobs, and then had to hold back a few of my own.

After she hung up, I leaned against the wall to collect my thoughts. After pulling myself together, I walked back into Cap's office. His mood hadn't improved.

"Nice of you to rejoin us, Nighthawk. Did your Swedish contact ever get back to you with the results of his tissue samples from the European biter? Or is he out ice-fishing somewhere?"

Goddam. I hated this job.

"Sandy's been missing since the night he took the samples. The lab sent a security guard to check on him yesterday. His back door had been kicked in and his home had been ransacked. The police have started working the case. His associate, Dr. Christian, stepped in to run the tests."

Cap glared at me. "You didn't think I needed to know that, Nighthawk? You need to keep—"

"Keep you posted, right?" I felt the vein in my temple pulsing. "That was Sandy's secretary, Ilse, on the phone just now. They found Sandy stabbed and turned deadhead. No bite marks and no injection sites. They had to put him down this morning. Dr. Christian performed the tissue sample tests for us since Sandy was...since Sandy wasn't there. He found a new, previously unidentified DNA sequence in the virus. He doesn't know its origin, but he's working on it. What he *can* say is that the virus didn't organically mutate. It was manipulated. The presence of the unidentified DNA strand confirms that. How's that for a timely update?"

I grabbed the edge of his desk and the picture of his wife fell over.

Cap lightened his tone. "I'm sorry, Nighthawk. I know you were friends."

"I don't need sympathy," I said, holding back tears. "I need to find out who's behind all this."

Rico motioned toward my chair. "Then sit back down and let's start with what we know. Miriam was stabbed, injected with the Z-virus, and despite not having the marker, turned anyway. BOLO Guy killed both Miriam and the mob boss, Joey Fingerello, then somehow turned into a biter and had to be put down. We still don't know BOLO Guy's real name, who he worked for, or why he murdered Miriam and Joey. Nighthawk raised Joey Fingerello, who told us he was in town to lean on Miriam, so she'd give up Leo's location, but she was already dead before he got to her. And last, but not least, we found out the Z-virus has been manipulated by...who the hell knows."

Weston rubbed his eyes. "Somebody give me a play book."

"It's not that hard, we just need to ask the right questions," Rico said. "Who has the ability to manipulate the Z-virus? Nighthawk, you said yourself that there are only a handful of people who know this shit. Who are they?"

I sat back down, tilted my head, and stared at the ceiling. "Well, there's Dr. Kimmel at the CDC, and with Sandy gone, maybe Dr. Christian at the European CDPC. There's Dr. Sato in Japan, and Ariel Sanchez in Brazil. And all of these scientists have research assistants who might be capable of introducing a new strand of DNA to the virus. But the source of the DNA sequence is unknown. That means that they'd have to engineer the DNA first."

Cap snorted. "Well, somebody sure as hell knows what they're doing, or this wouldn't be happening."

"What about other corpse whisperers?" Rico asked. "You told me once that they're not all as...moral as you. Who's on that list?"

I felt my face flush. "It's not like we have a Facebook group, De Palma. The good ones don't wear white hats and the bad ones don't wear black. Some of them might even switch hit on occasion, depending on the circumstances. Now that we know the virus is being manipulated, I'll start reaching out. Maybe I can narrow down the list."

Rico's phone rang, providing a welcome interruption. By asking me specifics about which corpse whisperer could be involved, he was pulling me down a path I wasn't prepared to travel. In more ways than one.

"De Palma," Rico said and eased out of his chair to leave the room. But he didn't get far. "He did? When?" Seconds passed while he listened. "How bad is it?" Finally, he shook his head. "Damn it. We'll be right there."

He hung up and grabbed his jacket from the back of his chair. "That was Ortega from the safe house. Leo had another seizure." He slid his phone into his pocket. "We need to get over there, Cap."

Cap turned his eyes to me. "If this is the end, you let me know, pronto."

"Got it," I said, scrambling out the door.

I rode with Rico, lights, sirens, the whole production. Once we turned onto Jora Lane, I called Ilse. Even knowing how hard she took Sandy's death, I was hoping to find her at the lab. She answered on the second ring.

I exhaled long and hard, unaware that I'd been holding my breath. "Hi Ilse, how're you doing?"

I prayed she wouldn't tell me the truth. Not because I didn't care, but because I didn't have time to chat. I held my tongue, and let her go on a bit, before breaking in.

"Ilse, I'm so sorry, but there's another reason why I called. Leo's had another attack. Can Dr. Christian offer any suggestions? Tell me what I need to look for?"

She placed me on hold and put Dr. Christian on the line. "Hello, Ms. Nighthawk, is Leo still seizing now, or has the attack passed?"

"Let me check, Doc."

Rico pulled up in front of the safe house, and I bounded up the front steps, two at a time.

After bursting through the door, I took one look at Leo and skidded to a halt. "Oh, Jesus, Doc. He's lying on the living room floor, twitching, with his eyes rolled back in his head. This is way worse than his last one."

Dr. Christian sounded detached, even clinical, like a seasoned ER physician. "Give him an extra two mils. Put it directly into his heart, not his leg. We want it to pump through his system as quickly as possible."

Rico grabbed one of Leo's syringes and tossed it to me. I primed the needle to work out any air bubbles, and then jabbed it into Leo's heart. He bucked once—hard, like a rodeo bull—then fell completely still.

"*Leo*," I said, tapping his face. "Leo? Wake up."

He didn't move.

"Leo! *Come on, Leo.*" I gave him an all-out slap up the side of his head.

"What the... What the fuck?" he moaned. "Stop beating the shit out of me, will ya?"

He rolled onto his side, coughing up a lung.

"Damn, that shit hurts when you stab it into my chest. Somebody get me a glass of water, huh?"

"Dr. Christian, thank you so much," I said, breathing like I'd run a marathon. "Any other instructions?"

"Happy to help, Nighthawk. Keep him calm today. Sadly, this being his second episode, the meds may be losing their efficacy. Watch for increased tremors, sporadic slurring of his speech, and God forbid, another seizure. I'm here if you need me."

I hung up the phone and swallowed hard, dreading the day there would be no stopping the inevitable.

Since our shift at the house was due to begin anyway, we sent Powell and Ortega home, and settled in for a quiet afternoon with Leo. He dozed on and off, beneath a blanket on the couch, snoring loud enough to drive Rico and me into the kitchen.

It was quiet without Leo's non-stop verbal diarrhea. Rico checked his phone for messages, and I pulled up the Internet to catch some news. Later that afternoon, we ordered a pizza with everything but anchovies from Ricardo's.

Out of the blue, Rico said to me, "So, now that it's just us, maybe you can tell me what you held back in Cap's office. You know these renegade corpse whisperers. You have to, at least some of them. There has to be a name that shoots to the top of the *Most Likely to Fuck Up the World* list. Who is it?"

Little Allie cajoled me. *Tell him. Just tell him.* The problem was, that although I had my suspicions, there was no way for me to know for sure. And I didn't want to stir up that nightmare of a hornet's nest, unless it became absolutely necessary.

While I silently debated coming clean, Toby sprinted up the front steps with our pie. Rico jumped for the door, so Toby wouldn't wake Leo ringing the bell. But the smell of incoming pizza roused Leo from his nap anyway.

He sat up, stretched, and lay his head on the back of the couch with a groan.

Toby handed the pizza to Rico. "Not feeling good today, Uncle David?"

Leo didn't answer.

"*Uncle David*," I said, patting him on the head. "Toby asked if you weren't feeling well today."

Leo's eyes flew open. "Oh, hiya, kid. Yeah, I'm feeling pretty rough today. Must've been that Kimchi I had last night. Thanks for asking."

Toby smiled. "I know it's none of my business, but have you guys noticed the black Lexus parked up the street today? I've made a couple of deliveries this way already, and it's been sitting about fifty feet up the block all afternoon. But the minute I pulled into this driveway, it took off. It could be nothing, but I thought you'd want to know."

Rico glanced at me, I looked him, and Leo stared at us both.

"Maybe you'll stop delivering pizzas and make detective someday," I said with a grin. "You didn't happen to catch the plate number, did you?"

"As a matter of fact, I did." He pulled a slip of paper from his pocket. "What's it worth to you?"

Rico yanked a twenty out of his wallet and gave it to Toby, along with a high-five. "Way to go, kid. Keep your eyes open. There's more where that came from."

"Really?" Toby deadpanned. "Couldn't prove it from your tips. But, I digress. Here you go, dude."

He flipped Rico the plate number, then turned to Leo with a wink.

"You feel better soon, Uncle David. *Ciao*."

Toby got back into his beater with the Ricardo's pizza banner strapped on top, and rumbled down Jora Lane.

Rico went into the kitchen, got some plates and napkins, and tossed them to us on the couch.

"Go ahead, eat while it's hot," he said. "I'll be right in. I want to run this plate number first."

I turned on the TV since Leo was awake, and sat next to him on the couch. We each grabbed a slice and turned our eyes to the screen, just in time to catch a tantalizing promo for the Channel 10 evening news with Jade Chen.

"Meatbag melee at the M.E.'s office. Find out what our local cadaver diver, Allie Nighthawk, has been up to today and hear the latest damage estimate caused by Hurricane Allie. Details at six."

"God, I hate that bitch."

Leo flinched as I threw my water bottle at the TV. Magically, it hit the power knob and Jade's botoxed mug disappeared as the screen went black.

"That chick needs a riding crop," Leo said. "She rides your ass like Eddie Arcaro."

"Shut up, Leo."

Hand to God, people. It sucks being me sometimes.

13

FOR THE LOVE OF LASAGNA

L eo bit into his pizza and wrinkled his nose. "Does this pie taste funny to you? It tastes funny to me—like tinny. Ricardo's must be slipping. How 'bout asking Nonnie to send me another lasagna?"

"I'll get right on that," I said, taking his plate with his half-eaten slice of *everything but pineapple and anchovies* out to the kitchen and dumping it into the trash can.

The pizza tasted fine to me. Maybe his senses were changing due to the virus. I'd been watching him like a hawk, every sneeze, every cough and every twitch, waiting for *the* sign —the one that would tell me it was time.

I hated myself for that.

Before Leo, my cases had always been a combination of *raise this corpse* and *waste that rotter*. Quick in, quick out; no muss, no fuss. I'd never gotten close to a rotter-in-the-making, to anyone who was holding off the disease with drugs.

I tried to tell myself that the tinny taste could be from upping his dosage, or maybe the pizza did taste tinny, and my taste buds were off. Then again, maybe it was like he said. He was just freaking tired of pizza.

This assignment was wearing on me. Leo was wearing on me. But the day would come, not too far off, when I'd move on to a new case and Leo would be gone. He'd be a ghost, a strange collection of memories and Leo-isms.

Nonnie's lasagna sounded pretty good, and the comfort of homecooked food was the least I could do for him. I'd ask her to fix him one tonight when I got home.

I glanced back into the living room and found him nodding off again, so I sat at the kitchen table across from Rico, and checked the web for news flashes about increased zombie activity. A few posts popped up about sighted zombies and the virus changing across the globe, but like my prior search, nothing turned up about actual manipulation.

So, I messaged Philipe, a mercenary corpse whisperer who always had an ear to the ground. He was a reliable source for intel—at a price.

True to form, when he answered my message, he cut to the chase.

Nighthawk! Can't say I'm surprised. I know what you want. The question is, what are you willing to pay for it?

At least he was consistent. I hovered my fingers over the keyboard and thought before typing my response.

The pay is good karma. Tell me who's behind the virus manipulation, and you could save a lot of lives.

His answer flashed.

You know me better than that.

He was right. I did know him. And while I didn't have any money, I had something he might find even more valuable.

I'll owe you one.

Specifics, please. That could mean a great many things.

I winced. No kidding.

A favor. Someday, somewhere to be repaid. Best I can do.

Seconds passed before he answered.

I'll take it. I don't know who he is, but you'll find his rhetoric here: www.duat.onion. Enter the password: Ammit.

Finally. A baby step at best, but still progress. He was taking me to the dark web. The site name *Duat* came from the realm of the Egyptian Gods of the Underworld. *Ammit* was a soul-eating monster, a dispenser of divine retribution.

A few seconds later, another message appeared:

If this ever comes back to me, we're both dead.

No shit.

Understood. Thanks, Philipe.

Do not thank me. This is not a gift. You owe me.

Without a doubt, one day that would come back to haunt me.

Rico glanced at me over his phone. "What's up? You look like you swallowed yesterday's sushi."

"Or worse," I mumbled. "Did you run the tag on the Lexus?"

"Yeah. It's registered to Stanous Electric."

I shrugged. "They're renovating that four-family brown-stone near the corner of Jora and Paxton, right where Toby saw the car. I'm glad the kid had his eyes open, but sometimes a Lexus—"

"Is just a Lexus. I know."

I wanted to dig into the onion site Philipe had given me but I would have to use Tor, a protected web browser, to access it. I'd have to bring my laptop back with me tomorrow, to see how good Philipe's intel was.

Leo walked into the kitchen and grabbed a bottle of water from the refrigerator. He cranked the cap off with his teeth and chugged half the bottle there, beneath the fluorescent kitchen light. He looked a little yellow, but then, everybody looked yellow under those ugly-ass lights. On the upside, he seemed more relaxed, more like himself. If you could call that the upside.

He tossed me the bottle cap. "I think *Dancing with the Stars* is on in a few minutes."

Rico looked over and groaned, then turned back to his phone.

Finally, the night was looking up. If I'd been at home, I'd have fixed me a big ole Jack Daniel's slushie and plopped on the sofa next to Headbutt.

Instead, I poured myself a Coke Zero and settled in next to Leo, on the plasticized couch.

It was just as well. I could sense I'd been crowding Rico in the kitchen. Still in the dog house with Jade over blocking her access at the Coroner's Office, no doubt he had a mouthful of crow to swallow. He probably wanted some space to chat with the conniving little wench.

Out of nowhere, Leo reached across the couch and took my hand. Not in a romantic way. It was more...needy. I'm not the touchy feely type. In fact, I had to fight the urge to pull away from him. But, knowing what he was going through, I didn't have it in me to reject him.

We sat for a while, neither of us saying a word, watching the dancers, when he finally spit out what he wanted to say.

"Thanks for saving me today, Nighthawk. I know one day you won't be able to. And I just wanted to tell you that's okay. When the time comes, you do what you got to do. No hard feelings, huh?"

It was hard to talk, what with the golf-ball sized lump in my throat, so I just squeezed his hand and mumbled, "No sweat, Leo."

When he leaned over to grab his water bottle, I wiped my eyes with my shirt sleeve.

Damn him, anyway.

Leo cranked up the volume on the TV. Len Goodman was chastising some celebrity schmuck, telling him he moved like a wounded elk.

Leo flipped Len the bird. "Goodman. What does that old fart know anyway? Thinks he's the greatest dancer ever, slinging insults at these guys, like a monkey flinging turds. I could dance circles around that smug bastard any day—any dance."

I snorted. Leo, a dancer? No way. Our hand-holding Kodak moment officially came to an end. "Gimme a break."

Leo raised his brows. "You think I can't dance? My mother taught me to dance when I was a kid. I even taught at Arthur Murray's for a while before, well, you know, I went full-time with the Family. I got moves that hoity-toity klutz ain't even thought of."

Some people grew up wanting to be astronauts, some firefighters and some ballerinas. Me? I wanted to be Ginger Rogers. My dad and I used to watch all the old Fred Astaire movies on TV. Who wouldn't want to be Ginger, gorgeous and graceful, floating through life wearing chiffon, heels and opera-length gloves?

On any given day, I'm lucky to be sporting clean underwear, a T-shirt without holes, and biter-proof boots. Everyone dreams. Even me.

"Look," Leo said. "Maks and his partner are doing the waltz. Now there's a guy who's graceful *and* manly. A real guy's guy."

I couldn't have said it better myself, except I would have added a few other yummy adjectives.

Leo pointed at the screen. "You want to know how to waltz, Nighthawk? Watch her, head back, elbows high. Count the beat. One, two, three, one, two, three—"

My phone rang. Normally, during *DWTS*, that's an automatic *send to voicemail*. But I was on duty, so I looked at the display. "Hey Nonnie. Wassup?"

Leo heard her name and mouthed the word *lasagna*, making like he was shoveling food in his face.

I listened to Nonnie, while Maks and his perfectly-coiffed partner floated across the stage. I nodded here and there, throwing in a few well-placed *uh-huhs*, trying to move her along. But Nonnie wasn't going anywhere. She must have been lonely.

We were out of milk, she said. And the bird seed was running low, so Kulu kept dipping into Headbutt's food bowl, which started animal Armageddon in my kitchen. Yack, yack, yack, duck's ass, more yacking.

"Nonnie," I interrupted when she caught a breath, "somebody here wants to say hi."

I flung the phone at Leo.

"*Mia bella*, Nonnie! How are you?" he said. "I was just telling Nighthawk...Allie...earlier, how much I miss your lasagna."

Yack, yack, yack, duck's ass, more yacking. Flirty laughter. Ewww. Enough of that. I tuned Leo out and focused on Maks.

Screw his Barbie doll partner. She could have been wearing a bag over her flammable beehive, for all I cared.

By the time Leo finished running his mouth and hung up, *Dancing with the Stars* was over.

He let out a big yawn and stretched as he headed for the hallway. "I think I'm going to turn in now. Must be more tired than I thought. G'night."

He was usually more of a night owl, and more often than not, awake when Powell and Ortega arrived at midnight.

"You okay?" I asked.

"Yeah. Really. Just ready to turn in. See you, tomorrow."

"Night, Leo," Rico called from the kitchen

"Goodnight," I said, watching him pad down the hall.

When Leo closed his door, Rico strolled into the room. "Is *Dancing with the Dweebs* over?"

"Yes. The cooties are gone. You can return now."

His ever-present phone was noticeably missing.

"You patch things up with Jade?"

He took Leo's seat on the couch and shrugged. "I guess. She's got boundary issues. She can't just show up in the middle of a crisis and expect special press access, just because we... date."

"Is that what the kids are calling it these days?" I tried hard to keep the smirk off my face. *Allie: One. Jade: Zero.* "I'm sure it'll all work out for the best. Just give it time."

Time to crash and burn. Not one to gloat—well, that's a big fat lie—I changed the subject and flipped between our three available channels, hoping something good might pop up. Bingo. An episode of *CSI*.

About five minutes in, I realized it was a repeat, the only episode I'd seen all season. With nothing better to do, I sat through it, rolling my eyes at how easily their cases came together, and when it ended, I watched yet another episode. By the time the eleven o'clock news came on, I was rooted to the couch like a redwood tree.

Rico's eyes looked heavy. Too much burning the candle at both ends. He wouldn't get any pity from me.

I flicked him with a rolled-up section of newspaper. "Hey. When do you think they'll schedule the grand jury hearing for Leo? I'm a little worried he might not make it if they hold off too long."

"I was thinking the same thing. I don't know," he said. "We'll have to get with Cap and see how the FBI's investigation is going. Christ, I'm tired. I could use some caffeine."

"Me too." I headed out to the kitchen to nuke us a couple cups of stale coffee and heard a thump outside.

I drew Hawk, and turned to see Rico coming to my side, his Glock at high ready.

"I think it came from alongside the house," I said.

He flipped off the lights to even the playing field.

It took a minute for my eyes to adjust. I peered out the kitchen window, into an endless blanket of pitch.

"I can't see a thing," I whispered, checking the lock on the back door.

Rico squatted below the picture window and scanned the front yard. "Same here."

He checked the deadbolt on the front door and then crossed to the hallway, where he opened the door that led to the second-floor dormer. We weren't using that space. Leo had taken the bedroom on the ground level, but someone could gain access through an upstairs window.

I stood in the darkness, letting my senses take over, every sound a warning, every movement a threat.

Then came another thump, louder, from down the hall.

Leo's room.

"Rico!" I yelled, and took off down the hall.

I skidded to a stop in front of Leo's room and turned the knob.

Damn it. He'd locked the door.

I thought about shooting off the lock, but Rico reached my side and threw his shoulder into the door. It burst from its frame and crashed against the wall.

I went left and Rico went right.

The room was pitch black and completely silent.

And the window was wide open.

"Cincinnati PD," Rico announced. "Put your hands up."

No movement, no sound, just a slight breeze blowing through the room.

I motioned to Rico, then knelt beside the bed, sucked in a breath and shined the light from my phone underneath it.

There was Leo, covered in red, lying motionless on the floor beneath the window.

Shit, shit, shit.

"Hit the light," I yelled.

Rico groped his way across the wall and flipped the switch.

I dove across the bed and peered down at Leo, expecting the worst.

Onion and garlic fumes from his marinara-stained shirt assaulted my nose.

The window screen had been carefully propped against the bedroom wall, and a crumpled aluminum pan of leftover lasagna lay splattered across the floor.

If Leo hadn't already had one foot in the grave, I'd have killed him right then and there.

I pulled him up by his shirt collar.

"Now, don't go doing anything stupid, Nighthawk. I just wanted a little lasagna. You heard me say that earlier, right? Man does not live by pizza, alone. Nonnie called, and said she was fixing me a dish to send over tomorrow. But I didn't want to wait. For God's sake, I'm a dying man here! All I wanted was some freaking lasagna."

"I thought you were dead." I brought Hawk up, close and personal, so Leo could get a good look at him.

"Rico! Rico, man, take that gun away from her. I think she's going to shoot me."

"If she doesn't, I might," Rico said. "What the hell's wrong with you? We're trying to keep you alive and you go sneaking out your window in the middle of the night? We might have shot you as an intruder. How stupid can you get?"

"Sorry, guys. It gets so boring here, you know? Nothing to do but think about dying."

He got up from the floor and hung his head. "I didn't mean to scare you. I wasn't thinking, that's all."

He looked at the lasagna splattered across the hardwood floor. "How 'bout a little help here, huh? Nonnie made an extra dish. She's giving it to you tomorrow."

I grabbed a towel from the hallway bath and threw it at him. "You're on your own, twinkle-toes. Make it snappy, before Powell and Ortega get here. And not a word. You hear me? Not a word."

That was all we needed, Cap getting wind of this little episode. That was a disturbing visual.

An ugly thought crossed my mind: *I wonder if they need corpse whisperers in Siberia.*

14

SHIT GOT REAL

Powell and Ortega called to say they would be a little late. So much the better. It gave us enough time to get the house—and Leo—back under control.

Leo cleaned up the lasagna and threw the dirty towels in the wash, while Rico lectured him about the stupidity of his great escape. By the time Powell and Ortega walked in around twelve-thirty, it was situation normal.

Now, I needed to go home and address the other end of that escapade—Nonnie.

When I walked in the door, most of the lights were out, and the terrible twins were sound asleep. Nonnie sat at the kitchen table with her head high and her jaw set. She clearly expected a ration of shit.

I was happy to oblige.

"Nonnie, you can't drag Le...you can't drag David away from his work. What he's doing is very important and top secret. If you want to make him a lasagna and send it over with me, fine. But you are never to lure him away from his work again. Do you understand?"

Nonnie arched her brow and shot me the stink-eye. "You think Nonnie can't read below the lines? Nonnie did not just fall out of bed yesterday, you know."

Despite the garbled idioms, I got her drift. The jig was up, and my seventy-year-old neighbor was about to hand me my ass.

"His name not David. Is Leo. He good man, dying, cooped up in that house like criminal. He likes me. And my lasagna." Her cheeks blazed. "Shame, shame on you, Miss Allie, for not telling me what you do. You...you turn dead people into zumbas! Leo told me."

Strike two, Leo.

Rule number five of corpse whispering, never let your neighbors know what you do. Granted, my neighbors had seen a lot of weirdness at my house over the years, and they'd have gladly paid for the moving van if I decided to leave, but they've never known exactly what I do—until now.

I took a deep breath and stared her down. "What I do, this gift I have, came from God. I only raise the dead under very specific circumstances, in situations where the dead have information the living need. And I put the people I raise back down, Nonnie. I don't leave them zumb...zombies, to wander the earth. That would be wrong. Do you understand the difference?"

She nodded.

"Everything Leo told you is confidential, about him *and* me. Do you know that word? It means secret. Leo should never have told you any of it. And you can't tell anyone else. It would put all of us—you, me, Rico, and Leo in danger. Tell me you understand?" I took her by the shoulders. "Swear to me you will never tell another soul."

Nonnie's mouth fell open, and she jerked away from me. "What kind stoolie you think Nonnie is?"

Stoolie? I chuckled in spite of myself. "Nonnie, with all the English words you don't know, where in the world did you pick up a word like *stoolie?*"

"I married to Mortie Nussbaum, God rest him, thirty-five years before he pass. First, my name Nonnie Vitale. I'm born in Palermo, Sicily." She waved her hand. "Where you think lasagna recipe come from?"

Palermo, Sicily? The brain bitch went Pavarotti in my head.

"Nonnie," I asked, pinching the bridge of my nose, "Do you have relatives connected to La Cosa Nostra?"

Her gaze drifted up and to the right. "Well...there is Vitale family of Palermo. This is known. It is...possible...we are relations. But, as I say," she smiled sweetly, "I no stoolie. *Capiche?*"

Oh, sweet Jesus. Nonnie tied to a mafia family? Rico would have a meltdown. I'll bet Leo didn't know that little tidbit when he was busy, blabbing his business.

"Do you involve yourself with family business?" I asked.

"*Bah*, no. Men playing men's games. Is boring. Sometimes, I hear talk from womens in family, but they yap, their mouths, how you say, Miss Allie? Run like duck's ass."

"I need you to stay away from them, until this is over. Promise me, you won't talk to them. You don't want Leo hurt, do you?"

"No. Of course, I not hurt Leo." Nonnie pinched her lips together. "How long I cannot talk to family?"

"As long as it takes." I stared at her, waiting for an answer.

"I promise. Nonnie no liar."

Next, I needed to find out if the Vitales and the Giordanos were allies or enemies. That was a Rico question—for tomorrow. It was two in the morning, and I needed to decide what to do with Nonnie.

"You go on home, now," I said. "It's late. Thank you for

taking care of Headbutt and Kulu. Remember, when it comes to Leo, you know nothing, and you won't talk about what you don't know with *anyone*. Right?"

Nonnie, an amazing, lonely, old Italian-Jewish woman, who baked the best lasagna in town and whipped my pets into shape with the *chutzpah* of a drill sergeant, nodded her solemn vow, and plodded across the yard to her house.

Once I saw her safely inside, I turned off the lights and crawled into bed, wondering what other surprises she might have in store for me, but quickly kicked that thought to the curb. I'd do better counting sheep than pondering the enigma that was Nonnie.

I called Rico's cell at eight the next morning. Who do you think answered? That bitchy she-devil, Jade.

"Rico can't come to the phone right now. He's...in the shower."

The dig behind those words was loud and clear.

"Any message?"

"Tell him to call me, pronto."

"Something wrong?"

I gripped the phone a little too hard. "Nice try, sweetheart. Go put some more product in your hair. Then you can twist that waist-length mop of yours into a giant strand and use it to stab more people in the back."

"Oh, I take it you caught my headline the other night. The ratings went through the roof."

I pulled the phone cord into a garrote. "Just have him call me."

"Sure thing."

I slammed the receiver down, absolutely certain that he'd never get the message.

Surprisingly, he called me back within the next ten minutes.

"What's up?" he asked.

"You need to come to my house. We have a...situation."

"Really?" Rico's voice sounded odd.

Jade giggled in the background. "Things are popping up everywhere today, Miss Cadaver Diver."

My face blazed.

"Be there in twenty...ah...make that forty," Rico said, hanging up with a chuckle.

I needed to Lysol my phone.

———

True to his word, Rico arrived in forty minutes, and sat at my kitchen table, scratching Headbutt's ears, while he listened to the tale of Donna Nonnie Vitale Nussbaum—the Sicilian Godmother.

After I relayed the entire, mind-bending clusterfuck, his head hit the table with a thud. "We are so screwed."

"Not necessarily," I said. "Nonnie will keep her mouth shut because she doesn't want to hurt Leo. How about you? Think you can keep Nonnie's mob ties out of your pillow talk?"

"What kind of question is that?" Rico's eyes were bloodshot and puffy. "I can't do this with you right now, Nighthawk. How about some coffee?"

"The cups are in the cabinet. Get it yourself." *Asshat.*

While he tried to resurrect himself with copious amounts of caffeine, I spent some one-on-one time with Headbutt and Kulu (or is that one-on-two time?). No doubt, they were happy to see me, but overall, I had to admit they were much better behaved after spending time with Donna Nonnie, our apparent pack leader.

When I returned to the kitchen, Rico was on the phone,

checking into the availability of another safe house. After Leo's antics the night before, we couldn't afford to take chances.

It was unlikely that his location had been compromised, but better safe than sorry. Besides, all three of us wouldn't mind a different house. Maybe one with cable or DISH.

I sat across from Rico, opened the onion router on my laptop, entered the web address Philipe had given me, *duat.onion*, and put in the password *ammit*.

I held my breath and prayed.

When the screen changed, I'd accessed a site named *Legion*.

The site's graphics were horrific, featuring the dead rising together, in some outrageous, sci-fi, rotter rapture.

Little Allie went apeshit once she got a load of the alt-crazy rhetoric. Things like: *People are sheep, walking corpses in need of a leader who will shepherd them toward a common goal. The enlightenment is coming. The course of human history will change. And I will accept the mantle of leadership.*

Damn. Was Philipe holding out on me? I thought he'd have had something more valuable than the ramblings of a madman. Nothing on the site made a direct reference to the virus, or what role the virus might play in changing the course of human history. But, on the other hand, whoever wrote this just spiraled to the top of the whacko-whisperer list. Who was he?

If Philipe did know more than he was willing to tell me, maybe he was afraid of poking the bear—a 'whispering' bear who could corpsify him at will.

Whisperers who walk the dark side do their best to fly under the radar. This nut-job might have been throwing his hat in the ring for world domination, but he wasn't telling us who he was. Surprisingly, he had over three-thousand followers. Did those idiots simply like the site's macabre graphics and think it was some dark, comic blog?

The thought of a raiser like me, angling to dominate the world, made the hair on my arms stand up. There wasn't anything in the site that clued me in to his identity. I slammed my laptop closed and then rubbed my face with my hands. With all that tradecraft and high-tech finagling, I didn't know anything more now than I had before visiting the site.

Rico, no longer on the phone, sat drinking his coffee.

"Do they have another safe house for us?" I asked.

"I told Cap we'd been on Jora for a while, and it might be smart for us to move. I didn't tell him why. He said he'd check and get back to me."

There was a lull in the conversation, a good time to circle back to the issue of just how confidential Leo's situation remained, with Jade Chen slathering herself all over Rico, seducing him with her hero worship and perfect looks. She wanted him for his body and for his inside scoops. No doubt about it. Why wouldn't she? Rico was hot. He'd be a catch for any girl.

I stared him down hard. "Level with me. Are you dishing details of this case to Jade?"

Rico's voice turned cold. "What I do or do not discuss with Jade is none of your damned business."

"It is when my life and Leo's are on the line."

"You honestly think I would do that? Do I look that gullible?"

"She's got you wrapped around her little finger so tight, I have no idea *what* you'd do for her. She's playing you. Can't you see that?"

Rico's steely eyes skewered me from across the table. "Sounds like somebody's jealous."

Oh no, he did not just say that. I could feel the burn in my cheeks. Little Allie slapped me upside my brain, screaming, *hell yes, you're jealous.*

Stupid brain bitch. Not only was she a loud-mouthed pain in the ass, she was also confused. I shoved myself back from the table, balled my fist, and took a quick step toward Rico.

Then Nonnie walked in the back door. "Good mornings. How my friends this day?"

Rico pushed back his chair and stood with a forced smile. "Good morning, Nonnie. No unauthorized conversations with or about Leo to anyone. Got it?"

Her cheeks turned rosy and she lowered her eyes to the floor. "I not hurt Leo, or you, for anything."

"Good." Rico didn't even glance in my direction. "C'mon. It's time to go to the safe house."

I threw on my jacket. "I'll drive myself."

Rico harrumphed and stomped outside.

Nonnie shot me a knowing smile. "Ah. Mens troubles."

"Bite your tongue," I said, slamming the door on my way out.

I pulled into the driveway of the safe house, within seconds of Rico, and caught him as he walked around back. The kitchen door was ajar. We drew our weapons.

Rico nosed the door open further. "Powell? Ortega?"

No answer.

I walked in behind Rico. "Leo?"

An odd stillness filled the house. Little Allie moved to high alert.

"Jesus, Greg!" Rico, gun at high ready, pushed into the living room where Powell lay motionless in a massive pool of blood.

Rico stooped and felt for a pulse. When he looked back at me, the pained stare on his face told me all I needed to know.

I bit my lip and motioned for him to move on.

Together, we cleared the house, moving down the hallway, taking each room in succession. He went left and I went right.

Leo's room was at the end of the hall on the left. It seemed like an eternity until we reached the last two rooms. As I cleared the bedroom on the right, Rico let out a yell from Leo's room.

I raced across the hall to find Ortega's lifeless body lying on the floor. Half of his head missing. And Leo was gone.

15

TICK-TOCK, TICK-TOCK

Doc Blanchard and the forensic team arrived within twenty minutes and began buzzing through both the grounds and the safe house itself, although I wondered what good would come of it. This house had been occupied, from time to time, over the past thirty years. It wasn't in immaculate condition. Any number of fingerprints would surely show up. But, at least, we could run them through AFIS.

If the assassins (and I say *assassins* because it would have taken more than one to get past both Powell and Ortega) were mob connected, we might get a hit in the database. But if the killers had something to do with the Z-virus manipulation, the prints would likely stay anonymous. Paranormal perps with these talents weren't likely to show up in AFIS.

The theory of a mob hit made sense. They had reason to want Leo dead. But the zombie killings seemed to follow in Leo's footsteps and the timing of the two cases was bizarrely coincidental.

Cap's car careened into the driveway, spraying gravel into the yard.

Rico and I exchanged frowns and waited for the endless shit stream that was sure to come.

He got out of his car, walked past us without a word and headed into the house, motioning for us to follow. When he got to the living room, he squatted on his haunches next to Powell's body and peeled back the sheet.

Powell had been shot center mass, with what appeared to be a large caliber bullet, based on the hole in his chest. Cap took a knee beside him and closed his eyes, lingering a moment.

Rico took my arm and whispered, "Powell was in Cap's Firearms Instruction class at the Academy."

Cap got to his feet and silently made his way down the hallway, to Ortega's body. The top of Ortega's head was gone and the blowback on the wall behind him looked like a Jackson Pollock painting. Cap sank to his knees, teary-eyed, and rested his hand on top of Ortega's.

When he rose, his lips were thin set and his gaze stone cold. "De Palma, you find the SOB who did this. You find him and you bring him to me. Nobody gets away with killing my men. Nobody."

The hardened look in his eyes turned flat. "From the moment Leo came under our protection, things have spun out of control. I've got a lot to answer for. *You've* got a lot to answer for. We'll get our chance soon enough. The FBI is on its way."

Rico looked pasty, like he was about to hurl.

I wanted to toss my cookies too, but more than that, I was pissed. "We can play the blame game later. If whoever took Leo wanted him dead, they could have killed him right here. But they didn't. That makes me believe he's still alive, at least for the time being. We need to be out there looking for him, not here, kowtowing to a bunch of suits."

I strode over to Cap and stood him, toe-to-toe. "Remember,

Leo needs his meds to stay alive, so he can testify before the grand jury. Rico and I need to move. Now."

Doc Blanchard, who was lingering nearby, jotting notes in his coroner's report, said, "She's got a point. Why didn't they kill him here?"

Cap shrugged. "Maybe they were worried that Nighthawk could just raise him, and get all the information the prosecutors needed anyway. They wouldn't want to take that chance. Who knows? Maybe they wanted to find out what info Leo had given up before they killed him. Other than the books he turned in, that is."

The books.

I grabbed Cap's arm. "What if Leo had an extra set of those books?"

My question was met with a round of blank stares. While we considered that theory, a black sedan pulled into the driveway.

Cap stood a little taller. "The Feds are here. Let me do the talking,"

Two suits wearing Oakley's marched up the gravel driveway, staring us down every step of the way.

"I'm Assistant Director William Horton, FBI," said suit number one. "And this is Agent Tucker. Which one of you clowns lost our snitch?"

I started to speak, but Rico stepped forward, blocking me. He reached behind and grabbed my little finger, giving it a good twist to keep me quiet.

Cap held his chin high. "Agents Powell and Ortega were watching Mr. Abruzzi at the time of the incident."

The Director gave Rico the once-over. "You must be Ortega." Glancing down his nose at me, he added, "I guess that makes you Powell, doesn't it, honey?"

Why? Why do these assholes insist on testing me? Don't they communicate with each other? Instant Message or something? Little Allie didn't stand a chance of shutting my mouth.

"Zero for two, ass-munch. Believe it or not, there's more than one Latino officer on the CPD force. This man," I said, motioning to Rico, "is not Ortega. He's Detective Rico De Palma. Ortega is dead inside, in the hallway, missing half his head. And I am not Powell, or your honey. I'm Nighthawk. Powell's in the kitchen with a big-ass hole in his chest. Care to use your finely honed FBI skills to make any other discriminatory assumptions—honey?"

Suit number two, Agent Tucker, piped up. "Nighthawk? As in *the* Nighthawk? No shit."

He took an involuntary step backward. That made me smile inside.

The Director scratched his chin and then smirked. "I've heard about you. You're the infamous, Voodoo-priestess, she-bitch...what's your title...Paranormal Crimes Specialist? Well, now. What kind of bullshit is that?"

He turned to walk away, then stopped and called over his shoulder. "De Palma, you and Nightingale go wait for me at my car."

The Director wandered into the house with a hulking, cock-sure gait that made me want to rip out his adenoids out through his eyelids.

Once he was out of earshot, Cap gave us our instructions. "We don't have a lot of time. You need to cooperate with this asshole. You give him all the information you have. All of it. A man's life is at stake. But, in the meantime, while he's busy retracing every step we've taken since we got here today, let's revisit the topic of Leo's books. It makes sense he would keep his own copy. For security. You know?"

Rico nodded. "As long as he has a copy in his possession, they can't afford to kill him. And for all we know, he might have given the Feds a fudged copy, just enough to get a deal, and he's holding the real books as his ace-in-the-hole. Leo's a lot of things, but he's not stupid."

I leaned in, keeping my voice low. "You're assuming it's the mob who kidnapped Leo. Granted, they have a hell of a strong motive to go for him, but we can't rule out a Z-virus connection. These two cases are chasing each other in one big circle-jerk."

"We'll find Leo," Rico said. "And after we do, we'll ask about an extra set of books, and dig deeper in-house, figure out who our mole is and who he, or she, works for. That'll lead us in the right direction."

"If we don't find Leo soon, it won't matter. Quiet," I said under my breath. "Here comes Dickhead."

The Director charged us like a bull. "De Palma, Nightshade, let's chat. Tell me what happened here at the house. Anything. Everything."

Well, damn, Sam. Weren't we about to take a trip down the stinking rabbit hole?

Rico squared his shoulders. "It's all there in the daily reports, Director Horton. Every visitor, every call."

"C'mon, De Palma. The guy was mobbed up. He had a vice. What was it? Booze? Gambling? Women?"

A thought bubble filled with lasagna floated over my head and burst, when I heard Rico's next words.

"Now that you mention it, he did have a weakness for Italian food."

What the hell! Not only did Rico throw us into the rabbit hole, he brought a damn Ditch Witch down with us and dug a Grand Canyon we would never get out of.

He spilled the beans about Nonnie, her lasagna, and Leo's late-night excursion, sneaking out his bedroom window for a plate of pasta.

Holy crap. Hearing Rico tell the story out loud, we came off looking like a couple of dill weeds.

When Rico finished confessing everything but original sin,

the Director's face turned a color I'd never seen before. Kind of purple, kind of gray, with sixteen shades of pissed-off, in between.

The Director shook his head. "That took some guts, De Palma. *Total* incompetence is hard to come by in this business. Usually there's at least a hint of brain activity."

He turned to Cap and said, "From here on, CPD and these two numbskulls are off this case. Completely. The FBI's calling this ball. In particular, me."

"You're dismissed," he said, waving us away. "And take your medical examiner and the forensic analysts with you. I have my own team. They'll be here in five."

"As for you, Nightstalker," he said, looking directly at me. "Try not to bust their balls on the way out. This group is handicapped enough."

Cap exploded. "Who the hell do you think you are? You can't order us off the scene. You have a kidnapping to investigate, but we've got a double murder to solve, the murder of our own officers. We're not going anywhere."

"The hell you aren't."

As if getting reamed by the FBI wasn't bad enough, members of the press began to arrive, including Jade Chen, who hovered at the edge of the crime scene tape, watching the whole sordid debacle, while Rip recorded it for posterity.

The brain bitch tried to stop me. Like she even had a chance.

"Now wait just a damn minute, Director. There's a clock ticking here. Leo needs his meds. No medication means a dead state's witness, and a dead witness means no case for the grand jury. I'm going back inside to get his meds."

I stomped toward the house, with Director Horton chasing after me.

He snatched my arm and whirled me around. "Don't you worry about that. You hear me? We'll handle it."

I felt my fingers flexing into a fist. Little Allie tried her best to hold me back, but this time, she was out of her league.

"Fine," I said. "Have it your way. But, before I leave here, I need to raise Powell since Ortega doesn't have a brain anymore. Powell's a material witness whose testimony can't be obtained any other way."

The Director skirted around me, blocking my path to the house. "Like hell you are, you Voodoo whack job. Get out of my crime scene. Now!"

Hell hath no fury like an Allie scorned. I was ready to spit nails and shit shrapnel.

With a glance at Jade, who was furiously scribbling notes from outside the yellow crime scene tape, I yelled, "Here's another inside source for you to sleep with Jade. Did you get his name? It's Director William Horton. That's Horton, with an H. Or have you done him already?"

Rico gawked at me wide-eyed, as if I'd lost my mind. Jade's cameraman, Rip, who'd been filming the fray, had to stop when one of the FBI agents took his camera away and made him erase the footage.

Thank God. That hadn't been one of my finer moments.

Doc had already exited the house and was walking toward us, as the Director passed him on his way back inside.

I brushed past Doc and whispered, "Go back in there and grab Leo's meds from the kitchen. Shove them into your pocket. He's going to need them."

Doc, no doubt feeling pissy himself about being displaced in this shitstorm, wasted no time turning around and making a pretense of having to retrieve some forensic tools he'd left inside.

The smile on his face as he ambled back out told me he'd been successful.

I breathed a sigh of relief.

Rico turned to Cap. "You aren't going to let that jackass Director get away with this, are you?"

Cap bit his lip and shook his head. "There isn't much I can do here onsite, once he claims jurisdiction and throws us off the case. But that doesn't mean we can't get a court order to raise Powell, much as I detest the thought, and compel them to share their forensics, so we can investigate our murders. You can run your own investigation on the side—just stay out of their way."

Cap turned to me and let out a long, exasperated sigh. "Do us all a favor, Nighthawk. Don't go out of your way to tell Director Horton that you guys are conducting your own investigation. Suck it up for once. Make my life easier. Can you do that?"

Seriously, folks. What were the odds of that happening?

16

DAMN IT, I'M BUSY

Having been evicted from the safe house by Director Douchebag, we regrouped at the precinct to form our action plan for finding and rescuing Leo.

Once again, we found ourselves sitting in Cap's office, awaiting a monumental tongue lashing. Cap had told us to meet him there. But he was late, damn him. We couldn't afford to waste time.

Rico, bursting at the seams with his own private agenda, didn't bother to wait for Cap.

"What the hell is wrong with you, Nighthawk? How dare you attack Jade? And on air, yet! You're like a fucking rabid dog when it comes to her. If you can't contain yourself—"

"*Contain* myself?"

He shoved his finger in my face. "If you can't contain yourself, I'm going to ask for a transfer. I'm not putting up with your psycho horseshit anymore. You're out of control."

My jaw dropped. "Jesus! Are you blind? She goes out of her way to insult me, and make me look like a fool on the goddam news, every chance she gets."

"You do a good enough job of that on your own."

I jerked as if he'd slapped me.

He took a deep breath and lowered his voice. "For God's sake. Like it or not, what you do—what we do—is news. She reports the news. Don't forget, I'm not coming out of this situation smelling any better than you. Get over your sensitive self and grow a pair."

He clammed up tighter than a nun in church, leaving me to think about his words. Of course, that's when the stupid brain bitch decided to grace me with her two cents worth. And once she got started there was no shutting her up. God help me, she was enough to make me want to dig into my head with a spoon and perform my own bitch-ectomy.

Since Rico decided to be a passive-aggressive butthead and give me the silent treatment, I picked up Cap's desk phone and called Nonnie. "Hey, yeah, listen. I may be late tonight."

She cut me off, telling me about her day.

Knowing it wouldn't get any easier, the longer she talked, I finally blurted out, "Nonnie, Leo's been kidnapped."

She took it hard. I could hear her sniffling.

Her voice sounded shaky. "Who do this?"

"We don't know yet. But we're going to find him. Okay? We won't give up until we do. He'll be back at the kitchen table, eating lasagna, in no time."

Rico shot daggers at me and shook his head. I know. I shouldn't have gotten her hopes up. But she sounded scared for the Leo—love him, hate him, screwball Leo.

She wasn't the only one.

Nonnie's gentle sobs drifted through the phone.

I don't handle tears well. It was time to bounce. "Got to run now, Nonnie. I'll be home when I can. Kiss the twins for me, huh?"

Cap appeared as I hung up the phone. We'd been waiting nearly a half-hour, and I was testier than a monkey on Red Bull.

When I jumped out of my chair, I forgot all about using my indoor voice. "Where the hell have you been? We need to be out there—looking for Leo, not sitting here, twiddling our thumbs."

"Sit," Cap said, sliding behind his desk. "I had something to do. Now—"

I stopped, halfway down to my seat, and stood back up. "Something to do? What could possibly be more important than finding Leo?"

"*Sit!*" Cap yelled, waiting for me to comply. After I plopped back into my chair, he said, "I was delivering the death notification to Powell's wife of five years and their two babies. Any other questions?"

I closed my eyes, and wished for once that the stupid little brain bitch had done a better job of saving me from myself. She gets all high and mighty over stupid stuff, and leaves me hanging when I need her. Hell, in her defense, there's only a fifty-fifty chance I'd have listened anyway.

Cap planted his elbows on the desk, and put his head in his hands. "Officer Weston was good enough to speak to Mrs. Ortega for me. How do you tell someone their spouse's head's been blown away?"

Cap looked up, his face pale and haggard, and got to the ass-whooping part.

"Now, I don't know how the kidnapping happened, or how the responsible party got past Powell and Ortega, but you two..." His words hung in the air.

After a long, deep breath, he continued. "How in the hell did that Italian meatball sneak out of the safe house on your watch? The key word being *watch*. God help us, if Leo dies or comes back too far gone to testify. We'll get crucified."

I sat on the edge of my chair and leaned over the desk, into his face. "That's why we need the court order to raise Powell, *now*."

"I already called the D.A. He's backing our play. He agreed that the FBI has proper jurisdiction over the kidnapping case, but the murders of Powell and Ortega are ours. We can proceed as needed. He's getting a court order from the judge, even as we speak, just to have it in our hip pocket, if Director Horton feels the urge to get pissy...again."

"And you," he said, fixing me in a cold stare. "If you *ever* spout off to Jade Chen, or any other member of the press again, you're gone. *Finito.* I won't have it. Our jobs are hard enough without intentionally harassing the media. Look at me. Nod your head and tell me you understand."

I stared at my shoes, trying to will my face from turning purple. Judging by the searing heat in my cheeks, I hadn't succeeded.

"I'm talking to you, Nighthawk. Answer me. Tell me you heard me. Tell me it will never happen again."

After fidgeting in my chair for a moment, I cleared my throat. "Yes, Cap. I understand. I won't embarrass you or the department like that again."

Why not? Throw him a bone. I hadn't promised that I was finished jousting with Jade in private. That wasn't splitting hairs. It was more of a white lie comb-over.

Someone rapped on Cap's door. Whoever it was, I could have kissed. Anything to bring that bout of humiliation to an end.

Cap cast me one last withering glance, then turned and barked, "Yes?"

Weston opened the door slowly, like he was afraid of interrupting. He must have heard Cap's every word. *Bugger.*

I slunk down in my chair, as he walked into the room and nodded at Rico and me.

Then, he turned to Cap. "Hey, sir. I spoke to Elena, Ortega's wife. She's a mess," he said, rubbing his eyes with his hand. "I called her sister. She's coming to stay with Elena and the kids tonight. When I left, the department psychologist was there with her. I told her anything we can do, you know?"

Weston looked tired. Beyond tired. Shell-shocked. Weren't we all?

He leaned back against the door and changed topics. "The forensics guys were able to get some samples before the Director ran them off. I figured you'd want to know. Like we anticipated, they got a lot of prints. They're running them, but it's going to take a while. Same with the trace evidence they collected. They asked me to collect prints and DNA samples from Rico and Nighthawk, you know, for exclusionary purposes."

He pulled a couple of print kits and some swabs in plastic bags from his jacket pocket.

Rico nodded, inked his fingers, and let Weston roll them across the print card. Then, Rico opened his mouth while Weston swabbed the inside of his cheek and bagged it.

Weston peered at me from the corner of his eye.

I sighed and gave him my hand.

"Does this mean we're engaged?" I asked, just because, well, just because I'm me.

Weston rolled my fingers across the card. When I opened my mouth with no further objection, he came at me slowly, like he was about to do a cheek swab on a pit bull.

"Just do it already," I said. "If I wanted to bite you, I'd have done it a long time ago." As his hand neared my mouth I said, "But it's way past lunch time and I haven't eaten, so—"

He jerked away with a frown. When I laughed, he jammed the swab into my mouth, yanked back his hand, and bagged the sample.

Weston got up to leave but Cap motioned for him to stay put. "You need to hear this, too. Before we were ordered off the scene, I sent some officers to canvass the neighborhood, hoping we'd turn up some information. One of our guys spoke to a local man, who was out walking his dog around seven-thirty this morning. He heard what he thought were firecrackers in the distance and continued on his way. About fifteen minutes later, he came across a scene that struck him as odd. He said a black Lexus and a white Crown Vic, with city plates, were pulled to the side of the road. The driver of the Vic had exited his vehicle and was leaning into the driver's side window of the Lexus. As dog walker got closer, dude from the Vic turned his head and glared at him. Dog walker got a hinky feeling and pretended he hadn't been paying attention. He went on home and didn't think anything more about it, until we knocked on his door."

Weston sat on the edge of Cap's desk and bit his lip. "Did he get a plate number on the city car?"

"Only a partial. CCE3 something. Said he got scared and turned his eyes to the ground. But here's the thing. He mentioned that he'd seen the black Lexus around there before."

Rico's head snapped up. "Did the dog walker give a description of the drivers, Cap?"

"Not much. He only saw their faces for a second. He said the driver of the Crown Vic was tall and had light hair. But he saw the dude in the Lexus handing the guy in the Vic a brown paper bag."

We all exchanged glances, no doubt sharing the same suspicion: *money.*

Cap sat a little taller and laid down the law. "I know you all want to be out there looking for Leo. And you will be. But first, we're going to figure out where we stand with the pending investigations. Obviously, the biter attack at the range, the deaths of Miriam and Fingerello, the mob boss, and BOLO Guy must be connected to Leo. Any theories, people? And that freaking black Lexus. What's the story on that?"

I threw a side glance at Rico, whose fingers had dug into the arms of his chair.

His words came out with an edge. "We got a tip from...an informant...who said he'd seen it parked up the street from the safe house all day. He even gave us a plate number. We traced it, Cap. It's registered to some outfit called Stanous Electric. There's construction going on up the block from the safe house. The Lexus was parked along there, with twenty other contractor's cars. It seemed legit, so we gave it a pass."

Cap rubbed his eyes. "Jesus. Put another BOLO out on the damn Lexus, with the plate number this time. And find out everything you can about Stanous Electric. Any more on the biter attack at Brasshole's?"

I figured I'd field this one since Rico looked ready to implode.

"It's like we said last time, Cap. It could have been anyone with access to the Perptown schedule, to know when I was going to be there. Someone who knew where the security cameras were. Someone with a key. That narrows it down to most anybody on the force. To be honest, with Leo and everything else that's been going on, Rico and I haven't been able to take it further."

It was time for a little game of hot potato. "Weston, if I recall, you were digging into that. What'd you come up with?"

Weston looked like I'd drilled him in the face with a tuna. "I... I... Well, what Nighthawk said, Cap. Short of investigating every single cop in the district, we may never find that out."

"And BOLO Guy," Cap said. "Did we ever figure out who he works for?"

"Actually, no," Weston said.

"Did we at least figure out who he was, based on his prints, DNA, or facial recognition?"

You could have heard a pin drop.

Cap's face puffed up like a big red blowfish. "Did I, or did I not, give you an order? And I'm including you in this rant, Weston. What the fuck have you people been doing?"

"Babysitting Leo," I yelled.

The flaw in that response was obvious the minute it came out of my mouth. But damn it, Cap had us by the cojones and it wasn't sitting right.

"How about we move on to new business," Cap said, ignoring my outburst. "We now have a white Vic with a partial city plate to find. Rather than ask you...*overworked*...folks to chase that lead, I've requested the daily logs from the various city departments to find out who had that car. That's one less lead for you princesses to follow."

His mouth opened like he was about to go for round two, but his phone rang.

Thank you, Jesus.

Cap picked up the line, grunted several times and hung up. "That was the morgue. Powell's body is back and the D.A. got his court order. Time for you to do your thing, Nighthawk. That is, if you aren't too busy."

17

END OF WATCH

We might have had a court order to raise Powell, but Little Allie made it clear there was a matter of moral importance that needed to be addressed, before we began.

Denise Powell, Greg's widow, stood behind the glass walls of the conference room in the City Administration building, watching Rico and me approach.

Someone needed to explain what was about to happen to her husband and why. That someone was me. Rico had known Denise for years, so I asked him to come with me. I hoped he could comfort her. And maybe me, too.

It was late in the day. Denise's husband had been dead for almost ten hours. And while that wasn't long enough for her to fully grasp the impact of his death, she'd already witnessed the shameless intrusion of the pandering press—which included Jade Chen, uber-bitch.

When we walked through the conference room door, Rico immediately moved to Denise and wrapped his arms around her. He was sturdy as an oak, eyes flat, lips taut, as she sobbed against his chest. She struggled to compose herself, then sat in a chair and turned to me with sad, inquiring eyes.

I spoke softly and chose my words with great care. "Thank you for meeting with me, Mrs. Powell. Please accept my condolences. Your husband was a wonderful officer, and although I didn't know him well, he struck me as a caring, selfless man, who devoted himself to his family as well as his job. He will be missed by all who knew him."

Denise's unblinking eyes never wavered.

"Greg was working with us on a special project for the FBI. He died before he could give us information about his attackers. We need to raise Greg, to find out who killed him and Officer Ortega."

She sucked in a breath and waited for me to continue.

"I want to personally assure you that I will handle this raising with the utmost respect and decorum."

Denise let out a muffled moan. "No! No, you won't. Leave him in peace. He's given his life. Isn't that enough? What are you? Some kind of freak? Some kind of monster?"

Although I'd wondered that myself on occasion, I doubted she cared to hear that. I tried to find an answer she could accept, but the words wouldn't come.

Rico sat in the chair beside her and took her hands. "I know this is the most difficult decision you've ever had to make in your life, Denise. But ask yourself what Greg would do."

"I don't care! He's my husband," she cried. "You're not going to desecrate his body. You're not going to destroy his sweet... face."

With that she collapsed against Rico's chest, and clung to him like a lost child, crying with a sorrow so deep it pained me to watch.

"I want to see his face," she whimpered. "I want his family to see his face at the funeral, to say goodbye. You can't take that away from me, too! *You can't.*"

"Denise, you can still have an open casket, if that's what you want. I will use all of my skills to make sure that can happen."

This was getting more complicated. The only way to give her his unblemished face was to take him at the back of his neck. That was a lot to promise.

She turned to me, her head still resting on Rico's chest, and murmured, "We're Catholic. What you do, this thing you do, where does the power come from?"

I knelt beside her and looked straight into her eyes. "It comes from God, Denise. It's this amazing, inexplicable power from God that helps me right wrongs. Something Greg did every day. Please, Denise. Please. Other lives depend on information only Greg can give us."

I was starting to doubt my decision to talk her through this. The last thing I wanted to do was pull rank on her, by whipping out the court order. Not because Jade and the press would shred me, although they would. But because I didn't want to cause this woman another minute of grief.

Rico gently pulled Denise back and looked in her eyes. "Honor his memory, Denise. It's what Greg would choose if he were here."

Denise pulled herself upright and smoothed her hair. Her voice shook, but rang clear. "You promise me that if you raise him, we can all see Greg's face at his funeral."

Promise was such a strong word, given the unpredictable nature of raising, but I stuck out my neck and said, "Yes."

Rico wrapped his arms around Denise's shoulders and escorted her out of the office.

I stood at the door and watched him pull one of his cards from his wallet, and write what must have been his personal number on the back. He showed it to her, slipped it into her coat pocket, and kissed her cheek.

She climbed into the passenger seat of a cruiser and let the officer take her to her empty home, where she could dream of kissing Greg, just one more time.

God help me, if I couldn't deliver on my promise.

Rico and I walked into the city morgue wondering what kind of reception we'd get from Doc Blanchard.

Sure, earlier at the safe house we'd been working in tandem, singing *Kumbaya,* doing our level best to smuggle the trace evidence we'd collected past Director Dickhead. We were on the same team, the team that got kicked to the curb by the FBI. It was all for one and one for all, right?

But my recent efforts at the morgue had resulted in...significant...damage. The insurance adjuster declared it catastrophic, but what did she know? She'd never witnessed the havoc that I...that raising a corpse could wreak.

Doc hurried out of his office to meet us in the foyer. It was time to find out how tight we'd bonded in our battle against the Evil Director.

"Nighthawk, if it weren't for us losing two good men today, I wouldn't let you within fifty feet of this office."

Well, that was short-lived. I'm not a bonder anyway.

"I'll try to keep the scene contained," I said. "You know the drill. Is Powell restrained now?"

Doc sighed. "Yes, much as I find that distasteful. Powell was a good, good man. Let's make this as fast and painless as possible."

Jesus. Did he really think he had to tell me that? Did he not realize that this was ten times harder for me than it was for him? Taking a soul at rest, the soul of a "good, good man" and bringing it back to a pitiful state of fear and confusion? Sometimes, it seemed like my *gift* was more of a merciless monster.

All the other bodies had been put away in the morgue drawers, with the exception of one aging corpse that was stored in the freezer.

Rather than risk contaminating the inside of the freezer, I decided to take my chances raising Powell on the open morgue room floor. If a clean-up was necessary, at least the bodies would still be properly stored to ensure their integrity.

Such a sterile environment, the morgue, with its stainless-steel sinks and sparkling white tile.

Powell rested on a gurney parked about twenty feet from the vestibule door. Blinds covered the window for privacy. I picked up a scalpel from an instrument tray, then glanced at Rico, standing beside me, and nodded that it was time to begin.

Cap walked through the door and took his place next to us, in a gesture of solidarity.

I bowed my head and prayed.

Rico turned away. I didn't blame him, really. He had been longtime friends with Powell and knew him far better than I did. In that split second, I got a taste of what raising a loved one is like for civilians who happened to be in attendance.

Can't say I liked that feeling any better than I liked my own kettle of fish.

Greg Powell was one of the few officer's corpses I'd ever been asked to raise. And he'd been dead less than twelve hours. It gave me hope that the humanity that made him both a good, decent man and a stellar officer, still glimmered inside him.

Eyes closed, I centered myself, and made the sign of the cross.

Then I took off Powell's restraints and channeled the strange, awesome power God had given me.

Energy coursed like blood through my veins.

I placed my hands on Powell's chest, and began. "*In the name of God, I command you to rise.*"

Powell's body twitched.

"Rise, Greg Powell, Rise!"

He moaned low and long, then bolted upright on the steel table, dazed, confused, an empty husk of the Powell he had been, only hours earlier.

His tongue was thick. "Cold. Cold."

Rico grabbed a linen from the supply shelf and wrapped it around Powell's shoulders.

"It's Nighthawk, Powell. Can you see me?"

Powell, shivering, cocked his head toward me.

"Who did this to you? Who killed you and Ortega?"

"Sleep," he mumbled trying to lay back, but I stopped him.

"Powell, answer me. Who did this? What did they look like? Anything. Tell me anything you can remember."

Powell's body tensed. He flailed his arms and tried to climb off the table.

"No! No! *Stop.*" He thrashed like a fish tail and screamed. "Don't shoot!"

Oh, God. He was reliving his death.

"Stay with me, Powell. It's Nighthawk. That's all over now. Who were they, the men who attacked you?"

His eyes swept from side to side. "Don't know."

"Help me, Powell," I begged. "What did they look like?"

"Didn't see," he whimpered.

My heart sank. After all this, he really didn't know a single thing that could help us.

"Nighthawk?" he said, his fingers brushing against mine.

I looked in his eyes, and for a moment, the Powell I knew stared back at me.

Tears trickled down his face. "Am I dead?"

Oh, sweet God. If you want me to do this, you're going to have to help me.

I sat behind him on the gurney and cradled him against me. My voice quivered as I offered what little peace I could.

"It's okay, Powell. Can you feel me holding you? I'm not letting go." I leaned my head against his and whispered, "Denise loves you. She'll be seeing you again, someday. It's end of watch, buddy. Time to go home."

When I felt him relax against me, I pulled out the scalpel and drove it deep into his brain stem.

He went down easy. Denise would get her wish.

Rico stepped away and vomited in the sink, then sat down beside it, staring at the floor.

I took Powell's precinct pin off his shirt, then brushed his eyes closed and walked toward the door.

"Where are you going?" Cap asked.

"Give me a moment," I muttered.

"Nighthawk, we need to get these bastards. For Powell and Ortega."

I stopped and turned, flipping Cap Powell's precinct pin. Denise would need it for his dress blues. "Consider it done."

18

BITCHES AND SNITCHES

I walked out the door to the coroner's office, and the media-razzi descended on me like a swarm of locusts.

Naturally, Jade led the charge. "Nighthawk, what happened inside the morgue? And what happened earlier today on Jora Lane? Why were you there?"

Little Allie cautioned me to zip my lip.

"No comment," I said, making a beeline for Rico's car.

While the Feds had kept the media behind the crime scene tape at the safe house, and they'd confiscated Rip's videotape, a few reporters managed to record the scene unnoticed, including the removal of the body bags, and my little dust-up with Director Dickhead. I wasn't about to put my size-ten foot in my mouth like that again.

Exhausted to the point of dizziness, I crumpled into the passenger seat, locked the door and instantly regretted my choice. All that stood between me, and the media horde, was a thin sheet of glass that did nothing to filter the barrage of questions.

"Who was killed on Jora Lane today?"

"Why were the Feds called in?"

"What is your involvement in the investigation?"

And of course, "What were you doing in the morgue?"

The stink flies found a new target when Rico walked out the door. Jade pushed and shoved her way back toward the building, angling to get closer to Rico.

She bowled over a female newscaster and grabbed Rico by the arm. "Detective De Palma, tell us what happened on Jora Lane today."

"No comment." He walked past her without as much as a glance.

But Jade wouldn't be ignored. *"Excuse me, Detective De Palma. The city has a right to know."*

Rico fixed Jade in an icy stare and opened his car door. "Ms. Chen, the city will find out when CPD is damn good and ready to release that information, and not one minute sooner."

He sank into the driver's seat, started the engine and pulled away from the curb, leaving the swarm behind.

"Where to?" I asked.

"Home. We need some rest."

"But Leo...his meds. We need to find—"

"We're not going to do him any good if we can't think straight."

Rico was right. I was exhausted. For me, raisings are like marathons. Every ounce of energy inside me is spent when I'm finished.

Just a few short hours of sleep, I told myself. *Just a few.* Even the brain bitch didn't argue.

Rico dropped me off at home. I figured the house would be dark and Nonnie would have left, to crash in her own bed. But the kitchen light was on.

Although Headbutt and Kulu barely budged when I walked

through the door, Nonnie, sitting at the kitchen table, jumped like I'd scared at least ten years off her life. A cigarette hung from her bottom lip.

By the number of butts in her make-shift ashtray (an empty half-gallon container of ice cream) and the smell in my house, she'd taken to her new habit with the conviction of a crack addict.

"Jesus, Nonnie. It stinks in here. When did you start smoking?"

"This morning—when you tell me Leo kidnapped."

"Maybe you could do that outside. There's a mushroom cloud at the ceiling."

She ignored me. "You not find him. I know by look on face."

I walked through the nicotine haze and patted her shoulder. "Were you waiting up, hoping he'd walk through the door?"

She dabbed at her eyes with a tissue. "Yes. And make sure you both in one pieces."

At least someone was worried about me.

"We both need some sleep, Nonnie. Go on home. I'll see you in the morning."

I squeezed her hand as she plodded toward the door. "Thanks. You know, for everything."

She gave me a wan smile, crinkling her puffy red eyes, put on her coat and trekked across the yard. I turned off the porch light, once she made it inside.

God, I needed sleep. I kicked off my boots and threw myself across the bed.

The night was filled with tossing and turning, worry about Leo, and wondering if he was seizing. Or, in the worst-case scenario, would he be dead by the time we found him.

Somewhere around three in the morning, I fell asleep and dreamed.

Leo and I sat next to each other on the plasticized couch at the safe house. He stared straight ahead, refusing to look at me.

Angry, I grabbed his face and turned it toward me. The half of his face that had been closest to me looked normal.

The other half had rotted away, with most of his cheek missing, his jaw bone and teeth jutting through the festering hole like jagged white rocks.

He snaked his tongue through the putrefied flesh and licked pus from the hollows of his cheeks.

My hands, still holding the sides of his face, were covered with maggots. When I jerked away, he pounced on me, jaws wide, teeth barred.

I bolted awake and stared into the darkness, waiting for my heart to settle down. As the visions in my dream drifted away, a foreboding voice whirred in my ear.

Soon...soon.

So much for sleep.

It was close to five, at least two hours earlier than I usually climb out of bed and crank up the coffee maker. I woke Headbutt from a sound sleep, called him up to my bed, and scratched behind his ears. Neither one of us was the cuddly type, but if one of us needed affection, the other always obliged.

It was a bit too early to wake Rico. I couldn't help smirking at the fact that he likely spent the night alone, given the ration of shit he'd given Jade at the coroner's office. I grabbed a shower and fed my animal posse.

Rico called around six, saying he'd drop by to pick me up about seven. I could have driven to the station on my Low Rider, but it was easier (and more enjoyable) to ride with Rico —not to mention that, if by some chance, Jade saw us together, it would irritate the piss out of her.

That's what I called a win-win.

Nonnie walked over when she saw Rico pull in the driveway. It seemed like she'd just gone home. The days and nights were beginning to run together.

We drove toward the precinct in silence. I'd actually started to doze off when Rico's phone rang. He glanced at the number, frowned, and sent the call to voicemail.

I smelled trouble. Jade Chen kind of trouble. Maybe he was beginning to think with his brain instead of his pecker. Or maybe it was their first lover's quarrel. The brain bitch told me to stay out of it, that it was none of my business. Fat chance.

"Trouble?" I asked.

Rico kept his eyes on the road and cleared his throat. "It's nothing."

"Why didn't you answer it, if it was nothing?"

"Drop it. I don't want to talk about it."

I knew it. It *had* been Jade. Thankfully, Rico missed the smirk on my face. He didn't say another word, until we got to the precinct.

By the time I hit the coffee machine and found his desk, he had already pulled up his computer and googled Stanous Electric. Strike one. The search came up empty. Then he checked for a phone number. Strike two. An electric company with no phone number. Something smelled fishy.

Rico stood and grabbed his jacket. "At least we have an address from the DMV registration I ran at the safe house. Let's take a ride."

He pulled the printout from his pocket and frowned. "It's in the 1400 block of Republic Street. Why does that sound familiar?"

Republic Street, in Over-the-Rhine, could be a dangerous place. One by one, the neighborhood streets being rehabbed, making the area a popular place for urban dwellers. Almost overnight the area was reborn with family-friendly

Washington Park, restaurants and bars. But some streets, like Republic, with its battered three-story walk-ups and boarded windows, still harbored pockets of violence and crime.

Rico turned off Liberty Street onto Republic, and pointed to plumes of oily black smoke a few blocks ahead, on the left. "That's right around the 1400 block." He whistled as we reached the corner and pulled to the curb. "Would you look at that?"

There, in an open lot, was our black Lexus, right down to the plate, fully engulfed in flames. Not a soul in sight, no sirens sounding in the distance.

Rico called it in.

Two engines and paramedics arrived on the scene, within minutes. I sucked in a breath while the firefighters extinguished the blaze. *What if Leo was inside the car?*

Once the flames had been knocked back, we could see there wasn't a body in the cab. But there was one more place to check. A member of the fire crew raised a shovel high above his head, and slammed it down onto the trunk latch.

The lid sprang up and I exhaled. No body there either.

Rico called in a forensics team, hoping to turn up some trace evidence that might point us in a direction. But the truth was, we were twisting in the wind, grasping at straws.

All I could think of was Leo. *Was he dead? Alive? Maybe seizing?*

Rico checked in with Weston to see if he'd come up with any leads. He was out on the street, calling in favors from every snitch he and Rico had developed over the years. Beating the bushes was a little broad stroke for my taste, but it was as good a plan as any, since we had squat to go on. To save time, Weston agreed to take south of Vine Street. Rico and I took from Vine Street, north.

We had our work cut out for us. Every corner and every dive on Vine Street had resident snitches. And Rico knew them all.

We hit up Krueger's, Fifth and Vine, The Lackman, and at least a dozen smaller, grungier places, I'd never stepped foot in before—or ever would again, if I was lucky. And I knew grungy when I saw it. I'd worked at The Blue Note Lounge, once upon a time, not so long ago.

By two o'clock, my stomach growled. It was time for a quick lunch.

"I know a place," Rico said, "Right around the corner. Decent food, good service." He grinned and picked up his pace. "Not to mention Ronnie Russo. Ronnie always has an ear to the ground."

We walked into Enzo's, another hole in the wall dump I'd never seen before. At first glance, the place looked like it couldn't have been more than thirty feet deep, but a closer look revealed a narrow hallway at the end of the bar that led to the johns and a back room.

The walls were nothing more than an assortment of dart dings and bullet holes, connected by patches of crumbling drywall mud. Stuffing poked out of the ripped, red vinyl bar stools. The woodgrain laminate on top of the bar was mostly missing. A yellow haze covered the mirror behind the bar back. The place wouldn't have been complete without the unmistakable stink of stale smoke, hot sauce and piss.

All things considered, it was my kind of joint.

The bartender, a big-boned, bottled-blonde female, tall enough to hunt geese with a rake, leaned over the bar and yacked with a couple of geezers, who were staring at her cleavage through the ties of her lace-up leather vest. A tattoo of a flaming skull, with spark plugs coming out its eye sockets, covered her left bicep. The tat read: *The Hard Run Fast.*

Rico and I stood at the end of the bar and waited for her to turn around.

When she ignored us, Rico put his fingers in his mouth,

whistled as loud as he could, and yelled, "Yo, skank. What's it take to get a drink around here?"

Bionic Blondie spun on her heels, wrapped her man-hands around a fifth of Fireball, raised it high and barreled straight at Rico.

I stretched across the bar and threw a hard right to her jaw, then tried to yank the bottle from her hand.

My punch didn't even slow her down. She wasn't about to let go of that bottle of Fireball. Neither was I.

Before it was over, she'd pulled me over the top of the bar and onto the floor in front of the sink.

She wrestled the bottle away from me and brought it down against the edge of the bar above my head. A deluge of whiskey and glass rained down on me.

She swept her frizzy blonde hair out of her eyes and said, "Had enough, you half-pint ho?"

Seriously? Game on, Amazon.

I kicked her in the jaw.

She sat on me and balled her hand into a fist, so she could knock me senseless.

As she punched me in the face, I used my hips as leverage to flip her off me, and then kicked her in the side, to roll her onto her gut.

I put a knee in the middle of her back, reached for my cuffs, and said, "Now, I've had enough."

The guys at the end of the bar whooped and hollered.

Rico hopped over the bar and screamed, *"Everybody stop!"*

He worked his way in between Blondie and me and pulled us apart.

"Nighthawk, stop. *Ronnie.* Hey, girl. Look at me. It's Rico. Chill."

Blondie did a double-take, and dropped a fistful of my hair. "Damn, De Palma. Is that how you greet an old friend? Call me names and insult me? You're lucky I didn't put a permanent part in your skull."

The two of them hugged it out while I shook the glass shards out of my hair and wrung the excess whiskey from my clothes. The side of my head throbbed, and had grown a knot. *Perfect.* But her jaw had an ugly purple knot on it, too.

Damn straight, I can hold my own.

"Nighthawk, this is Ronnie Russo, the owner of this dump. Ronnie, meet Nighthawk, my partner."

Ronnie wore a sheepish grin. "Sorry for the Fireball bath. No hard feelings, huh? If I'd have known it was Rico, I wouldn't have rushed him with a bottle. Guess I need to start taking my Xanax again. Nice to meet you."

She stuck out her gorilla mitt and shook my hand, hard enough to crush blood vessels.

Rico plopped down on a bar stool. "How 'bout a couple burgers, Ronnie? The ones with avocado, cheese and onion?"

I followed suit and sat down, my eyes burning a hole through Rico. *Way to almost get us killed, dumb ass. Don't mind me sitting here, dripping hundred-proof on the floor and picking glass out of my scalp.*

"Here you go, honey," Ronnie said, tossing me a towel.

The two old farts sitting at the other end of the bar snickered.

"What are you looking at?" she said. "Crawl back into your shot glasses. I'm taking a break."

She called our order back to the cook and then turned to Rico. "How long's it been? Three years? Five?"

"Four. I bailed you out on your assault charge against that pimp." He leaned across the bar and lowered his voice. "You owe me, remember?"

Ronnie leaned over the bar, stuck out her chest, and shoved her massive mammaries in Rico's face. "Any day, any time, pretty boy. I'm all yours."

Even the brain bitch wanted to barf. I laid my head on the bar and said, "It's okay. Just act like I'm not here."

"I *am*," she said.

Rico moved toward Ronnie like he was going to plant a kiss on her cheek, then whispered, "Sorry. I need a different kind of currency. The mob snatched a guy. We're looking for him. Whatcha got for me?"

Ronnie tilted her head toward the back hallway and said, "I'm going to go check on your food. Walk down there like you've got to take a whiz, and meet me in the back room."

Off she went, and a few moments later Rico wandered down the hall, leaving me with Dumb and Dumber at the other end of the bar.

Dumb didn't waste any time. "Hey, sweet stuff." He smiled, showing me his gnarly grill. "You handle yourself pretty good. I got some moves of my own. Why don't you come down here and let me show you a few?"

I got off the stool and shook more glass out of my hair. "Why don't you shut your yap and leave me alone. If you're lucky, I might let you live." I pulled my Ka-bar. "Or not. You decide."

Rico returned to his seat as I stuck my knife back in its sheath. Then he glanced down at Dumb and Dumber, both gazing silently at their drinks. Rico closed his eyes and sighed.

Ronnie came back out with our burgers wrapped to go. Rico put a twenty on the bar and told her to keep the change.

"Good to see you, baby boy. Don't be such a stranger. Nice to meet you, sweetie," Ronnie called as I stepped outside. "Hey, the Fireball's on me, next time you come in."

Damn straight it will be.

"Yeah. Thanks for..." Luckily, Little Allie intervened, "lunch."

I climbed back into the passenger seat of Rico's car and got a whiff of myself. "Run me by my house for a minute. I need to change."

"No shit, you need to change."

What the hell did he mean by that?

"I sure as hell hope she had something for you, after all that."

Rico chuckled. "Ronnie always comes through. She said a couple of Giordano's button men were drinking there last night, low talking about some guy they're holding at a place called *The Ultimate Tapper.*"

"What's that?"

"How the hell should I know?"

"Okay. *Where's* that?"

"Not a clue."

As we pulled from the curb, the brain bitch lectured me that even clueless, we were Leo's best hope.

The poor bastard.

19

WE DON'T NEED NO STINKING PLAN

Even with the windows down, Rico's car...well...I reeked of Fireball Whiskey. As we pulled into the driveway, I invited Rico in, hoping he'd keep Nonnie occupied while I showered and changed.

We stepped through the back door to find Headbutt stretched out across the top of his favorite air vent. One blood-shot eye opened, taking note of our arrival, and then slowly slid closed.

Nonnie, at the kitchen sink, cleaning the bird cage, turned to us expectantly. She dropped the cage into the soap suds, causing Kulu to mutter curse words from her perch on the curtain rod above the window.

Nonnie squished her eyebrows together and poked her gnarled finger toward Kulu. The sassy little pecker-head stopped in mid-squawk.

Impressive.

While drying her hands on a dish towel, Nonnie asked, "You find Leo?" Her nose curled as I passed by. "Why you stink of cinnamon?"

"Not yet, and I had an accident at lunch," I said, tossing my phone onto the kitchen table and cruising down the hallway toward the bathroom, without even slowing down.

What the heck did I have left to wear?

Washing clothes had taken a back seat the last couple of weeks. Hell, it always takes a back seat. But having not been there much, I couldn't have done it anyway. For practical reasons, other than my emergency loads, I have two grades of laundry. *Semi-Dirty* (everyday dirt) and *Name That Stain* (bio-hazardous waste).

Thoroughly convinced that my only options lurked in a semi-dirty mound beneath my bed, I was amazed to find my freshly laundered jeans and T's, stacked on my perfectly made bed.

Thank God for Nonnie. If I'd actually been paying her, she'd have deserved a raise.

After a quick shower, I threw on my *Zombies eat brains. You're safe.* T-shirt and a clean pair of jeans. As I walked back down the hallway, my nose caught a whiff of fresh-baked rugelach.

No, I wasn't hungry; we'd just eaten. Yes, of course, I would have some on our way out the door.

By the time I made it to the kitchen, Rico was working on his second slice.

Nonnie stood before me, holding a plateful of rugelach, and fixed me in her sad, puppy dog stare. "Miss Allie, let me help find Leo."

"I wish you could," I said, shoving a piece of pastry into my mouth.

I wish you could? Well, that was a big fat lie. Involving Nonnie in the investigation was the worst idea in the history of bad ideas.

"Thanks for the treat," I said, "and for doing my laundry, and taking care of the twins. You're more help than you know."

Rico crammed his piece of rugelach into his mouth and reached for another.

"Tick-tock, De Palma. We need to make this a to-go order."

Nonnie slid the pastry in a plastic bag and gave her plea one last shot. "Please. Let me come. I cannot sit here only worrying. Let me help."

Her voice conveyed a feeling of helplessness. There was a lot of that going around.

"I'd take you with me," I said. "But you're a bigger help here."

Crushed, Nonnie turned back to the sink. "Fine. I cook. I clean. Go be hero. But do faster. For Leo."

Rico pushed back his chair. "C'mon, partner. Let's go find The Ultimate Tapper. Whatever the hell that is."

Nonnie's back straightened. "What you say?"

"The Ultimate Tapper." Rico frowned. "Why? Do you know what that is?"

"Where you hear this?"

"Enzo's Bar." Rico walked toward Nonnie and gently spun her around. "What do you know?"

"Enzo's. On Vine Street, yes? Peoples from old country, they go Enzo's." She took Rico's hands. "Is not The Ultimate Tapper you look for. Is *l'ultima tappa*—the last stop." Her eyes flew open wide. "Leo is at *l'ultima tappa*?"

I grabbed her so hard I almost knocked her over. "What is that?"

"Is last stop. If someone from La Cosa Nostra take you to *l'ultima tappa*, you not come back. You know," she said, as she slashed her finger across her neck. "You...how you say it...sleep with fishes."

I think I peed my pants a little. "Nonnie, look at me. Where? Where is *l'ultima tappa*?"

"Is empty warehouse, Fourteenth and Clay."

No freaking way. Could Nonnie be right?

Rico's foot never left the gas pedal on our way to the warehouse. He parked down the block on 14ᵗʰ, on the opposite side of the street. The building was old, maybe 1800s, judging by the architecture. Solid brick, small casement windows (most of which were broken), one door in the front of the building on 14ᵗʰ and a loading dock around the corner on Clay.

Breeching options were limited.

When Rico reached for his phone, I knew who he was going to call, so I tried to bat it out of his hand. "Don't call Cap. He'll make us come back to the office and waste our time developing a *plan*."

Ugh. That four-letter *P-word*. It's what people do when they're scared. Not me. I'm an *act now and regret it later* kind of chick.

Rico looked at me like I'd lost my mind. "You can't just go barging in there. That building's five stories tall. Even if he is inside, we have no idea where. We need a viable plan. We need SWAT."

I squirmed in my seat, like a four-year-old. "But that will take too long. Leo's been without his meds for," I looked at my watch, "Oh, God. Almost thirty-six hours. We need to move *now*."

Rico shook his head. "Leo could be dead for all we know. But if he is still alive, busting in and getting killed won't help him."

Quick to blow off my objection, Rico called Cap and told him what we'd learned.

"It's the only solid lead we've got, Cap. There's a lookout scumbag on the outside, but we need to know who's inside with Leo and exactly where they are." Rico listened then gave a quick nod. "Be there in ten. Four Boy Fifty-Two clear."

I smacked the dashboard. "Dammit! I told you not to call him."

He pulled away from the curb and turned onto Clay Street. "Relax. We'll get Leo. And with some planning, we'll all get out alive."

By the time we reached Cap's office, it was standing room only. Cap, Weston, Jerry Armitage (a captain with the fire department), and Craig Stovall (the SWAT commander), were waiting for us. Jerry had a rolled-up blueprint wedged in the crook of his arm.

Cap waited for us to cram inside his office and close the door. "Let's get started," he said. "We're on borrowed time here."

Jerry Armitage spread the blueprints across Cap's desk, and used his finger to outline the building's features.

"We've got five stories, copper piping, copper 110 wiring, and a basement housing a boiler room and a coal chute. One ingress/egress on 14th Street, a loading dock on Clay, and a total of thirty steel casement windows measuring 24" by 48" across the exterior perimeter. One fixed ladder with roof access runs up the west face of the building. Two chimneys, one pulley-operated lift-gate elevator, running up the center of the building behind the central staircase, and additional stairs along the east and west perimeters. Duct work from the original coal furnace is still in place, condition is unknown. The rooftop is obscured by the building's facade, but the prints show it's flat with metal casement roof windows at its center."

Jerry paused and looked up at the group. "The property was purchased by Queen City Restoration Services in July 2014, and a building permit was issued for rehabilitation purposes. CFD has since sent two registered letters to the owners, citing the property as a blight to the community, and asking that the building be demolished, or that the permit be renewed, and the work needed to bring the property up to code be completed."

He looked up and shrugged. "To date, we've received no response to our letters. The last CFD inspection prior to the building's sale was in June 2013. In short, I can't tell you what condition the building is in now."

Jerry glanced at Rico and me. "On the upside, your vic and whoever is holding him captive are currently inside, and we haven't received any rescue calls. That suggests that the structure could be stable."

No sooner had Jerry taken a breath than Ottis, the squirrelly janitor, barged through Cap's door and pushed his garbage bin over the top of Rico's foot.

Rico grabbed the bin with both hands. "What the fu—"

"Sorry," Ottis mumbled.

"Ottis!" Cap turned to him and sighed. "We've had this discussion before. Knock first, then enter *if* I give you permission. Can't you see we're busy here? Come back later, for chrissake."

Ottis turned crimson and muttered an apology, then backed out of the room, taking his bin with him.

Cap rolled his eyes. "Where were we?"

Stovall from SWAT cut to the chase. "So, we know the layout of the building, but not its condition. This is where I come in. I'll send in a drone to take pics through all the windows—including the one on the roof. The drone's silent, so less chance of tipping our hand. We'll see how many bogeys we find, and hopefully where they're holding your vic."

He glanced at his watch. "It's six-thirty now. I can have the drone up in thirty minutes and back here in sixty, give or take."

"Go," Cap said. "Get me enough for a warrant. Let's take these bastards down."

Stovall rubbed his chin. "Look, I heard you guys got kicked off this case by the Feds. It's a kidnapping. The FBI called the ball. They've got jurisdiction. No offense, but I'm not willing to lose my job over this. Either you call them in, or I will."

Cap rubbed his face and sighed. "Yeah. I know. I'll take care of it."

I started to pitch a fit but decided to hold my tongue instead. It wouldn't have done any good. Cap had to call in the Feds, he didn't have a choice. Arguing wouldn't get Leo rescued any quicker. But that didn't mean I had to like it.

In fact, Little Allie kept yammering that the bigger this operation got, the bigger the chance of a leak.

For once, we agreed on something.

With roughly an hour to spare before Stovall returned, Rico and I hustled to the M.E.'s office to grab Leo's meds out of the morgue cooler. We walked through the outer doors and down the hallway, to Doc's office.

He was typing furiously on his laptop and didn't hear us knock. When he finally glanced up, he seemed startled and slammed the laptop closed.

"What's up?" he asked.

Rico leaned against the doorway. "We're here to pick up Leo's meds."

"You found him? Where?"

"Hope so," Rico said, sidestepping the question.

We followed Doc into the morgue. He pulled the bottle out from the cooler, grabbed two syringes, and then went for a third.

"Just in case. Good luck. Hope it's not too late." He held onto the medicine and hesitated. "Sorry, but if it *is* too late, make sure you do him there. I've got a full house here. No time for cleanups."

How thoughtful.

"Sure, Doc," I said, ripping the bottle and syringes from his hand. "Why don't I make things easier for you? How about I just find him, spike him in the head, and be done with him? I mean, he's almost ready to croak anyway. No need making a mess in your nice clean morgue. It's all about you, isn't—"

Rico grabbed my elbow and pulled me out the door. "You really need to work on your people skills."

"I've got a better idea," I said, yanking myself free. "I'll handle the dead ones. You handle the living ones. It's easier that way."

We made it back to the precinct in plenty of time and threaded our way through the station, passing Ottis the Amazing Squirrel, still emptying trash cans. Weston was in an empty office, on the phone. Rico motioned for him to join us.

I thought I'd lose my mind while the three of us waited outside Cap's office for Stovall. The minute he rounded the corner, Rico knocked on Cap's door and we all gathered round to hatch a freaking plan.

Director Dickhead of the FBI arrived on cue, and strutted in like he owned the place.

My hackles raised.

Stovall spread out the blueprint once again, and got down to business. "Okay. The drone got pics of each floor. It identified two bogeys on the first floor and two on the third. The pics shot through the roof window show that Leo is being held on the fifth floor. He's got two guards. Counting the external lookout, that's a total of seven bogeys, all carrying assault rifles—"

"Let me see those pics," I snatched them from Stovall's hand and focused on the photos of the roof and the fifth floor. The roof window was open at a forty-five-degree angle. Leo was on a chair in the middle of the room, his hands and feet restrained, head back, mouth open. His face was bloody, his eyes black. The bastards had beaten him.

Director Dickhead ripped the pictures out of my hands.

"Make no mistake. The FBI is in charge now. This is a federal operation. And with the content of these pics, we don't need a warrant. We've got probable cause."

He turned back to the blueprints on the desk. "For a target this size, we've got inner and outer perimeters. We'll need C-4 to blow the main entrance and roof windows. We'll send in the Hostage Rescue Team, using mutual aid from SWAT. Starting with the first floor, we'll breach and sweep upward, floor by floor. We'll have the roof team rappel down from a chopper, and send a flashbang down through the sky window. Once the flashbang is deployed, the roof team will rappel inside to the fifth floor, sweep, and effect rescue. This is a precision operation, people. We don't want to risk any crossfire between our ground and air teams. Any questions?"

He gave it a three count, then said, "Go time is 0100 hours."

"Wait a minute," Rico said, "What about Nighthawk? She should go in. Leo's condition is critical—every minute counts. He needs to have his meds before he's extracted. Nighthawk worked with the scientists who developed the drug. She knows how and where to inject it, depending on his condition. None of you do." Rico glanced over at me. "And if she goes, I go. She's my partner."

"Negative," Dickhead said, glowering at Rico. "Neither one of you will be involved in this extraction. There will be no mutual aid from CPD. Of any kind. Especially from you two. Is that clear?"

That arrogant son of a bitch.

Dickhead pointed at the door. "Nighthawk, De Palma, you're excused for the remainder of this meeting."

We marched out of Cap's office and down the hallway, dismissed like a couple of losers from the cool kid's club.

I threw my hands into the air. "Zero-one-hundred hours? That's one a.m.! That's four hours from now! He'll have been without his meds for close to forty-six hours. He won't last that long."

"Nighthawk, stop. Look at me," Rico said, grabbing my arm and grinding us both to a halt. "He could be dead already. You need to be prepared for that."

"But what if he isn't? We might still be able to save him."

I pulled Rico up the hallway, and shoved him through the next door we came to, the ladies room.

Then I jerked my hand out of my jacket pocket. In it were Leo's medicine and the syringes.

"Screw Dickhead, and screw that *it-takes-a-village* rescue parade he's planning."

It was nine o'clock. Sunset had long passed. Dickhead be damned. This time I was calling the ball.

"Operation Nighthawk commences now, at twenty-one hundred hours. With or without you, partner."

20

OH, NO SHE DI'NT

Rico could spout all the lip service he wanted to about being my partner. Right here, right now, was the time to prove it. Either shit or get off the pot. Kind of appropriate, given that I'd taken him hostage in the ladies room.

The brooding look in his eyes suggested he might be having second thoughts. No great surprise. He'd have been crazy not to. I was asking a lot of him. Insubordination isn't the way to win friends and influence bosses. Even if we saved Leo, there would be repercussions. That's code for *hell to pay*, resulting in possible suspension or termination.

That was no skin off my nose. I was a sub-contractor. I could do what I did without the CPD's blessing. It was just easier with it. Not to mention, CPD actually paid for my services. But with Rico, it wasn't just a matter of losing a job, or a paycheck. Being a cop was in his blood. It was all he knew. All he wanted. Forcing him to make this choice wasn't fair.

But when was life ever fair?

Rather than risk seeing rejection in his eyes, I turned away and walked into one of the stalls.

Rico cleared his throat. "I'll, ah, just wait for you out there... in the hallway."

It took me a minute to realize that it didn't matter whether he was along for the ride or not. That if the career he'd built was more important than stepping outside the bureaucratic box to save a life, I would be better off without him. My fingers curled around the lock on the stall door and froze.

Why was I balking? Leo's life was in danger. *With or without you*, that's what I'd told Rico. The ball was in his court, not mine.

I strode out the restroom and into the hallway, prepared for the worst. I found Rico leaning against the wall, playing with his phone.

He threw on his jacket and asked, "What took you so long? We're wasting time."

I should have known he would never let me down, never leave me hanging. He was a true-blue partner, like Harry Delk had been. For a moment, I couldn't wipe the grin off my face.

Then we got in the car.

"I'll take the front door," I said, unsnapping Hawk's holster. "You take the loading dock. We'll meet in the middle and clear each floor as we go."

Rico did a double take. "Jesus, Nighthawk. There are eight of them scattered throughout the building—at least there were, when the drone took the pictures, but that was hours ago. There could be more of them now, or they could have all moved to the fifth floor with Leo. We can't just go in blind, guns blazing. We need a plan."

Plan. That sucky four-letter word.

"You and your plans. How about you create a diversion

outside? When they get distracted, I'll sneak in from the loading dock and work my way up to the fifth floor."

"What if that doesn't work?" he asked. "What if only some of the scumbags come out to see what's going on? You'd have a close-quarters shootout with whomever was left in the house—by yourself."

"So?"

"So, if anyone should go in, it's me."

"Really?" I asked. "And why is that? I'm as good a shot as you, any day."

"Maybe. But your weapon retention sucks. I've been with you three times when the shit's hit the fan, and you've lost your weapon every time. First, the twitcher at the shooting range knocked your gun away. Then, Miriam whapped your arm and sent your knife flying. Then Joey Fingers pulled the morgue room shelf over on top of you, and you lost your gun again. Zero for three, Nighthawk. That's pathetic."

Well. That was uncalled for, even if it was true. He could have had the decency to at least cringe, like he expected me to slap the crap out of him, but instead, he stared, waiting for a response.

The best I could manage was: "Shit happens."

"Shit doesn't just happen to you, Nighthawk. You're like a fucking fountain of shit...the font from which all shit flows."

Rico took a couple of deep breaths and massaged his neck to work out the kinks. "We're getting off topic here. When this case is over, we'll work on your little...training opportunity. Right now, we need to come up with a viable plan to get to Leo."

With the warehouse in sight, Rico pulled over, parked along the curb on Clay Street, and turned off his lights.

I crossed my arms and glared at him the dark. "What's your strategy, Mister Grand Poobah Planmaster?"

Rico fell silent, staring at the warehouse, eyes narrowed and face frozen. I'd seen that look before. The hamsters in his brain were working overtime. It wasn't long before his lips curved into a thin smile.

"Look at the top floor," he said. "The one where they're holding Leo. The electricity's turned off, right? But there's a light up there. It's dim, but if you look close, you can see it."

Sure enough. I squinted and he was right. There was a faint glow inside. That made sense. Whatever light source they were using had to be dim, to keep from attracting attention.

"You think they're up there, hanging out with Leo?" I asked.

"Could be. Or maybe they're still where they were earlier, and we just can't see them from this angle. When we got here this afternoon, I checked the place out. There were broken windows on every floor and a ledge running beneath them. The side of the building closest to us had a fixed ladder."

He hesitated, like he was putting the finishing touches on his plan. "There was one perimeter guard, right?"

I shrugged. "Yeah. But who knows how many are camped out there now."

"Fair enough. We'll do a little close-up recon before we go in. If everything's copacetic, we'll wait until the guard moves to the opposite side of the building. Then we'll climb the ladder to the fifth floor, work our way across the ledge, and crawl inside through one of those broken windows on the back side of the building. That way, we won't be dropping in right on top of them. If we're quiet, no one will even know we're there. We rescue Leo, you dose him up, and we'll all be on our way."

Climb the fire escape ladder? Fifth floor?

"Ah, nope. That's a big negatory. No can do."

"It's a good plan. What's the problem? "

"Ladders and heights, well...mostly heights."

Rico laughed. "Heights? Of all the shit you do, you're afraid of heights?"

My cheeks blazed. "Yeah. That and public speaking. Remember? Want to make something of it?"

"This is the only plan that makes sense. Getting up to the fifth floor will be the easy part. Time to grow a pair, Nighthawk, and be the cast iron bitch everyone thinks you are. Like it or not, you're going vertical."

Holy shit. Just the thought of being five stories up had me sweating like a pig. "But...but what if they're all on the fifth floor, like you said?"

"They might be. Rescues are highly fluid situations. We'll have to play it by ear. At least this way, we're both inside, backing each other up. Get your ass in gear," he said. "This was your idea. Remember?"

My phone vibrated. I was thankful for the reprieve, until I looked at the call display. It was Jade Chen. I answered anyway. Not because I wanted to talk to her, but because I was curious why she was calling me. And besides, every minute I was listening to her, I wasn't climbing that damn ladder.

Even so, my greeting came out a little cold. "What?"

"Nighthawk, something just came across the wire. Your guy at the European CDCP, Dr. Christian, is reporting that there's been a 1.3 percent rise in the spread of the zombie virus across the European Union. And he confirmed that the virus was manually manipulated. What's your take on that?"

"I'm a little busy here, Jade."

Rico jerked his head at the sound of her name.

"With Sandy gone, Christian is probably the world's leading authority on carovescology. If that's what he's reporting, go with it."

Jade wouldn't let it drop. "Think about it, Nighthawk. 1.3 percent. Do you have any idea how many new cases that is? Something strange is going on, and I'm betting you know what it is. Spill."

Of course, I did. To a point. Christian had already

confirmed that the virus had been manipulated. He just hadn't released that information to the public. The list of possible suspects who were capable of bioengineering the Z-virus was limited.

With Leo's kidnapping, I hadn't had time to dig into that yet. And Jade would be the last person on earth I'd toss conjectures to anyway. I didn't trust her any further than I could throw her. Not to mention, she hated my guts. I didn't have time for kibitzing.

"Sorry, Jade. Talk to Christian. I gotta run—"

"Wait! Let me talk to Rico."

"What makes you think I'm with Rico?"

Rico rolled his eyes and motioned for me to wrap it up, but Jade wasn't finished.

"Because, you paranormal freak, if he weren't there with you, he'd be here with me. I've got him wrapped around my finger so tight he doesn't know whether he's coming or going."

Oh no, she di'nt.

I went in for the kill. "Sorry. You were breaking up. What'd you say?" I pushed the speaker button on my phone.

"I said if he weren't there with you, you freak, he'd be here with me. He's wrapped around my finger so tight, he'll do anything and everything I ask him to. Now give him the damn phone."

Nighthawk: One. Jade: Zero.

Amateur.

Rico's face flushed. He pressed himself up against the car door and waved his arms, warding me off.

I considered tossing him the phone anyway, but we didn't have time for fun and games. We needed to rescue Leo.

"Maybe you don't know Rico as well as you think you do," I said. "He isn't here, Jade. Gotta run, now. Bye."

I hung up and smirked at Rico. "It's all right. I'll buy you a new pair of balls for Christmas. There's always a BOGO sale somewhere."

No sooner had I hung up, than Rico's phone vibrated. Guess who? He glanced at the lit display in the dark.

I could almost see his thoughts scramble: *To answer or not to answer?* That was the question.

He raised the phone to his ear and I groaned. Bad choice.

"De Palma." His tone was pancake flat.

I couldn't hear her exact words, but she had the lilting voice of a woman who had no idea she'd busted herself. He let her ramble a bit and then cut her off mid-lilt.

"Jade, honey. I'd tell you what you want to know, but well... people might think you've got me wrapped around your little finger. They might even think I don't know whether I'm coming or going. You should probably ask some other shmuck." He started to hang up, but had second thoughts. "Oh, yeah. One last thing. Lose my number."

He disconnected, set the phone on vibrate, and slipped it into his pants pocket.

I didn't say a word.

He leaned back against the head rest. "Somehow, she found out we were thrown off the case and wanted me to comment."

He grabbed some extra mags from the glove compartment and shoved them into the pocket of his jacket.

Before I could tell him how lucky he was to be rid of her, my phone went off again.

I checked the number, then turned toward Rico and bit my lip. Jade, no doubt mad enough to claw me a new one with her acrylic nails.

I sent her call to voicemail, turned off my phone, and shoved it into my back pocket.

Rico got out of the car and started to slam the door, but stopped. We were officially in stealth mode now. Phase one of Operation Nighthawk had begun.

"Shit," he whispered. "Look up the street. Two black sedans on the opposite side. Looks like the Fed's advance team beat us here."

He eased the door closed, with his finger to his lips, as I climbed out of the car, still amused at having bested Jade Chen. Who was the uber-bitch now?

Rico walked over, fixed me in a steely-eyed stare, and murmured. "Go ahead. Yuck it up, Nighthawk. Get it all out of your system now. Because once that guard is out of sight, your ass is going up that ladder."

Son of a bitch. I was hoping with everything that had just happened, he'd have forgotten all about his ridiculous high-rise rescue idea.

Didn't it figure? Me, five stories up with no net. Pretty much the story of my life.

21

AIN'T NOTHING BUT A THING

The mob lookout, not twenty feet from the ladder, lit up a fresh smoke. Rico and I crouched behind a truck parked along the curb, waiting for him to finish. Damned if creeping down 14th Street, ducking for cover, didn't bring back memories of my qualification test at Perptown. That same adrenaline rush coursed through me now. It would be easy to move too quickly. To get careless. This time, there could be consequences.

I studied Rico in the moonlight and wondered if his heart was hammering like mine.

He focused, peering through the darkness, fingers moving to unsnap his holster, without as much as a glance. He was cool. He was ready. The kind of ready that comes with training. Although I'd never tell him so, we made a damn good team.

When the scumbag finished his smoke and rounded the corner, we scrambled from the edge of the street and sprinted through the parking lot, to the side of the building.

"Show time," Rico whispered. "Ain't nothing but a thing, Nighthawk. Don't look down."

He started up the ladder and I followed close behind, hands sweating, stomach lurching. I swallowed the urge to puke with every step, eyes glued straight ahead, spotting the mortar lines between the bricks to keep from falling, but my vision started to swim.

And then the brain bitch started flapping her gums. *You lily-livered pussy. You spineless weasel. You gutless...*

"Fine. Okay. I'm a wussy," I said. "Now get the hell out of my head before you make me fall."

Rico glanced over his shoulder. "What?"

"Sorry. Never mind."

See? Shut up you little buttinsky before you get us killed.

You should be ashamed of yourself, Alliyah Marie Nigh...

You know how much I hate that name.

Whatever. Care to look where you are? Take a moment. Enjoy the view, Alliyah Marie.

Holy shit. I was two flights up already. Every rung under my belt meant one less rung to climb. Three flights down and working on number four.

What do you know? I can do this.

You're welcome.

God, she's a smug little witch.

Four flights up, I started feeling my oats. "Think the Feds are watching?"

Rico stopped and turned his head. "Yeah. But that's all they'll do. The Director's no fool. They could blow the whole operation, trying to stop us now."

The visual of Director Dickhead blowing a gasket made me laugh. My left foot slipped off a rung and dangled in the air.

I tried not to pee my pants. "Shit. Shit. Shit."

"You okay down there?"

"I hate you, De Palma. I hate you. I hate you."

"Just checking," the bastard said, not even hesitating on his way up the ladder.

When I caught up to him at the fifth floor, he motioned

toward the fourth window on the left, broken, with most of its glass gone.

"We're going to climb across this ledge right here and slip into that window," he said. "The ledge is straight across from this rung. Just step over, then slip into that window. Easy-peasy. You with me?"

I threw him an icy stare. "Well, I'm sure as hell not climbing back down the ladder."

"Watch me. You can do this," he said, creeping across the ledge to the window. "See? Step with your left leg out to the ledge, use your left hand to grip the wall, then bring your right leg out to the ledge, and your right hand to the wall. From there it's just left-right, left-right until..."

"*Shhh,*" I whispered, "Someone's coming."

Rico tucked and rolled inside the window.

There I was five stories up, one foot on the ledge, the other on the ladder, butt sticking out like a nun in a whorehouse.

The guy stopped right beneath me, yapping on his cell. "Joey. It's Dom." Dom went quiet, like Joey was giving him an earful.

Stick a sock in it, Joey, I thought, glancing down at Dom's bald head. *I can't be hanging here forever.*

"Dude. Shut the fuck up already," Dom said. "I got something important. Snowflake called. The Feds are coming at one. We're outta here. Got it?"

Snowflake? Who the hell's Snowflake?

Dom shoved the phone into the pocket of his hideous, canary yellow sport coat and walked toward the corner of the building.

My right hand had gone numb, so I adjusted my grip on the ladder. My foot slid on some loose concrete, near a chipped section of the ledge. Tiny concrete pebbles showered to the ground below.

Dom spun on his heel, drew his gun, turned left, then right, and peered through the darkness.

Don't look up. Please. Don't look up.

He chuckled and shook his head, then holstered his gun and continued walking, until he finally rounded the corner.

Rico's head popped out of the window. "That was close."

I pulled my right leg to the ledge, then flattened myself out against the side of the building and wriggled, Flat Stanley style, toward Rico. He stuck out his arm and pulled me through the window.

I did a face plant onto the floor and was surprisingly relieved, until a rat scampered past my face. At least my butt wasn't a bullseye, waving in the breeze for target practice, anymore. I might never have gotten to my feet again, but Rico's phone vibrated.

He pulled it out of his pocket, looked at the display and sighed. He didn't say a word, just held the phone to his ear, wincing periodically, and eventually mouthed the word, *Cap.*

"You can yell at me later," Rico murmured. "The mob knows about the raid. Uh-huh," he whispered with a nod. "Uh-huh. Uh-huh. I know. I will. Uh-huh. Bye."

Rico leaned in close. "Let me see if I got this straight. You and I are toast. I'll be riding a safety patrol car, by the time Cap's finished with me, and you'll be raising the dead in Hoboken. The Feds I saw out front have called in the cavalry. Oh. They also video'd you hanging from the ladder, and made book on how long it would take you to fall."

Masochistic mouth-breathers.

"I see. Anything else I should know?"

"No. Those were the, ah...salient...points."

"Then move your ass."

Rico led the way, gun at the ready. I pulled Hawk and held him high, fingers wrapped around the grip, thumb forward, right hand stabilizing from beneath. No way, no how, was this gun coming out of my hands. Not this time.

Creeping through the warehouse was tough, with only the moonlight and the dim glow of Rico's phone to guide us. The concrete floors, cracked and worn, were littered with debris and animal scat. Tangled wiring hung from the ceiling, like snakes slithering across our heads. And Jesus. The smell. Even on a chilly spring night, the musty odor of mold, mildew and animal feces made me gag.

I walked through a ginormous spiderweb, and had to shake the urge to squeal like a little girl. The brain bitch must have been sleeping. God help me if she ever got wind of that.

We'd advanced maybe thirty feet when we got our first glimpse of light ahead. That had to be where they were holding Leo. Another forty feet further and we heard voices.

Rico doused the light on his phone, and we listened in.

"How the hell are we supposed to move this schmuck? Is he even breathing?"

I looked at Rico and bit my lip.

"Like I know?" came another voice. "Check his pulse, moron."

Seconds later, "Yeah. He's breathing. Throw some of that water on him. Wake his ass up. I ain't carrying him down five flights of steps."

Rico and I crept forward, hugging the wall, and positioned ourselves on opposite sides of the doorway to the holding room.

A low moan broke the silence.

Leo.

My heart leapt. Footsteps trotted up the stairs and echoed off the walls. We leaned back in the shadows, out of sight.

Someone asked, "He give anything up yet?"

I knew that voice. It was Dom, the ugly yellow jacket guy.

"Nah. He's half-dead," said voice number two.

"He ain't giving up shit," came a third voice. "Tough guy, this one. Got some big stones on him."

Rico held up three fingers, signaling three bogeys in the room.

"Save yourself some grief," Dom said. "Spit it out now, dumbass, and I'll do you quick."

Leo croaked, "Go spit."

Next came a loud crack, and what sounded like a chair crashing to the ground.

"You stupid mother. The only thing keeping you alive is knowing that if I kill you, before you spill what you leaked to the Feds, I'll end up in the same block of cement as you. That don't mean I can't use you for a little target practice in the meantime."

Rico nodded at me and burst through the doorway, taking out Dom, then sliced left and shot again. The second bogey went down. I sliced right through the doorway, as the third skell drew a bead on Rico.

I leveled my gun and said, "Over here, D-bag."

The bogey spun, raised his Colt, and pointed it at my face. Not today, ass-munch. I squeezed Hawk's trigger, and drilled him between the eyes.

Three down. Who knew how many more to come? But one thing was for certain. The element of surprise was gone.

Rico slammed and locked the door behind us. "Thanks. He had me dead to rights."

I nodded and dashed toward Leo, tied to a chair, in the center of the room.

My knees hit the floor beside him. I didn't want to look. But I did. Face and clothes drenched with blood, eyes swollen, cheeks split and teeth missing.

Jesus.

"Leo. Leo. It's Nighthawk. Can you hear me?"

He moaned, but didn't open his eyes. Foam bubbled out of

his mouth and he began to seize. Even if the medicine worked, no way he was walking out of there.

Rico crouched on his haunches, shielding Leo and me from anyone who might come through the door.

Then he called Cap. "We've got Leo," he said. "They did a number on him. We're going to need help getting him out of here."

Someone kicked at the door.

"Soon, would be good," Rico said, hanging up.

Unable to do anything more, he leveled his gun at the door and waited for the inevitable.

"Leo, look at me," I said, tapping his swollen cheek. "Open your eyes."

My fingers fumbled as I loaded the syringe with his medicine. *Calm down, now. Chill out.* I breathed deep and forced myself to slow down. Then I tried again. Bingo.

I jammed the needle directly into his heart. "C'mon, Leo. Open your eyes, damn it."

A flicker? Did they flicker?

"One more time, Leo. Do that one more time."

His puffy eyes peeled open slowly, as if he wasn't sure he wanted to see who, or what, was in front of him.

"Nighthawk," he whispered, with a wan smile. "What took you so long?"

I grinned and cut the zip ties that bound him to his chair.

Next, came yelling and cursing, and the sounds of an army of feet running up the stairs. Rico moved beside the door and leveled his gun.

He nodded toward Leo. "Move him over here, away from the door."

I bent down and slung Leo over my shoulder, nearly coming to my knees. "Holy crap, lard-ass. No more lasagna for you."

No sooner had I schlepped Leo across the room, than a stream of bullets blasted through the door.

"How long does it take for the HRT team to scramble, anyway?" I yelled over the gunfire.

In seconds, the gunmen would take out the lock, or manage to leave more holes than wood in the door, and kick it in. The shooting lulled momentarily and Rico slid, on his stomach, across the floor to the far front corner.

I knelt in front of Leo, shielding him as best I could.

The door gave way, and a jumble of mobsters burst in. I winced, thinking we were goners. But, before they got off a single round, an explosion knocked us all on our asses, blinded, ears ringing and dizzier than bed bugs.

A flurry of Feds rushed the room and began rousting the bad guys. The disoriented mobsters were cuffed, hauled to their feet and dragged, half-walking, half-crawling from the room.

I pushed back some nausea and struggled to my feet, trying to shake off the effect of the blast. Then, I straightened up and worked my way over to check on Leo. He was breathing, but unconscious.

One of the Feds said an ambulance was five minutes out. At least, I think that's what he said. I had to read his lips.

With Leo taken care of, there was one more thing I needed to do. Something a little shady. Something covert. Something that if Rico did, he'd probably get shit-canned for. But me? I was a sub-contractor. What were they going to do? Not use me anymore? Fine. *Sayonara, chumps.* I'll save some other corner of the world from the zombie apocalypse.

I leaned against the wall, and staggered around the perimeter of the room, toward the big yellow splotch on the floor. Dom. I tried to crouch down beside him, but fell on my ass instead. Before anyone could ask what I was doing, I slipped my hand inside his pocket and went fishing.

Let the Feds have the mobsters. All I wanted was Dom's phone. Dom, the guy in the Tweety Bird sport coat, who stood beneath me when my butt was hanging off the ladder, flapping in the breeze, five stories up.

I lurched toward Rico, who stood in the doorway, rubbing his ears, chatting with one of the HRT guys.

He looked over at me and laughed. "You don't look so good."

I wanted to hurl, but at least I could see again, and my balance was coming back.

"Flashbangs." Rico smirked. "They get easier once you know what to expect."

I pulled him over to the wall, slipped Tweety Bird's phone out of my pocket, and showed it to Rico.

"Why do I want to look at your phone?"

"It's Dom's," I whispered. "I think I know how to catch our snitch."

22

CAN'T WE ALL JUST GET ALONG?

Clearing the warehouse, floor by floor, was a painstaking and time-consuming process. Designated members of both the SWAT and HRT teams funneled out of the holding room to lend a hand, while the EMTs shouldered in past them, lugging their equipment.

They had already begun their evaluation of Leo, when Director Dickhead burst through the door, eyes wild, face blanched and spittle flying. He stomped across the room toward Rico and me, sneered, and delivered the shellacking we'd both known was coming. He didn't use his indoor voice, either.

"What the hell were you thinking, Nighthawk?"

I wobbled and grabbed the wall for support, stuck my finger in my ear, and pulled out some blood. "Standing right here, sir. No need to yell."

He didn't skip a beat. "It wasn't just your own life you risked, you smart-assed little show-boater. You fouled up a strategic operation, and risked the lives of every member of the rescue team. What have you got to say for yourself?"

Strategic operation? What a load. Leo would have been dead if we'd have waited for the sun and the stars and the moon to align.

Unable to bite my tongue, I responded the way I'd wanted to respond to him since the moment we met. I threw up on his shoes. That might have been a physical manifestation of my feelings toward Dickhead, but to be honest, most of the credit lay with the flashbang.

Dickhead, not expecting a puke bath, moved a split-second too late, then shook his soiled shoe in disgust.

"And you, De Palma," he said, scraping his Gucci against the baseboard, "You're a cop, for God's sake. You *know* better than to go in without backup."

Rico, red-faced, gamely met Dickhead's gaze. "If I may, sir. I'd like to point ou—"

"No. You may not. Do not interrupt me when I'm addressing you."

Cap appeared in the doorway. "I'm sure you aren't dressing down one of *my* officers, Director Horton. That would be a grave mistake."

"Hey, Cap," I mumbled, wiping the puke off my chin.

"For God's sake, Nighthawk," he said, shaking his head. "Go sit down."

I sank to the floor with a thud. "Good idea, sir."

Cap strode over to Dickhead, never breaking eye contact with him. "I think perhaps what Detective De Palma intended to say, is that had he and Nighthawk not gone in when they did, your entire operation would have ended up in the crapper. And just so you're aware—the mob knew about the raid in advance."

"That's impossible. There were only so many people present when we discussed this mission."

"Exactly."

"A mole?" Dickhead puffed out his chest. "Surely, you're not suggesting it's one of my men."

"Well, it was *somebody* in that room."

As the EMTs wheeled Leo toward the door, Dickhead nodded to one of his men.

"Ferris, you're babysitting now. Stick to this putz like tar paper, and don't even think about blinking. You understand?"

Ferris? I took a closer look and grinned. Sean Ferris. I'd met him several years ago, at a training seminar. Solid guy. Hot too, though I doubted he remembered me.

Leo strained against the straps on his gurney.

"*No way, Jose.* I want Nighthawk." He swiveled his eyes toward me. "Don't let 'em do this, Nighthawk."

"Not after this fiasco, Abruzzi," Dickhead said. "I want one of my men with you at all times."

"*Your* guys? *Your* guys?" Leo wheezed. "If Nighthawk and De Palma hadn't shown up when they did, I'd be dead by now. Screw your guys."

Leo coughed and struggled to catch his breath. "I'm not fucking around here. You take Nighthawk off my detail and our deal's history. Period."

Dickhead smirked, and flicked an invisible speck of lint off the sheet covering Leo. "Nice try. But we both know how much you need that medication. You'll stick with the deal. If for no other reason than you want to live longer."

"Watch me," Leo said. "Those drugs get less effective every day. Some things are worse than dying. I can take myself out, any day. And I'll do it, too. I got nothing to lose. Your call, you big blowhard."

Damn, Leo. Way to play hardball. Leo had Dickhead by the short hairs.

"Fine. It's your funeral," the Director said with a snort. "Nighthawk stays. De Palma, too. But Ferris here stays with them. That's the only way—"

Gunfire and screams erupted from the floors below.

"Stay put!" Rico shouted at the EMTs. "Wait here, until we tell you it's safe to leave."

Cap, Rico, Ferris and I sprinted to the top of the steps and listened, trying to nail down the location of the gunfire.

"Third floor, maybe. Could be second," Ferris said.

Dickhead trailed behind us, as we hugged the wall, and took the steps down to the fourth floor.

Screams echoed up the stairwell.

"Third floor," Rico yelled, taking the steps two at a time.

Cap, Ferris and I caught him at the third-floor landing. A final round of gunfire rang out in the hallway to our right, followed by a chorus of gut-wrenching shrieks that quickly tapered off.

After Rico cleared the corner, we entered the long, narrow passage, lit only by our phones and an odd smattering of beams scattered along the floor, maybe twenty yards down the hallway.

We pushed forward and a copper tang hit my nose. Two more steps. I slipped in something wet. I didn't want to look at the sticky floor beneath me, or the chaotic tangle of shapes and forms that rose from the center of the light beams.

Cap advanced, shined his phone into the jumble, and gagged. The blood-soaked bodies of both SWAT and HRT members, ravaged beyond recognition, lay strewn across the floor.

"Sweet Jesus," Ferris murmured. He rested his hands on his knees and sucked in air, as I walked among the dead, systematically pumping bullets into their brains.

Frenzied sounds filtered toward us from a room beyond the pile—wet, tearing sounds I'd heard before—the sounds of deadheads devouring human flesh.

How many were there? Were they all in that room?

Only one way to find out. We retrieved the Maglites off the fallen officers, and moved on.

I breached the doorway, with Hawk cocked and locked. Something growled to my right. I spun, coming face to face with a deadhead, a multitude of gunshot wounds in its chest. It leapt at me and I fired. Dead bang. Right between the eyes. One down.

Rico, Cap and Ferris filed in at my six. Rico cut left, leaving Cap and Ferris to cover the middle. The room, massive and black beyond the range of our flashlights, could have held one biter or a hundred.

Growls and the sound of shuffling feet echoed around us, making it impossible to know where the rotters were. But they were close. I could smell them.

I swung my Maglite across the room, and a pocket of dead-heads scattered like roaches into the darkness, leaving their feast of entrails and flesh behind.

Cap, eyes focused on the shadows, advanced and tripped over a severed leg. No sooner did he fall, than a biter dropped from above and pinned him to the floor. Cap wrestled with it, rolling back and forth, struggling to keep clear of its jaws, trying to get out from beneath it.

Rico leveled his Glock. *"Give me a clear shot,"* he yelled.

Cap leveraged his shoulders against the floor, and pushed the biter slightly off center. Rico fired and nailed the back of its head. The front of its skull exploded, splattering gray matter and decomp all over Cap, who lay on his side, gasping for air.

"You okay, Cap?" Rico asked, as he pulled Cap to his feet.

"Never...better." Cap panted, wiping zushi off his face with his sleeve. "Where the hell did that thing come from? The ceiling?"

I aimed my light at the collection of copper steam pipes that snaked back and forth above our heads. No more biters.

"It's as if they drew us into this room, so they could attack from above, and pick us off one at a time," I said.

"When did they start to strategize?" Rico asked.

I bit my lip and sighed. "I didn't know they had."

The remaining biters grew louder, bolder—and closer. The

four of us stood shoulder to shoulder, peering deep into the void beyond the reach of our flashlights.

They attacked from all sides. Cap squeezed off one shot and then another. The deadhead sailed backwards, like a rag doll. Rico fired a couple rounds into the advancing horde. One of the biters broke through and jumped Ferris. He blasted a hole in its chest, barely slowing it down.

"Head shot," I screamed. "Shoot the head!"

The biter took Ferris down, but he brought his Glock to bear and put a bullet into its eyeball.

Two of the meatbags double-teamed me, one coming at my thighs, the other at my face. I kicked the one near my legs, and sent him tumbling across the floor.

The one coming at my face ended up with no head, thanks to Hawk. The biter I'd kicked lay face up, arms and legs flailing, trying to right itself.

I scrambled beside it, and drove my Ka-Bar through its brainstem.

The room went strangely silent. No more growls, no more shuffling. Only six decommissioned deadheads that had decimated an entire tactical team, because the officers hadn't shot for the head.

I choked on the bile in my throat and the feeling of helplessness that welled inside me.

The tactical teams had been trained to go for center mass. It was a game of percentages. The larger the target, the greater the odds of stopping the threat. But, damn it, when were these guys going to start listening to me?

My stomach rolled, and I thought I might retch, but Dickhead wandered into the room and my brain changed gears. He'd been with us on the stairs, maybe a step or two behind at most. Where the hell was he, while we were fighting for our lives?

"Zombies." He spat out the word like it tasted bad. "Fucking piles of decomp. What the hell are they doing here?"

The brain bitch didn't even try to sensor me.

"That's a good question, although none of us has had time to ask it yet. We were busy trying to survive. What about you, Director? What were you doing?"

"You impudent little shi—"

An odd, high-pitched mewling rose from behind him. Before he could turn, a rogue biter threw him to the ground.

So help me, as he struggled to break free, a part of me wanted to let him sink or swim, but you can guess what the damn brain bitch had to say about that. There'd be no living with her, if I walked away.

I moved into place above the rotter, glared at Dickhead, and said, "Move it or lose it," shoving Hawk's barrel against the biter's skull.

Dickhead pushed himself out of the line of fire, giving me the shot. Against my better judgement, or maybe because of it, I pulled the trigger. And I won't deny it, seeing Dickhead covered in zushi was the only good thing that happened that day.

Dickhead slid out from beneath the corpse and popped to his feet, chewing nails and spitting barbed wire. "*Jesus H. Christ, Nighthawk.* Couldn't you have used your knife, like you did on the last one?"

"Oh. That's right," I said, standing over the top of him. "You had a front row seat to what happened in that room, didn't you? And you didn't lift a finger to help us. Yeah. I took that last rotter out with my knife. But basting you with biter juice gave me a lot more satisfaction."

"I'll have your ass, you insubordinate bitch. No one ta—"

Before anyone could stop me, I dropped onto his stomach and straddled him. "Listen, you pompous ass. If you, or your men, knew the slightest thing about taking down deadheads, you'd know that center mass hits *don't fucking work. You need to take out the brain.* How many more officers have to die before you halfwits at the top get the message, and start training these guys right?"

I climbed off Dickhead and wiped the sweat from my face. "What I do, raising the dead, is a gift. I do it, because it's the only thing I know how to do—that I was born to do. And I do it really well. There's a madman out there, manipulating the Z-virus, and trying to overrun this country—the entire world—with zombies. Somehow, he's connected to Leo and this case. These biters didn't wander in here by accident. And here's something else to keep you awake at night, Director. The dead-heads that attacked us today seem to have developed intelligence, an ability to problem solve."

I exhaled long and slow, then extended my hand to help Dickhead up. "Look at me, Director Horton. I'm Allie Nighthawk. The best of the bad-ass zombie hunters—and the only hope you've got. If you stop working against me, maybe we can catch this monster and get Leo to the grand jury alive, in the process."

That was as close to an olive branch as he was going to get from me. But would the moron be smart enough to take it?

23

NO WONDER HEALTH CARE IS
A MESS

W ith the last of the rotters down, the EMTs would be able to safely transport Leo. They'd head for University Hospital, one of the facilities located on Pill Hill in nearby Clifton.

Two of us would need to be there to guard his room. It was three in the morning. The night had been long and exhausting. What I really wanted was sleep.

We trudged through the hallway of the warehouse and back to the third-floor landing, a collection of characters more disheveled than the biters we'd put down. Ferris's five o'clock shadow made him look pasty and gaunt. It wasn't the dark circles beneath his eyes that drew my attention, but the haunted look inside them. New to this game, he'd seen things that night that he'd never seen before. Yet somehow, he'd not only handled himself well, he'd stepped up, in spite of it all.

"I'll go take the first shift," he said. "One of you guys can go home and get some rest."

Good man, for a Fed.

I volunteered to go with Ferris, then turned to Rico and

asked, "Think you can head to the hospital around 10:00 a.m. and spell me?"

"Sure thing," he said, starting toward the stairway.

He stopped when he reached Ferris. "Good job today, man."

Ferris flashed a weary smile and clapped Rico's shoulder as he walked by.

As Rico started down the steps, Ferris and I trekked up to the holding room on the fifth floor. I knocked on the door.

The voice on the other side warbled, "Wh...who is it?"

"Biters," I called through the door. "It's lunch time. Which one of you should we eat first?"

Ferris snickered.

The door creaked open and one of the EMTs greeted us with a sigh of relief.

While Ferris was letting them know they were good to go, I made straight for Leo. His face had blossomed from the beating he'd taken, making him look like Quasimodo, but at least he seemed more alert than when we'd left him. And his seizures had stopped.

Could the medicine have returned him to his pre-kidnapping status? Only time would tell.

After stopping by the 51st for a shower and a quick change (Ferris had to raid the lost and found), Ferris and I arrived at University Hospital. We entered the underground ambulance bay and took the freight elevator to the emergency room, away from the prying eyes of Jade Chen and the rest of the news hounds. No doubt, given the raid at the warehouse, they were sniffing out details like bloodhounds on a scent.

We waited with Leo in his partitioned examination room, where he drifted in and out of consciousness. Eventually, a physician arrived. She said he had a concussion and was dehydrated, but he also needed blood work and several tests, including a CT scan to identify possible skull and facial fractures.

When they wheeled Leo off for testing, I stepped outside and called Nonnie, wanting to hear the relief in her voice when I told her Leo was safe.

"Oh, thank heaven. When he home, Miss Allie?"

"I'm not sure yet. I'll let you know as soon as I hear something."

"He come to your house. I care for him there."

I hadn't thought that far ahead, but involving Nonnie in Leo's care posed a serious risk.

"Probably not," I said. "Leo's a target, Nonnie. You could be in danger."

The tough old bird argued with me, until I finally agreed we would discuss the idea more when I came home.

The hours in the ER passed more like days. We watched *Judge Judy*, reruns of *Two and a Half Men*, and *Martha Bakes*.

Ferris yawned, then stretched out on an empty couch and took me by surprise. "You were fucking awesome out there tonight."

I looked up from a magazine to find Ferris staring at me, wearing an enigmatic smile.

I nodded and returned the compliment. "You were pretty amazing yourself."

"So, what's the story with you and De Palma? You two... involved?"

I nearly choked. "No. We're just partners. He's dating Jade."

"The reporter?"

"Go figure."

"Good." The mysterious smile settled on his lips, as he closed his eyes.

Minutes later, the doctor came back to tell us Leo had a broken nose and cheekbone.

No wonder the healthcare system is a mess. I could have told her that before they did the testing. The fact that his nose was sideways, and his right cheek the size of a grapefruit, should have been the first clue.

They decided to keep Leo overnight for monitoring and to give him fluids.

Dickhead had already arranged for Leo to have a private room, number 414. Two tortuous-looking metal chairs awaited Ferris and me, outside his doorway.

When the medical staff whisked Leo into his room and closed the door, we sat in the chairs and did our best not to nod off.

"You don't like my boss very much, do you?" Ferris asked, stretching his legs across the over-waxed linoleum floor.

I couldn't help but laugh. "Is it that obvious?"

"Yeah, well. Just between you and me, there's a lot of that going around. The dude couldn't find his ass with a roadmap."

Ferris was turning out to be a stand-up guy.

"How can you work with that turd?" I asked.

"He may be a turd, but he's an ambitious turd. He knows how to play the game. Sooner or later, he'll move up, out of the line of fire. Ain't nobody going to shed a tear over that."

Ferris started down the hallway to find the vending area, then turned with a wink, promising to bring me some Doritos along with a Jack and water. Apparently, my reputation had preceded me.

"That's Coke Zero," I said. "Not water."

What I really wanted to say, was just bring the Jack.

Ferris hadn't been gone but a couple of minutes, when the medical team came out of Leo's room.

Questions swarmed out of my mouth like angry bees. "How's he doing? You know he's contracted the Z-virus? I have his daily meds. Do you need them? Or do you have a supply on hand? When can he go home?"

The house doctor narrowed his eyes. "I'm sorry, I don't see a medical release on file. I can't give you that information."

Shit. Shit. And double shit.

"FBI," I barked. "We need this information for ongoing critical care issues, once he's released into our custody."

"Very well," said the doctor, buying the manure I'd just shoveled. "Assuming there are no complications, he can leave in the morning. We're going to get him hydrated and make sure he's voiding properly."

Always with the voiding, these docs. You could be hemorrhaging like a stuck pig, but if you can pee and poop, you're headed out the door.

I called Nonnie and gave her the good news.

"Room 414," I said. "But how about we let him get some sleep tonight?"

After the care team scattered in separate directions down the hallway, I went into Leo's room and shut the door behind me. His eyes were closed, but as usual, his mouth was not.

"Nice of you to drop by, Nighthawk. Now that you're up to snuff on my bowel movements, how 'bout you tell me *what the hell took you so long to find me*. You guys. You act like you're doing me this big favor, keeping me alive. I'm the one doing the favor. Without my testimony, the D.A.'s got jack. The least you can do is keep me from getting the shit beat out of me." He pushed the button on his PCA pump.

"Actually, Nonnie led us to you," I said, filling him in on her life-saving translation of *l'ultima tappa*.

Leo smiled in spite of himself. "*Mia bella*, Nonnie."

My eyes darted to his IV. "Bet they've got you on some sweet pain meds."

Leo harrumphed, pulled up his blanket, and stared out the window.

"Look," I said, "I really am sorry. The truth is, it was an ugly scene busting you out of there. Six members of the tactical team died trying to rescue you. Biters got to them."

Leo's eyes snapped back to me. "Biters? Where the hell did they come from?"

"That's what I want to know. Suppose you tell me."

Leo toyed with the edge of his blanket. "What do you mean?"

"You heard me. Everywhere we turn, biters keep showing up. What aren't you telling me?"

"Nothing. I swear."

He answered a little too fast. A little too...practiced. Was he afraid of something? I debated pushing him harder, but his heavy eyelids told me the pain meds were kicking in.

Another time.

Rico, ready to take his watch, appeared in the doorway, along with Ferris, who handed me my Doritos and a Coke Zero.

"How's he doing?" Ferris asked, pulling his crappy folding chair into the room.

"As feisty as ever. He'll live, for now."

This Ferris guy impressed the hell out of me. He respected the relationship I had with Leo and didn't try to insert himself. Good instincts.

"So, why do you think the biters keep showing up?" Rico asked, pulling the other chair alongside Ferris and taking a seat.

I bit my lip and shrugged. "I don't know. I keep running over it in my head. The mob and biters. Everything the mob does involves money. They can't make their own zombies, right? So, who's supplying the biters and where are they coming from? And why?"

Rico leaned forward, elbows on his knees, and nodded. "You're right. If we follow the money, we'll figure it out."

Try as I might, I couldn't hold back a yawn. "I guess I'll take off now. Ferris, is somebody coming to relieve you? We have to be back at Cap's office by three-thirty."

"My relief should be here any minute." He looked at his watch and sighed. "See you in...five hours."

I turned to say goodbye to Leo, but his eyes were closed and he was starting to snore, his mouth curved into a smile. He must have been dreaming about Nonnie's lasagna.

Nonnie cornered me the moment I walked in the door. I told her about the broken bones in Leo's face, and reassured her that he'd be getting out in the morning, assuming all went well overnight.

She seemed more concerned with his long-term prognosis. So was I.

"His virus. Is it worse?" she asked.

I didn't have an answer for that. No one did. He seemed about the same, but who knew what kind of impact his having gone without meds would have down the road—or how long that road would be.

There'd come a time when I'd have to brace her for the inevitable. But not now. Now, I needed sleep.

"Ms. Allie, Leo stay here. I not charge extra to care for him."

How could I explain to her that Dickhead would never go for that—inserting a civilian into the scenario? Yet another battle to fight, with Dickhead on one side, Nonnie on the other, and me in the middle. He was exhausting. She was relentless. I didn't have the strength to think about it. Dickhead would be at the three-thirty meeting. We could discuss Leo's care and safety then.

I asked Nonnie to wake me at two, crawled into my bed and crashed. The last thing I remember was Headbutt curling up next to me, and Kulu sitting on her perch, head under her wing, settling in for a nap.

Two o'clock came and it seemed like I'd just closed my eyes. Nonnie shook my shoulder and rousted me out of bed. I stumbled into the shower and put on some fresh clothes, including my *Zombies—the Organic Low-Carb Diet* T-shirt.

I downed a monster cup of coffee and called Dr. Christian, to ask whether the European biters were exhibiting the same intellectual ability as the deadheads in the warehouse.

"Such as?" he asked.

"Problem solving. Strategizing. That sort of thing."

He hesitated before answering. "No. Not intellectual behavior. Remember, Ms. Nighthawk, the dead have no ability to reason, like you or me."

I told him about the pack attack at the warehouse.

"It is possible that someone could direct their actions remotely," he said. "Say, through an ear piece or some other mechanism. But, no, I do not believe their brains are capable of strategic thinking."

Remote direction hadn't even occurred to me. If that were the case, what were the chances any of the ear pieces would still be lodged in the biters' ears, after transporting them to the morgue? I'd have to check that out after the meeting.

Headbutt and Kulu eyed me, as I threw on my jacket and slid Dom's confiscated phone into the pocket. The terrible twins thought they could guilt me into staying home.

"What?" I said, through a mouthful of rugelach. "I'll be back as soon as I can. Don't look at me that way."

Nonnie walked me to the door. "Don't forget. You bring Leo home."

"I'll see what I can do," I said, closing the screen door behind me.

If I got a move on, I could stop at the hospital and check on Leo before the three-thirty meeting. I told myself I'd done enough running for one day and decided to go straight to the precinct.

The brain bitch had other ideas. Damn her and that megaphone mouth of hers. Never a moment's peace. She had me turning onto Clifton Avenue, toward University Hospital, before I realized what I was doing.

When I reached the fourth floor, some guy was sitting in one of the chairs outside of Leo's room. I'd never met him before and figured he must be Ferris's relief. For some reason, Rico wasn't sitting there with him.

"Nighthawk," he said, sticking out his hand, "Nice to meet you. Frank Martin."

Why do these guys always shake hands like it's a dick measuring contest?

I yanked my hand out of his death grip and glanced at Leo's closed door. "Where's Rico?"

"Somebody named Jade called. Girlfriend, maybe? He's down the hall," Frank said, pointing past the nurse's station.

Damn that boomeranging biatch, anyway.

"Why is Leo's door closed?" I asked.

Frank yawned and stretched out his legs. "The nurse is in there. Maybe she's examining him."

I poked my head through the door and saw a nurse messing with Leo's IV.

"Hi, there. We haven't met," I said, offering her my hand. "I'm Allie. And you are?" I glanced at her scrubs. No hospital ID.

She blushed, shamefaced. "I'm Angie. Silly badge. Always seems to be on my dirty scrubs instead of on the pair I'm wearing. If you'll wait outside, you can visit in a minute, after I finish up."

She reached up toward his IV again, and the sleeve of her

scrub top inched up her arm. Part of a tattoo peeked out. Just the bottom of it. Even so, it looked familiar.

She seemed to sense that I was still there, let go of the IV bag, and turned toward me. "I'll only be a minute. Go on, now. Wait in the hall. I'll let you know when I'm finished."

I stood my ground.

She pursed her lips. "I really must insist."

Where had I seen that tattoo?

"Leo," I said, "Has Angie been in to see you today—before now?"

"No," he said. "Just the original nurses from when I got here."

He spooned some ice chips into his mouth. "Freaking hospitals. Running on skeleton crews. One nurse to like a thousand patients. Seriously. Try hitting the call button. Paint dries faster than you can get a bed pan in this place. No offense," he said, glancing up at Angie.

She turned to me and pointed toward the door, waiting for me to leave. Not that I gave a rat's ass. Besides, I was still stuck on skeleton crews.

Skeleton crews. Skeleton crews.

"I've asked you nicely," she said. "Am I going to have to call security?"

Nurse Crab-Ass was twerking on my last nerve. Even Little Allie wanted to slap her six ways to Sunday.

"That's okay," I said, retreating to the door. "I'll be out here, Leo."

When I pulled the door open, she turned back to Leo.

I let go of the door and let it close, with me still in the room.

She reached for Leo's IV again, this time baring a little more of the tattoo on her arm. And it came to me. *Skeleton Crews.*

The tattoo was a skeleton. And not just any skeleton. It was a skeleton with a cane. I knew that image. It was the Vodoun Lord of Death, Baron Samedi.

A light switched on in my head. The mob, zombies, the virus mutation, and now, Voodoo. I didn't have it all put together yet, but the addition of Voodoo took this case in a familiar and terrifying direction.

Angie pulled a syringe from the pocket of her scrubs, primed it, and went for Leo's IV port.

"Hey," I yelled, diving across his bed.

Startled, she dropped the syringe and then sidestepped.

I sailed over Leo's bed and did a face plant onto the floor. The syringe lay inches from my left hand.

Angie and I both went for it. I grabbed it first and squirted whatever had been inside it across the floor. Then I jumped to my feet and whirled around.

The last thing I saw was Leo's bedpan crashing down on top of my head.

24

NIGHTHAWK DOWN

y left eye peeled open, then my right. I lay on the floor, head throbbing, stomach lurching, the empty syringe still in hand.

The room spun like a Tilt-a-Whirl, and voices swirled overhead, Leo's loudest of all. *"Forget Nighthawk. Grab that nurse."*

Frank's face loomed over mine. For some reason, he slapped me. Hard.

"Nighthawk. Wake up."

Never rouse an unconscious person by smacking them in the face. It leaves them miffed.

Rico hovered behind me, peering down.

I grabbed Frank's hand as he came in for a third slap. "Touch me again and you're a dead man."

Rico winced. "Rookie mistake, dude."

Frank slowly backed away from me, as if I were an IED that might explode, and mumbled, "Just trying to help."

I gathered my legs beneath me and wobbled to my feet, cradling my head with one hand, pointing to the door with the other. "Then get your ass out of here and follow that fake nurse."

Happy to escape, Frank set out down the hallway.

I sat on the edge of Leo's bed and patted his leg. "You okay?"

"Better than you," he quipped.

Rico picked up one of Leo's ice packs and handed it to me. "You aren't using this, are you, Leo?"

"Not anymore."

"What the hell did I miss?" Rico asked. "I was just down the hall."

When I finished the blow-by-blow, I handed him the empty syringe. "We need to dust it for prints, other than mine, and find out what was inside it."

"How'd you peg this Angie for an imposter?"

"Just a feeling. And a tattoo on her arm."

Rico raised an eyebrow. "A tattoo? Of what?"

I shrugged and shifted my gaze to the doorway. "Just a Voodoo thing I've seen before. When I tried to stop her, she whacked me over the head with Leo's bedpan. It could have been worse."

"How so?" Leo asked.

"It could've been full."

Jade Chen entered the room and I scowled. "Talk about full of shit."

Rico threw me a glare.

"What's going on?" Jade asked, kissing his cheek. "You scared me when you rushed off our call."

I stared a hole through Rico. Stupid, clueless Rico, the fish dangling on the end of Jade's hook. "Yeah, Rico. Tell us. What *is* going on?"

He couldn't even look me in the eye. He must have been thinking about his last conversation with Jade. The one where she totally emasculated him. I know I was.

"What're you doing here?" he asked Jade. "And how'd you get here so fast? We just hung up."

"Actually," Jade said, "I'm looking for Nighthawk, to get her thoughts on the Z-virus mutation. But that can keep. Who's in the bed?" Her eyes lit up. "Does he have anything to do with the virus mutation?"

"Wait a minute," I said. "How'd you know I was here? And don't say you're a reporter. You couldn't follow a clue if it left a trail of bread crumbs."

Jade flashed a triumphant grin. "Well, Nonnie told me, of course. She's a chatty little minx, isn't she?"

Sweet Jesus. What had Nonnie told her?

"Honey, you can't be here," Rico said, whisking Jade out of the room and closing the door behind them.

Her voice filtered in from the hall. "But why? Who's that in the bed? What aren't you telling me, baby?"

Baby? Now, there was a bell I couldn't unring.

While I waited for Rico to give her the boot, I leaned over Leo's sink and splashed some water on my face, instantly regretting it. My head began to spin.

I copped a squat on the edge of Leo's bed and heard a knock at the door. It was Weston.

"What are you doing here?" I growled.

"I'm here to watch Leo while you guys meet with Cap and the Director."

I looked at my watch. Three-ten. We needed to get a move on or we'd be late. The door opened again. I assumed it would be Rico coming back to collect me, but it was Frank, sweating like he'd just run the 800.

"She's gone," he said, panting. "I'll confiscate the security footage. Grab a still shot, see where she went. Maybe get a plate number from the parking lot, if we're lucky."

Weston eyed Frank. "Who the hell are you? Somebody want to tell me what's going on here?"

"Frank, Bill. Bill, Frank," I said, making introductions. "Frank, why don't you bring Bill up to speed on today's events?"

I slowly rose from the bed, steadying myself against the nightstand, and grinned at Leo.

"Gotta run, buddy. Rico and I have a meeting. But first, I need to rescue him from that two-legged black widow of his, before she eats him alive."

Leo eyeballed Weston and Frank. "You're not leaving me here with these schmoes? No offense, guys, but I don't know you from Adam. My own nurse just tried to kill me. My, whatchamacallit, *circle of trust*, is shriveling up faster than balls in ice water."

Leo turned and pointed at me. "Just so's you know, when I get sprung from here, screw *safe* houses. Fucking *unsafe* houses, that's what they should be called. So many dead bodies, you need a score card to keep up. No, I'm going home with *you*, Nighthawk. You and Nonnie. She's the only reason I'm still alive."

Weston shook his head. "She's a civilian, Leo. Bad ide—"

"My life. My rules. Either I go to Nighthawk's or the D.A. can kiss my testimony goodbye." Leo set his jaw and turned away, signaling the conversation had ended.

Freaking Leo. The smug bastard had us all over a barrel.

25

THE BEST LAID PLANS

R ico and I drove separately to the precinct. It was just as well. After I left the hospital room to rescue him from Jade, I found them playing tonsil hockey in the vending area. Rico might have been entitled to fall for that manipulating she-shrew, but the last thing I wanted was a front row seat to the main event. Riding to the meeting on my Harley gave me a chance to process the situation.

Rico knew how I felt about Jade and it didn't make any difference. I told myself it wasn't his fault that he was too bone-headed to realize she was a man-eating succubus. She had all the blood in his body going to his little head, instead of his big head.

No wonder he was a moron.

By the time we reached the precinct, I'd filed the memory of their kiss into my *Things I Can Never Unsee* file and locked the door. That's not to say the brain bitch wouldn't haul that sucker back out and throw it in my face, when the mood suited her. She's devious that way.

It was standing room only in Cap's office, with Jerry Armitage from the fire department, Craig Stovall from SWAT, along with Dickhead, Rico and me. The same crowd that had planned the warehouse raid. Good. I reached into my pocket and fingered Dom's phone, the perfect bait for catching our snitch.

Cap had called this debriefing meeting, but Dickhead let us know up front who was running the show. He sat on the corner of Cap's desk, sporting raccoon circles beneath his eyes and Einstein hair that defied gravity. Yesterday's five o'clock shadow had morphed into an eclipse, and he wore the same frumpy Fed clothes he'd worn the night before.

Although his voice was soft, his words were anything but. "I don't know what happened at that warehouse last night, but make no mistake. Before this meeting is over, I will. Six law enforcement officers, two SWAT team members and four federal agents died fighting those...those...creatures. That makes the investigation into their deaths a Federal operation. Now, I don't believe in Hoodoo, or Voodoo, or any of that *Serpent and the Rainbow* bullshit, so somebody's going to have to tell me what really happened in that warehouse—the science of it. How it's possible. Much as it galls me, I suspect that person is you, Nighthawk. So why don't you keep that tongue of yours in check and bring us all up to speed."

What a spoil sport.

"Fine. You want a crash course?" I asked, looking around the room. "Then listen up, guys. What I'm about to say may save your lives."

Their eyes instantly fixed on me. Good. Maybe they were listening.

"Carovescology is a newer bio-science dedicated to the study of zombieism. The biter population, which had remained fairly static for decades, has increased world-wide. And in the last several weeks, the increase has been unprecedented. In Cincinnati alone, the biter population is greater now than it was for the entirety of last year. The 'zombie' disease, Carovescitis, is spread by the Z-virus.

"Up until now, there were only two ways of contracting the Z-virus: being raised from the dead by a whisperer like me, or being bitten by a raised corpse—and then, only if the victim had a certain genetic marker that predisposed him to turning. That's why only some bite victims turned, while others got sick or died, depending on the severity of the bite. That's also how, over time, the zombie population remained relatively static.

"When Leo was bitten, he turned because he had that genetic marker. While we do not have a vaccine against the virus, we do have a drug named Nacarotoxin that can slow the onset of the disease. Leo is taking that drug, and hopefully, with its help, he will be able to testify before the grand jury as planned.

"If you take away nothing else from today's Zombie 101 class, remember this: There is no cure for Carovescitis. If you are bitten, the odds are you are either going to die or turn. When you shoot to kill a biter, or use hand-to-hand, whatever the situation calls for, you go for the brain. Center mass hits are useless. Those officers who died, died because they aimed for center mass. Are you clear on that?"

The somber faces staring back at me suggested I'd hit a nerve.

"Since Rico and I were put in charge of Leo Abruzzi's witness protection, we've encountered cases of the disease that spontaneously occurred in people who were not raised or bitten, namely Miriam, Cap's secretary, and BOLO Guy, her as yet unidentified murderer. Studies have proven that these changes were not caused by a biological mutation of the virus, which only leaves one option. The virus was manually manipulated. In other words, some lunatic out there is altering the virus to make it spread more easily."

I shot daggers toward Dickhead and went for broke. "You've

completely separated the Z-virus manipulation issue from Leo, but the truth is that zombies have been swarming around him ever since he arrived here. We need to find the connection between Leo and the zombies."

Rico joined in. "The mob's primary function is to make money. Leo was the Giordano Family's money launderer. Sometimes, the mob buries money in a pyramid of shell companies. Sometimes, they funnel it through legitimate businesses. And sometimes, they finance black-market operations. What if someone is borrowing money from the mob and paying off the loan with biters, in lieu of cash?"

Dickhead sprang to his feet. "That's ridiculous. Who the hell would want those walking puss-bags?"

"You're asking the wrong question," I said. "You should be asking who would want disposable soldiers to do their bidding. That brings us back to the mob and money laundering again, doesn't it, Director? When Leo was taken into custody, he had a set of books with him. I want those books. They should tell us who's into the mob for big money."

Dickhead dug his heels in. "Absolutely not. We're not corrupting the chain of evidence, so you can go off on some wild goose chase. Those books are in the custody of the prosecutor's office and that's where they'll stay."

"Jesus," I said, throwing up my hands. "Don't you see? Those books could tell us who we're after. Those *walking puss bags* were either directed to attack those agents, or they did it on their own."

That reminded me of my conversation earlier in the day with Dr. Christian.

"Let's find out which," I said. "Cap, can you pull up the autopsies of the biters we put down in the warehouse?"

Cap glanced at me, hesitating, like he was trying to figure out my angle, but he did as I asked.

He stared at the files on his computer. "What am I looking for?"

"Check to see if there were any earbuds or microphones in their ears, something that could be used to control or direct the biters."

"Surely, Doc would have pointed that out," Cap said, scanning the documents. "No. There's nothing like that mentioned."

Damn it. There went Dr. Christian's theory.

"Then what we have," I said, "is another proven change in the zombie virus strain. Those biters attacked us strategically, with no external guidance whatsoever. They demonstrated the ability to problem-solve. That's new and more frightening than you can even imagine."

Dickhead's eyes were hard to read, but I thought I saw a flicker of apprehension in them. He cleared his throat and stared at his hands, twisting his watch, as though he were debating his next move.

"All right then," he said. "From here on, we have a dual focus. The mob and the biters. Armitage, Stovall, thanks for your assistance. I don't think we'll be requiring your services from here on. If that changes, I'll be sure to let you know. The rest of you have your orders. And now," he said, "I'll turn the meeting over to Captain Dorsey."

Cap sat forward, a pinched expression on his face. "Now that we've reviewed our case for the Director's benefit, I'd like to take this meeting in another direction. I understand you were attacked in Leo's room today, Nighthawk. What happened?"

"A woman, posing as a floor nurse named Angie, tried to inject Leo with something. She and I scuffled. Luckily, I managed to empty the contents of the syringe on the floor. She got away, but we confiscated the syringe."

"I dusted it for prints," Rico added. "And sent it to the lab just before our meeting. We're hoping to identify the residue left inside it."

"That reminds me," I said. "Cap, can you please pull up one more group of autopsy photos for me? I want to look at the pics for BOLO Guy."

Dickhead sighed. "How could they possibly be germane to what happened today?"

I ignored him and waited for Cap to finish pulling up the photos. And there it was. BOLO Guy's bicep had the same tattoo as Angie, the skeleton with the top hat and cane, Baron Samedi. Whoever was pulling the strings behind the Z-virus manipulation had ties to Voodoo. That narrowed the list of possibles down considerably. Who was on that remaining list, was a discussion I wasn't ready to have just yet.

"So what?" Dickhead asked. "So, two perps, who may or may not be connected to each other, have the same tatt? It stands to reason that whoever tried to kill Leo today will try again. The guy has one foot in the grave, anyway. I say we get a deposition from him now. Just in case."

I jumped up, nearly knocking Rico over. "*No.* Leo is recovering. His condition is nearly back to what it was, before he was kidnapped. Just when *is* this grand jury going to convene anyway?"

Dickhead snarled. "When the prosecutor has sufficient evidence to make his case."

"I'll get Leo to the damned hearing. Don't you worry about that," I said, locking eyes with Dickhead. "In the meantime, when he's released from the hospital, he wants to go home with me."

Dickhead's face turned seven shades of ugly. "Not happening. I told you, he's under our watch now. You had your shot and you blew it."

I bristled. "Turns out, it doesn't matter what either one of us wants. Leo said he needed a score card to keep up with all the dead bodies in the so-called *safe* house. He said we either do it his way now, or, and I quote, 'the D.A. can kiss his testimony goodbye.' We can make it work, Director. You can send your guy, Ferris, over. He and Rico can alternate shifts with me."

Judging by the color of his face, Dickhead was ready to implode.

"What are you planning to do?" I asked, "Send Leo to a different safe house and wait for another leak? At least this way, it'll be easier for me to protect him and keep an eye on his condition."

Cap's door crept open and squirrelly Ottis wandered in as if on cue, looking for trash cans to empty. Before Cap could banish him, I picked up the can, rolled my eyes, and motioned for Ottis to come get it.

Then, I slid Dom's cell phone out of my pocket and down the side of my leg. With an anxious glance at Rico, I pressed redial. If my hunch was correct, it would ring right there in the room. In Ottis's pocket to be exact. Because I had pegged Ottis as our snitch, Snowflake.

But Ottis's pocket didn't ring. Maybe he wasn't the snitch. Or maybe he was the snitch, and he reported up the food chain to the real Snowflake.

Someone did answer the call, though. Down alongside my calf, I heard a muffled voice say, "Yo."

I'd heard that voice before, but I couldn't place it. I ended the call, watched Ottis mosey out the door, then turned my attention back to Dickhead, who had never stopped babbling.

"I'm tired of arguing with you, Nighthawk. You know what? You want him. You got him. But you can bet your ass a federal agent will be with you, at *all* times. It just so happens that the hospital called, right before I walked in here. They're releasing Leo tonight. I'll sign the order remanding him into your custody." His eyes fired liked coals. "You'd better pray he doesn't get whacked before that grand jury hearing."

Dickhead glanced at Cap. "I'll be assigning one more agent to Leo's detail, who can alternate shifts with Ferris, and another two to assist with your investigation into the warehouse biters. If we can identify them, or even your BOLO Guy, we might develop a lead. For now, you're in charge of the task force. Nighthawk, while you're babysitting, shake the bushes to find out what you can about the increase in cara...carato...whatever you called that disease. See if that ties in somehow to the warehouse biters or BOLO Guy."

Having given Cap and me our assignments, Dickhead stomped out of the room, signaling that at least his portion of the meeting had come to an end.

One by one, the attendees filed out in silence, past Ottis, who was still futzing around outside Cap's office.

Rico stepped through the doorway, pulled Ottis back into the room by his collar, and kicked one of the chairs in his direction.

"Have a seat, Ottis." Rico said. "We need to have a chat."

26

TROUBLE IN PARADISE

Ottis sagged onto the chair, with an uneasy smile, and swiveled his head when Rico pushed the door closed with his foot.

I strolled across the room and came to a stop behind Ottis, resting my fingertips on his shoulders.

He flinched and grabbed the arms of his chair, squeezing them so hard, his knuckles turned white.

Cap glanced from me to Rico, Rico to Ottis, and then back to me. "Fine. I'll bite. Why is Ottis back in here?"

I held up Dom's phone and smiled. "Well, look what we've got here."

"It's a phone, Nighthawk." Cap leaned back in his chair with a sigh.

"But not just any phone. It belonged to Dom, the dead mob enforcer, with the ugly yellow sport coat at the warehouse. I... relieved...him of it at the scene."

"You stole evidence."

"Potatoes, *patahtos.*"

"Other than you annihilating the chain of evidence, why do I care about this phone?"

"Remember when I was hanging off the ledge? This Dom guy's standing below me, yacking on his phone, saying somebody named Snowflake called and ratted us out." I swung my eyes to Ottis.

Cap rubbed his face, then stared at me over the top his hands. "You think Ottis is Snowflake?"

Ottis's jaw dropped. "Huh?"

"Really?" Cap asked, inspecting Ottis as if he were some alien being. "He doesn't look like a snitch."

"A what?" Ottis's eyebrows squished together, giving him that *lost ball in high grass* look.

"Quiet," I said, smacking the back of his head. "No one asked you."

Cap swept his hand in my direction. "Get to the point, Nighthawk."

"While we were in the meeting a few minutes ago, I pressed redial on Dom's phone. The same group of people from today's meeting were present when we planned the warehouse raid, including Spuds McSquirrel here, when he coincidentally wandered in for your trash can."

Ottis's right leg shimmied. "Bu...but that's m-my job."

"I don't get it," Cap said. "I didn't hear a phone ring."

"That's because it didn't ring here," I said. "But it did ring somewhere. A man answered. I'm not sure who, but the voice sounded familiar."

I moved out from behind Ottis and resumed my seat across from Cap. "Think about it, sir. Even if McSquirrel here isn't Snowflake, he could still be feeding intel to a handler."

Ottis blinked. "Feeding...*what?*" Sweat poured from his temples. "I-I'm not feeding a-anything. Am I in t-trouble?" His eyes grew moist. "Can I g-go back to work n-now? I don't like this."

Cap frowned and shook his head. "This is thin, even for you, Nighthawk."

I had to admit, one look at the sniveling squirrel told me my theory sucked rocks. He didn't have the guts, or the brains, to be a stool pigeon. Ottis couldn't find his way out of a paper bag without a map.

I'd scared the crap out of a simple guy, doing his simple job. And now, I felt like a shitheel. And Little Allie, who should have stopped me in the first place, decided to get all high and mighty, making me feel worse. The brain bitch needed to either stay tuned in or butt out. Her ADD was killing me.

"Sorry about the head slap, Ottis," I mumbled. "My mistake."

Cap walked around his desk and lifted Ottis out of his chair. "You haven't done anything wrong. Go on back to work, now. Just one more thing before you go. Don't forget. When you see my door closed, always knock from now on before you come in. Okay?"

Ottis threw me a withering glance. "No problem."

He slunk out the office, side-eying me every inch of the way.

Cap closed the door behind him, then turned back to me and asked, "Have you lost your mind?"

I explained that Ottis was conveniently present at all the strategic moments of the case, but my words fell on deaf ears.

Cap shooed Rico and me out of his office, with instructions to pick up Leo and take him back to my place.

Rico pulled me out of Cap's door, even as I continued to plead. "Somebody answered that phone, damn it. And when I figure out who, I'll have our snitch."

Cap yelled from his office, "Be sure to log that phone into evidence."

"Will do," I called, then I grinned at Rico and whispered, "Right after we use it to find our snitch."

"Jesus," he sighed, leading me out of the precinct doors. "You'll get me fired, yet."

I dropped my Harley off at the house and then Rico drove us to the hospital to pick up Leo.

Weston grinned like a fool, the minute we walked down the hallway.

Rico stopped outside Leo's door, to let Weston know he'd been allocated to the unit responsible for identifying the warehouse biters and BOLO Guy.

I walked on past them and into the room, but I couldn't help overhearing Weston's sigh of relief, and something about Leo being a royal pain in the ass.

Leo couldn't wait to share his feelings, either. "What's with that Weston guy? He's like a mannequin, only stupider, and with no sense of humor."

After we gathered Leo's things, a nurse rolled him to the front door in a wheelchair, while he yammered on, a mile a minute, thrilled to be "busting out of this joint."

Weston parted ways with us at the curb and strolled across the parking lot, a lightness in his step, presumably due to being "Leo-free."

The ride home featured Leo unplugged. I was surprised at how much I'd missed that.

We reached my house, and hadn't even made it out of Rico's car, when Nonnie flew through the screen door, arms open wide, homing in on Leo like a B-52. I was afraid she'd knock him over, but he latched onto her and gave her a big smooch on the lips.

"I have lasagna for you," Nonnie said, beaming. "And some rugelach for dessert. The guest bed is made up for you, too. Come, come," she said, hustling him into the house.

The guest bed? I didn't have a guest bed.

And while I'd worried about Headbutt's reaction to Leo,

given that he had the Z-virus, Headbutt escorted him up the driveway, wagging his tail stub, treating him like his new best friend. Even Kulu was on her best behavior, greeting Leo at the door with, "*Buongiorno*, Leo."

Leo wandered in and gawked at the pictures of my family, hanging willy-nilly on the walls.

"Nighthawk," he said, his head on a swivel. "Your mother... and father? I'll be damned."

Good Lord. Had the man thought I'd been hatched?

We sat at the kitchen table and ate lasagna until it came out of our ears, smiling and laughing, Leo's arrival feeling like a homecoming of sorts. Leo's color was good, even if the usual glint hadn't returned to his eyes. Once his belly was full, he yawned, clearly ready for a nap. Nonnie led him down the hall-way, to the bedroom across from mine. Until now, I'd always referred to that room as *The Arsenal*. And the door to the arsenal had been locked.

The last time I'd been in my house, only a day or so earlier, there was no bed in that room. I threw a side-long glance at Nonnie, which she completely ignored, then I moved to the doorway, almost afraid to look inside.

I peeked through my fingers and stifled a gasp. *Good God. What had she done with my napalm?*

The room now hosted a double-bed, complete with sheets, pillows and comforter, as well as a night table and matching dresser. This was not my stuff, but one look at Nonnie's face told me who it belonged to. She was happy and feeling needed; Leo was relaxed and comfortable.

On the far side of the room, a padlocked metal cabinet took up most of one wall. Nonnie stepped beside me and forked over the key. I unlocked it and peeked inside. She had managed to move all my weapons and munitions into the cabinet, without blowing my house to bits. A woman of many surprises, our Nonnie.

While Leo slept, Nonnie cleaned our lunch mess and started making veal scallopini for dinner. If I continued to eat like this, I wouldn't be able to outrun an eighty-year-old corpsicle. Headbutt, who followed Nonnie around like she had a pork chop tied to her neck, had already put on a few pounds.

Rico and I excused ourselves and walked outside to analyze the security of my house. Or lack thereof.

"Other than locks on the doors and windows, I got nothing," I said. "There isn't a soul in this neighborhood who would even think about screwing with me. And when it comes to random riff-raff, Headbutt doesn't take any prisoners."

But it was different this time. It wasn't just my life at stake. We weren't talking about screwball kids with attitudes anymore. Gangsters and biters boosted the security needs up a notch. Motion sensor lights seemed reasonable, as did an alarm system. Sweet. I'd be sending that bill to the D.A.'s office.

We'd gone back inside and were reviewing home security systems on my laptop, when someone rang the doorbell. Headbutt growled and jumped up and down in front of the door, his usual greeting. I looked through the peephole and sighed. Even on the best of days, trouble eventually found me. Today's trouble took the shape of Jade Chen.

I opened the door and summoned every ounce of control I had left inside. "What the hell are you doing here?"

Jade smiled sweetly and handed me the newspaper from my driveway. "I come in peace. No microphones, no cameraman. Just me. May I come in?"

I stepped aside and let her pass. "I'll let Rico know you're here."

"Actually, it's you I want to talk to," she said, sitting on the couch.

Rico walked into the room and she smiled.

His eyes narrowed. "What's up, Jade?"

"I know it's early, and you're supposed to pick me up at seven, but I really stopped by to see Allie."

Rico's eyes darted back and forth between Jade and me, making what was already an awkward moment downright uncomfortable.

As if that weren't bad enough, Leo, apparently awakened by the doorbell, appeared in the hallway, pointed his finger at Jade, and said, "I know you! You're the news broad who gives Nighthawk shit all the time. Cadaver diver! Ha! Good one. You're sharp. And you've got some big-ass, hangy-down things. Two thumbs up, *chica*."

I scowled at Leo. "Go back to your room, *Uncle David*. This is a private conversation."

"No. Wait," Jade said. "Allie, I know who he is. He's a mob accountant named Leo Abruzzi, who's turning state's evidence against the Giordano Family."

Nonnie rounded the kitchen doorway and burned holes through Jade with her eyes.

I snapped my head toward Rico, seconds from making him wish he'd never been born, when Jade jumped up and stood between us. "I know what you think. But Rico didn't tell me anything. I swear."

I rolled my eyes. "Please. Don't insult my intelligence."

"Oh, c'mon, Nighthawk," Jade said. "Don't be so naive. Grand juries aren't the secrets you think they are, when you have the right sources. There's something else I wanted to talk to you about tonight. Something only you can help me with. The wires are full of stories about an increase in zombie activity and biters that seem to be evolving. I want to know more about that."

She took a deep breath. "No, actually, I *need* to know more about that. One thing's for sure. If Leo's here, and you're here, those two things have to be related. And that's news." She paused and lifted her chin. "It's dark. It's gritty. And I want in on the ground floor. I want to write an exposé on the Z-virus."

Oh no, she did not just say that.

I laughed, in spite of myself. "And because we're such close, personal friends, you thought I'd buy into this ridiculous load of crap."

"Oh, hell no. That ship's sailed. But I'll run my copy by you before I air it, to be sure I'm not giving away any secrets. Agreed?"

"No way, Jade." I yanked the front door back open. "You'd be in so far over your head, you'd never come up for air again. It's time you leave now. And if one word of this gets out, I'm coming for you. Personally. You can count on it. A man's life is at stake."

Jade looked down and bit her lip. "I know in the past I've been...harsh. But to be fair, so have you. I've thought...what you do...is cruel. I didn't understand it. I'm not sure I do now, but I want to. And I want the public to understand it, too. No more jibes, no more insults. I promise. And not a word will go to print, until you say the word. Deal?"

I held the door open and glared at her.

"No," I said. "No deal. And I meant what I said. If one word of this gets out, there isn't a corner of the world where you can hide, where I won't find you."

Jade nodded and walked slowly to the door, then turned to me and said, "I'm going to do this with or without your help, Nighthawk. With, would make it a whole lot easier."

I pushed the door closed behind her and stared accusingly at Rico.

He didn't look away. "You know me better than that," was all he said.

Leo wandered into the kitchen with Nonnie, probably trying to stay out of my path. The next hour passed in awkward silence, as Rico cleaned his gun and I scanned the internet for security systems.

The doorbell rang again at six o'clock. Thank God, Ferris was here for the start of his shift.

Without so much as a glance at me, Rico let him in, squeezed past him, and slammed the door on his way out.

"Whew," Ferris said. "Trouble in paradise?"

27

DID SOMEONE SAY DARK AND GRITTY?

The smell of Nonnie's scallopini quickly derailed Ferris's curiosity about the spat between me and Rico. Either that, or he decided I'd fill him in on whatever he needed to know. Smart cookie, that Ferris.

"Something smells good," he said. "Don't tell me you're domestic, Nighthawk. That would completely shatter my image of you."

"Not a chance. Nonnie's the chef," I said, pointing to my chief cook and bottle washer, as she rounded the kitchen corner.

"Ah! You like? You must be Ferris. I, Nonnie Nussbaum," she said, grabbing both his hands. "Miss Allie's assistant. I cook the scallopini. Dinner almost ready."

Assistant? Suddenly, she had a title.

Ferris took a deep sniff and sighed. "Smells amazing, Mrs. Nussbaum. Can't wait."

Nonnie, head held high, strutted back into the kitchen and shooed Leo out from under her feet, into the living room with Ferris and me.

Still smarting from my spat with Rico, I let the two of them chatter on about finance, while I sulked in the corner.

"You're a young guy," I heard Leo say. "Don't be afraid of global funds. They'll pay off over time."

My mind began to drift. And damned if the brain bitch didn't hijack the opportunity to harangue me.

Rico's a damn good partner. He'd never put Leo at risk. What were you thinking?

Although no one would have ever guessed it, I was capable of being a bit...rash...sometimes. Was it possible that Jade was a better reporter than I gave her credit for? Could she have gotten plum lucky and stumbled into this mess, all on her lonesome?

In the end, it didn't matter. I knew inside that Rico hadn't breached confidentiality, just like I knew it would be my responsibility to keep Jade's surgically-altered, upturned nose out of harm's way. Refusing to help her with the exposé had been the right move.

I relaxed a bit during dinner as the mood lightened. And when Leo asked Ferris about his background, his answer intrigued me.

"Mostly military," he said. "I did a couple of tours in Afghanistan, explosive ordnance detail. Got recruited by the FBI, not long after I came home. That's been five years, now."

I pictured Ferris's sandy hair, caked with mud, steely blue eyes peering out from above several day's growth, his six-foot-four frame decked out in combat fatigues, massive football player hands, strong but dexterous. What would they feel like on my...

"Isn't that right, Nighthawk?" Leo asked.

"Sorry. What?"

Leo shoved the last forkful of veal into his mouth. "I was telling Ferris here, you and De Palma, you're like oil and vinegar. Polar opposites. It's a wonder one of you ain't dead yet."

"We've kept you alive so far, haven't we?" I said, carrying my plate to the sink.

Ferris pushed his chair back and followed me. "I'll do the dishes, Mrs. Nussbaum, and Miss Allie here will help me. Sit down and relax."

The guy was bucking for sainthood. Nonnie and Leo kibitzed in the living room, while Ferris washed and I, shamed into action, dried.

Ferris's blue eyes twinkled as he sidled up alongside me. "I'm not much for doing dishes, but I was running out of ways to get you alone, *Miss Allie*."

Something that resembled a giggle bubbled inside me. I squelched it before it escaped. He might have been tall, blonde and ripped, but that didn't give him the right to mess with me.

"You don't remember me, do you?" I asked.

"The National Law Enforcement Training Center. Hand-to-hand combat training. Two, no, three years ago."

"Impressive."

"I thought you were. But I would have laid bank you didn't notice me. You were all business."

"Oh, I noticed you."

"Yeah? Is that good or bad?"

I turned away, red-faced, trying to hide a smile. "Just wash the dishes."

He scrubbed a plate, dunked it into the rinse water, and then held me captive with his baby blues. "Seriously, Allie. You were amazing. You didn't have military training, you weren't a Fed, or even an officer. You were a freakin' zombie hunter, with some hella impressive skills. The way you wiped the floor with the instructor, when he thought he had you dead to rights. How hot was that? I will never forget the look on his face. Five years with the FBI and pulling this detail...I gotta say, it's the first time I've actually looked forward to babysitting a witness."

Even Little Allie was speechless.

I grabbed for the plate he'd been washing. Our fingers touched. He didn't pull away, and neither did I.

"Okay, Ferris, I'm calling rank on the plate."

"Call me, Sean," he said, smiling as he released the plate.

"Other officers call you Ferris," I said, drying.

"They aren't as pretty as you."

I laughed. "They damn sure aren't as pretty as you, either." Him and his impossibly blue eyes. "You can call me Allie. Sometimes. If you use it judiciously. And not in public."

"Wouldn't dream of it," he grinned. "I like the name Allie. It suits you. It's tough, like you, but it's also...fun."

Was he liking me, as much as I was liking him, right now? Or was this all in my imagination? Was he just a nice guy, who was trying to find common ground with the person he was assigned to spend a shitload of time with? Or was he feeling the same sparks I was?

I could feel him leaning toward me, just slightly. It made me wonder if he was about to tell me one whopper of a secret, or if the potential for more...maybe even something like a kiss...was lurking just around the corner...

Headbutt snapped to attention, peaked his ears, and uttered a low growl, ruining the moment.

Seconds later, the doorbell rang. Director Dickhead stood on the other side of the peephole. So much for sparks.

I opened the door, and he barged past me into the house. Headbutt, apparently unhappy with the Director's alpha behavior, barked, promptly hiked his leg, and doused the Director's shoe.

Ferris, sporting one hell of a poker face, pretended not to notice and moved beside me.

"Jesus," Dickhead said, shaking his foot. "Teach that dog some manners."

"Sorry, Director." I took Headbutt by his collar. "Come on in. We're just finishing up dinner."

Nonnie offered the Director some scallopini, but he declined.

He crossed the room and introduced himself to Leo. The only other time they'd seen each other, Leo was being carried out of the warehouse on a gurney, semi-comatose.

"You folks carry on with your evening," Dickhead said, nodding at Nonnie and me. "I'd like to talk to Agent Ferris for a bit. He'll be right back."

When the Director ushered Ferris out the door, Nonnie moved to start a new pot of coffee. For the first time that day, Leo and I had a few minutes alone together.

I plopped beside him on the couch, with an agenda of my own. "Something's been gnawing at me for a while now, Leo."

He cocked an eyebrow and waited for me to continue.

"When you turned yourself in, you gave over the mob's books, right?"

Leo nodded once, eyeing me, no doubt wondering where this conversation was going.

"Smart guys always have a second set of books. You know—the dummy books to protect their clientele. And the real books. And the really smart guys, like you, keep a third set. Maybe a duplicate of the books you turned in." I looked him dead in the eye. "Leo, where's your set of the books?"

He squirmed. "I don't have any books. I turned them in. Why the hell would I keep a set? What would I use them for?"

"You tell me. Insurance, maybe?"

"Honest. I swear. I don't got any books."

I let out a sigh. "'Fess up, Buddy. There's been a trail of zushi a mile wide, following you ever since you got here. The Mob's after you because of what's in those books. Somehow, some way, whatever is in them has to be connected to the zombie influx."

I paused, giving him time to reconsider, but his stony stare signaled we were at an impasse. Time for a different angle.

"Leo, has it ever occurred to you that your being bitten wasn't some random, cosmic joke? That maybe you were targeted? If I can look at the books, maybe I can figure this whole mess out."

Leo's eyes turned dark. "I told you, I was in the wrong place at the wrong time. *Cosmic joke?* You might consider me getting bit a joke, but I sure as hell don't. For the last time, I don't have any damn books. Period. Now let it drop or I'm going to bed."

I had no doubt that Leo could lie with the best of them. And I was sure he was lying to me. But why? Was he protecting someone?

Short of beating it out of him, my only option was to try to get him to open up. But that would come another day. His drawn face and bloodshot eyes told me he'd had enough. I changed the subject and turned on the TV.

"Guess what I taped last night?" I said. "*Dancing with the Stars.* I've taped every episode this season. I never know when I'll get the chance to sit down and watch it."

As we settled back on the couch, Ferris returned alone from his conversation with Dickhead, and Nonnie carried in the fresh pot of coffee.

She kissed Leo on the cheek. "Is beauty parlor night. Wash and set," she said, primping her blue-tinged hair. "*Buonanotte, Leo.*"

He smiled and kissed the back of her hand. "*Grazie, signora dolce.*"

I watched her walk across the yard, and then turned to Ferris and asked, "What did Dickhead want?"

"Micromanaging. Making sure I was here and that Leo was secure. He also told me that my replacement at midnight is Andy Capple." Ferris chuckled. "Andy's one of the old guard. He'll enjoy Nonnie's cooking, just don't count on him hopping over any fences to chase bad guys."

Sedentary security, courtesy of Dickhead. I might have known.

Ferris flopped beside me on the couch and sat quietly, while Leo and I, catty bastards that we were, took potshots at the *Dancing With the Stars* judges.

"That Len," Leo said, waving off the TV. "He's so full of shit. Gives no points for originality."

Leo sat up straight and tilted his nose in the air, mimicking Goodman. "*With all that gyrating, I didn't see the basic steps. You've got to include the basic steps.*' Ah, blow me, you old fart. Get out of the forties." Leo's eyes lit up as he leaned forward, hands on his knees. "Nighthawk, one of these nights, I'm gonna take you dancing. Show you how it's really done."

I damn near spit out my coffee.

"Thanks for the invite," I said, looking down at the steel-toed, zombie-stompers on my feet, "But I don't even own a pair of heels, let alone dancing shoes. Me doing the paso doble in these clodhoppers? There's a disturbing visual."

Ferris busted his gut laughing.

Leo harrumphed and rolled his eyes. "Slacker. How you ever gonna learn ballroom, without dancing shoes? You lack commitment, Nighthawk. That's the problem."

By ten o'clock, the stars were finished hoofing it. Leo looked relaxed and content, but tired. He plodded down the hallway to go to sleep, leaving me and Ferris to pass the time alone.

Not much of a small talker, I wasn't sure how comfortable I'd be, waiting for the minutes to pass until the changing of the guard at midnight. Something else to look forward to. Another stranger in my house.

But Ferris seemed at ease, and chatted like we'd known each other forever. We fell into an easy rhythm, complete with natural breaks in our conversation that didn't need to be filled. We were...sympatico. That boded well.

I asked him what it was like working bomb disposal and before he could answer, the doorbell rang again.

What the hell? It was after eleven o'clock.

Ferris pulled his gun and peeked out, from behind the blinds on the living room window. "It's De Palma. And he's with that news chick from Channel Ten."

"Yeah. They're...dating." The last word scratched like sandpaper on the way out.

I opened the door, loaded for bear, thinking Jade had returned to take me on for round two of the exposé argument. But one look at them told me this wasn't a social call.

Rico's face and shirt were bloody. Jade's dress, wet and torn, clung to her legs, and her long black hair hung in tangled strands down her back.

"Lock the door behind us. We've got a situation," Rico announced, as he hustled Jade inside. "We were leaving Fountain Square, and a couple of biters popped out from between parked cars."

He stared at me incredulously. "Nighthawk, they came right at me. They actually plowed through a group of people to get to me. People scrambled through the street, pushing and shoving, trying to get away. Absolute chaos."

"I got knocked into the fountain," Jade whined. "Look at my dress."

"Wow. What a shame," I deadpanned.

"Let me grab you a towel," Ferris said, shooting me a disapproving grin, as he headed toward the bathroom.

Rico wiped his face with his hand and it came away bloody. "The bastards caught me by surprise. One of them knocked me flat and I smacked my eye into somebody's side view mirror on the way down. I pulled my backup piece from my ankle holster and nailed them both, before they could do any real damage."

My heart went into overdrive. "You're sure? No bites, no scratches?"

He walked to my freezer, pulled out a bag of frozen corn and held it to his eye. "No. I'm fine. But this shit's getting real, fast."

Rico was right. Things were escalating, but whoever was pulling the strings knew Rico could handle a couple of rotters. If the bastard had wanted Rico dead, he would have killed him. This had all the markings of a warning shot over the bow. *My bow.*

Fine, then, I thought. *Come and get me, asshole. I'm right here.*

Ferris returned with a bath towel and handed it to Jade. The pretty little princess dried herself off, shaking and sniffling, like the world's biggest wussy.

Little Allie couldn't have shut my mouth with super glue.

"So, Jade," I said with a smirk. "How good's that biter exposé looking now?"

She fixed me with a smoldering stare. "I'm more determined than ever. Just try to stop me."

Damned if that chick wasn't a freaking albatross around my neck.

28

EENY, MEENY, MINY, MOE

R ico checked the lock on the kitchen door and switched on the backyard light.

"These biters," he said, as he tried the window over the sink. "They were freshies. And not just freshies, they were suits. You know? Like if they hadn't been dead, they could have passed for Feds. Dress shirts, jackets, ties."

"Did they have tatts?" I asked.

Rico squinted at me from behind the frozen corn. "I didn't notice any, but then, I was a little busy."

Jade wanted to shower, so I showed her to the bathroom and gave her fresh towels and a clean set of clothes.

Leo wandered out of his bedroom, eyes blinking against the bright hall light. "What's going on out here? You trying to wake the dead?"

"Sorry," I said. "No worries, Leo. Go on back to bed."

He blew me off and padded barefoot down the hallway to the living room, stopping short at the sight of Rico, sporting the bag of corn over his eye.

"What the hell happened to you?" Leo asked.

Leo didn't need to hear about the night's attack. He had

enough problems of his own. I tried to signal Rico, but he ran his mouth before I could stop him.

"Some biters blitzed me tonight, while I was out with Jade."

Leo's mouth gaped. "And all you got was a black eye? I'd say you got off lucky. What about your hotsy-totsy news chick?"

"She's fine. Just taking a shower and getting cleaned up."

Despite the fact that it was closing in on midnight, I put on another pot of coffee. The four of us sat at my kitchen table, throwing around theories.

Rico touched his cheek and winced. "Obviously, this was a targeted attack. We must be getting close to something. From now on, boys and girls, best have eyes in the back of your heads." He held the bag of corn against his face. "But why come at me? No offense, Nighthawk, but I would think you'd be the target of choice."

Now there was a fun thought. Maybe tonight, Rico had simply been a target of convenience, a way to toy with me. Maybe I had a big old bullseye on my butt.

But the little brain bitch with the mega-mouth suggested otherwise.

"What if," I asked Rico, "they weren't targeting you—or me?"

The four of us slowly eyed each other.

"Well, don't look at me," Leo burst out. "I'm already bit."

Rico cast me a skeptical eye. "Say that again?"

"What if they were after Nancy Newshound there?"

I swept my eyes toward wet-headed Jade, who had walked into the kitchen dressed in a pair of my boy shorts and a tee that read *Queen of the Damned*.

"Time to come clean, Jade," I said. "Who have you been interviewing for your zombie exposé?"

She leaned against the wall and struck a pose, as if playing to the camera. "My sources."

"What sources?" I was milliseconds from mauling the smirk off her face.

"You know I can't tell you that, Nighthawk. What kind of self-respecting journalist would I be, if I divulged my sources?"

And just like that, the gloves came off. "You might be the living kind, unless I get tired of your narcissistic, entitled little—"

Rico cut me off. "Jade, if you won't give up their names, at least tell us what kind of sources they are. Are they specialists of some sort? Scientists? Other whisperers? Government officials? What kind, baby. Just tell us that much."

"I went a completely different route," she said. "A...darker route. And that's all I'm going to say."

Darker. The one word I didn't want to hear coming out of her mouth. I knew darker. *Darker* could get her, and everyone around her, killed, including me. Especially me.

I've got a thing about being thrown into holes dug by other people. I don't like it. If not for Little Allie and Rico, I'd have said to hell with it, and pulled the names of the sources out through her nose, right then and there.

Instead, I pointed at Rico and said, "She's got her head so far up her ass, she can see her belly button. You'd better talk some sense into her, before it's too late."

Rico got up and poured himself another cup of coffee. "We've taken this subject as far as we can tonight. Somebody pick another topic."

"Fine," I said, with more 'tude than I'd intended. I swiveled my chair toward Jade. "There's a hair dryer under the sink in the bathroom. Help yourself."

She flashed me a thumbs up and disappeared down the hallway, giving me a chance to discuss the investigation without worrying that she'd blast it across the evening news. Still, I waited until I heard her turn it on. Couldn't be too careful, with a sneaky-ass bitch like Jade in the house.

"How's Weston coming along with identifying the ware-house biters?"

Rico leaned back against the counter and crossed his arms. "So far, they're coming up empty. I called him tonight, before I picked up Jade. They're still digging, though. Director Horton will have their asses, and mine, if they don't come up with something soon."

He carried his coffee to the table, sat in his chair, and asked me, "Have you had any more thoughts on the identity of the snitch?"

That was the question of the week. I was so sure it had been Ottis. It almost had to have been.

"No," I said. "But we've still got Dom's phone. My plan will work. I just need to hit redial at the right time. The snitch's phone will ring and we'll have him."

I was glad Rico didn't ask how I'd know when the right time came along. I was kind of hoping the brain bitch would clue me in at the operative moment.

Midnight arrived and so did Andy Capple. I could see what Ferris meant about not expecting the guy to scale any walls. He looked to be in his mid-50s, maybe 6'2", 280 lbs. and balding. With his round-frame glasses, he could have been a computer nerd. Or a really big minion.

I offered him some coffee, but he had a Coke slurpee with him. An instant pang hammered in my heart. I missed my nightly Jack Daniel's slushies.

Ferris introduced Capple around, and then asked him, "So, how much do you know about the case?"

Capple looked at Jade, questioningly, and Rico asked her to wait in the car.

"No way," she said.

"Pick somewhere," I said. "The grown-ups need to talk."

She glared at me. "Fine. I'll go fix my make-up."

She stomped down the hall to the bathroom, slamming the door shut behind her.

Capple walked with us back to the kitchen, took off his jacket and draped it over the back of a chair, revealing the biggest shoulder holster I'd ever seen. He carried a Glock. Good gun. He automatically got bonus points for that—assuming he could use it.

"So, back to the case..." I said.

He pushed his glasses up his nose and smiled. "I don't know much. I know Leo will be testifying before the grand jury and I'm filling in on babysitting detail. That's about it."

Ferris covered the lay of the land, and reviewed the exits and entrances, then he opened the cabinet door next to the refrigerator and pulled out a syringe.

He held it up in front of Capple's coke-bottle lenses. "Leo was bitten by a deadhead a while back. This is his medicine. He needs to take it every day—and any time he has a seizure, in-between doses. If, for some reason, Nighthawk isn't around and that happens, you'll need to know where it is. Small seizure, it goes in the thigh. Big seizure, it goes straight into the heart."

Capple's eyes grew wide and he asked, "He's not...contagious...is he?"

Leo flinched. So did I. There went those bonus points.

"No. No, he isn't," Ferris said, walking Capple back into the living room.

Ferris continued to talk, his voice fading as he rounded the corner. "There are a few things you need to know."

I couldn't hear what more he said, but I was sure it had to do with the ins and outs of contracting the virus—and not talking about Leo like he wasn't in the room.

I glanced over at Rico and we both grinned. I didn't have to be a mind reader to know that we were thinking the same thing. Ferris was stepping up. He hadn't known this zombie shit coming into this case, but he'd been a damn quick study and he always treated Leo with respect.

Rico and Ferris? They were two of the good guys.

Capple returned to the kitchen, a slight flush on his cheeks. The kind of flush that comes from getting dressed down.

He made a point of smiling at Leo, nodding his head, and saying, "Nice to meet you, man. You let me know if you need anything. Okay?"

Leo rose from his chair and gave him a quick nod, then walked past him, clapping him on the shoulder as he passed by. "You too, Capple. I'm going back to sleep now. Later."

Rico fished Jade out of the bathroom, and announced they were calling it a night.

"Hang on a minute," I said, running back into the bathroom.

I grabbed Jade's dirty dress off the floor and shoved it into a plastic trash bag. Hey, I don't even do my own laundry, I certainly wasn't going to do hers. And neither was Nonnie.

I closed the door behind them and then turned to Capple, stifling a yawn.

"There's still some coffee in the pot, if you want some later. I'm headed off to bed. Call me if you need me."

I grabbed Hawk out of my shoulder holster and carried him into the bedroom with me. Nothing like a cold, hard piece of steel to keep you warm at night.

Although, as I drifted off to sleep, a wistful smile on my face, I pictured a couple of hot officers who could crank up my thermostat nicely.

29

BY THE LIGHT OF THE SILVERY MOON

At 2:00 a.m., my eyes flew open. Dogs barking outside. Headbutt, who had been curled at the foot of my bed, now stood at the window, eyes unblinking, ears peaked. I lay still, listening.

Another sound.

Thump... Thump... *Crash.* The garbage cans?

Damn raccoons.

A growl thrummed in Headbutt's throat.

Nonnie's porch light switched on and shone against my bedroom wall.

I climbed out of bed and peered out the window to find a full moon, not a cloud in the sky. Things looked right enough. But Little Allie wasn't convinced.

A few minutes later the sound came again. Thump... Thump... *Thud.*

What the hell?

Something, or someone, was in my backyard.

I threw on my Wonder Woman robe, shoved my phone into the pocket, then grabbed Hawk from the nightstand.

Stepping softly down the hallway, I nearly collided with Capple, as he rounded the living room wall.

"Shit," he hissed, lowering his weapon.

Footsteps padded out from the darkness in the hall behind me. "What is it with this neighborhood? Don't you people *ever* sleep?"

"Damn it, Leo," I whispered. "Go back to your room, lock the door, and don't come out until I tell you."

Leo's eyes grew wide at the sight of Hawk in my hand. He did a 360 and retraced his steps down the hall, feeling his way along the wall. His door closed softly, followed by an audible *click,* as the lock tumbled into place.

I turned to Capple and said, "You take the front yard. I'll take the back."

Capple nodded and disappeared into the living room, while I crept into the kitchen. The glow from Nonnie's porch light filtered in through the curtains on the back door, illuminating not only the ugliest linoleum floor ever, but the shadow of the person standing outside my door.

I darted forward, and took cover beside the refrigerator.

Then Nonnie's unmistakable voice blared through the door.

"Miss Allie?" she said, banging on the door. "Someone out back. *Let me in.*"

I raced across the kitchen, unlocked the door, and threw it wide.

"Come here," I said, pulling her inside.

Headbutt howled and scooted past me, then tore, bulldog-style, across the backyard. Only one thing could make him move like that.

Nonnie wrenched her arm loose from my hand, pushed through the door, and scrambled after Headbutt.

I flipped on the backyard floodlight, and sprinted after them both, pulling out my phone and speed dialing Rico.

"Get over here, now," I yelled. "Ferris, too! Code... Oh, what the hell. We got biters!"

Headbutt bayed furiously and disappeared behind the tool shed, with Nonnie trailing, maybe twenty yards back.

Next came the sounds of breaking glass and Headbutt's frenzied snarls.

I raced past Nonnie, yelling, *"Get back inside, now."*

After rounding the corner of the tool shed, the source of the commotion came into view, and I skidded to a halt. A dead-head, of the corpsicle variety, flailed helplessly, impaled on a jagged spike of glass rising up from the broken window frame.

Despite my order for Nonnie to return to the house, she had followed me, wringing her hands, sobbing hysterically. One look at the corpsicle found her crossing herself and slowly backing away.

Leo, the last to arrive, put his hands on his knees and gasped for air. Nonnie launched herself forward and wrapped her arms around him, nearly tackling him in the process.

Those two would be the death of me yet.

"Damn it, Leo. I told you to stay in your room."

Headbutt sunk his teeth, gum-deep, into the rotter's leg and shook it like a rag doll.

The biter writhed against the serrated edges of the glass, shearing off bits of zushi that splattered like chum bombs on top of Headbutt.

Every time that crazy dog jerked his head, flesh flayed off the rotter's leg in long wet strips, exposing degloved muscles that glistened like fish bellies in the moonlight.

I leveled Hawk and took aim, but had second thoughts. It was the middle of the night. The homeowners association already hated me. One more hundred-dollar fine and I'd have moths flying out of my pockets.

So, I pulled open the door to the tool shed, reached in, and wrapped my fingers around the first object I came to—a hoe.

I owned a hoe?

What the hell, the business end of that thing would shred a biter into coleslaw faster than a Veg-O-Matic. I turned, raised the hoe high, and whaled it down on the deadhead's skull.

Brains and bone splattered like blowback from a gunshot. The biter's body sank deeper into the jagged glass and severed at the ribcage, leaving its top half still impaled on the glass, leaking liquid decomp on two generations of worthless shit shoved inside the shed. Its bottom half slid slowly down the shed's vinyl exterior, painting it, and my yard, zushi red.

Damn it. A middle of the night, make-it-go-away-before-dawn kind of clean-up. Jimmy at Splatz would charge me an arm and a leg for this mess. So to speak.

Thoughts of the clean-up cost disappeared when Nonnie screamed on the far side of the shed.

I tore around the corner and found her backed up against the siding, another corpsicle gnashing its teeth, inches from her neck.

Leo pulled on its arm to keep it away from her, but the arm came off in his hand.

Freaking corpsicles fall apart faster than pork roast in a crockpot.

"Leo. Get back to the goddam house," I screamed. "I've got this."

The rotter turned and lunged at me. I swung the hoe like a Louisville Slugger and took its head clean off, sending it into the Winstel's backyard, leaving a juicy trail in its wake.

Well, *crap.* Another job for Splatz. After tonight, Jimmy should dedicate a wing to me.

Nonnie headed straight for me, waddling faster than any gum-grinder I'd ever seen. I put my arms around her and told her everything would be fine.

Then Leo moaned.

I let go of Nonnie and whirled around to find him curled

into a fetal position on the ground, his muscles randomly contracting.

"Nighthawk," he whimpered. "Help me."

Oh, God. No. No. Not now, Leo. Not now.

I knelt down and swung his arm across my shoulder. "Stay with me, Leo. Let's get you inside, so you can take your meds."

Everything was falling apart, dammit.

C'mon, Rico. Where the hell are you?

I glanced up to find Capple ambling toward me, his weapon at his side.

I felt the heat rise in my cheeks. "Where the hell have you been?" I asked.

"Securing the front yard. Like you asked."

"Were there any biters out there?"

"No," he mumbled, eyes glued to the corpsicle's jawbone that lay at his feet.

I reeled at the sound of footsteps. Rico and Ferris sprinted toward us from the side yard. *Thank God.*

I turned back to chew Capple a new one for taking his sweet time, but the words caught in my throat. A biter had grabbed Capple from behind, its teeth inches from his neck.

I had no choice but to pull Hawk and squeeze off a shot, drilling the rotter's forehead. The bullet blasted out the back of the deadhead's skull, blowing biter bits all over Capple.

"Grab Leo," I yelled to Rico. "He's having another seizure."

Rico and I carried Leo back into the house, with Nonnie in tow, while Ferris and Capple cleared the yard, making sure we'd seen the last of the biters.

If my neighbors hadn't been awakened by the barking dogs, the crashing garbage cans, or the sound of breaking glass, the gunshot might have succeeded. But they'd seen and heard some weird shit at my house over the years. Two-to-one, they'd rolled over and gone back to sleep.

We got Leo into the house and laid him on the kitchen floor.

His muscles had stopped contracting, but the whites of his eyes had turned a sickly beige, and his irises, a golden yellow.

"Nighthawk," he rasped. "You look funny."

"It's okay, Leo." I held him and jabbed the medicine into his thigh. "Just relax. You should feel better any time now."

He lay in my arms, looking at the ceiling, tears welling in his eyes, no doubt wondering what muscle contractions and visual changes meant. It was probably better that neither of us knew.

Misplaced or not, the anger that burned inside me exploded. I slid out from beneath Leo and jumped to my feet.

"What the fuck were you thinking out there, Crapple?"

"It's Capple," he said with a snarl. "You want to tell me what you mean by that?"

I poked my finger in his face. "Nonnie moved faster than you did. What the hell took you so long? You trying to get me killed?" I took a deep breath and tried to calm down. "If you're going to work with this team, you'd better get somethi..."

The power cut off. I dropped to the floor and dragged Leo beneath the kitchen table, then pulled the chairs in as far as they'd go, to hide him.

"Nonnie," I whispered, "Crawl under here with Leo. And whatever happens, keep quiet."

"Wait," she said, yanking open the cupboard door above the stove.

"What the hell are you doing?"

She pulled out a giant box of quinoa and plunged her hand inside it. "A gift from my Mortie—God rest his soul. I bring when Leo tell me about zumbas. Just in case."

She slid her hand from the box, pulling out a .44 Magnum and a gallon-size baggie of ammo.

God help the zumbas—and anyone else within range.

Almost as an afterthought, she grabbed the cast iron skillet from the burner on the stove.

"Now, I ready," said Nonnie, the world's only two-fisted zumba killer.

While my eyes adjusted to the darkness, I heard Rico, Ferris and Capple scrambling for cover in the living room. Once they got into place, an expectant hush fell over the house.

I crawled away from the table, feeling my heart beat quicken. With Leo and Nonnie hiding there, that was the last place I wanted to be when trouble started. But my options were limited. I crept across the room and hunkered down between the refrigerator and the stove.

Spread out, in the dark, not knowing exactly where my guys were—that's as dangerous as it gets. God help me if I took one of them out by accident.

"Rico?" I called softly.

"Here," He said, raising his arm high enough for me to see that he was concealed behind the arm of the couch.

Fingers drummed against the side of the entertainment center that held my fifty-two-inch pride and joy. "Over here," Ferris whispered.

"Here," muttered Capple, followed by the unmistakable cocking of a gun.

I followed the sound and choked back a laugh. Moonlight, streaming through the picture window, illuminated a lone drapery panel that stuck out a good eighteen inches further than the others.

For the third time that evening, the sound returned: Thump...thump... *Bam.* Thump...thump... *Bam.*

Sweat trickled down my forehead.

Thump...thump... *Bam.* Again. And again. And again. Then more of the same sequence, faster, and over-running the sequence before, until the expectant hush that had filled the house, only minutes earlier, had been replaced with an incessant, relentless pounding.

In one horrible moment of clarity, I realized what they were doing. They were trying to break down the doors.

But, just as quick as the pounding started, it stopped. The four of us stepped out from behind our cover and silently huddled together, back to back, in the center of the living room, guns at high ready, peering into the darkness, waiting for whatever was coming.

The kitchen door splintered and a corpsicle broke through. I fired, sending its head airborne. Another deadhead tumbled in behind it. And then another. And another. Then the picture window exploded and a tide of biters rushed inside.

I brought Hawk to bear and wondered what it would be like to be eaten alive.

30

GOTCHA!

Capple, positioned closest to the picture window, fell in a matter of seconds, his screams nearly swallowed by the frenzy of the horde.

Rico, Ferris and I fired into the scrum on top of Capple, but it was a waste of ammo. Capple's screams had stopped almost as soon as they'd started. He was either dead, dying, or destined to turn.

Headbutt, stationed at my feet, snapped and growled, spoiling for a fight. I worried for him. All heart and no brains, that dog. Whether it was one rotter, or dozens, made no difference to him. Headbutt would stand with me until the end—and take out more than his fair share of deadheads along the way.

On the other hand, Kulu, whose cage had toppled during the onslaught, was nowhere to be seen. The cage door, now slightly bent and open, probably unlatched when it hit the floor. Kulu, bird of prey, would have to fend for herself. I was up to my eyeballs in rotters. And since she wasn't in my line of sight, at least for the moment, she was out of the fray.

For once, Leo and Nonnie did as they were told, and stayed hidden beneath the table.

Deadheads tumbled into the house in waves, first the corp-sicles, then the flesh-eaters, and finally, the freshies. The attack had a definable strategy. The first wave, corpsicles, were nothing more than expendable battering rams, their sole purpose being to gain access into the house.

Once inside, they either continued on, or if too damaged by the initial impact, were overrun by the flesh-eaters. The freshies, the least decayed of the lot, struck last, moving quickly and at will.

Was Dr. Christian seeing that same cooperative pack mentality in Europe?

I fired one round, then two, then three. The closer they came, the faster I shot. And still, they came.

Headbutt charged and sank his teeth into the foot of one of the corpsicles, its rotting muscles and tissue giving way instantly to the crush of his bite. Festering flesh peeled down its foot in jagged strips. With one last snap of Headbutt's jaw, the zombie's foot severed, coming loose in his mouth. The biter toppled over, but continued to pull itself across the floor, using only its hands.

Kulu reappeared, swooping down with a screech, and proceeded to peck out the rotter's eyes. She kept on drilling, too, until she hit brain matter.

That's my bird.

Another deadhead advanced from the kitchen. I squeezed the trigger again but the gun misfired. The son of a bitch *jammed.* I racked the slide, chambering a new round.

But the rotter was a freshy, quick and agile. It lunged forward, grabbed both my arms, and then threw me to the ground. I fired off balance, halfway to the floor and missed it completely.

Shit. Bad time for my Ka-Bar to be holstered in my room.

Headbutt went for its leg, but the rotter kicked him hard and sent him sailing.

Bad move, meatbag. "Oh no, you did *not* just kick *my* dog."

"Ferris," Rico screamed. "Help Nighthawk! I've got Leo."

Ferris, maybe twenty feet away, raised his Glock and took the head shot. But the biter moved, pouncing on me like I was a breakfast burrito, its dead eyes staring into mine, its death stink wafting up my nose.

How many rounds do I have left?

I pushed up on the rotter, putting as much distance as I could between it and me, and then closed my eyes. *Please don't be empty,* I thought as I brought Hawk to bear, squeezing his trigger.

Booyah, baby! Tango down. Nailed that sucker right in its temple. I'd have bragged about that kill for the rest of my life, if I wasn't pretty sure I'd peed my pants.

Ferris, now at my side, rolled the biter off me and pulled me to my feet.

"Just how big are your balls?" he asked.

"Bigger than yours." I reached into my pocket to check for more mags and came up empty. "How many mags you got left?"

"One."

I hollered over to my shoulder to Rico, "How many mags you got?"

"Two."

"Ferris, watch my six," I said, as I battled toward the kitchen.

A corpsicle shambled straight for me with outstretched arms.

"He's mine," I called to Ferris.

Our ammo was dangerously low, no need wasting it. I side-stepped and threw a roundhouse to the biter's head. It splatted like a leftover Halloween pumpkin.

Two more bogeys attacked. Flesh-eaters. Their heads wouldn't fly from a kick, so I squeezed Hawk's trigger and prayed. But he was empty.

Ferris took them both out, one-two, with his Glock.

Having finally made it to the kitchen table, I bent down and yanked up the tablecloth.

Click. The cold, hard steel of Nonnie's .44 pressed against the bridge of my nose.

"*Nooo,*" I screamed, knocking her hand aside.

The gun went off like a cannon and Nonnie fell over backwards, taking the table and chairs with her, wiping out the next wave of biters.

"Give me that gun." With a quick grab, and a twist of my wrist, I took it from her and handed it to Leo. "Whatever you do, don't give this back to her or I'll shoot you myself. Now, both of you, get behind me. *Quick.* We need to move."

Nonnie grabbed her skillet and scrambled to her feet, followed by Leo. They sandwiched themselves between Ferris and me. Headbutt remained at my side, ever loyal, snarling and snapping at the new wave of rotters as they advanced.

I nodded to Ferris. "Help Rico take out the rotters, so we can move down the hall. My ammo's in Leo's bedroom. We can hold them off from in there."

Together, Rico and Ferris picked off the biters that blocked our path.

I whaled on the ones behind us with a broken chair leg, to drop the backline of deadheads that charged us from the kitchen. One down. Two down. Then three. But they kept coming. And coming.

One of the fallen corpsicles clambered back to its feet as we moved past it, and latched on to Nonnie's left arm, pulling her dangerously close to its mouth.

Nonnie screamed and powered through, with a deadly right skillet to its face. Its head exploded like a piñata, producing a spectacular spray of zushi.

Another biter zeroed in on Nonnie.

Leo pulled the .44 and aimed way too close to my head for comfort.

If he was off an inch or two, I'd be the next corpse on the floor. I ducked.

He fired, taking out the rotter, nearly losing his balance from the recoil.

Nonnie caught him by the collar of his pajama top and we continued our push toward the hallway.

"*Kulu. Kuulluu.*" Nonnie called.

Damned if that bird didn't come right to her and perch on her shoulder. What the hell was her secret? I couldn't make that pissy little pecker-head take a drink of water if she was dying of thirst.

The battle raged for what seemed like an eternity, although it was only a matter of minutes and most of our remaining bullets, until we cleared the hallway.

Then Rico and Ferris joined me at the rear of our group, holding off the endless swarm of rotters that followed us, as we funneled down the passage.

Leo reached the bedroom door first and threw it open. We all piled inside and slammed the door shut, locking it behind us. Rico and Ferris slid the dresser in front of the door, to hold the horde at bay.

The wooden door shimmied in its frame as the biters flung themselves against it, over and over again. Each time they pushed forward, the door creaked and groaned. It would only hold so long.

Where in the hell had I put the key to the weapons cabinet Nonnie installed?

No time to figure that out. I shot the lock off the cabinet and pointed to the stockpile of ammo inside it.

"Leo, take our empty mags and fill them with 9 mils."

Leo plopped on the floor and started filling our empties. The hinges on the door were beginning to give. Leo struggled to fill our mags, his hands shaking so bad, he kept fumbling the bullets.

Rico and Ferris scoured the cabinet for alternative weapons and I joined Leo on the floor.

"You're doing fine, champ," I said. "How 'bout tossing me a mag, so I can get in on the fun."

Nonnie's eyes gleamed when she spied the flamethrower propped inside the corner of the cabinet. She dove for it and Little Allie screamed, nearly bursting my eardrums.

"Don't even think about it, Nonnie," I scolded. "We're not sending my house up in flames."

My house—with its busted windows, flattened furniture and wall-to-wall zushi. Splatz wouldn't know what hit them.

Sirens roared in the distance. Lots of them. No sooner did I breathe a sigh of relief than the top hinge on the door broke free. Rico and Ferris pushed the dresser tighter against the door.

I tossed a fresh mag to Rico, as a lone biter smashed through the door, toppling the dresser and knocking Rico over.

The airborne mag sailed over Rico's head. The biter fell, landing on the overturned dresser, inches from Rico's neck.

It rolled off the dresser to its knees, and lunged for him.

I slapped a fresh mag into Hawk and took aim, but Nonnie obliterated the biter's head with a single swipe of the skillet.

Kitchen Accessories: Two. Biters: Zero.

Tires squealed and gravel pelted the house as cars roared up the driveway. Loud voices and rapid fire burst through the house. Bullets strafed through the bedroom wall and we dove for cover.

"It's us!" I screamed. "For God's sake, stop. We've got live ammo in here."

The shooting slowed to an occasional shot and soon stopped altogether.

I climbed to my feet and walked to what was left of the

doorway, hung back from the opening, and called, "Friendlies. Coming out."

We wandered into the hallway and beheld the carnage. My house. My battered, beaten, block of Swiss cheese house. Rotters lay on top of rotters, piled three deep, in some places, even higher.

Leo and I stood at the end of the hallway, heads on a swivel.

"You payed up on your homeowners?" Leo asked.

Something plopped on my head. I glanced up and cringed. *Oh. This was so going to suck.*

Hundreds of biter bits dangled like spitballs from the ceiling, waiting for gravity to work its magic. One by one, the bits fell in random order, bombing everything in their path.

I took Leo by the arm and meandered to the couch, shoving a pile of dead rotters off the cushions, making room for us. There we sat, me leaning over him, sheltering him from the rot bombs.

Dickhead, Cap and Weston finally arrived and entered my house through the gaping hole where the back door used to be.

Dickhead hung at the opening and hollered in. "How's Leo?"

The lump in my throat made it hard to swallow.

Leo was horrible. Leo would probably die soon. But one look in his proud, tired eyes and I realized that I would rather cut off my arm than give up on him.

"Leo? Leo's a fucking hero," I said. "Not to mention a kickass zombie hunter. He helped keep us alive. But I think he should go to the hospital, now. You know. Just to make sure he's okay."

The EMTs were already there. Rico and Ferris said they would ride with Leo to the hospital and take the next shift.

I winked, my tears nearly spilling, as they carried Leo out. "You're tough as they come, buddy. See you in a bit."

Nonnie walked alongside him to the ambulance, and then

stooped to kiss his forehead. "You come home tomorrow. I make lasagna."

She glanced back at what was left of my kitchen, and added, "Maybe, my house."

Dickhead and Cap trailed after Rico and Ferris, no doubt hell-bent on getting their debriefing at the hospital, while Leo was being evaluated.

Weston stayed behind, taking pictures of my house...the crime scene.

The sun would be up soon.

I dialed Splatz. "Hey, it's Allie. Oh, you heard on the scanner. Yeah, it's bad... No. Way worse than the morgue. Like the morgue times infinity. Bring a carpenter...and a drywaller...and paint...and primer. Lots of primer. See you in five."

I started to hang up, but stopped. "Hey, I almost forgot. Before you get started here, hit my neighbor's back yard. The Winstels. The ones on the right. Okay?"

Jimmy asked me where to send the bill.

I looked at the phone and blanched. "Sure as hell not to me. Send it to Director Horton at the FBI office, here in town. One more thing. This place has to be livable within twenty-four hours."

I waited for him to stop yelling.

"Bullshit," I said. "You work miracles every day. Just do your magic and make sure the walls and doors are up. The finishing work can wait. Thanks, man."

I leaned back on the couch, closed my eyes, and took a deep breath for the first time in hours. It wasn't long before I drifted off.

Damned, if Weston's phone didn't ring, rousing me from my nap. He answered it on the third ring. "Yo!"

Yo? Yo...

Yo! The brain bitch screamed. I bolted awake and craned

my neck toward Weston, who was already immersed in conversation.

What do you know? The answer had been right in my face all along.

Now, where did I leave that phone?

31

WHY?

I opened my bedroom door to search for Dom's phone and
held my breath, steeling myself against the damages that
lay in store for me.

As it turned out, my bedroom was the least ravaged room in
the house, with the possible exception of the bathroom. Dom's
phone lay on my dresser, right where I'd left it after my failed
attempt to finger the mole during Cap's meeting.

I picked it up and walked back through the hallway, ripping
myself a new one with every step.

How had I not figured this out earlier? Why hadn't my
instincts served me better? Little Allie never missed a trick.
She...I...should have seen this coming. But then it occurred to
me that I actually had.

When Weston first arrived at the safe house and I raised a
red flag, a certain cop, whose first name begins with Rico, and
last name begins with De Palma, blew me off and vetted the son
of a bitch. It would be a long time before I let De Palma live that
down.

I stopped at the end of the hallway and pressed redial. Not

twenty feet away, Weston, who'd been using his pen to flip shell casings into an evidence bag, answered the call.

"*Yo.*"

That moment didn't feel anything like I thought it would. I expected to feel pumped, even proud that I'd finally nailed the mole. But all I felt was sorrow. Sorrow for Rico, who had been blindsided by an old friend, sorrow for Cap, who would see someone he trusted fall, and sorrow for all the people who died because of one man's unimaginable betrayal.

How could a good cop go so wrong?

"Hello?" he said, holding the phone to his ear. "Hello?"

Weston must have sensed me in the archway. He turned and stared at the burner phone in my hand. Our eyes locked and the color drained from his face. His shoulders slumped.

So many questions, so many thoughts swirled through my head, and yet the only word I could utter was, "Why?"

"Does it matter?" he asked.

"It does to me."

Weston didn't offer an explanation. He simply slid the burner phone back into his pocket, pulled out a fresh evidence bag, and continued to scoop up shell casings, as if the events of the last few minutes had never happened.

"Put your gun on the floor and kick it over to me now, Weston. Careful," I said as he reached for his holster, "One finger. Cuffs, too."

"For what it's worth, Nighthawk, I'm sorry."

He nudged his .44 across the floor with the toe of his shoe, tossed me his cuffs, and then turned back to the carpet, sweeping his gloved hands lightly across its bloody, soiled nap, feeling for any brass he might have missed.

After a moment, he stood up, with his back to me, squared his shoulders and said, "Did you know I was the youngest badge to ever make detective at CPD? I beat De Palma by two months."

"No shit," I said.

"Yeah. It was always like that with us. We pushed each other, but in a good way. You know?" He bent back down and continued to hunt for casings.

What the hell was he doing? We both knew he was going down. But if I let him settle into it, maybe he'd tell me something important. Or maybe not. What the hell did I know? My gut said to give him some space.

So, I backed off, slipped into the hallway and called Cap to fill him in, while Weston continued to work the scene.

From where I stood, it looked like he'd found all the brass. But he seemed almost desperate to find more. Like, as long as there was one more casing, he could stay there indefinitely and never face the ugly road ahead of him.

I needed to be at the hospital with Leo. Time was at a premium. "Listen, Weston, I—"

"Please," he said, without looking up. "Let me finish. I haven't gotten to the kitchen, yet. It won't take long."

"Someone else can do that. C'mon, now. Let's go."

"*Please.*" His voice quivered.

He turned to face me, a shadow of the man he'd been only minutes earlier.

"I wanna finish," he said. "I was a good cop, once. Let me go out with my head up." A sad smile tugged at the corner his mouth. "That's not too much to ask, is it? Besides, Splatz'll be here any minute. Somebody's got to let them in."

There were still a few badges milling around out front. They could escort Jimmy and his crew inside. Did Weston really want to go out with a little class? Or was this some kind of ruse to catch me off guard?

"Ten minutes, tops," I said. "Cap's sending a car for you." I looked at Weston, sizing him up. "You aren't thinking of running, are you?"

His red-rimmed eyes looked weary. "Where would I go?"

He was right about that. There was nowhere to hide. Too many lives had been lost.

Oblivious to Weston's situation, Jimmy and a dozen or so of his guys burst through the door, dragging their industrial strength hoses behind them.

Jimmy quietly totaled the cost, as he strolled through the house surveying the carnage, and then let out a whistle.

"I ever tell you how much I love you, Nighthawk?"

"Bite me, Jimmy."

"I never bite the hand that feeds me, baby." He threw me a wink. "But I'll be chowing down good tonight."

Within minutes, Weston's police escort appeared and eyeballed the scene, then skirted around Jimmy's guys and closed in on Weston. His ten minutes were up.

"You ready, Weston?" I asked.

"Yeah. Thanks for...you know." He stood tall and stuck out his wrists.

"Take off your jacket," I whispered.

He handed it to me and we locked eyes, as I slapped on the cuffs, then draped his jacket across his hands and led him out of the house, through the yard, past seven or eight of CPD's finest. Weston's peers.

One of the badges called out, "Hey, guy. Beer and wings at Chicken on the Run. Eight o'clock, tonight. Be there."

Weston stopped and smiled back. This was the last time they would see him as an equal, the last time they would be proud to have served with him. He lingered in the moment.

Committing it to memory, maybe? What the hell. I'd give him that much. But only that much.

My neighbors gawked at the scene from beyond the caution tape, so I blocked their view by stepping in front of him, as he climbed into the back of the squad car.

"Damn you, Weston," I whispered. "Just...damn you."

We waited in the chairs across from Cap's desk, listening to the hustle and bustle of the 51st just outside his door.

Weston fidgeted and picked at the upholstered arm of his chair. Every so often he let out a sigh, tilted back his head, and stared at the ceiling. Minutes ticked by and sweat began to glisten on his forehead.

A half hour later, Cap walked in, closed the door, and strode to his desk without so much as a glance at Weston. For the first time I could remember, Cap had a three-day beard. His clothes were rumpled, and his eyes were bloodshot.

He cleared his voice, as if he intended to speak, but instead, remained quiet and stared at his hands, folded on the desktop. After a long, awkward silence, he raised his eyes and shot Weston a withering glare.

"Why?" Cap asked.

Weston squirmed and fought for his voice, eventually spitting out the answer we'd all been waiting for.

"Fifty large," he mumbled. "I was in fifty large to Connie Hodges."

I glanced at Cap.

"Conrad Hodges," he explained. "A local bookie."

Weston shrugged. "I like the ponies."

He put his elbows on Cap's desk and lowered his head into his hands. "Don't ask me how I got in so deep. It was like falling down a fucking rabbit hole. Fifty big ones. I don't have that kind of money. I got a wife and kids. What the hell was I supposed to do? Then this guy emails me, from out of nowhere. Says he's got $50K with my name on it. All I have to do is stall the biter investigation and tip him off if the heat turns up. That's all I did. I swear."

Cap's eyes flickered. "What was his name?"

"I don't know. I never even saw the guy. All I had was an email address."

Jesus. This was sounding like a spy novel. It was time to play *follow the money.*

"How did you get paid?" I asked.

Weston slumped in his chair. "A box of cash, in the mail. Along with the burner phone."

Cap nodded and then paused, wiping his eye with the heel of his hand. "And Miriam?" he asked quietly. "What about Miriam?"

Weston frowned. "What do you mean?"

Before Little Allie could stop me, I sprang from my chair and grabbed Weston by his collar. "You killed her, you clueless son of a bitch."

"I didn't kill anyone!" His voice turned pitchy. "I would never have killed Miriam. That...that BOLO Guy killed her." He grimaced and his eyes began to water. "Jesus. Why would you even say that?"

"Because you did kill her," I said. "Just like you killed Powell, and Ortega, and Capple, and those FBI agents in the warehouse. You killed them all, the moment you sold your soul for $50K. Christ, you make me sick."

I sank back into my chair, desperately hoping I wouldn't puke on Cap's floor.

Weston self-imploded in front of us, rambling on about how he never meant to hurt anyone and that he'd only done it for the money.

I would have loved to have stayed there and bitch-slapped him a few times, telling him his greed made the killings all the more senseless. But I had to get to the hospital. Leo needed me.

"One more thing," I said, as I walked to Cap's door. "All those biters at my house. How in the hell could they have marched through my neighborhood, sight unseen?"

Cap took a deep breath and leaned back in his chair. "There

were some semis parked up the street, behind the Hyde Park Shopping Plaza on Paxton. A patrolman noticed them and called it in. Said he was going to do a drive by. When he didn't report back, another unit was dispatched. They found him dead. Shredded by biters, the semis gone. We checked with the shop owners. None of them had overnight deliveries. It's a short walk from the plaza to your place. It was the middle of the night, and people were asleep."

Cap shook his head and then stared at his desk blotter. "Trailers hauling rotters. Lethal and low-tech. Scary shit, huh?"

On my way to the hospital, I couldn't get Cap's words out of my head. If this attack had happened at any other time of day, the results would have been catastrophic.

I pictured hundreds of zombies, eating their way through the streets of Cincinnati, killing, maiming, and potentially spawning more and more deadheads with every bite. And all it would take to make that happen was a few semis.

So simple. So brilliant. So incredibly evil.

The bastard behind all this understood the meaning of terror.

32

SOME DAYS SUCK WORSE THAN OTHERS

For the second time, I scrambled to the fifth floor of University Hospital, not knowing Leo's condition. I hated walking into his room blind. What if he wasn't bouncing back? What if this was the end? If not today, that day was coming soon.

The promise I'd made to Leo weighed on me. But how much worse would it be, if for some reason, I wasn't there to stop him from turning? I didn't want either one of us to go through that.

As I rounded the corner to Leo's room, I realized there was another reason I dreaded today's visit. Rico was there. Even though part of me wanted to rub Weston in Rico's face, the bigger part of me knew how crushed Rico would be. And I'd be the one doing the crushing.

The room was dark and still. I stuck my head inside to find Ferris and Rico, minus the zushi they'd been wearing when they left my house. They were dressed in scrubs, sitting in the visitor's chairs, with their feet propped up on the trash can.

The steady rhythm of Leo's heart monitor pulsed from

behind a privacy curtain; light from his muted TV flickered on the wall.

"How's he doing?" I whispered.

Rico shook his head and my heart sank.

Ferris motioned me toward the door. The three of us walked out into the brightly-lit hallway, and let the door drift closed behind us.

"What's the story?" I asked.

Rico rubbed his chin and glanced away. "It's not looking good, Nighthawk. They ran some tests as soon we got here. We're waiting for the results."

Shit.

I borrowed an extra chair from the hallway and sat next to Leo's bed. His skin was sallow and his lungs rattled when he breathed.

He opened his eyes and attempted a smile.

"Hey," he whispered. "Look what the cat dragged in."

"Yeah? Well, you don't look so good yourself."

There were a thousand other things that could have come out of my mouth. And I went with that. No one ever said I had a good bedside manner.

Within seconds, Leo had closed his eyes again, and drifted back to sleep.

A doctor walked into the room and eyeballed the three of us. "Which one of you is Assistant Director Horton?"

"None of us are," I said. "Why?"

"Mr. Abruzzi's test results are back in."

Rico extended his hand. "Hi, Doc. Rico De Palma, CPD. Mr. Abruzzi is in our custody. What have you got?"

"I'm Dr. Kelly," the man responded, ignoring Rico's hand. "Mr. Abruzzi is my patient. Unfortunately, as I explained to that

Channel Ten newswoman earlier, I can't release information to anyone who isn't specifically authorized, if we don't have a signed release. HIPAA laws, you understand."

Damn that Jade. Always sticking her nose in where it didn't belong. If she got in over her head, it served her right.

But something else Dr. Kelly said didn't sit right, either, so I asked, "If you need a release, why did you ask to speak to Assistant Director Horton?"

The doctor cleared his throat and made a show of studying Leo's chart. "The Director claimed access to Mr. Abruzzi's medical records, under the provisions granted by the Patriot Act."

Ferris nearly choked. "The *what?*"

Dickhead strolled into the room, a smug smile plastered across his face. "The Patriot Act, Agent Ferris. I happen to consider the Z-virus to be a weapon of mass destruction. And I consider whoever engineered that virus to be a bio-terrorist. Either premise grants me legal access to Mr. Abruzzi's records."

Ferris, who wasn't in a position to take Dickhead on, pursed his lips and dropped his eyes.

I didn't have to worry about crossing any lines with the Director. He wasn't my boss.

I shook my head and looked him in the eye. "You're reaching a bit, aren't you? That's ridiculous."

"Is it?" His face turned dark. "You said, yourself, the disease is spreading. We need to understand the nature of the virus if we're going to stop it. Access to Abruzzi's medical records will help us."

I forced a laugh. "Leo would never sign off on that."

Dr. Kelly flipped Leo's chart closed. "Mr. Abruzzi wasn't capable of signing off on anything. He was unconscious when he came in."

"Abruzzi doesn't have to agree," Dickhead said with a wave of his hand. "This is an FBI investigation. If you aren't comfortable releasing the information, doctor, I can call a federal judge and get a warrant here in less than thirty minutes. Shall I make the call?"

"These are Leo's records," I said. "What say does he have in all this?"

"Hello!" Leo rasped. "I'm right here, people. Don't let the closed eyes fool you. I ain't dead yet."

He struggled to sit upright but fell back, exhausted. "Maybe Director Horton does have a legal right to know what those tests turned up. But those are my medical records, and I say everybody in this room can hear what you have to say, Doc. Go ahead. Let 'er rip."

Dr. Kelly frowned and opened Leo's chart. "Very well, Mr. Abruzzi. I am sorry to say that your heart is no longer functioning within normal limits. We believe that the injection of the Nacarotoxin directly into your heart muscle may have damaged the tissue. We are currently delivering your medication through an IV that allows for administration of a rapid, yet regulated, dose. In fact, your system should actually tolerate a higher dosage now, than you were able to with direct injection."

It's not like we had a choice, injecting Leo in the heart. It was either that or watch him turn in front of us. Still, hearing the doctor say that, felt like a knife in my chest.

"So, like how long can we do this IV thing?" Leo asked.

Dr. Kelly sat on the edge of Leo's bed. "Mr. Abruzzi, I'm afraid the Nacarotoxin is losing its efficacy."

Leo rolled his eyes. "English, Doc."

"It isn't working as well as it did initially." Dr. Kelly's voice softened. "You do understand, this drug is not a cure. The time is coming when the medication will fail, and no longer keep you from...turning."

Leo nodded and looked away.

"How much time?" Dickhead asked.

If Little Allie had a set of hands, they'd have been wrapped around Dickhead's neck.

"What is wrong with you?" I asked. "The man is sitting here, right in front of you, you pompous, inconsiderate ass. Show some tact."

Dr. Kelly ignored my outburst. "This is uncharted territory for me—and for most of the medical community. Nacarotoxin is so new. I've never treated a patient with Mr. Abruzzi's...condition...before. But given his presentation, I would say...days. Maybe a week or two, at best."

Leo continued to stare into space. Either he couldn't hear us or didn't want to.

Dickhead shifted his eyes to me. "I don't have time to be polite. I told you, if Abruzzi started to decompensate before the grand jury convened, we'd have to schedule a deposition. I'll arrange for a court reporter to come here to the hospital."

"No," I said. "Doc, can Leo go home with me, if we have a nurse stop by to help with the IV?"

"Certainly," Dr. Kelly said. "I can make the arrangements."

Dickhead's cheeks flamed. "Hold on, here. You don't call the shots, Nighthawk. I do. Your house is a now a biohazard. Besides, I want Abruzzi here, where he's getting the best care possible, until after his deposition. If you want him after that, knock yourself out."

My fingers curled into a fist. "You mean, after you've gotten everything you want from him. And for your information, the cleaners are already working on my house, taking care of business."

I stopped short of telling Dickhead he'd be getting the bill.

Leo finally spoke up. "If it makes any difference, I'd rather be at Nighthawk's. You can send the court reporter there, right?"

Dickhead turned to Leo. "Mr. Abruzzi, I really think you'd be better off..."

"Actually," Dr. Kelly said, "There is no medical reason for Mr. Abruzzi to stay here. I can arrange for Home Health to provide the nursing assistance he needs. And frankly, the longer Mr. Abruzzi stays here, the bigger the liability risk he poses to patients, hospital staff and visitors. If he should happen to turn..."

Dr. Kelly stopped and cleared his throat. "On behalf of the hospital, I must insist that Mr. Abruzzi spend his final days elsewhere. We will keep him here overnight, while I make arrangements for his in-home care. He'll have to leave here tomorrow morning, after we administer one more round of IV infusion. Is that clear?"

Dickhead shrugged. "Fine, Doc. Nighthawk, go ahead. Take Leo back to your house, tomorrow. I'll arrange for the court reporter to take his deposition there."

Oh, Nighthawk," he added as he walked to the doorway. "I almost forgot. Congratulations. I heard you caught the snitch. Weston, the son of a bitch. He played you all for fools, didn't he?"

Rico's eyes flashed.

I grabbed him by the arm, and stopped him from taking Dickhead down, much as I would have preferred otherwise.

Rico stared at me and waited for an explanation, as Dickhead's footsteps receded down the hallway.

33

THE WEIGHT OF THE WORLD

"You mind telling me what the Director was talking about?" Rico finally asked.

Why did I have to be the one to tell him? Damn Weston for being such a douchebag. And damn Dickhead for being so arrogant.

The recap I offered was short and sweet. "Weston's phone rang while he was processing my house. He answered the call, 'Yo.' The same word, the same voice I heard in Cap's office that day when I redialed Dom's burner phone. When I hit redial this time..." I swallowed hard and spit out the rest. "It was Weston who answered. I'm sorry."

"What if you're wrong?" Rico asked. "You only heard one word. How could you possibly be sure?"

"He admitted it." I softened my tone. "I know he was your friend. And I'm sorry you had to hear it from Dickhead. I was going to tell you myself, but he burst in before I had the chance."

It might have been easier to watch him take a bullet, than to see the hurt in his eyes. That was enough suckage for one day as far as I was concerned.

"I need to get back to the house," I said. "To make sure everything's ready for Leo tomorrow."

Rico didn't respond. I glanced from Ferris to Rico, and back to Ferris again. Ferris winked, and nodded me toward the door.

One more time, he'd come through, not only by agreeing to cover my shift with Leo, but by hanging there with a shattered Rico. Stand-up guy, Ferris. Little Allie wanted to know if he was my kind of guy. I wondered that myself.

———

I still had to tell Nonnie that Leo was dying. Everything seemed to fall on my shoulders. It always has, but this time I wondered if my shoulders were strong enough for the job.

I pulled into my driveway around three in the afternoon. The Splatz crew was still hard at work. The picture window and back door had already been replaced.

They'd made good headway inside the house as well, sucking up the zushi, lickety-split. Two guys roamed from room to room, spackling bullet holes, and priming the walls. Huge fans blasted air to quicken the drying time.

Jimmy had outdone himself. Things would be fine by morning. Now for the hard part, filling Nonnie in.

Amazingly, and not for the first time, Nonnie surprised the hell out of me. I broke the news to her, and her eyes welled.

After a moment of silence, she patted my hand and said, "*Memento mori*, Miss Allie."

I shook my head, lost.

"It means, remember, you, too, shall die. So must we all, someday. Leo be at peace, no? For this, we be grateful."

Her blue-haired, Yoda-like wisdom might have comforted her, but part of me was circling the drain. To the rest of the world, Leo would simply die. But I would have to kill him again.

Not wanting to dwell on that, I changed the subject. "Can I borrow your car tomorrow to pick up Leo? He can't handle a ride on my Harley."

Nonnie nodded.

"And I'm a little concerned about the way Headbutt and Kulu might react to Leo, now that his medication isn't working right. I don't want to risk them feeling threatened and attacking him. Can they stay here with you until—"

Nonnie smiled. "Yes. Of course. I make lasagna for dinner tomorrow. Leo will like."

She bustled back to her kitchen sink, did the dishes, and went on with her life. Nonnie had grit. That funny, feisty old broad could teach me a thing or two about resilience.

She asked me to stay the night at her house, saying she was afraid the zumbas might come back. But I suspected she knew I didn't want to be alone with my thoughts.

The paint fumes at my house would be obnoxious anyway, so I stayed, and sacked out on her couch, Headbutt curled up beside me, and Kulu perched nearby in her cage.

Sleep came easier than I thought it would. I was exhausted.

Rising when the first bit of sunlight peeked through the drapes, I left Nonnie a note, telling her I was at my house, checking on the progress and getting Leo's room ready, and that I would call her when Leo was home.

It was way too early to go to the hospital. I considered calling Rico, but he would have been relieved at midnight, by whoever Dickhead had decided would replace Capple. Better to let De Palma sleep in.

So, I changed the sheets on Leo's bed and vacuumed the entire house. Then, I settled in with a mug of coffee and watched *Dancing with the Stars* on my DVR. I'd missed a lot of episodes.

Given the recent zombie uprising, I took Hawk and my Ka-Bar knife with me when I left the house at ten. I'd be packing from here on. Just in case.

Leo was dressed and waiting, his IV already removed. He looked older and smaller than his 5'6" frame, his skin crepey and his shoulders hunched. Even so, he still had a hell of a 'tude.

"Jesus. I shoulda took a cab. I thought I was gonna die and go rotter before you picked me up. What took you so long?"

He dozed on and off, as we drove home. It took me a while, but I got him into the house and set him up on the couch with his pillow and a blanket. Then, as promised, I called Nonnie.

She walked through the back door in less than five minutes, the heavenly smell of lasagna wafting around her like a cloud. Nonnie dished Leo up a plateful, and handed it to him with a kiss on his cheek.

He smiled and picked at it mostly, but managed a few bites to show his gratitude. "Where are the terrible twins?" he asked, with his mouth full of food.

"They're at Nonnie's. You know, with all the paint fumes and dust here, it's better for them over there. And I didn't want them bothering you." So, I lied. It was one of those little white ones that don't even count.

The IV nurse arrived and hooked Leo up in a matter of minutes. If the injection site turned red, we needed to call her. Otherwise, she would come back to change it out in eight hours.

Leo lay back on the couch for a nap, and Nonnie returned to her house, to clean up her kitchen.

No sooner had Leo drifted off to sleep, snoring like a wounded rhino, than he was awakened by the ringing of my doorbell.

Dickhead, the D.A., a videographer, and the court reporter had arrived. I opened the door and District Attorney Mark Andrews walked in like he owned the place.

He breezed past me, hand outstretched, and headed straight for Leo. "Mr. Abruzzi, thank you for allowing us to take your deposition during this difficult time."

Leo glanced at Dickhead and shrugged. "It's his party. He invited you. Not me."

The D.A. shot a skeptical glare at Dickhead, and then sat beside Leo on the couch. "This is a deposition, Mr. Abruzzi. You have the right to legal counsel, if you so choose. In fact, I would encourage it. I can have an attorney summoned here to represent your interests. Just say the word."

Leo rolled his eyes. "What am I going to do, incriminate myself? I'm dying, here. You've already got my set of books. I don't need no counsel."

The court reporter and the videographer set up their equipment.

Andrews pulled me aside and said, "Ms. Nighthawk, as much as we appreciate you giving us access to the witness in your home, I must ask you to leave before we begin the deposition. Mr. Abruzzi's testimony is confidential. We'll make this short and sweet. I expect we won't need more than an hour or so. Director Horton will remain here for the security of Mr. Abruzzi."

I scowled and glanced at Leo. "You okay with that?"

Leo kicked back on the couch and waved his hand. "*Eh...* What's the worst that could happen? I could die. Go on. I'm fine."

I grabbed my jacket, picked up my keys, and left the house, having no idea where to spend the next hour. Nonnie's house was always an option, but it had been a rough couple of days. Tough as she was, the poor woman could use some down time.

Besides, I'd had enough of watching the clock tick. That

was all I could do with Leo anymore, wondering what moment would be his last. He was on my mind constantly.

I smiled, remembering the night he said he wanted to take me dancing. So, I drove into Montgomery Village, thinking I might check out the Arthur Murray Dance Studio. I sat in my car and watched through the windows as the students danced inside. They looked so...elegant.

I was strong for my size and agile, too. But nobody in their right mind ever called me graceful. Dancing was for graceful people. I left without even going inside, Leo's words ringing in my ears. *You lack commitment, Nighthawk.*

I told myself I'd left because it was time to get back home. That sounded a lot better than the *you sorry piece of chicken shit* crap the brain bitch was spouting.

Dickhead stepped outside as I pulled into the driveway.

He met me at the front door and blocked my path. "They're almost finished. Another few minutes at most."

He peered at me over the top of his sunglasses. "I assume you still have De Palma's services, if you need a break from Abruzzi. Given his condition, you don't need Ferris anymore. I'm pulling him from the case."

I sneered. "There's a shocker. Now that you've got Leo's testimony, he's not worth protecting anymore."

The D.A. opened the door and announced they were finished. One by one, the deposition team filed out of the house, carrying their equipment and nodding at me as they passed. Andrews, the last one to leave, made a point of thanking me again.

"It's Leo you should be thanking," I said, as I closed the door in his face.

Leo's color was awful, and the whites of his eyes were tinged with a pale shade of yellow. A very, very bad sign. We couldn't inject him with Nacarotoxin since he was already receiving it through the IV. In short, if and when his eyes went yellow, there would be no coming back.

What he needed now was rest. But I needed some answers of my own first. "Leo, you were under oath and you swore to tell the truth. Did you tell them what you've been holding back?"

"What the hell you talking about?"

"Did you tell them what you wouldn't tell me?"

"Quit badgering me, Nighthawk. You're worse than them. I answered every question they asked me."

"You're protecting someone. That's the only explanation, Leo. Who is it?"

He sat forward on the end of the couch and shook his head. "Nobody. Knock it off. I'm tired."

His eyes were wide, and his chest heaved. He was breathing too fast. Leo was scared. But of who? And why? He was already a dead man. What was left to fear?

"Who are you protecting, Leo? Tell me. I can help you."

He fidgeted and rubbed his hands through his hair. Then, he began to hyperventilate. I found him a paper bag and held it to his lips, giving him my *Come to Jesus* speech while he caught his breath.

"Listen to me, Leo. Whatever you're afraid of, I can handle. I'm sure you think by holding back, you're protecting someone, but consider this. If you don't tell me who's in danger, I can't protect them. Please. Let me help you. I promise, if it means that much to you, I'll protect whoever it is with my life. Hell, Rico and Ferris will as well. Just like they protected you."

Leo's breathing returned to normal, but tears filled his eyes.

"You swear," he said. "You swear on your mother's grave, if I tell you, you'll do that? You'll protect them?"

"Leo, look at me," I said, taking his hands. "I don't make empty promises."

He collapsed back against the cushion and exhaled. "His name is Vincent Arturo Abruzzi. And he's my son."

34

THE LAST DANCE

S *hit the damn bed, Louie.* In all the time I'd known Leo, he never once mentioned he had a child.

"He's twenty-one," Leo said. "Vinny and me, we're like you and De Palma, we don't mix. Too much alike, I guess. Wants nothing to do with me. He goes to school at Tulane. Lives in Monroe Hall. Remember that."

"Why is Vinny in danger?" I asked.

"I laundered money for a living. Some of the guys I did business with, they're not so nice. You know? This one guy, I never knew his real name. Called himself Stanous. He was into the mob, big. The bastard must have got scared that I was going to talk, 'cause next thing I know, I'm bit, and he sends me a message. *You tell the Feds about me, your son gets it next.* I couldn't do that to Vinny."

Leo lay his head back on the couch and stared at the ceiling. "Jesus. Who could do that to anybody? Let alone his own son."

Stanous. As in Stanous Electric. I shook my head. Leo probably did answer every question the D.A. asked. But the D.A. wasn't asking the right questions. The Feds wanted to know who was fronting the money. They didn't give a rat's ass who was borrowing it. But someone the Feds weren't interested in was willing to kill, to keep his name out of the investigation.

Why?

Leo lifted his head and peered into my eyes. "I give you what you need, you swear you guys will protect Vinny?"

"With our lives."

Leo let his eyes linger on mine, then nodded, and dug his hand into his pocket, pulling out a thumb drive. "This is my set of the books. Take it. Do whatever you need to do. Just remember you, De Palma and Ferris are on the hook for my son."

Leo laid it in my hand and then wiped his eyes.

"You're doing the right thing, Leo," I said, shoving the drive into the pocket of my jeans. "Who knows? Maybe it'll help us catch the fucker who's responsible for this mess."

Leo lay back against the couch and exhaled. The air in his lungs rattled out in a long, slow wheeze.

Oh, God. My poor fucking heart.

"You know what I have?" I said, forcing a smile. "DVR's of the entire season of *Dancing with the Stars.* How 'bout we watch it together?"

"Why not?" he murmured. "That reminds me. There's a bag on the shelf in my closet. Go get it, would you?"

I grabbed it from his room and handed it to him.

"This...this is for you," he said. "Nonnie ordered it for me, since you wouldn't let me online."

He pulled an envelope out of the bag, gave it to me, and said, "Life's too short, Nighthawk. Don't leave nothing on the table."

Inside the envelope was a gift certificate for ballroom lessons at Arthur Murray's.

My eyes welled. "What am I going to do with this, huh? Dancing's for graceful people."

"Bullshit," he said, handing me the bag. "Open it."

I reached inside and pulled out a box of bright yellow dancing shoes. Salsa shoes, according to the label. Words failed me, but for the first time in weeks, I smiled. Really smiled. I slipped them on and laughed.

"Yellow was all they had," Leo rasped. "You know how hard it is to find women's size ten dancing shoes?"

The celebrity couple on TV was dancing the waltz. I reached for Leo's hand. It trembled in mine. "How about one dance. For me."

He smiled and I helped him to his feet.

"See," I said. "You really did take me dancing. Just like you said you would."

We hung on to each other, swaying to the beat. We kept on swaying, too, even after the music stopped.

Then Leo went limp in my arms, and looked at me with eyes that were nearly as yellow as my new shoes.

"I don't feel so good," he whispered.

Oh, God. I can't do this. I just can't.

"Where'd you go, Nighthawk? Turn the lights back on, huh?"

"I'm here," I said, sitting us both back on the couch. "Right here."

His voice cracked. "You remember your promise. Don't you let me—"

I blinked back tears. "I got you, Leo. I got you."

"And my son. You'll watch over him?"

"Him, too, buddy. I swear. You just lie there. Get some rest."

Within minutes, his tortured breathing stopped altogether.

When his head fell to his chest, I summoned every ounce of strength inside me, pulled my Ka-Bar, and drove it into his brain stem.

"Thanks for the dance," I whispered, laying him back gently. "I wouldn't have missed it for the world."

Less than twenty-four hours later, Leo was buried at The United Jewish Cemetery in Montgomery, Ohio. Nonnie helped me with the arrangements, and per Leo's only request, made sure we recited Kaddish. Only six people showed up. Cap, Rico, Jade, Ferris, Nonnie and me.

I called Vinny in his dorm room at Tulane and told him about his dad's death. I was hoping Vinny would make the trip up for the funeral. No dice. A real hard case, this Vinny. A Grade-A, know-it-all, pain in the ass. The apple sure didn't fall far from that tree.

I told him his dad asked me to watch over him, and why. The kid wanted nothing to do with his dad or me. Fine. I'd keep tabs on the little shithead anyway. What he didn't know wouldn't hurt him.

Director Dickhead had the gall to show up at the gravesite, toward the end of the service. Probably just to make sure Leo ended up six-feet under. I wanted to boot Dickhead's ass to the street, but the brain bitch wouldn't let me. *Pansy-ass wussy.* Maybe that was because she'd figured out the real reason he'd come. It surely wasn't for Leo.

Dickhead motioned me aside. Keeping his voice low, he said, "I thought I'd find you here. We need to have a chat."

I walked with him to his car, where he reached into the glove compartment, pulled out an envelope, and shoved it into my hands. "We've had our differences, you and I, but you seem to know this Hoodoo, Voodoo crap better than anyone else. You were the first to suspect that the Z-virus had been manipulated. And statistics have shown you were right about the rotter population being on the rise."

He shifted his weight from foot to foot, and then sighed. "The FBI wants to keep you on the task force. They're offering you a contract as a paid consultant. But only on retainer and only until we get a handle on this mess. It's nothing permanent, so don't get your hopes up."

"What's the catch?"

A smile played at the corner of his mouth. "For the duration, you'll be reporting to me."

I should have known there'd be a turd at the bottom of the punch bowl. But things had been awfully tight lately, and I enjoyed eating as much as the next guy, so I asked, "What's the pay?"

"It's all in the contract. You've got forty-eight hours to make up your mind."

I wouldn't even need forty-eight minutes. Of course, I'd accept. Whatever the pay, I needed the money, but the thought of letting Dickhead stew about my decision for the next couple of days gave me a certain amount of childish satisfaction.

"Let me think about it," I said. "I'll get back to you."

Dickhead got in his car and drove off.

I rejoined the others at Leo's grave, having no idea how to explain Dickhead's mysterious appearance.

"What did he want?" Cap asked.

I smiled and shrugged. "Nothing important. What do you say the five of us throw Leo a wake? I think he'd like that."

Cap let my flip answer to his question slide, and he begged off the wake, saying he had a pile of work on his desk that he needed to get back to. Jade had to get back to the station. That only left six of us, Ferris, Rico, Nonnie, me, Headbutt and Kulu, a small but determined bunch, dedicated to celebrating the life of the mobbed-up moneyman with a heart of gold.

Rico volunteered to stop at the liquor store, but Nonnie said she had a leftover stash of Mortie's Chianti in her basement. What better way to toast the crusty Italian-Jewish gangster than with vino from the homeland? We would drink multiple toasts to Powell and Ortega too, before the day was through.

Not only did Nonnie supply the Chianti, she also brought

sandwich trays and chips. Lucky for us. She knew I sure as hell wasn't going to cook. Nonnie set up the food, and then announced she was returning home. Leo had no one else, she explained, so she decided to sit shiva for him.

After she left, I walked back to the bedroom to change into my jeans. I slid them on, stuck my hand in the front right pocket and pulled out the most important piece of evidence we had.

Leo's thumb drive.

"I've got something to share with you," I said, walking back into the living room with the drive in my hand. "Something Leo gave me on his deathbed, in exchange for a promise."

I told Rico and Ferris about Vinny—and about the collective promise I'd made that involved us all.

Ferris stared at my hand. "Is that what I think it is?"

Rico, tossing back some wine, turned to me wide-eyed. "Leo's books? No way. Are you shitting me?"

I plugged in the drive and pages of data populated the screen.

"Look at all these names," I said.

Rico whistled. "Look at all that money changing hands."

I scanned page after page, searching for the name I wanted —needed—to see.

"Bingo!" I yelled. "Here it is. Stanous Electric. Big as day. And check out the amount of that loan. Five million dollars."

I sorted the list by totals. That was the largest loan in the book. I was closing in on something. But what? Stanous Electric meant nothing to me. The longer I stared, the more frustrated I got.

Then, I remembered Leo said he never knew the client's real name, so I grabbed a pen and started moving the letters around.

Holy crap.

There it was, after all this time. The name of the demon

who'd been stringing us along, playing us for fools. It was the same demon who'd been haunting my dreams for the past three years. Somewhere in the back of my mind, where I shove the shit that terrifies me, maybe I'd always known.

"Toussaint Le Clerc," I whispered, although by then, my mouth had gone bone-dry.

Rico shrugged. "Never heard of him."

"You wouldn't have."

"Who is he?" Ferris asked.

"Just a ghost from the past," I said unable to meet his gaze. "An evil, fucking ghost."

"Screw it, then," Ferris clapped his hands loudly. "It's still early. I say we bring that ghost down now."

"Not tonight." I closed the laptop and shoved the flash drive back into my pocket. "Tonight is for Leo."

We ate too much and drank even more, toasting lost friends and comrades like Leo and Harry Delk. I even flipped on the DVR of *Dancing with the Stars*, and laughed while Ferris and Rico danced the worst Argentine Tango in the history of tangos.

It wasn't long after that, that Rico's phone rang. I could tell by the look on his face, Jade was on the line. He moved into the kitchen to take her call and Ferris scooped me into his arms, for an impromptu waltz.

Everything was fine, until my size tens tripped over the leg of the coffee table and we fell onto the couch, laughing.

He pulled back just a bit and stared into my eyes. Then he kissed me, like I'd never been kissed before, long, slow and deep.

When the kiss ended, and I came back down to earth, I noticed Rico standing in the doorway watching us. He glanced away quickly, and retreated to the kitchen.

Ferris, oblivious, rolled to his feet giggling, excused himself, and wandered down the hallway toward my bathroom.

I walked into the kitchen and found Rico staring out the window into the darkness.

"Everything okay?" I asked.

"Yeah. Just Jade," he muttered.

"*Just* Jade? That sounds...ominous."

Rico studied me with unreadable eyes. "She's been after me to move in with her."

Move in with her? What was wrong with this guy? She was such a user. With everything that had happened between them, he was too good a cop, too analytical, to not see that. He was pissing me off. And yet, for some reason, my heart was in my throat. That pissed me off even more.

I sucked in a breath and asked, "So, what did you tell her?"

"That I need some time. That I'm not sure."

Ten seconds, pal. That's all the time it should have taken to give her a big, fat, definitive no. But he was in love, and love brings out the stupid. Still, he was hesitating. Why?

"Is there someone else?"

Shit. Shit. Shit. Those words came out of my mouth before the brain bitch could pull them back.

He paused and glanced at Ferris approaching from the hallway. "No, of course not. When would I even have time? All I do is work."

Ferris staggered and banged into the kitchen archway with a chuckle. "What're we talking about now, boys and girls?"

"Your dancing ability," I said, poking my finger into his chest. "The consensus is, you can't lead for shit."

Ferris looked back and forth between Rico and me, then winked at me and stumbled back to the couch. Even drunk, it seemed nothing got past Ferris.

The guys left around midnight. I'd taken Ferris's keys away hours earlier, so Rico drove him home. I locked the door behind them and soon found myself standing in the hallway, peering into Leo's room.

For years it had been the arsenal, a place to store weapons, ammo, and other assorted crap. Somehow, in a very short period of time, it had become Leo's room. Freaking loud, obnoxious, warm, wonderful Leo.

Not yet ready for a trip down memory lane, I returned to the couch beside Headbutt, grabbed my laptop, and googled Toussaint Le Clerc. I hadn't lied about his being a ghost from the past, but I had neglected to mention he was a necromancer whose powers rivaled mine—and whose heart was black as pitch.

My search came up empty. I sighed. Of course, it had. Toussaint worked in the shadows. I shut down the computer, sipped the last of my Chianti, and watched the screen go black.

The air grew thick, almost expectant, and a hush fell over the house. Headbutt rose to his feet, ears peaked, hackles raised, a low growl humming in his throat.

"What is it, boy?" I scanned the living room, then craned my neck to peer down the hallway.

Finding nothing, I settled back in my seat, and stifled a scream. Toussaint taunted me from the darkened laptop screen, beckoning me with a crook of his finger. On his left bicep was the same Vodoun tattoo I'd seen on BOLO Guy and the fake nurse at the hospital.

I closed my eyes, and when I opened them again, he was gone.

Damn him. He had surfed my mind and manipulated my thoughts, like he had in the old days, before we went our separate ways. I slammed the laptop closed, and spun around, half expecting to find him standing behind me.

When I found myself alone, I hurled a message of my own through the cosmos. *I'm coming, you son-of-a-bitch. I'll find you wherever you are. And this time it won't be over until one of us is dead.*

H.R. BOLDWOOD

EXCERPT: CORPSE WHISPERER SWORN

H.R. BOLDWOOD

"Get your hands off my Harley."

I leveled my gun at the bastard's bald head and racked the slide, producing the metallic *click-clack* that commands instant attention.

Baldy froze, inched his hands into the air, and pivoted toward me. "You...ah," he squinted under the street light at the paper in his hand, "Allie Nighthawk?"

I walked to within a few yards of him and then planted my feet shoulder width apart. "I'm not going to say it again. Step away from the Low Rider."

He backed off, shaking his head. "Bank One says it belongs to them, now. You should've made the payments."

It was a warm Saturday in May, just after midnight in Cincinnati, and the weekend was already full-tilt in the crapper.

"They'll get their money," I said, keeping him in my crosshairs. "Go on, now. Leave before my friend Hawk here has second thoughts."

"Nice piece," he said, backing up, eying my gun. He turned and climbed into the cab of his flatbed. "Semi-auto?"

"Custom nine-millimeter. Nighthawk."

Baldy cranked the engine. It turned over slow and then backfired, the sound echoing against the houses on Pitty Pat Lane.

Little Allie, the head-squatting voice that lives in my brain, offered: *Maybe the neighbors will think that was a firecracker.*

By now, the blue-haired biddies on my street were surely peering out their windows, watching the live edition of *Repo Man Uncut*. Come morning, the HOA's mail box would be bursting with a fresh batch of complaints against me.

It's hard to blame the gum-grinders, really. When you live down the street from a corpse whisperer, you see some strange shit.

"I'll be back," Baldy yelled, as he rumbled away in his truck.

"We'll be waiting," I shouted, waving goodbye with Hawk.

Read the rest of the story in
Corpse Whisperer Sworn
(to be released in 2019)

ACKNOWLEDGMENTS

I would like to express my gratitude to the many people who helped bring this book to life:

Christiana Miller, your drive and focus gave *The Corpse Whisperer* wings. I couldn't be happier with your efforts.

Joseph Daniel Back, my spouse, whose eagle-eye and tireless logic rein in my ridiculously right-sided brain when it wanders off. Thanks for understanding.

My brother, Robert M. Burdick, the countless hours you spent reviewing and analyzing *The Corpse Whisperer* cannot go unmentioned. I'm sure by now you can recite the story by heart. Thank you for giving *The Corpse Whisperer* copious amounts of your time, your literary expertise, and your devotion.

The network of authors and beta readers who critiqued *The Corpse Whisperer*, the authors who offered suggestions, and those who encouraged me. You are too numerous to mention individually, but you know who you are. I will treasure your support and friendship always.

ABOUT THE AUTHOR

 H.R. BOLDWOOD is a writer of horror and speculative fiction. In another incarnation, Boldwood was a Pushcart Prize nominee and was awarded the 2009 Bilbo Award for Creative Writing.

Boldwood's characters are often disreputable and not to be trusted. They are kicked to the curb at every conceivable opportunity. No responsibility is taken by this author for the dastardly and sometimes criminal acts committed by this ragtag group of miscreants.

You can send H.R. Boldwood a message at hrboldwood@gmail.com. To learn more about H.R. Boldwood, visit her website at: www.hrboldwood.com.

facebook.com/hrboldwood
x.com/BoldwoodH
bookbub.com/authors/h-r-boldwood

ALSO BY H.R. BOLDWOOD

NOVELS

The Prodigal

The Corpse Whisperer

Corpse Whisperer Sworn

Corpse Whisperer Torn

ANTHOLOGIES

Killing it Softly (Volume One)

Killing it Softly (Volume Two)

Hyperion and Theia's Saturnalia

Toys in the Attic

Floppy Shoes Apocalypse II

Carnival of Horror

Bete Noire

Pilcrow and Dagger